The Golden Pig

El Cochino de Oro

The Golden Pig

El Cochino de Oro

Frits Forrer

Holland's Glory   PO Box 488, Gulf Breeze, FL 32562

This is a work of fiction. Names, characters, places, and incidents either are the product of the author's imagination or are used fictitiously. Any resemblance to actual events or persons, living or dead, is entirely coincidental.

Copyright © 2007 by Frits Forrer

All rights reserved. No part of this book may be reproduced or transmitted in any form or by any means, electronic or mechanical, including photocopying, recording, or by any information storage and retrieval system, without permission in writing from the author.

This edition was prepared for printing by
Ghost River Images
5350 East Fourth Street
Tucson, Arizona 85711
ghostriverimages.com

Cover illustration by Betty Shoopman
bcshoop@bellsouth.net

Contact the author at:
fforrer@bellsouth.net   or
www.fritsforrer.net
850-916-7566
Fax 850—916 1861

ISBN 0-9714490-8-2

Library of Congress Control Number: 2007932574

Printed in the United States of America

First Printing: August, 2007

10 9 8 7 6 5 4 3 2 1

Contents

New York's Finest 9
The Fifty-First 16
Manhattan Court 23
Washington Heights 27
The FBI Connection 32
The G-man's Story 37
Hello Mobay 42
Jamaica Farewell 47
Julia, all of her. 50
Washington D.C. 54
The Julia Goof 61
Deep, Deep Doodoo. 67
Judas? 72
The Bermuda Triangle. 79
Bermuda 83
Lucky's Wrath 90
Fred's Turn 96
Jersey, here we come! 102
Cruising the Caribbean 111
Colombia, South America 117
The Pilot 125
The Chase. 132
The Trap 139
Medellin 149
Flight from Evil? 156
The Propeller Jock 163
Two in a Row? 170
Georgia On Their Minds. 177
Flashing Blue Lights 181
The Penthouse 186
The Wrath of Lucky Vargas (Again) 191
Island Hopping. 197
The New Jersey-Bogota Connection. 203
The Deal. 209
Cashing in on Gamblers. 216
Betting on a Long Shot. 224
The Dragnet. 230
Ambush 237
Way Down Yonder. 243
The Prison Ward. 249
Dog Fight On The Bayou 255
Target Practice, Anyone? 262

(continued)

Harbor Patrol 267
How Lucky Can You Get? 275
Cuartel Militar de Cartagena 286
A Taste Of Hell 293

Epilogue 300

About the Author 319

Other books by Frits Forrer

Five Years Under The Swastika
Growing up in Holland under German occupation.
ISBN 0-9714490-0-7

The Fun Of Flying
Jet fighter training during the Korean Affair
ISBN 0-9714490-3-1

Someone's Smiling Down On Us
A love story
ISBN 0-9714490-1-5

Tampa Justice, No Money, No Justice
Injustices in the Florida penal system
ISBN 0-9714490-5-8

Smack Between The Eyes
A suspenseful murder mystery
ISBN 0-9714490-6-6

To Judge or Not To Judge
Another fine mystery in the Forrer style
ISBN 0-9714490-7-4

www.fritsforrer.net

AUTHOR'S NOTE

This is a work of FICTION, pure and simple. Exciting, but simple.

Many thanks to my number one spelling genius, my Katy.

Also, thanks to the dedicated members of the West Florida Literary Federation that make up the "Writers Anonymous", Joe Hefti, Jack Beverly, Andrea Walker, Dr. Joe and Marilyn Howard and Jack Beach. My English improved daily under their watchful eyes.

The critique from my buddies in the Belles & Beaux was very helpful and inspiring. True buddies, Jerry, Kay, Selma, Fred, true buddies indeed.

Many thanks,

Frits.

Chapter One

New York's Finest

Midtown Manhattan
12.35 pm

"Let's go pester Alberto!"
The two brothers, Fred and Ted were enjoying a two-martini lunch on one of their rare get togethers in the middle of the Big Apple.

"Yeah, like we used to fifty years ago? How's the old bugger doing?" Fred hadn't been in Spanish Harlem in twenty years and wasn't even aware that Alberto was still alive.

"He's still hanging in there. He's starting to look like a short version of Cesar Romero because he's totally gray by now, but he's hanging in there. He had a prostate scare, but that's probably because he doesn't get a chance to get laid often enough any more, the poor sucker. Magali cut him off a few years ago when he came up with a dose of the clap and she's still madder than hell at him because she thought he might give it to her."

"How do you know all of that?" Fred was flabbergasted that his brother Ted would have all that intimate information.

"Oh, Gympy talks to her mother in Harlem all the time. She still lives on East 108th in the same apartment and she tells her daughter all the gory details, every chance she gets."

"You're still talking to Gympy?"

"Twice a month maybe, sometimes more, sometimes less. Usually about the girls, but she keeps me informed about all the juicy gossip and I love it. I still laugh when I think about the beautiful little girls, four, five years old, coming up to the truck, going: *"Meester Sostee, Meester Sostee, da me un i-crean?"*

"You got money? *Tienes chavos?*"

"*No, no tengo chavo, da me one free, please Meester Sostee?*" I'll never forget those beautiful dark eyes flirting with me! Gorgeous little creatures and I'd tell'em:

"No chavo, no i-crean!"

"*Fuck you, Meester Sostee!*" Ted doubled up laughing, just thinking about it.

More than fifty years ago, shortly after getting off the boat in Hoboken, the Van Dijk brothers from Holland found themselves involved in the MISTER SOFTEE ICECREAM business in New York, first as driver/salesmen, later as owners of the trucks and they selected Harlem as their territories. Fred worked his area from 125th street north and from 7th Ave east to the Harlem River. Ted worked Spanish Harlem from 125th down to 110th and from 7th to the river. Some people thought it was a dangerous area, but the Dutch boys thought it was exciting and prosperous and they raked in good money. On his route, Ted met the love of his life, Gimriella (Gympy) Oliviera, She was a real Latin Beauty, born and raised on east 108th street by a Puerto Rican mother and a Cuban father; Alberto.

Alberto owned a bar in the middle of the Spanish Harlem jungle, **El Cochino de Oro,** on Madison between 113th and 114th. streets.

In the off-season, when the brothers had a little time on their hands, they would go into Manhattan and *'pester'* Alberto by walking into his bar and bumming a free beer. After all, Ted had married Gimpy and provided Alberto with two beautiful granddaughters, so that certainly entitled them to a beer, but the brothers had enough money to buy their own, so *pestering* involved something else. When two white, blond men walked into the dumpy bar, more than half of the customers would scurry out of the back door, thinking a pair of undercover cops had walked in. All the petty drug dealers, the pimps and guys with outstanding warrants would get out so fast, it was like the Exodus in double time.

Ted and Fred would laugh, but Alberto would ask; "What you guys do to my business.?"

"We just wanna see if you're still okay, Alberto. *Da me un cervesa, por favor!*"

(A beer, please.)

Finishing their lunch and with time on their hands, it sounded like a good idea. Their wives were in Westchester County somewhere at a huge shopping mall and that gave the beloved brothers an opportunity to go exploring on their own. Ted had driven down from Foxboro, Massachusetts in his SUV, but Fred had gotten a rental car at the airport and they decided that the smaller car might suit them better in Manhattan.

Ted still had a head full of blond curls and a somewhat stocky build. At five-seven, he weighed about two hundred pounds and he would have looked better if he shed about twenty of them. Fred was two inches taller and was nearly totally grey. Actually white. He could stand to lose about ten pounds as well, mostly around the waist. Both of them felt and acted as if they were still twenty-five.

So off they went. Traffic wasn't bad at mid-day and in Spanish Harlem, parking spots were readily available at the parking meters that lined the street.

"A couple of quarters beats twenty-two dollars I just paid on 49th for only fifty-five minutes in a parking garage." Fred was grumbling about the high cost of living in New York.

"Oh, it's only money." Ted didn't worry about little details like that.

"The streets don't look any cleaner than they did fifty years ago!" Fred was commenting as they walked back two blocks from their parking spot.

"Not much has changed. More Cubans now though. When we were here it was like little Puerto Rico, now it's been taken over by Cubans, including the whole Yorkville section that was all German at one point."

"You mean no more Hofbrauhaus and oompah bands?"

"Nope, all Cuban nightclubs now. The biggest difference is that the Cubans work for a living and the Borinqueños (Puerto Ricans) subsist on welfare, so from 90th down, there are lots of pretty modern condos nowadays." Ted kept up with his old stomping ground.

"Here's the joint. Let's tell him that he needs to paint his pig again. There's hardly any gold left on that animal." Fred was referring to the sign that at one time sported a dazzling golden pig, but now was tarnished and grey.

The brothers opened the door and strolled along the long wooden bar, looking for a seat. It was like old times. Dozens of people, mostly men, left their seats and split through the rear exit.

"*Hola, Alberto, como estás?*"

"*Ay, Teodoro! Mi amigo, que tal?* And you Fred? You good?"

They reached over the bar and shook hands with the Cesar Romero look-a-like, at least as far as the face was concerned. He was about half as tall as Cesar was in his hay days, but he wore the years very well.

"*Alberto, quantos anos tienes?*" (How old are you?)

"I now eighty-one, nearly eighty-two."

"When are you gonna look for a steady job?" Ted used to tease the old bar owner all the time and things hadn't changed.

"Whats you doin' in town? You move back?"

"No Alberto, we're visiting Michelle, the girls' cousin in White Plains and…"

"The girls come to see me, no?"

"I don't know, they do their own thing. They have their own cars, so they may come see you and La Vieja, (Grandma) I don't know. Thanks…." He accepted a tall glass of beer and started to put money on the bar.

"No, no. My treat. And how are you Fred? Where you live now?

Still in Tampa? "

"No, I now live in the Florida Panhandle and…"

"You still fly?"

"Sometimes. Not regularly any more. Just for fun now and then. Good beer. No more Rheingold or Balantine, right?"

"No. No more Knickerbocker or Schaeffer either. Them days is long gone. Now you drinkin' Bud. I have some Dos Equis or Becks in bottles if you want it. You can have anything you want. It's just good to see you. Maybe twenty jears. Maybe twenty-fibe, who knows. You guys look good! WHAT THE HELL IS THIS?"

Alberto shouted at ten or twelve New York City cops that stormed into his place through the front and back door simultaneously.

"HANDS ON THE BAR AND THE TABLES! Everybody! Stay put! Don't move!"

Ted and Fred had turned away from Alberto and looked in amazement at all the action until a burley cop shouted at them; "Turn around. Hands on the bar."

"Well, we might as well." Fred obliged nicely, but Ted said; "Come on! All we're doing is having a beer."

"Shut up and turn around." The burly cop, accompanied by a Latin looking sergeant, started shouting right in Ted's face. "Put those hands on the bar and start walking backwards. Spread your legs."

"Like hell I will. What do you think you're doing?"

"Ted! Listen to them." Fred was panicking. "Cooperate, goddamit. It'll be over in a minute!"

"You're right buster. Got an ID on you?" The sergeant was frisking Fred by moving his hands up and down his legs and feeling around his waistline and under his arms.

"Sure. In my left pocket." Fred started to reach for his pants pocket, but the cop snarled; "Keep those hands on the bar. I'll be right back at you."

Ted wasn't that cooperative. "What right do you have to order me around? Did I commit a crime or something?"

"Shut up and move back."

"All I wanna do is drink a beer in peace and unless you tell me what you're up to or what I'm guilty of, I won't have to listen to your orders. I know my rights."

"Oh yeah? Cuff 'em." Within seconds, the two policemen grabbed Ted's hands, slung them behind his back and smacked handcuffs around his wrists.

"COME ON! WHAT IS THIS?" Ted was shouting at the top of his lungs, but it didn't help one bit. The cops simply lifted his arms, forcing Ted's face down on the bar.

`"Oh, Officer. Is that really necessary?" Now Fred got into the act.

"You shut up or otherwise you'll get the same royal treatment." Fred decided to shut up.

The rest of the customers seemed more used to the routine. They produced ID's and were allowed to sit down or in some cases, cuffs were snapped on them and they were marched out of the front door. Nobody made a ruckus like Ted did.

The sergeant came back to Fred and said; "Show me your ID. Slowly." Fred slid his hand in his left pants pocket, produced a money clip and pulled his Florida Drivers License from between the bills. The cop looked over it carefully and back up at Fred to check the resemblance and asked, "What in the hell are you doing here?"

"Well, the owner here," he pointed at Alberto, "used to be my brother's father-in-law and we decided to say hello, since we're in town anyway."

"That's your brother?" The sarge pointed at Ted.

"Sure is!"

"What's the matter with him? Why couldn't he shape up? We have a job to do and all he had to do is stand there with his hands on the bar for a few minutes. Who's older? You or him?"

"Thanks, Sarge, I am by four years."

"Well, at least you're the wiser one."

The burly cop was still holding Ted's arms up in the air and his face down on the bar. The sergeant signaled him to let him up and

The Golden Pig

that proved to be a mistake. Ted swung around and shouted; "I'm gonna sue you miserable sonofabitches. Your badge says 1024. I'll remember that. You can't go around treating innocent people like that. I'll sue you and the police department for all you've got and…"

"You better shut up buddy or we'll haul your ass to the station house from where you can call your lawyer, so …"

"You haven't even read me my rights yet,.." The brother interrupted again.

"Oh Ted, shut up, will ya? Let them finish up in here and we'll finish our beer and all will be over in…"

"No way!" Ted again. "Did you see how they treated me? I'm still in cuffs and I don't have to take that shit from New York's finest. I'm…"

"Mister!" The sergeant again. "Either you shut up and we'll turn you loose or you keep threatening and we'll take you in. Your choice."

"Don't think I'll forget the numbers. Yours is 344 and his is 1024 and I'll sue you for police brutality.."

"Take him in!" The sergeant barked his order and started to walk away, but Fred stopped him and asked, "Please sergeant. I'll keep him under control. This is not necessary. Just let him go."

"Would you like the same treatment?"

"No, no! I'll follow you to the station house and bail him out. Where are you taking him?"

"Fifty-first precinct, 126 street."

"Alberto, I don't believe this."

Chapter Two

The Fifty-First

Fred couldn't find a parking space on 126th or 127th, couldn't park in the police lot behind the building, was afraid to leave the car at a fire hydrant and risk being towed.

Finally, at a gas station on the corner of 125th and Third, he left the little rental and walked back three blocks to the dilapidated police station.

Getting to talk to someone was difficult and getting his brother out was impossible. He was asked to sit and wait. He was told to show patience and he was threatened to be locked up as well, if he didn't behave himself. The waiting room was crowded with people, all black and mostly female. Apparently, the women had been called to the station on behalf of their husbands or lovers or whatever the case might be.

The big black corporal behind the bulletproof glass called them over one by one and after that they disappeared behind a connecting door or they walked out of the station into the street. It had to be a routine thing, because there were no hysterics or yelling, everyone acted like a lamb in a slaughterhouse.

Fred finally got his turn at the window. "My name is Fred Van Dijk and I'm here to bail out my brother Ted, who was arrested at the El Cochino de Oro bar."

The Golden Pig

"You caaint bail out nobody from heah, you gotta aks the judge."

"The judge? Where can I find the judge?"

"Downtown. Night court at 8 P.M.. Register wif the bailiff when you come in." The corporal waved at the next person to approach him,

"Wait a minute. Wait a minute! I need to talk to somebody. Who's in charge of this station? Who's the captain? I need to talk with somebody!" Fred was getting panicky.

"What's your name?" Fred repeated his name and the black face answered: "Von Dike?"

"Close enough."

"Sit." The corporal pushed a button on the phone in front of him and said something Fred couldn't hear. Looking up, he repeated; "Sit!"

Fred sat… Five minutes… Ten minutes… He started to pace and sat down again. Eighteen minutes later, the Latino sergeant came out, the same one who had been in the bar.

He didn't offer his hand, but sat down next to the exasperated brother and said: "I'm Sergeant Rodriguez and I'm sorry your brother got caught in this mess, but you have to understand what we're up against."

"Like what? All we were doin'…"

"I know, I know. But what you don't know is that we had the bar staked out for a long time because we had a rumor that a major drug lord, Lucky Vargas, was personally gonna investigate some infringements on his territory and probably would do some enforcing if necessary…."

"What did that have to do with us?"

"Well, you see, we don't know what Lucky Vargas looks like, but we do know he's not a youngster any more, so when you two walked in, someone spotted you and thought one of you might be Lucky, so we moved in."

"Oh, you gotta be kidding!" Fred couldn't believe his ears.

"No, no, no. I'm dead serious. You see, the drug scene is very competitive and when a new king pin or a major pusher starts to expand his turf, the bullets usually go flying and a lot of people get hurt, including innocent bystanders. You see, I don't give a shit if they kill one another. It saves us a lot of trouble and the taxpayers a lot of money, but we can't take a chance on other people getting hurt, so..."

"But for crying out loud, my brother is obviously not Lucky Vegas..."

"Vargas."

"Okay, Vargas, so what's the point in arresting my brother Paul."

"You see, sir. Crazy as it may seem, your brother acted just like a real suspect would have acted and we couldn't take a chance, so we booked him."

"You booked him? On what grounds?"

"Oh, just something minor. 'Resisting arrest without violence!' You see, that's enough reason for us to hold him and question him and check his identity for real. A judge may just reprimand him or fine him fifty bucks and that's it. He'll be free to go."

"Can't I just post some kinda bail and have him come out with me?"

"No, you see, it's too late to get him on today's docket, so he'll be one of the first heard in night court and he should be free to walk."

"You mean, he's staying locked up here until tonight?"

"Not really. You see, he'll be brought downtown in a paddywagon and they'll do all the recording and the paperwork at the court and if you're smart, you get there at about seven-thirty and register with the clerk and he may be one of the first to be heard."

"In other words, I have to hang around this town till evening? Good morning! What a mess." He rested his head in his hands for a moment and spoke up again: "Sarge, how bad is the drug problem here?"

"Bad, man, bad. Real bad. You see, there's a lot of money to be made in that business and teenagers manage to come up with oodles and oodles of dough and of course, that beats working. They don't even try to get a decent job. Too hard and too little reward. You see it's real glamorous to flaunt big money and fancy duds. My own boys get challenged by that sometimes, but between church and a strict mother, we've kept them in line so far, but it ain't easy. Our Captain is trying hard to get it all under control in his precinct, but the drug network is so cleverly ingrained in the local population, that it's hard to make any inroads."

"Who's this Lucky Vegas?"

"Vargas."

"Okay, Vargas. Who's he?"

"We don't know for sure. You see, rumors come and go, but one thing's for sure; he's real potent. We heard he's from Columbia, a big land owner. We also heard, he's college educated in this country and we hear other rumors that he grew up in the slums of Chicago, the hard way. Early street gangs and robberies and killings, but we don't know, but we do know we don't want him messing on our turf. Your brother is a little bit the victim of some nerves that have been on edge for a long time and you see, the pressure from Captain Esposito makes us all a little jumpy. Sorry sir. I really gotta go, so good luck with your brother." The sergeant got up and started to leave. "Where's the courthouse exactly?"

"Lower Manhattan, near City Hall." He disappeared.

"Thanks, I think. What a mess. I may as well go back to Alberto. I never even finished my beer."

"That's a lot of crap, Fred!" Alberto refilled the beer glass for the third time. "The only thing Esposito is trying to do is protect his little conglomerate he has here.

He's making sure no other drug dealers get into this territory and undercut his percentages. He gets a rake-off on every reefer and every gram that's sold in his precinct and he intends to keep it that way. That guy 'Lucky' may just be a figment of his imagination. I certainly have never heard of him."

"How do you know all that?" Fred found that hard to believe.

"Remember when you were working around here and Robert Wagner was mayor? Remember when he started the anti-police-corruption program? Just a minute." He walked over to wait on another customer. When he came back he asked, "Where was I?"

"Robert Wagner."

"Oh yeah. Well, I was being hassled all the time by the cops for *'protection'* like the mafia does in the other parts of town, so I contacted Brave Bob's taskforce with a guarantee of anonymity. I listed the names and the numbers of the cops that demanded payola all the time and within days, I was raided just about every day, I nearly lost all my customers, I was arrested a few times under false pretenses and just like Teodoro, got locked up all day and then I finally got turned loose by the courts at night while my employees robbed me blind. By the time I was called to testify to a secret grand jury, I chickened out, because I nearly lost my business and from there on in, life went on just the same. A couple of the cops got transferred and I wasn't bugged as much any more. With the advent of the big drug business, things changed. Now the cops don't need penny-ante payers like me any more, so I just keep my nose clean and survive. I paid off my mortgages years ago and now I just come in a few hours a day. That tall guy at the end, Ernie, he's my partner and he's buying me out. If his credit wasn't so lousy, he could float a loan and cash me out completely, so I could move to Miami, but that'll have to wait a few more years."

"So Ted got locked up because the cops want to scare possible drug dealers?"

"Yeah, and because he acted stupid. He gave them a perfect excuse; *'interfering with a police operation.'*"

"Now I have to wait till after eight this evening in order to get him out of there…" Fred figured there was no way he could drink beer all afternoon and make it downtown by car and then back up to Westchester.

"Oh, they let him go alright. They know they have no case and they want no publicity whatsoever, so…"

The Golden Pig

"Are you telling me this goes on all the time?" It seemed hard to believe.

Not to Alberto. "This has been going on for ages. Before I ever opened this bar I had an *after hour* joint in the Bronx, way up on the fourth floor in a tenement walk-up right along the EL. It bothered nobody, I opened at midnight. Most of my customers showed after the local bars closed at one and I provided a haven for lovers, drunks, lonesome cats and out-of-luck singers. The noise of the EL rattling by blocked out most of the noise of the joint anyway and I made a good buck. By five in the morning, I closed up and I made more money than I had ever made in my life." He chuckled; "That was before I knew Judy's mother. Plenty of gals came up, man. It was a happy life, Fred. You should have been there." He chuckled again.

"What happened?" Fred felt like he was left hanging.

"Oh, yeah. That's what I started to tell you. One day I got a visit from a nice, friendly New York City Policeman. I was busy restocking and when he knocked I thought it might be an early customer. Wrong! I opened the door and all I could do was offer him a drink, 'cause I said I was setting up for a private party. Well, he said; 'That's nice', had a drink and told me: "We've been watching your operation and that's fine, but you should think about our brother police officers and share a little. So the Captain decided that he doesn't feel you're really breaking any major laws, so with a little contribution on your part we're going to let you continue your private venture without a city license and all you do is give the captain $400 a week…"

"Four hundred a week? I don't even make four hundred a week! I can't do that. You guys have to be reasonable with me about this." He shook his head as he replayed that scene in his head. "Well, he said he'd talk to the captain and two days later in the middle of the night, they raided the place, arrested me, took all my inventory of liquor and beer and sodas and glasses and everything. And they took all my money, including what I had in my pocket and they said if I just pleaded *"nolo contendere"*, no contest, I could just walk away that night and I could look for a better location. Can you believe that? They took enough money and liquor for three Christmas parties at the precinct and the judge had no notion what was going on and let me go. Can you believe that? That's New York for you, baby. That's New York."

"Wow, remind me to stay in Florida. I may as well say hello to Magali, get something to eat and head downtown. No point in going back up and down to White Plains. Thanks for the beer, Alberto."

"De nada! Don't be a stranger now."

Chapter Three

Manhattan Court

Fred was ready to kick somebody. First of all he had a ticket on his windshield after he left Alberto and he swore he still had at least ten minutes left on the parking meter. The red flag showed "Expired", but his watch said he hadn't been gone for more than 45 minutes. "I betcha, these bastards kick these poles, so they'll jump the minutes on the clock." He knew if he didn't pay, the rental car company would get his ticket and by then it would show late payments and penalties and the car company would just charge it against his credit card. There was no escaping. "The bastards," he said again as he kicked the meter pole, but it didn't change a thing.

Then he decided to eat somewhere in Little Italy, but nothing looked the same anymore. The Village had no parking facilities it seemed and by the time he did find a garage, he realized that he would spend more money on parking than on food.

"That stupid brother of mine," he fussed as he tried to find his way around the courthouse. He had never seen a mess like that in his life. The place bustled like Grand Central Station and apparently nobody kept office hours in there. People in suits and ties, probably the lawyers and prosecutors, mingled with the strangest assortment of people in the most varied variety of clothing. It seemed that the United Nations had turned loose their poor and unemployed from all over the world and they were all gathered in the monumental halls of the courthouse.

"Good God, I hope we get out of here before midnight."

By eight o'clock, he had found the right courtroom, registered with the proper clerk and was sitting in one of the first rows reserved for spectators. The registration was necessary in order to represent his brother or claim him.

"Do you represent him?" seemed like a dumb question, but if he were going to say anything to the judge at all he would have to be registered as *'representing'* him.

"Okay, I represent him."

"What's your affiliation? Attorney?"

"No, I'm his older brother and that's worse."

"I beg your pardon?"

"Forget it. You want my driver's license? Okay..." He slipped over the document and said to himself; "Okay, okay! I wish I could still beat him up..."

Ted was about the fourth *criminal* to be brought in before an unusually young judge. According to his looks, he couldn't even be twenty-five, but he was introduced as the Honorable Judge Bernard H. Bernstein. He seemed to know his business though. The defendants appeared before him, he glanced at their dockets, asked a question or two, ordered a fine and it was over. Next!

Ted looked haggard. He also looked mad. Fred worried about the way he would react to the judge. "Let's hope he doesn't run his mouth again."

Wrong! The judge glanced up from the papers in front of him and asked, "Mr. Van Dyke? Van Diek?"

"Van Dijk", Ted proclaimed " and I want to lodge a complaint before this court. I've been held against my will without..."

"Mr. Van Dike, just answer my questions, please and we'll have this concluded in just minutes." Ted wasn't gonna give up that easy.

"Your Honor. I have committed no crime, but I've been shackled, locked up and held in custody..."

"Mr. Van Dike, this is a final warning. Either you control yourself or I'll hold you in contempt and you'll be returned to your cell. Do you understand me?'

"What kind of system is this? You grab innocent people..."

"Mr, Van Dike!'

"Your Honor!" Fred jumped up in the front spectator row. "Your Honor, may I approach?"

"Who are you?"

"Your Honor, I'm Fred Van Dijk, Ted's older brother and if I may, may I approach and take over and speak for him and introduce some common sense into this whole situation?"

"Well, that would be refreshing. Come forward." The judge even smiled.

Fred moved through the turnstiles and stopped when he was right in front of the judge. "Your Honor, this whole affair is nothing but a misunderstanding and if my dear brother had shown a little patience instead of challenging the officers, this whole thing could have been avoided."

"Very well, tell me in your own words what's involved here."

Fred started to relate the events of the afternoon, when Ted interrupted; "I know my rights and.."

"Hou je smoel!" Fred shouted at him

"What was that?" The judge wanted to know.

"I just told him to shut up, Your Honor."

"What language was that?"

"Oh, that was Dutch. We're from Holland."

"How long have you been here?"

"Here? In the U.S.? Since '57 and I became a citizen in '63. Anyway, Judge, all Ted would have to do is cooperate with the police for a few minutes, put his hands on the bar and keep his mouth shut, so the officers could complete their mission and everything.."

"They can't just order people around like that..." Ted had to put in five cents again, but the judge cut him short; "Mr. Van Dike. Keep your mouth shut and you may be out of here in five minutes.

Go ahead Mr. Van Dike" He turned back to Fred. What were you doing there in the first place? In a bar on Madison and 113th?"

"Oh, the owner used to be Ted's father-in-law until he divorced his daughter or when she divorced him. Either way, he always remained friends with his in-laws and whenever we're in the New York area, we drop in to say hello. That's all. This time, the police raided the place while we were there and…"

"Mr. Williams?" The judge turned to the young black prosecutor who had read the initial indictment, "What's the word?"

"No charges on our part."

The judge banged the gavel. "Case dismissed. Mr. Van Dike, listen to your brother from here on in. Have a good night. Next!"

Ted opened his mouth again, but Fred turned him around fast and led him to the clerk, who returned personal belongings, had him sign some papers and they were in the street.

"I hope you have enough money to bail out my car." was the first thing Fred had to say and Ted's answer was; "I have enough money to buy your car and a dozen drinks, so let's do first things first. I see a beer sign over there and let's tie one on. I'm so thirsty, I think I lived in the Sudan for twelve years!" They crossed the street dodging taxicabs and entered a crowded dark saloon. Once they had gotten their beer, Ted raised his bottle and toasted: "Let's drink to the greatest, most conceited brother anyone could possibly ask for. Here we go! *Drink Up All You Happy People!*"

Thank God, the people in the bar couldn't even hear his Frank Sinatra rendition of the old torch song, 'cause they might have thrown him out or taken him up on his offer to buy the whole house a drink.

After that bar, only two more got them all the way to White Plains.

The wives didn't believe a word they had to say.

CHAPTER FOUR

Washington Heights

"You mean there really is a *Lucky Vargas?*"
"Rumor has it that there is such a person and that he's really shaking up the drug trade in the City. Maybe even in other parts of the country."
"Where do hear those rumors?"
"Right here. In the shop."
They were sitting in Ray's Donut and Soft Ice Cream Shop in Washington Heights.
When Ray had opened the shop the whole neighborhood was white. Jewish, Armenians, Italians and a mixture of other European nationalities, but over the years, it had gotten to be more Spanish and Black. What started out as a CARVEL soft ice cream shop became a donut shop as well. During the cold winter months business became so slow that Ray looked into supplementing his income by putting in a donut machine. The CARVEL company took Ray to court over FRANCHISE infractions, but a sympathetic judge ruled that Ray was entitled to make a year-round living as long as he paid his franchise fees. After all the legal hassles were over, Ray bought out his CARVEL franchise, changed to another ice cream mix supplier and lived happily ever after. He added coffee and sodas, little tables and chairs to the sidewalk, a waitress and became a neighborhood

fixture. For more than thirty years, everyone in a ten block radius had been in his shop and enjoyed the camaraderie and friendly service. Consequently, Ray knew everybody and heard all the gossip and got to know all of the people. Legitimate business men and women, hustlers, pimps, housewives and teenagers, they all needed a donut from time to time and some cool ice cream in the summer.

Like the Van Dyke brothers, Ray had started off in the MISTER SOFTEE business too and they had remained pals all through the years. Now the two happy Dutchmen had decided to visit their old friend, while the wives had more important things to do, like 'shopping'.

"We don't hear much about dope where we live except for news reports when somebody gets caught again with some crack or pot. Here it's a different scene though, isn't it?" Fred had just finished telling Ray the hilarious events of the night before and even Ted had a good belly laugh when they recounted the scene in the courthouse.

Ray agreed; "Here, it's big business. There are hundreds of penny ante dealers and it's nearly impossible for the cops to keep tracking 'em down and arresting them. In the theater and music world, cocaine is the big seller and the money rolls in. In just about any nightclub, dope is available and because the profit margin on that stuff is so high, they can afford to buy off anybody they want. The bouncers, the owners, the cops, anybody. It's frightening. When my kids went through school, it was a continuous nightmare for Sarah and me, worrying about the kids when they were on a date or even at a ballgame. We stayed right on top of them and now they're married and they can start worrying about their kids in a couple of years. We were lucky, I guess." He sighed a deep sigh, expressing all the frustrations that now laid behind him.

"Talking about lucky, in Pensacola Beach, right under our noses, a cocaine ring was busted up a few years ago and we knew a bunch of the people involved. Prominent people too. Hard to believe. But, going back to *Lucky Vargas,* how can one man just muscle in on somebody else's territory and get away with it?" Fred seemed fascinated by the subject.

"Money, baby! Big money. Oodles of money! Money buys loyalty, money pays for getting competition knocked off. Money pays for police protection. Money talks in that business. What's your interest all a sudden?" Ray grinned at him. "Wanting to get in on the game?"

"No, no. no! I've taken up writing again and maybe I can concoct a good novel about the subject, if I knew a little more about it."

"Why don't you fly to Colombia and go to work in the mountains and learn the business from the ground up?" Ted thought he was funny.

"Seriously?" Ray ignored Ted's sarcasm.

"Yeah, I couldn't just start writing through a hole in my head. I would ha...."

"Why not? You have so far." Ted never stopped.

"How do I obtain facts and figures? The amount of dopies in the City, the amount of coke that comes in here and how, and how the money is channeled? There's so much to know and I really know very little..."

"We all know that..." Ted again.

"Seriously. I couldn't just walk into Captain Esposito's office and say; 'Captain, how about a lengthy interview about police involvement in the drug business?' and expect to get the time of day, could I , Ray?"

Ray chuckled; "Not likely. He probably has too much dirty laundry in his past that he can't afford to air any of it. Guys like that just want to retire without blemishes on their records or any nasty newspaper reports that could expose him. No, better forget about him."

"Then how do I get started? Buy some stuff myself? Risk the chance of getting caught and get to interview a little penny-ante pusher who only knows the guy he gets the stuff from? His supplier? And then what? Find his supplier? Get shot one day for being too nosey? How do I get to the inside of that trade?"

"You got the right idea. Become a junkie so you can understand the junkies." Ted's sense of humor never quit. It might get annoying, but it never quit.

"I wouldn't go that far. Don't start from the bottom. Start from the top. Contact Bob Martinez or some other Drug-Czar and then work your way down."

"Sure! I pick up the phone and call.... Who's the Drug Chief now?"

"I don't know. I have no idea. I don't even remember Bob Martinez. Who's he?"

"Ray, you're supposed to know everything..." Ted just can't control his mouth.

"Lots of local stuff? Yes. Big scale politics? No. Not the foggiest."

Fred seemed to have some of the answers; "He was Governor of Florida and then was promoted to Drug-Czar and he solved everything. No more drug problems today. Right?" He snickered sarcastically and continued: "Seriously, how often do I have to say 'seriously' before you take me seriously?"

"Seriously?" Ted again. "Maybe never. When have you ever known Fred to be serious, Ray? Except when he was a serious beer drinker, remember?"

"Yeah, I remember some of those days and it wouldn't hurt my feelings if we went out and livened up a few of the old familiar places."

"Well, lock the door and there's a pub just a few doors up, so we can get started in minutes." Ted must have been craving a beer in the worst way.

"No, you guys know, I can't do that, but if you're still around at seven, I'll be ready to buy a few for old time's sake, but not right now. Sorry, I have..."

"Getting back to seriously. I feel a story brewing that needs to be told, but I can't get a handle on it. How do I start?" Fred seemed to have a one-track mind.

Ray sat up straight and frowned; "Seriously?"

"Seriously." Apparently, Fred was serious.

"I'll tell you what. I have a neighbor who was with the FBI for many years and got early retirement because of some drug mix-up.

I don't know the details and I don't know if he's gonna wanna talk about it, but I'll ask him. I'll be home by eight for sure and if you call me at about nine, I'll let you know if he's interested in talking with you. That's the best I can do."

"That's fair. I have your home number. Do you also have a cell? Give it to me!"

"Hey, maybe! Wait, will you guys have a chance to drop by the house for a few cold ones tonight? I know Sarah would love to see you clowns and then I'll ask the FBI guy to drop by as well and then you can get acquainted and you can put your feelers out about his experiences. How's that sound?"

"Sounds like a winner to me!"

"Me too!"

"Good. I'll see you at about eight, eight-thirty, okay?"

"Ray, you're on!"

Chapter Five

The FBI Connection

8:20 PM
Ray's house
Westchester County

"Come in , come in, you bums! The beer is getting warm already. What kept you so long?"

"You said eight-thirty, didn't you?"

"Yeah, I did, but I also know when I mention beer, you guys show up an hour early. Come in. Sarah….. They're here!"

Hugs an kisses were exchanged with great enthusiasm and the two brothers were guided downstairs to the converted basement. It actually had become a playroom with a pool table, a long, western type bar and a huge television set. The whole place was paneled in dark mahogany and decorated with all sorts of nautical memorabilia. Flags, anchors, helm wheels, compasses, burgees and rods and reels. Absolutely stunning.

"What a place!" exclaimed Ted. "Where's the barmaid?"

"I'm afraid you'll have to settle for me." Ray answered with a laugh, "but I'm a good one. I even have Heineken on tap."

"Hooray for Ray!" Ted was ready to roar.

The Golden Pig

A half hour into the party, the ex-FBI neighbor showed up and introduced himself as Ralph Barron. Ray lifted his eyebrows in surprise and Ralph quickly explained; "That's my middle name and my mothers name, because if these clowns indeed start writing about me, I don't want them to inadvertently spill my real name in their story. I've had as much trouble as I'll ever want about my old job. By the way, which of you is the author? You?" He addressed Ted, but Ted shook his head and said: "I'm the reader, he is the writer." Pointing at Fred. "The one with the dumb face. I'm too smart to be a writer. I make money, he doesn't. Is there any good advice you can give him? He needs it as badly as he needs money. Hahahahaha!"

Just two beers and Ted was on a roll already. Actually, that was just two beers since they got to Ray and Sarah's. He had a few martinis before dinner and some red Chianti with his food. It brought out the best of him. His weird sense of humor that is.

Ralph walked over to Fred and shook his hand warmly. "Let me grab a drink and then we'll sit in the corner over there while your jolly brother hangs at the bar. Less interference."

Ray fixed Ralph a *Dewars* and water and the two, Ralph and Fred, meandered over to a cozy corner, formed by four leather club chairs and a coffee table that was once a shrimp boat's netting device. It was beautifully lacquered and the brass latches were gleaming with pride.

Ralph took the lead. "Before I tell you anything, I need to know a little more about you of course, but by the same token, I've been dying to get my story out, because it's the weirdest thing that ever happened to me and I still find it hard to believe. It's like it happened to another person. It's like I've read it somewhere or seen it on T.V., when you hear it, you'll agree with me." He took a swig and continued. "But first tell me about you. Where do you and your brother fit into this group? Ray just mentioned that you sold ice cream together, but that's all I know. What's your background?"

"Let me fill my mug a moment. I'll be right back." Fred obtained another frothy mug of Dutch beer and sat back down. "Briefly, my brother and I both grew up in Holland and survived the war years.

In the early fifties, I was sent to the U.S. for flight training with the Air Force by the Royal Netherlands Air Force and when I got out, I applied for an Immigration Visa and migrated to the States in '57. Later on I brought over my brother and sisters. My full name is Frederic and Ted's name is actually Theodoor with double o. I was known as Rick and Ted was known as Theo, but when we applied for driver's licenses and filled out job applications the clerks figured we didn't know how to spell, so we ended up as Fred and Ted and that sounds like a song and dance team, which we really are. Anyway, when I finally found the time, I wrote a story about us growing up under German occupation from 1940 to 1945 and enjoyed fair success with that book and still do. Then I wrote about my flight experiences during the Korean War, although I never made it to Korea. I flew fighters over Holland instead. Later I wrote a few more books, including Murder Mysteries and some involved FBI and CIA personnel and I'm intrigued by the drug problem in the U.S., especially since my daughter as a teenager was caught smoking pot on the school grounds. You may already have heard how my brother was arrested in a raid in a bar in Spanish Harlem and when we were telling Ray about it and I started asking questions about the drug situation, he suggested I talk to you or rather, listen to you."

"Alright Fred, like I said before, I've been dying to get my story out, but we have to establish a few rules, OK?"

"Sure! That makes sense. What kind of rules do you have in mind Ralph?" Fred seemed agreeable enough and savored his cold beer as he leaned forward.

"For one thing, my name has to stay out of it, okay? Totally! Okay?" He bent over and his brown eyes locked into Fred's blue ones. "Okay?" Fred nodded "And second, you don't publish a word without my consent. Not a word, okay?" I get to proof read every syllable before you submit it, okay?"

"I can live with that. Do you want me to submit something in writing for both of us to sign?" Fred seemed eager to cooperate.

"No, it may be dumb, but I'll take your word for it. Besides that, any signed piece of paper would create another paper trail and I can't afford that. When you hear my story, you'll understand why. I had too much shenanigans already, you understand?"

"Okay. Where and how do I hear your story and would it be best if you record it and I destroy the tape when I'm done with it or…"

"That's the risky part. There's no way you can write as fast as I talk, besides that, we would have to spend several days together, I'm sure and that may not be advisable, so lets talk about this for a minute. How long are you going to stay in this area and what is your schedule?"

"I'm flying out from MacArthur the day after tomorrow, so if we can get together tomorrow, we can at least get started. Do you have one of these little handheld recorders?"

"No, I don't and tomorrow would be great, but we can't meet at my house. You may not be seen at my house. We may ask Ray if we can meet right here in his cellar, since they're not home during the day and that should work. I'm sure he won't object. Let's ask him." Ralph got up with a little difficulty out of the deep leather chair and murmured: "Damn arthritis."

He was of average height, about five foot ten and stooped a little bit. He had most of his hair yet, just a receding hairline, but totally white. He kept it trimmed in a military style, the way he must have kept it most of his adult life.

Fred thought as he watched him get up; "Interesting! An FBI man is just like every other ordinary man, plain ordinary. Nothing to make him stand out from the crowd. Maybe that's the whole idea, blend in."

They both found a place at the bar and had to wait a while to get Ray's attention. Ted was bending his ear of course and the two of them broke into songs and laughter constantly. Reminiscing about the old times, Fred figured.

Finally, Ralph cornered Ray long enough to get Ray's approval and they agreed that Ralph would come over and hold the fort before Sarah had to leave for work at the nearby hospital. Fred would join him as early as possible, but he had to buy a cassette recorder before showing up. Things looked promising.

"What's your wife gonna say?" Ted wanted to know. "She's gonna think you'll be chasing some young broad across the county. Hahahaha! Like Hillary Clinton! Hahahaha!"

"As long as you don't put some of those crazy thoughts into her mind, I'm gonna be alright. So you just stay out of it, okay?"

"Who's gonna make me?" The beers were having their effect.

"Aw, come on! Let's sing one more song and go home. What's your favorite, Ray?"

Chapter Six

The G-man's Story

I'll start at the beginning, crazy as this is gonna sound. I was recruited by the FBI when I was still in college. I majored in languages and was planning on maybe working at the United Nations or maybe at a foreign embassy somewhere. The thought of adventure is what always appealed to me and somehow the FBI made it sound interesting. In retrospect, I should have joined the CIA. I would've seen more foreign countries and used my linguistic abilities a little more, but anyway. I joined the FBI.

I was single, there were plenty of girls around and I was in no hurry to get married. At first I got some boring assignments, but little by little, the jobs got more dangerous and more exciting and I was having a ball. I was stationed in different parts of the country from time to time and I loved it. The money and the expense account kept me very comfortable. I could afford to rent in nice affluent neighborhoods and again, the girls were aplenty. Some married, some single, some very young, some reasonably old. I had the time of my life. I worked fifty, sixty hours a week, but not having to mow the lawn or take kids to their ballgames, I had plenty of time to go dancing and partying. All on the up and up, mind you. Never got involved in anything illicit unless you considered some of my married girlfriends off limits. Well, what can I say? If they wanted to hit the sack with me, who was I to refuse? I didn't. Didn't even consider it.

By the time I hit thirty, I might have been ready to settle down, but I was still not in a hurry, so when I met this blond good looking thing at a party, I followed my usual routine, we got drunk together and hit the sack together. We were fabulous together. She needed it badly and I was eager to provide, we screwed our brains out. It started one of the longest affairs I ever had and whenever I was in town, we partied and stayed in the sack for hours on end. Couldn't get enough of it. What I should have noticed, but didn't, she drank all the time. When I'd pick her up, she was already half soused, but very loving and very clinging and I then joined in a few drinks and love and life went right on. No end to our lust. She told me she needed me and my sex, because she came off an unhappy longtime love affair with a married man who strung her along for years, promising divorce and marriage, but never made it true. When she found out he had another girlfriend on the side, she packed up, left town and settled down on the other coast, as far away as she could get. She was only twenty-three and broken hearted. Until I showed up. I was seven years her senior, but that didn't bother me and it didn't seem to bother her. Guess what? Of course you can easily guess. After six months or so, she turned up pregnant. Only a little bit pregnant.

Well, we talked about it and I guess I was ready for a family, so we got married.

Nice little private wedding with friends and close relatives. Couldn't have been nicer.

We rented a nice little home and she stayed home, getting ready for "baby".

The only problem was, I could not convince her to lay off the booze. I got the pediatrician to warn her about possible birth defects because of alcohol, but she never really listened to either of us. I cut down on drinking in front of her and wouldn't let her drink either, but I know she nipped the stuff when I wasn't home. I could tell. Just the way she acted, but all in all we had a good life together.

The Golden Pig

When the baby came, three weeks earlier than she had projected, she was fine, seven pounds, eleven ounces. A bouncy little baby girl. I went bananas. I was crazy about that beautiful little kid and had never been happier in my life. I never looked back. I didn't miss the nightclubs and the bar scene for one minute. My whole life revolved around my little family. Four years later we added a little boy and life couldn't be better. Except for one thing. Booze. She continued to drink all the time. Of course, I could have banned all liquor from the house, but I figured, 'you're a human being, you have a free will and you can control your actions. All your actions, including drinking.'"

Wrong! Instead of getting better, it got worse. As far as I was concerned, once I was home, we could fix a drink and enjoy the evening, the kids and one another. But that's not the way it worked. Half of the time, when I got home, she'd meet me with a lopsided grin and with a slurry voice, she'd say; "Howareyahoney?" and hug my neck and give me a sloppy wet kiss. Boy, that would make me soooo mad! If the kids were still up, I would control myself and act as if everything was honky-dory, but if the kids were already in bed, I'd get in an argument that I couldn't win, would sleep in the guestroom and not talk to her for days. Sometimes I would simply walk out of the door again and hit the corner bar for a few scotches, but that never left me with a very satisfied feeling, so I'd meander back home.

Dozens of times, we talked about the problem, dozens of times she promised she wouldn't drink by herself, but those promises never lasted very long. Other than that, we had a pretty good life. I had moved up in the force and we owned a nice home with a swimming pool in Northern New Jersey. I had landed a steady assignment and worked a pretty regular schedule without too much traveling involved. I had evolved into a happy family man.

Not quite. When she got pretty belligerent at a company Christmas Party, I really blew my cork. Same results, plenty of tears, plenty of regret, plenty of promises and we continued on our way. Until the next time. When we came home from a father's day party at my sister's home, where my darling wife fell flat on her face trying to demonstrate a Cha-Cha, my daughter burst out crying and fled the room in embarrassment. It was obvious something had to be done. The next Saturday we had a family conference. Present were my sister, her husband, my daughter, my wife and myself. We put our cards on the table and at first my wife played the teary role of the innocent victim, until my sister laced into her and told her things like: *ashamed of yourself, unfit mother, embarrassment to the family* and a few more choice words, she became more repenting and after a lot more tears and a lot of embraces by all involved, we turned a new leaf and we would cut down on drinking during the week and maybe even weekends.

Life was grand again. The kids were marvels as far as I was concerned and I couldn't have been happier.

Until.... until things started to deteriorate again little by little and when I reminded her of her promises, she called me an old *Stick-in-the-mud* and an old *Fuddy-duddy* who forgot to have fun in life.

The New Year's Eve party resulted in a hangover that kept her in bed for most of the New Year's day with a headache that didn't quit for two days. Unfortunately, she believed the only cure was cold beer.

I had it! I had absolutely had it!

We were scheduled for a conference in Miami at the end of January, the day after the Super Bowl game. A group of us old timers had planned to fly in early in the morning on Sunday or even the day before so we could get together in a hotel room for a genuine Super Bowl party.

I improved on the plan by making reservations in Jamaica on Friday preceding the party and flying to Miami on Sunday morning. Several of the men brought their wives at their own expense, so the ladies could enjoy the Florida sun and it gave us, my wife and I, a chance to be alone for a few days and iron things out. I was going to threaten divorce, getting custody of the children and any other nasty thing I could think of. This was it. In Jamaica we would either end or save our marriage. I was determined.

My sister came and got the kids, we took off for Newark in an ice storm, but we got there alright. We were on time, but the plane was not. We sat in the plane for two hours waiting for a de-icing truck to get around to us, but it finally happened and we were off into the wild blue yonder on our way to the sunny Caribbean. On our way to a different life.

We had no notion what lay ahead.

Chapter Seven

Hello Mobay

Jamaica was beautiful. Montego Bay was gorgeous from the air, it was exciting on the ground with the Steel Band at the gate and colorful on the trip to the beach hotel. The view from the balcony was stunning. Right at the beach, overlooking the snorkeling tourist and all the bikini-clad beauties, it was a sight to remember.

The Hotel was an older one, close to downtown *Mobay,* nearly under the approach to Montego Airport. We ate a nice lunch of tropical fruit and laid the foundation for our peace conference. I refrained from ordering anything alcoholic with lunch and told her that this was a decision making event. She pouted a little bit when I said: "This is a do or die situation. We're going to reach an agreement and go on with our life, or we're going to split."

When tears welled up in her eyes, I signed the tab and we went upstairs. On our balcony overlooking the gold, teal and blue waters of the Caribbean, I told her in no uncertain terms that this was it. The children were upset by her drunken antics, my family was disgusted with her and I was just plain fed up and out of patience.

She protested some, cried some, screamed now and then, blaming my long working hours and finally collapsed in a sobbing heap of human flesh on the bed. I was dying for a cold beer, but that might have triggered a negative response, so I stuck with fruit juice instead and that wasn't too bad either. I was tempted to go over and hug her and tell her we'd work it out, but we had gone that road so often, that I decided to stick by my guns and let her suffer a while.

As expected and hoped for, she calmed down, told me how sorry she was and how her life without me and the kids would be unbearable and she begged forgiveness and promised to never touch a drop of liquor again.

We hugged and cried, kissed and made up, resulting in a wild lovemaking session with the windows and balcony doors wide open. I still wonder if the people on the beach below could have heard it, but at the time, I really didn't give a damn if they did.

We must have slept for hours, got into our bathing suits and went out snorkeling right in front of the hotel. It was marvelous! The underwater forest of coral in a dozen different colors with all its beautiful array of tropical fish was the most stunning underwater scene I had ever encountered.

The taxi driver who had taken us to the hotel had recommended dinner in the BANANA BOAT, a Harry Belafonte style nightclub with good food and fabulous entertainment. A phone call from the lobby produced the same taxicab and before long we were sitting in a tropical club, complete with palms and bananas. It was set up like an arena, with rows of tables staggered along three sides, facing a rectangular dance floor.

Dinner was served before the entertainment would start and in between courses we danced our shoes off. We were the only couple on the floor. The rest of the audience seemed to be a bunch of over the hill snowbirds that only remembered polkas and waltzes. Nobody seemed to know Reggae, Cha-Cha, Rumba or Mambo. We did and we had a ball.

All went well until she ordered a glass of Chablis and I protested. I changed it to fruit punch and she called me a spoilsport, an old fuddy-duddy and begged: "What difference does one little glass of wine make?" I reminded her of her solemn promise of a few hours ago and if it weren't for the fact that I had already paid for two dinners and entertainment in advance, I might have walked out of the joint. It ruined our mood, but the entertainment sparked it right up again. It was fabulous. I was an ardent Belafonte fan and the singing and dancing was right up my alley. By the way, Belafonte was not there himself, but his imitators were outstanding. Great so far? Well, when I came back from a bathroom trip, she had switched drinks. She claimed it was a coke. Punch was too sweet. You guessed it.... it was rum and coke, a Cuba Libre. Hotdamn! I could have spit. Rather than walking out on her, I ordered a beer and made up my mind: "THIS IS IT! IT'S OVER! SHE GAVE ME A SIGNAL, LOUD AND CLEAR! IT'S OVER BABE!"

Right then and there I decided she was not going to ruin my trip or my life, I was simply going to start divorce proceedings when I got home and might as well enjoy my stay in paradise. We drank and danced, enjoyed the music and continued onto another club after the show. That club was an all native joint. Our taxi driver stayed right with us through the night although he never charged us for waiting for us. He assured us it was positively safe to visit that club and he claimed they had the best island music in Jamaica. It was rather dark, but the drinks were good and the music was fantastic. My wife didn't want to dance anymore, so she sat at the bar and drank with some nice black gentlemen and I danced my shoes off with some of the native girls. I'm not sure why we left. I seem to remember that one of the black dudes acted jealous or maybe my wife was starting to hiccup, anyway, we walked out and didn't find our driver, but it wasn't far to the hotel, so chewing sugar cane that we bought along the road, we worked our way toward our bed until another cab stopped and carried us the rest of the way. That was a good thing. The rum was starting to work and she could barely wobble, let alone walk. At the hotel, I helped her into the elevator and in our door and she collapsed across the bed and passed out.

So much for good intentions. I walked to a corner bar, had a few beers and went back. She never stirred. I slept on the couch.

In the morning I had breakfast by myself at 10 in the morning, slipped into my bathing suit and went snorkeling. She just snored. I didn't even check if she'd soiled herself. I didn't care. Not anymore. Her message was loud and clear: "I'm going to keep on drinking!" The underwater scenery was still unbelievable and I could have floated out there forever, with just my snorkel and my butt sticking out of the water.

My bladder and my throat finally forced me out of the water and after taking care of number one problem, I sat down on a stool at the tiki-bar asking for a cold beer. I really don't remember whether I made the first remark or if it was the Latin beauty who spoke first, but all of a sudden I was involved in an animated conversation with a young bikini clad girl under the palm fronds of the beach bar. She was about twenty-five, mature enough and wore an imitation leopard skin two piece bathing suit. It wasn't really as skimpy as a bikini, but the way she filled it out, it shouldn't have been much smaller or she would have spilled over it. Boy, oh boy! Was she luscious! We may have been talking for more than a half hour before either one of us said: "What's your name?" I gave her my real name, not Ralph, and she said her name was Julia or Julie. As the conversation wore on, she suggested we should retreat to her towel on the beach because she really wanted to get more of a tan. We took our beers and stretched out and talked. When she asked what I did for a living, I told her I was a sales rep for John Deer Tractors. Don't ask me why I said that, but I have a John Deer lawnmower and I wasn't about to tell anyone that I worked for the FBI. She introduced herself as Julia Robinson and when I asked her about her accent, she said she was from Columbia, studying nursing in Miami. When I asked "Robinson?", that's not very Columbian, she said she had adopted her mother's maiden name. because her father had married again and she didn't want anything to do with his last name nor his last wife. She told me that her mother was his second wife and that he had a total of thirteen kids, most of whom she accepted as siblings. Not the last few that were born by the third wife, the one she detested.

In turn, I told her about my situation, my hung-over wife upstairs, my disgust and my determination to end it all in divorce. She asked if I'd considered A/A and I admitted that I hadn't because I'd been told that the initiative has to come from the drunk, not any outsider. She also suggested I go up and check on her, but truthfully, I didn't want to lose sight of this beauty, in case I couldn't find her again. I asked where she was staying and I even suggested going out for dinner that night. Boy I was getting rambunctious! She told me that she had some commitment that night, but gave me her Miami address where she would be again after Monday. I promised I would call her.

Before we parted she said she wanted to show me something at the high-rise hotel where she was staying and my mind immediately dropped into the gutter because I thought she was gonna take me to her room and boy, was I ready.

Wrong! We walked over to the next building where on the first floor was a large beauty parlor/nail-shop. Through the huge showroom-like windows she pointed to a poster on the wall and asked, "Do you believe that?" It was a centerfold of Burt Reynolds from Cosmopolitan Magazine, stark naked, with his hand strategically in his crotch. She thought that was the funniest thing she had ever seen and I joined her enthusiasm. Somewhat. Not wholeheartedly. I had really expected to go upstairs with her and my imagination was already three miles ahead of me. She said goodbye, "See you in Miami", brushed my cheeks with her lips and was gone. I couldn't believe it.

Back at the hotel, I was faced again by a tearful wife, but this time, I only did what was civil, bought her dinner downstairs and went for a walk. I kept hoping to encounter Julia somehow, but I didn't and turned in fairly early with mixed, very mixed emotions.

Chapter Eight

Jamaica Farewell

On Sunday morning, we packed up and caught the flight to Miami. A dozen of my pals were already checked in and we got together in one of their rooms where beer, ice and liquor had already been set up for the football extravaganza. I ordered up some pizza and chips and we were soon in the spirit of the game. Where the wives were, I didn't know and frankly, I didn't care.

The game was a blast, the camaraderie amongst my fellow agents was nearly overwhelming and I temporarily forgot all about my worldly problems.

In the morning the various seminars and meetings kept us writing and running and not till lunch did I have a chance to check our room. She was there alright! All teary, looking like hell and ready to make two more years of promises, but I had to run off to a luncheon speech by one of our big shots, so I urged her to get something to eat and get some sleep.

During a speech, a few hints were dropped as to who was in the running for some awards that evening, but I was already aware that in my district nothing outstanding had happened all year, so I wasn't all that excited, although I was rooting for some of my buddies in other regions that were in the running. I loved those affairs. For the winners it was some overdue recognition for some of their hard work or their smart work during the preceding year. For the non-winners (I don't wanna say losers) an inspiration to do more or do better in the year to come. As I said. I love that kinda stuff. Makes my adrenaline flow.

When it was time to put on the tuxedos and get ready for the dinner awards presentation, my wife was all in red, hair in place, looking gorgeous. For a moment, I forgot about our squabbles and was in love all over again. She promised she would behave and that we would have a good time. I was elated. We went down and joined the rest of the gang at the cocktail lounge. I had beer and my gorgeous partner had a plain coke. I felt so positive, I didn't give the events of the last few days another thought.

After we filed into the dining room, a major problem occurred. Out of all damn things, just after everything was going so well, a cocktail cart came rolling through the aisle, offering drinks. If they had only stayed away, everything would have continued to be great, but when the cocktail waitress in her mini skirt asked my wife if she wanted a drink, of course she said YES and over my protests, she got her Seven/and/Seven, saying this was the only drink of the evening. Sure! Surrounded by my colleagues and their wives, I couldn't make too much of a stink and the results were predictable.

Throughout the awards ceremonies and the speeches, she kept ordering more drinks, because the stupid cart kept coming around and it was all free. All part of the program. She nor I had to produce a nickel and if we had been forced to pay for them, I might have curtailed it somewhat, but it was all beyond my control. What I probably hadn't mentioned was that she was not only pretty, she was a charmer. Everybody loved her and nobody seemed to mind that she laughed a little louder than before, but then again, everybody else was drinking too. One big happy family!

I just got madder by the minute and although the awards and the acceptance speeches were funny, sometimes even hilarious, I just started to boil underneath.

I had considered calling Julia, but I really didn't have the nerve. Not for long…. My resolve was starting to change rapidly.

Chapter Nine

Julia, all of her.

After the awards ceremony and the annual speech by our Director, a dance band took the stage and I got up and walked out. I had it, I had it, I had it!

Dressed in a gorgeous red gown, hair beautifully coiffed, she was slurring again and walking unsteadily. Normally I would have saved her and myself a lot of embarrassment and simply disappeared upstairs and gone to bed. It wasn't even ten o'clock yet and I was thoroughly disgusted. I dug in my wallet for the slip with Julia's address and phone number and after debating with myself for a while, I called her. She was home and invited me over. I couldn't believe it. I walked out the front door in my tuxedo, caught a cab and gave the driver the address. It took twenty minutes and more than twenty-five dollars to get there and I realized, I should have put more cash in my pocket. Too late now.

Julia lived in a second floor condo apartment and welcomed me as a long lost friend. I had nearly forgotten how beautiful she was, but now, with her black hair hanging down over a white silk blouse and in black shorts and bare feet, she looked like she was seventeen. Holy Moses! She didn't act like she was a teenager. She took my jacket, offered a drink and when I said thanks and kissed her lips lightly, she exploded. She grabbed my head and pulled my mouth hard onto hers and I spilled half my drink reaching around her back to mush her into me. When I think about it, I still can't believe that it all happened so fast. I put my drink somewhere, I don't know where and while our lips never disconnected, we wrestled one another out of our clothes and fell on the couch, banging our brains out. I never even got to take off my socks. We collapsed! After a while, we kinda got up. Kinda, because we tried to remain connected but when that didn't work, we sat up, I took my socks off and found my drink. She shared my glass and we started embracing again and before long we were so excited that we were ready to do it again, although this time she led me to the bedroom where we simply dropped down on top of the blankets and started our sexual wrestling match all over again. Somewhere along the line she asked me not to be so loud because her windows were open and the whole neighborhood could hear me. That's the last I remember until about five o'clock, when a bursting bladder woke me up and when I got off the bed, she woke up as well and flipped on a light. My she was a beauty! I shook my wise head as I relieved myself and thought: "Now what? Get dressed and go back to the hotel or try to knock off another little piece?"

    I wasn't really given that choice, because, after Julia made a bathroom trip, she kissed me again with those full hot-blooded lips and we went at it again. This time we didn't fall asleep and I told her I should be at a breakfast meeting by eight, so I'd better hustle and get going. We promised to get back together the next night and I asked to call a cab. She wouldn't hear of it, she slipped on her shorts (no undies) and her blouse (no bra) and after slipping into some flip-flops, we walked to her car, hand in hand. She dropped me half a block from the hotel and I promised I'd call as soon as I got out of the last meeting.

My welcome was worse than I expected. My beloved sat on the balcony, fully dressed and started to lace into me, threatened immediate divorce and even followed me into the bathroom while I shaved and showered and kept right on ranting and raving. I didn't know that she had a vocabulary that was greater than a dockworker's and when I finally got to say something, I said: "Here's your ticket, grab a cab, change your flight and I'll see you back in Jersey."

Well, that started the verbal avalanche all over again, so I simply walked out of the door and went to my meeting. After lunch I checked the room, but she hadn't left. I guess she was in or by the pool. I had really hoped she would fly out. She didn't.

She reappeared at cocktail time as we had a poolside cocktail party/barbeque going at the time , so I didn't even have to go to my room to dress. It was totally casual. All the seminars and lectures had been concluded and the following morning we'd have a group breakfast again with some inspirational speeches, I'm sure and after that we'd fly home. I happily guzzled beer, all the time hoping my darling wife would get sloshed again, but she didn't drink a drop. All my plans about looking up Julia again were fast going down the drain. I slipped out to the men's room and found a phone at the far end of the hotel, where I wouldn't get caught and called Julia. I was afraid she'd be mad or at least annoyed, but she remained calm and pleasant and asked for a number where she could reach me if she came out my way and I gave her my private number at the office. Nobody but me picked up that phone. She fully understood why I couldn't slip out again and we parted with a somber: "wish you were here."

The evening was pleasant enough with all the reminiscing with the old buddies about our past adventures and the party broke up early, 'cause everyone had to pack and get ready. All night I had the feeling that she kept an eye on me and I was surprised she hadn't followed me to the bathroom earlier. Anyway, we ended going upstairs at about the same time. I preceded her by a few minutes and when she wanted to start talking again, I cut her short by saying: "Everything that needed saying has been said and I have to get up early, so goodnight."

We remained civil throughout our departure and the entire flight. Our car was still covered by a sheet of ice at Newark, but it started and when the windshield finally defrosted, my mental harness defrosted a little too and we drove home in silence, lost in our own thoughts.

Being reunited with the kids was a pleasure as always and little by little we started talking to one another again, especially about the everyday things, like kids, food, bills and work. We didn't drink a drop, neither of us and life nearly continued as if Jamaica and Miami had never happened.

Not for long!

Chapter Ten

Washington D.C.

Everything about work, home, kids and wife had nearly returned to normal. Work was always exciting, the kids never ceased to amaze and amuse me and my beloved hadn't drunk a drop since our return from Miami. At one point she went as far as apologizing. That was a first. She always blamed it on me, my long hours and the fact that I was an old fuddy-duddy. This time she tearfully took the blame and said she was sorry for what she had put me through. Well, well, well! I was so happily surprised, that I hugged her and cried from sheer happiness. It was beautiful. We shed our pajamas that we started to wear after our Jamaica escape and made beautiful love together. I couldn't have been happier.

Then… like a bolt of lightning…. Julia on the phone. She had to be in New York. Something about her father's business and she had tickets to the Opera. "Did I like Opera? La Traviata?"

"When?"

"Next Tuesday. If you come by the hotel, we can have a drink before the performance, okay?"

Well, I hemmed and hawed and promised to call back, because I had to check my schedule. Sure! Boy, talk about mixed emotions. I vividly remembered the exciting night in Miami and on the other hand, things were going well at home. I couldn't think straight for the rest of the day. When I came home, I was halfway hoping that my wife would have been boozing, because that would give me a perfect excuse to take up with Julia again. No such luck. She was as nice and sober as could be and I convinced myself to call Julie and tell her: "Can't make it!" That was it. I had a good life, a good marriage, fine kids, secure job, everything a man could wish for. There was no way I was gonna screw that up. I didn't call back.

Friday night we brought the kids to my sister's house, because we were invited to a dinner dance of the Armenian Scholarship Society and we always enjoyed their food and the music. All these Armenians brought their home cooked meals and all we had to do was bring our own bottle. Set-ups provided. I was being cautious. I brought a bottle of Chablis and hoped that my bride would drink sodas. You're probably starting to think that I'm a glutton for punishment. You're right. Or maybe I'm unreasonably optimistic! Or both. Possibly both.

The music was great. One set of Armenian music and dances, (it was all Greek music to me), then a set of traditional American tunes, then a raffle and of course…. a belly dancer. It was marvelous. Except….. "Just one glass of wine….don't be such a fuddy-duddy all the time. You know I'll be good. Just one glass."

Sure!

On Saturday, I found an excuse to go to the office and called Julia. "What hotel and what time?"

On the way out of the door on Tuesday, I told the family that I had an important meeting in New York and I might be late.

"A drink before the theater?" Forget it. I didn't finish half a drink before we were in bed again. We never did see La Traviata.

This time we talked more. One of her older brothers (twenty years older) was an attorney in New York and she had to deliver some papers to him from her father. He lived on Long Island, but she wouldn't stay with him and insisted on staying in the city so she could catch the Opera. She said she could convince her father that her studies wouldn't suffer if she ran more errands for him and she might have more of these missions in the future. Could I ever join her in Washington or Chicago? Why? She had another lawyer brother in Chicago and a first cousin in D.C. who was also a lawyer. If I could manage to come over for a few days, we could really do things together. Things other than sex? My mind was reeling. I was at least fifteen years her senior. Why did she want to continue a relationship with me? Didn't she have different boyfriends right and left? Why me? Yet she seemed so genuine and I enjoyed her company so much that I said, "Sure, but give me enough notice, so I can work it out."

I left her at twelve midnight, got home at one and snuck in the door, grabbed some milk and eased into bed. Thank God, I wasn't asked to perform again, because I'm sure I couldn't.

Two weeks passed and a similar invitation came in about Washington.

Of course! Our headquarters was in D.C. and it was not unusual that I would drive off for a conference for a day or two. It took me less than three hours to get there and I couldn't wait. I checked into a room in the same hotel and my expense account would verify that I was there. My, I was getting to be good at that kinda game.

We talked in bed for hours. She was so comfortable with me in the nude, as if we'd known each other for fifteen years. As she moved around the room, stark naked, I'd just lie there and admire that beautiful shape. What a doll. We talked a lot that time. I learned she was from Cartagena and that her father ran an import/export business and had children, age forty through three, by three different wives. He insisted that all his kids got an education and mostly in the United States. She herself had a nursing degree already in Colombia, but she had to be certified in Florida in order to work there. She said she didn't want to live near her stepmother in Cartagena, but would find a job in the Miami area as soon as she graduated. It all sounded good. She had a definite affinity for the classics and we did take in some symphonies and operas. I'm now talking about a period of some years.

You see, Washington was just a two day, three night adventure,

The Golden Pig

but it had me completely hooked. I was so totally enwrapped by that beautiful talkative creature that I couldn't think of life without her any more. Crazy as it may seem, I managed to live a happy married life and about once a month, I'd meet up with Julia. Detroit, Chicago, D.C. again, New York of course and when we had another conference in Miami, I went alone and spent a bunch of time in Opa Locka, where she had bought a little condo. (Daddy must be doing alright.) Nobody had a hint of what I was doing. Not my wife, not my co-workers, not my friends, nobody. Julia never found out who I really worked for and I never new what she was up to. We just had a lot of fun, a lot of raw sex. I couldn't even find a hint of guilt on my conscience. I was totally content. This went on for years and no one ever caught on. My wife still hit the bottle, but mostly, just a drink or two, except at parties. Same problem. I put up with it. It was my excuse for what I was doing.

Of course, it had to burst sometimes. A couple of things started to happen. Julia called in hysterics one day. She had a car accident right near her home, someone hit her at a stop sign. That in itself was no big deal. She had insurance and got a rental car and that was when she realized that she had left $48,000 in the glove compartment of her wreck and when she ran by the body shop, the money was gone and nobody knew anything.

"Forty-eight thousand dollars? Why do you drive around with that kinda money?"

"Oh, it wasn't mine. I had to deliver it for my father."

"Forty-eight thousand dollars? Have you people never heard of checks?"

"You don't understand! That's how my father does business. He's very old fashioned."

"You can say that again!" I thought for a minute that she was gonna hit me up for a loan, but that never happened. She was just shook up and needed my shoulder to cry on. Cry she did. In D.C. one night, but not for long. It didn't seem like it was really such a big deal. I was flabbergasted. Then I accidentally noticed something else. She usually checked in as Robinson, this time she had checked in as Radowicz. I didn't question her at first, but while she was in the bathroom, I flipped through her purse and found two passports. Robinson and Radowicz. Later, much later, I mentioned something about the different name on the hotel register and she said: My older brothers are all Radowicas. That was before my father changed his name."

"Oh? Wasn't he originally Colombian?"

"No, he came over after World War Two and at first he kept his own name. Then he changed it to Robinson because he wanted to be regarded as an American, but now his name is Vargas. He became a Colombian National. So I was born Robinson and I have all my mother's looks and features because she was a native from the mountains. The high mountains. May even have had some Indian blood in her. She was a beautiful woman. You would have loved her."

"I believe that. If she looked like you, you'd better believe it."

We roamed around for nearly four years and we could have gone on forever. Except for two things. One, as you might have guessed, the drinking problem never went away. It got worse. In a different way. The kids were getting older and my wife had found a job. Great! In a way, yes! It was great, she liked her job, it didn't interfere with the kids school life and after school activities and it gave her no time to drink during the day. At that point in life I believed we would stay married forever or at least until the kids were grown and gone.

No such luck. On her job she befriended a middle aged girl, good looking and divorced and she brought her over sometimes and that was okay. She wore a little too much make-up, she smoked and laughed too loud, but basically was a good person, I think. Slowly, things changed. The girls would stop for a drink after work. Innocent enough to start with, but when the kids expected dinner on the table and mom was still in a bar somewhere, the situation became explosive. My daughter was pretty handy at fixing dinner and most nights I was home early enough, so we could eat together, with or without mom. I kept saying to myself: "I've got a bad habit and she has a bad habit, so we'll live on without making too much of a ruckus over it."

The kids had a hard time with it, especially my daughter and one evening, my son was already in bed, mom came staggering in, ossified! She fell across the threshold and we helped her up, my daughter and I and my daughter screamed at her: "Mom, why do have to drink all the time, look at you! You're stone drunk."

"Don't you lecture me Miss Prim. I can do what I want and you keep your snot nose out of it, you hear!"

That's when I made a mistake. I should've know better. You should never argue with a drunk, but I did that time. I hollered at her: "I'll tell you what! If you ever take one more drink of alcohol, you're out of this house, we've had it!"

"Oh yeah? Oh yeah? I get out of this house? No. no buddy, you get out! I'll divorce you and you get out!" She screamed so loud that our son woke up and came running down the stairs in his pajamas, crying: "No, No, No divorce, no divorce!" and clung to his mothers leg. She whacked him on the side of his head, screaming: "Aw, shut up you brat!" and the kid went flying.

Within a second, I slugged her, hit her smack across her chin and she toppled onto the couch where she crumbled into a crying heap. Well, my kids ran over and hugged her while crying "No Mommy, No mommy, no divorce. We love you, we love you, oh Mommy!"

Before long I sat right there with them, all bundled together, all crying, me included and it was a bit like a movie scene; someone's hysterical, someone else slaps her and the hysteria stops. Ever seen that? Same here. It was as if she was instantly stone sober. We cried, calmed down, put the kids back in bed and put ice on her jaw.

"We'll talk in the morning."

I called the office that I would be late, she called she wasn't coming in and we talked after the kids left for school.

We agreed. I had never hit a woman in my life and when the circumstances became such that I would actually hit a woman, no matter what the justification, I had to get out. She said, she had felt for a long time that I didn't love her any more and she wanted out. I wondered if her girlfriend from work had something to with it, but it didn't matter. We would sell the house, buy a condo for her nearby, so the kids could stay in the same schools and near the same friends. We would work out an alimony and child support arrangement and we could stay friends for the kids sake and we would alternate weekends with them. And that's what we did. Real friendly like.

Julia? You wouldn't believe this.

Chapter Eleven

The Julia Goof

Everything went fairly smoothly. We didn't get as much for the house as we had anticipated and the condo cost more than we had expected, so after everything was settled and organized, I had only a few dollars left. Less than eight thousand. Privately I had dreamed about getting a little cottage on the water nearby, close enough to the kids and close enough to the office. That thought had to be put on hold for a while and we went looking for a suitable apartment for me. When I say 'WE", I mean all four of us, Mom, Pop and the two kids. My daughter was not at all shook up about the separation because, as a typical teenager, she loved to be far away from dad's strict discipline.

We found a neat little place in Piermont, just above the New York State line. It was right on the Hudson River, it had boat slips and a boat ramp, because I had been dreaming about getting a ski boat, so my son and I could go ski-ing and fishing. The whole family agreed on the location and we set about the task of furnishing and decorating the place. We had divided everything evenly and my half of the furniture ended up in storage. We rented a U-Haul, emptied the storage unit and moved dear old Daddy into his bachelor quarters and the kids wanted to spend the first night with me in the spare bedroom. This worked out just beautifully! I was thrilled.

The complex had a nice pool and that made it even more attractive. Everyone was thrilled, including mama. She seemed to be happy with her new found freedom and the fact that I wouldn't bug her anymore about drinking. Kudos for everyone.

Of course, Julia came over within ten days. It was marvelous. No time pressure at all. She could stay until it was my week-end to have the kids and that was okay by her because she had work to do and studies to complete. I did wonder; she had been studying now for all the four years that I'd known her and she still hadn't finished. She was in the U.S. under a student visa and she was milking that for time, as best she could. I really didn't care. Life was great. The little condo that I rented belonged to a man who was overseas in Hungary, because he had immigration problems. I paid my rent to an agency, and I assumed, the agency would send the money to him. After three months of carefree living, a lady from the agency approached me and told me that her customer, the Hungarian, was having problems and needed to sell his property and I was given first option. How much? He didn't ask an extravagant price. As a matter of fact it was cheap in comparison. It was a great opportunity except for one thing; *he needed fifteen thousand down.* I had bought a used sixteen foot Larson bow rider for only four thousand dollars, so my money supply was real low. As fate would have it, Julia was there when the real estate lady came over with the proposal and of course she heard my stall. I had to work out some details with my bank in order to come up with that kind of money and the sales lady was very understanding, but she did say she would hold the deal for me with just a thousand dollar deposit. I still hesitated, but finally wrote a check for a thousand bucks and asked her to hold it for a few days, because I had to transfer some money to my checking account. No problem! I signed some papers and she left, congratulating me on being the proud owner of the condo. I didn't feel half as happy as she did, because I now had to scrape up some money. Julia snuggled up to me and asked: "Why aren't you happy? You look so worried."

"Because now I have to somehow scrape up a lot of money in time for the closing."

"How much?"

"How much? About ten thousand clams."

"No problem! I lend it to you. Give it back when you can."

"Oh, but I don't think I can do that."

"Yes you can. I write a check. Just a minute." She got up and got her purse. "I write you a check for nine thousand nine hundred and ninety dollars. Over ten thousand you have to report to the bank where you got it and the IRS steps in and that always spells trouble!"

"Now wait a minute. I can not accept that kinda money from you, I…."

"That's right! You can NOT accept it. It's not a gift. It's a loan."

"You carry that kind of money in your checking account?"

"Sometimes I do. Here. Congratulations. I like this place, you like this place, your kids like this place, okay? Everybody happy."

"I don't know what to say……'

"Say nothing, kiss me."

Well, what do you know? Just like that I owned a condo. In retrospect that turned out to be the stupidest thing I had ever done. It came back to hound me big time.

But at the time I was as happy as a duck in the pond. My son and I really took to the water in our little boat, but my daughter was too busy with boys, and I hardly ever saw her. So my boy and I spent nearly every weekend together..

This was how I met Ray, by the way. They had a thirty four foot cabin cruiser that they docked at the marina where I launched my boat and we got to be boating, partying and drinking friends. Everything was swell. I tried to round up the money to repay Julia, but she put no pressure on me whatsoever and time just flew by. She talked me into coming to Cartagena with her and meet her dad and his operation and take a week to tour Colombia. I had vacation coming, so why not?

It was great and it was strange. Great city, great trip, great countryside, great father, but a strange portside shipping operation. He ran a dilapidated operation out of a couple of hangar like buildings on the wharf and the only thing impressive was his air conditioned office and his big Mercedes sedan. It didn't really look like an operation that would support thirteen kid's college educations. Much to my surprise, he was a lanky six foot man, with a shock of gray hair and a German face. He even spoke with a bit of a German accent. His English was quite good, spiced with Spanish expressions and curse words. He made me very uncomfortable by asking too many questions about my work and about my background. It was as if he didn't approve of my relationship with his young daughter and we weren't invited to his home.

Julia explained that her stepmother wouldn't want us there anyway and we didn't worry about it, one way or the other. We took a hovercraft to Barranquilla, spent the night in that beautiful city and flew to Bogota the next morning. Wow! I loved that city! We walked around for two days and I couldn't get enough of the old culture, the cathedrals, the people, I was having a ball.

On the third day, everything came to a sudden halt. We walked out of the hotel, hesitated about taking a cab or a horse carriage, when a shot rang out and knocked me flat on my ass. Julia screamed, fell right on top of me and yelled bloody murder. The hotel porter came running, then fell on his face as if he was shot as well or as if he expected more shots. The driver of the carriage ran over as well and someone screamed: "Medico! Policia!" and I passed out. When I came to, I was lying on the floor in the hotel lobby, Julia's face was just two feet from my nose and a medical man, nurse?, doctor? was taping up my right shoulder and arm. I felt no pain. I was kinda numb, but common sense returned to my foggy brain.

"What happened? Julia, what happened?"

Through her tears she cried: "Honey, somebody shot you."

"Me? Why?"

"I don't know, I don't know. The ambulance is on its way. You'll be okay?"

"But who shot at me? I didn't do anything, did I?"

"No, you didn't. Here is the ambulance. I'm going with you." We left together and when she held my hand on the way to the hospital, I thought of my wallet and my I.D.s. They certainly would want to know if I had hospitalization and other insurance and who my carrier was and that would reveal that I was with the FBI. Julia might have a fit. It never happened. They didn't even check my pockets.

Later I learned, Julia paid for everything. At the hospital, they took me into the operating room, put me out, repaired my collarbone and stitched up my wound.

Three hours later, I was whisked away in a cab. Julia had gotten our luggage, changed our flight and we were leaving beautiful Bogota before three in the afternoon.

Once we were back in Miami, we moved into a nursing home, attached to a hospital and within an hour, I had been x-rayed, re-stitched, bandaged anew and put in a partial cast. By then I was feeling pain, but I was provided with pain killers, so it was bearable.

Once I was alone with Julia in a private room, I asked her again: "Who the hell would wanna shoot me?", but all she kept saying was: "I don't know, I don't know."

Something was very wrong. She was scared stiff. She didn't want to take me to her condo, she didn't want me to fly home and stay in my place, she simply wanted me to stay in that home and convalesce for about a week. I couldn't do that! I had to be back on the job and I certainly had to report that I was injured. She wouldn't hear of it. I think they slipped me a mickey, because I fell sound asleep. When I awoke at three in the morning, Julia wasn't there. Nobody was there. There was a phone next to the bed. I got the operator to connect me with the Miami FBI and told them to get me out of there and back to Jersey in a hurry. Of course, in the middle of the night that was a ridiculous request, but it set the wheels rolling.

"Man down!" spurred everybody into action and by five in the morning, I was hauled out on a stretcher, by seven thirty I was up in

the air in a Falcon and by eleven I was taken from Teterboro airport to the Hackensack General Hospital, where my bureau chief was already waiting for me.

Chapter Twelve

Deep, Deep Doodoo.

Every word was recorded.

I was asked if I needed something for my pain and when I answered in the negative, the questions started.

"Where was I shot?" "Why?" "By whom?" "What was I doing in Bogota?"

"Didn't I know that as an FBI agent I had to clear all foreign travel in advance?"

"Who was I with?" "What's the connection?" "Where else was I in Colombia?"

When I mentioned Cartagena, their ears perked up and when I told them that I met Julia's father, the reaction was astounding: "*You met Vargas? Lucky Vargas?*"

"Huh?"

My immediate chief, Bruce Bongers, leaned forward and repeated: "You met Lucky Vargas?"

"I don't think that was his first name. I think it's Herrmann or Johann."

"Good God! No wonder you were shot. You're lucky to be alive. These guys don't miss as a rule. How come they missed you?"

Well, I could only tell them what I thought had happened. Just as I bent over to call the carriage driver the shot rang out. If I had stood straight up he probably would have pierced my heart. I got the shivers just thinking about it. I must have turned white, because they stopped the recorder, offered me some orange juice and held my head up for a minute. I nearly passed out. The big brass walked out of the room and they let me rest a bit with only the recorder operator sitting on the far side near the window.

I did feel better after about ten minutes and the big boys came back in. First of all, my immediate boss, Bruce Bongers from our Secaucus office, Mark Slogan from our Manhattan branch and special investigator Phil Evans from D.C. The questions started all over again and finally I asked: "Gentlemen, please, what is the big deal? I took ten days off to go on a trip with a friend and you're acting as if I'm the criminal of the year."

"Well, consider that you are just that." This was Bongers speaking. "You're under arrest and you will remain in our custody for the time being."

"What for? " I nearly jumped out of bed, but two pair of hands put me back down. "What's my crime? What am I being charged with?"

"Conspiracy to transport cocaine."

"Who? Me? I've never even seen the stuff. I don't even smoke cigarettes? You have this all wrong, I'm telling you, you're all wrong!"

"Not based on what you've told us so far."

My whole world crumbled. At first they wouldn't let me see my kids, but after a week they came to see me in the hospital and they figured I had been wounded in a stake-out with some bandits and they walked out being proud of me. They didn't realize that I was under guard. I was not allowed to call Julia, but the attitude of my superiors started to change. At first they treated me like an arch criminal. The $9,990 check from Julia was certain proof that I had been paid for some underhanded activity. In a court of law it would certainly convict me. I still marvel at the way they figured all that out so fast. Well, after all, they are the FBI. Little by little, my story seemed to become more believable as they traced my travels with the Colombian bombshell. At first they thought she was the reason for my divorce, but my buddy agents who had known me over the years gladly confirmed that my marriage had been rocky for a long time. They had all seen my wife in action.

The one who seemed to believe me more than any other was my direct boss, Bruce. He listened as the whole story evolved, all the way back to Montego Bay. One morning he loaded me in his car and took me to my condo, which was a little dusty, but in fine shape. He let me collect my bills and my checkbook and I started to hope that everything could be worked out. While he was becoming more convinced that I was telling the truth, the pattern changed. I was discharged from the hospital and driven to D.C. In the J. Edgar Hoover Building, they started piecing things together. Who were the brothers? The lawyers? The cousin in D.C.? The lawyer? How often did Julia travel to deliver things? Paper or money? Did I know about her passports? What was her explanation? Did I never get suspicious? Didn't I ever question her?

I hated to tell'em that I was so busy enjoying my outlandish sex that I never thought about much else. Thank God, nobody shook their majestic heads in disapproval.

Of course the details about Vargas' operation was the main topic. By the time they were finished with that I believe they could reconstruct his buildings brick by brick.

It still didn't explain why I was shot or worse, why somebody wanted to kill me.

Their theory was that Vargas must have checked my background after he met me and decided that I was undercover and used his daughter as a shield in order to integrate his operation and that's why I had to be taken out.

"How could that guy check me out?"

"Remember his lawyer sons in the U.S.? They probably figured you out in one hour."

"Good God! May I finally ask, what's with Julia? Have you picked her up?"

"No and we're not going to. First of all, her dad may wanna deal with her, maybe cut her off financially, maybe bring her home permanently. He probably doesn't trust her anymore. Secondly, we're contemplating the thought of you taking up with her again in order to get deeper into their organization. We need your help."

The director himself had called me to his office and while I enjoyed the view of the Washington monument, he signaled me over to the seat next to his desk.

"Let's make something very clear. You are suspended from regular duty. You could be prosecuted and dismissed without a pension. We're not going to do that. We're going to give you early retirement, but not yet. You're going to earn your pension. You will follow our orders to a tee or else, you'll end up in the can, possibly for a long time. We're not going to ask for your opinion or your approval. You're going to work with us without questioning and without flinching. Is that understood?"

I sagged in my seat and nearly collapsed. I was regarded as a criminal, a stoolie, an undercover man with no recourses and no security. All of a sudden my shoulder hurt. My brain choked. What had I done that was so terrible? I didn't answer.

"Did you understand me, son?" He called me son! I perked up. It couldn't be all that bad. He was trying to impress me, scare me! But did I have a choice? NO.

"I understand you sir. Tell me what you want me to do."

To my surprise, he stood up and shook my hand. My left hand. That was quite a switch. I was starting to feel a lot better.

There were a lot more questions, a lot more details to remember and record, but finally, we left for home. Bongers instructed me on the way of what was expected from me.

He was a tall, six foot two, blond haired muscular man, with a fatherly demeanor about him. I would trust that man with my life. We were seated in the back of the company Buick and he outlined the plan. I was to get back in touch with Julia, but immediately admit that I was with the FBI, "don't deny that", because her daddy probably told her so already and explained to her why I had to be taken out. I was to tell her that I had the FBI get me out of Miami, because I feared for my life and in turn, the FBI kept me in custody because they suspected I was in on the drug trade. I was to tell her how they found out about her check and that I was being released on a partial pension and would start looking for a job as soon as my shoulder was healed. I was to tell her that I was not allowed to communicate with her anymore and not to see her at all. After that, I was to await her reactions.

Chapter Thirteen

Judas?

I have no idea how Judas felt when he betrayed Jesus, but I know how I felt when I was supposed to call Julia and take up with her again, but now as an undercover man for the government. I understand, that's how her father pegged me in the first place when he first found out that I worked for the FBI instead of John Deer. I still marvel at the intelligence systems those coke dealers must have. Within two days, they had figured my true identity and had an assassin all lined up to take me out. Good God!, We run around blindly in the belief that we have everything under control in the U.S., but apparently, crooks and terrorists have access to our best protected secrets as if there are no safeguards whatsoever.

I wondered if my car or my boat might explode underneath my butt one day, because I didn't think they planned to let me live after my unexpected survival. I had to learn a lot from Julia when I got a hold of her. When? If? I had no idea if her dad would let her live in Opa Locka any longer or if she had to be eliminated too. Her condo had been under surveillance, as well as her school, but she hadn't been seen since my sudden flight from Miami.

Here's the deal we worked out. I would pretend to live in my condo at Piermont, while in reality, the FBI set me up in a safe house in Westchester County across the Hudson River. (Not far

The Golden Pig

from Ray and Sarah by coincidence) My phone number remained the same and other than a message from Julia, two hours after my hasty disappearance, there were no messages from her. Her phone was still operative and I left word that I was on disability retirement and would be at the condo, in the pool or out on my boat: "So, please call!"

I also wrote her a letter, in case her mail was forwarded and from there on in, all I could do was wait. I got to take my kids to a movie, watched a few ballgames with my son and set up shop in my new modest little home across the river. I reported to the office at irregular intervals. Sometimes because I wanted to record some information that I thought might be helpful, sometimes because I was asked to report. In reality, I was mostly retired. They didn't give me any further assignments because I was to serve just one purpose: *"Bait for Lucky Vargas by means of his daughter."*

They failed to tell me that I would probably lose my life in the process, but I felt I had no right to complain. What seemed like a little mistake to me, was a major crime in the eyes of the organization and I was paying the price. In my new home I received stacks of information about the drug trade and why "Lucky" was so important to them. Since I had never been assigned to that department in our organization, I was really green and my eyes popped a few times when I read about murders within the cartels and between the cartels. It read like civil war. I also never had any idea about the size of our enforcements in the mountains of Colombia. CIA operations, Green Berets with helicopters, Colombian troops and local police, it seemed like they had a miniature war going on. Most of it was beyond the reach of the FBI, but when the stuff reached the States, it became our concern, along with the CIA. I was really baffled at the scope of the operations. Millions, maybe billions of dollars are involved in the importation and distribution network throughout the United States. I couldn't imagine how tons and tons of cocaine come into our country every day and how millions of dollars get collected and transported back to Colombia. I now had a fair picture how money moved within our borders. I had been a witness to that for years, without suspecting a thing. Boy, was I ignorant! I was itching to get more actively involved and my moods swung between sympathy for Julia and anger at her callous way of using me as a cover, a peon.

Part of me wanted to crucify her and part of me wanted to cuddle her, dry her tears and say: "You were an innocent victim like me. Let's make up."

The government had different ideas. She was definitely going to be *"bait"*, while I was definitely going to be the *"hook."* I was given no other choices. I guess I had to be grateful that I still received my salary, so I could make my condo payments and take care of my alimony and child support. I guess I should have been content. I wasn't.

Three weeks passed when I finally received a call. I wasn't in. She said she'd call again. Didn't leave a number, no address, nothing. Just: "I'll call again." Period.

I changed my phone message. This time my recorder added: "or call my cell at dadadada." Once she had my cell number, there was a better chance of catching me. My private number at my office wasn't mine any more, but though I checked with them on occasion, she had never tried to contact me there. Calling the FBI office might be considered a No-No.

Finally, just at four weeks, she got me as I was crossing the Tappan Zee Bridge.

She had gotten my letter. It had been forwarded to Naples, Florida where she was staying with a cousin. Good God? How many cousins and siblings did she have and were they all part of the network? I explained how I had gotten out of Miami so fast, because I feared for my life. She understood. (Surprise, surprise!) She had heard from her dad that it was necessary to eliminate me. She had screamed at him and told him I was not trying to spy on his operation and in turn he said; "Then why did he lie to you about his job. He lied to you for five years. How do explain that?" He was convinced she was set up and he ordered her to come back to Cartagena. She refused and went in hiding. How long that would last, she didn't know, because she couldn't contact any of her brothers in the U.S. and she was now totally cut off from all funds. I said I could try to raise the money I owed her, but she said that wasn't necessary yet. Maybe later. Getting together? Not immediately. I told her how I was reprimanded about leaving the country without clearance and how I was restricted to New York and New Jersey, It would be up to her to come in my direction and I urged her to work on it.

At least I planted a seed in her mind, that I really had no ulterior motives when I associated with her and went along to Colombia. It was up to her to believe it or not.

I called Bongers and he urged me to come into the office and report in person, rather than on the phone.

He was very cordial. I guess he believed me all along, but even more so now. I felt he could read my sincerity. He listened quietly and asked some questions, all that time taking notes. At one point he asked me: "May I see your cell?"

For a minute I thought he didn't trust me, but when he flipped it opened and scrolled to: *"Recent calls"*, I realized that I hadn't even thought of it. Her phone number was right there! He copied it down, pushed a button on his intercom and said: "Track down number so and so and report back to me as soon as you have it." I was dumbfounded. Was I really getting too old for intelligence work? Should that have been my first reaction? I felt sooooo stupid.

Bongers didn't react one way or the other. Asked about my shoulder, the new house, the kids and had I read all the literature he had given me? By the time I started commenting about that, an agent walked in with a print-out and when Bongers said: "That was close. She said Naples, but she called from Bonita Springs which is just north of there. Well, she might have been visiting there. Maybe another cousin." I had to laugh in spite of the circumstances.

We parted with the understanding that I was going to play a more active role shortly and that from here on in Julia was going to be under surveillance. He'd keep me posted.

My cast came off. X-rays were positive or negative. They were positively good and negative as far as bad results were concerned. In other words, I looked good. I could now drive with both hands again. Pain had always been negligible but the main advantage was I could toss and turn in my sleep again. So far, so good. I wondered if I could make love again like before? Why not?

Every time I took my boat out, an explosive expert, dressed like a marine mechanic would check my boat and my door was checked for booby-traps because we were sure the smugglers did not only find my identity, they must also have found my address. Nothing ever happened. We started to wonder if they believed they killed me or maybe, they felt that they had scared me off. Anyhow, they didn't try to eliminate me again. Not yet!

After another week, I was called in again, but this time for training. The brass in D.C. had decided that I should recruit Julia for our side, promise her witness protection and then train her how to obtain and forward information to us, especially about trafficking. Oh boy. I didn't think that was ever gonna work. Well.... They kept paying me. I might as well try to earn it.

The next time she called, I was to ask for her number. I had to act like I hadn't noticed it on my cell. Once I had her number, I had to start developing a plan to meet up with her, somewhere away from Florida. Too many cousins.

The meeting place was to be in Bermuda. During World War Two, Bermuda had been the international spy center of the world for both sides of the conflict and we still had swank locations that were perfectly bugged. When she did call, I told her honestly that I missed her terribly, because that was the truth. Besides that, if I didn't get some good sex very soon, I might break out in pimples. I didn't tell her that though.

First I suggested we'd meet in North Florida, because she could drive there, but she kept driving to a minimum, because she was afraid that the accident with the $48,000 was staged and that that could happen again. I asked about flights out of Naples or Fort Myers. Some place that she could get out of safely. Maybe we should fly to North Carolina? Anyway, I planted a seed. She hadn't heard from her father directly, but the cousin told her he was blowing a gasket. He felt he was being betrayed. Which he wasn't as yet, but I was working on it.

I asked her where I could reach her, but she told me it was better if she called me.

Okay, waiting for your call. I was tempted to say I love you, but we had never said that before, so I didn't. Might have sounded phony anyway.

Bongers noted the number down from which she called this time (I had gotten smarter) and said, "Good show. Talk to you in a little bit."

A little bit became a half hour and the news was, she was now on a cell phone and without being connected to tracking material, they couldn't figure out where she called from. He was very complimentary and told me that we were making headway.

Headway? A little maybe. The next time she called she did give me her cell number and she had checked on flights out of Naples. An easy one would be to the Bahamas if I could get there too, but she was afraid that her daddy's tentacles might reach into the Bahamas as well. I again suggested Carolina, the West Virginia mountains, anywhere but where I really wanted to go. I was hoping that SHE would suggest Bermuda, but she didn't.

My chance came when she called one day and suggested Alaska and I said: "Too damn cold, how about Bermuda, at least its warmer. Europe some place maybe?"

She bit! "Europe is too far. Bermuda sounds good."

"Let me buy the tickets, okay? You must be running low by now."

"No, let's pick a date and I'll meet you there."

"Okay, I'll get on the computer, find a nice place and fly in a day early, so I can pick you up at the airport. What day looks good to you?"

"How about if we meet on a cruise ship in New York and sail over there? It's only a two day cruise and that way we can relax and get reacquainted again."

"Wow! What a great idea. How often do these cruises leave for Bermuda? Do you have any idea? I don't have a clue."

"I'll find out. Do you have any problems leaving your kids? I mean, don't you have them every other weekend?"

"Theoretically I do, but the truth is; I have them most weekends, which is what I love and I should not have any problem switching with my ex. I'm sure I can work that out. And then there's always my sister nearby, if needed. No, don't worry about that. Check the schedules and let me know the cost, okay. I owe you a few."

"I'll see. Talk to you soon."

Chapter Fourteen

The Bermuda Triangle.

The thought: *Bermuda Triangle* flashed through my mind because there we would be.... The three of us.... The happy trio. Julia, the FBI and me. What a thought! For the first time since my "arrest and retirement" did I feel excited about being a part of the whole scheme of things. I was going to work again as an experienced G-man. Besides I would get back in bed with Julia. If anything would get me excited, the reunion with Julie certainly would.

As I had time to think about it, I actually marveled that after all this time, Julia and I had never used the word 'love' between us. Yet, I was under the impression, that she hadn't had another man in her life or in her bed since we first met. Why? I didn't know. I couldn't even fathom it. Why would a good looking chick like her string along with an old married man for some occasional sex? I'd better get my mind off the subject and call Bongers.

He was excited about the prospect and would line up a nice apartment or hotel suite in Bermuda, complete with all the listening devices. (cameras in the bedroom?) He would let me know within the day and I was to make the arrangement with my own credit cards under my own name. The word FBI should not be shown on any record. I would be reimbursed before I would even receive the bill. Halleluiah! I couldn't wait for her return call.

There were some other things to be clarified, Should I tell her that I lived in a house in Westchester County? What kind of protection plan could I offer her? What location? What guaranteed income? I'd better go in for a complete briefing.

I called the office and after being on hold several times for three or four minutes was told to come in at 1 PM the next day. Okay already! I was getting more excited by the minute.

The offer was as follows: Julia should cooperate with the government.

The government would provide her with a cozy condominium.

She would be provided with a Degree in Nursing and a Masters in Education in any state she wanted to live.

She would receive an annual stipend of $50,000 a year, to be adjusted if her nursing income started to exceed fifty grand.

Julia would receive a new identity. (A third passport?) and year-round protection.

What a deal? I was certain she would bite on that, of course depending on how badly she wanted to see her relatives again. Big question! At least I had something to work with.

I did ask them about cameras in the bedroom and they laughed a lot, implying they might start a porno film industry of their own. Seriously, no cameras. Listening devices all over the place. All I had to do now was to inform them of my departure date.

Two days later she called, Apparently, cruise ships leave New York for Bermuda kinda frequently. Generally, people book a trip to Bermuda, the Bahamas, Fort Lauderdale or Miami and back to New York. Booking for just a return trip New York-Bermuda was no problem. Being done all the time.

"When do we go? And who orders the tickets? I have the apartment all set in Bermuda, but can you still travel under your own name? And what name do you use for airline travel?"

"Can you ask one question at the time, please? Don't get over excited." She snickered on the other end of the line. "We leave next

Wednesday. Pier 40, Holland America Line. The Westerdam. Two cabins have been reserved. One in your name and one in name of Mrs. Robinson."

"Missus?"

"Yes, I now travel as a married woman. What did you expect? That I should travel as a KEPT woman? Shame on you." She was certainly her old self again. "Unless you gave me a phony name, you simply check in as yourself. Don't forget to tell'em you work for John Deer. Hahahaha!" Boy was she on a roll! She must have been excited about getting together again as well.

"You mean, you already paid for me?'

"All set, Romeo. Boarding time begins at nine. We sail at noon. Are you ready?"

"Not yet, but I could be ready in a half hour. Do I have to wait till Wednesday?"

"Your heart will grow fonder! Bye, bye!"

Was she ever in a rare mood. Made me wonder what happened on her end? Could she have made up with her dad? I'd better call Bongers.

The phone number she called from this time was different again. They traced it to Naples. The feds were already at that address. Talk about efficient. They had half the country under surveillance, it looked like. Well, at least she was well guarded. I could sleep in peace.

On Wednesday I left after nine and at that time of day, the Bronx River Parkway sailed me right into the city and within the hour I parked right off Pier 40. With my parking ticket in my pocket and my suitcase in my hand, I walked through security and used my driver's license for my I.D.. They didn't require passports for those trips. I wondered if Julia knew. My suitcase would be delivered to my room, but I did receive a key. They wouldn't give me Julia's cabin Number, but I sprung a surprise on them: I showed my FBI badge and then they told me. I'm still not sure if that was a stupid move on my part, but the purser didn't even flinch. They must be used to that kinda stuff.

Well, she wasn't there, so I hung out on deck with a complimentary Heineken in my hand, (they couldn't sell alcohol until they were three miles out.) and watched the passengers as they arrived. In the old days, guests could come aboard too, but that must have changed. Only ticketed passengers came aboard. At 11:15 she got out of a cab. She was half a mile away, but I knew it was her when she disappeared under the huge overhang. I raced to the ramp, but it still took twenty minutes before she strolled aboard.

I just grabbed her and held her. Maybe for five minutes. Just held her. Finally I asked: "How are you? You look great." She had aged five years and looked tired. I didn't say that. She answered as she pulled me close again: "I'm fine. Let's find my cabin."

I nearly blew it by saying that I already knew her number, but I caught it in time and we walked over to the purser's office and got her key.

Inside her cabin, it was like Miami all over again. We couldn't get out of our clothes fast enough and when we finally caught our breath on the narrow, one-person, bed, we readjusted and I let her rest on top of me, while I savored everything. The body itself, her hair, her lips, her perfume, everything! I was in Hog Heaven.

We settled down to normal, were interrupted by a bellboy bringing her luggage and finally, all dressed again, went to lunch. Leisurely lunch. We talked for two hours. We held hands, ate a little, talked some more and were finally chased out by the cleaning crew. We saw Miss Liberty floating by, but we really only had eyes for each other. How I had missed that girl! I couldn't believe it.

Like real tourists on a honeymoon, we dined and danced, we cuddled and kissed, we couldn't get enough of one another.

And then.... There was Bermuda! I don't know what I expected, but it looked different than the Caribbean Islands. Very neat and very proper. Must have been the British influence.

Chapter Fifteen

Bermuda

Neither one of us had ever been to Bermuda before and after we had settled in, in a beautiful one-bedroom Time Share suite, we rented a scooter for three days and started off with a tour of the island. The temperature was about eighty and on the scooter that was just great. We dined at the far eastern end in a native restaurant and tried out some delicious local foods. Before dark, we were back admiring a beautiful sunset and with a drink in our hands, we sat on the balcony, totally relaxed. I didn't know if microphones would pick up our conversations out there, but I didn't think that was very important at that point. We had talked on the boat about her dad and how mad he was at her and also, that she heard through a cousin that he wanted to make up somehow. Was it possible that their tentacles reached so far into our system that they found out about me being arrested and consequently being fired? If they did, that might have cleared Julia in his mind and me as well. Maybe that was why there hadn't been any other attempts on my life?

Anyway. I had to start on my undercover scheme. I asked if she felt she was in danger and if she needed protection? She wasn't sure. Then I slid into my story that the FBI had contacted me about giving her a new identity and hiding her in a perfectly safe protection program. I didn't say a word about cooperating with us or that I would be working with her. That could wait. First I had to let the thought sink in that she might have to sever all ties with her family.

We fixed another drink and drifted away from the subject. The front desk told us about three places nearby that had dance music and we selected the one with the piano bar. We weren't too much into disco, and Latin rhythm was not one of the choices available to us. As it turned out, the piano lounge was great. Casual dress, happy people and good music. To our delight, the combo did play some rumbas and cha-chas, so we were on cloud nine. The next morning we explored the other end of the island and by two we fell asleep at the pool site under an umbrella.

After dinner we got back into the conversation about her dad and I finally started to tell her all I knew about him. Two weeks of studying FBI files about her old man had painted a pretty nasty picture in my mind.

First of all, he was suspected of being a German SS officer, who had worked at the death camps.

Second, he had proven to be merciless in dealing with rival businessmen and cartels. The estimate was that he was responsible for at least fifteen deaths in Colombia (nearly sixteen if they had gotten me) and four in the U.S.. Maybe more, but four was all they could pin on him for sure, but there were so many unsolved ones, that the total might exceed twenty.

Third, he was running the second largest drug smuggling corporation in the world and in spite of all that, the FBI barely had a picture of him. What I hadn't realized at first was that I gave them more details about him than they had gathered over all those years.

As I halfway expected, the whole session ended in a crying spell by Julia, because even though she had expected a lot of those facts, she had secretly tried not to believe them.

This time we laid on the couch with her head on my chest and my arms tightly around her without getting aroused. I let her cry.

We let the subject rest and took water ski-ing lessons. This was a first for her, but she got up on the third try. I got up on one ski for the first time in my life and I was dying to show my son. We took a flight in a small plane around the island and I must say: That was exhilarating! I should take up flying and I just might!

At the breakfast table, the next morning, I outlined the details of the protection plan. I didn't say a word yet about her cooperation that was required.

She surprised me by asking: "Are you going to live with me?" because I hadn't considered that angle.

"What a great thought! Now remember, I'm under a sort of a protection plan myself, as a matter of fact, it's nearly house arrest, but I'm sure, these things can be worked out somehow,"

"I still don't understand about the crime you have supposedly committed. What have they accused you of?"

"For one thing, I met with your dad in person. Then another thing, I received drug money and…"

"The money I lent you for your condo? That was MY money, NOT drug money!"

"You know that and I know that, but it sure looked suspicious to them. As a matter of fact, I'm still not sure if they believe me."

"Even after you were shot?" She sounded incredulous.

"A lot of people get shot in that trade and that doesn't prove them innocent, but I'm getting back in their graces and they're still paying my salary, so maybe we shouldn't complain."

"So would you move in with me?"

"Of course! Of course! Come here!" I held her so tight she could hardly breathe.

"Would we make a baby?" She whispered.

I moved her away about a foot and looked deep in her brown eyes: "You mean that?"

"Yes, I think I'd like to settle down and have a family. To tell you the truth, I'm getting tired of the travel, the theater trips, living out of a suitcase, always on the go. It gets tiresome."

"Really? What a thought." I pulled her back into me and just held her. I was starting to think I really loved that beautiful bundle of sexuality. "What a thought!"

"Let's drink to that thought!" She was smiling from ear to ear.

"Okay! What'll be your pleasure?"

After I handed her a drink, she proposed a toast: "*Salud, Dinero y Amor y tiempo para gozarlos.*" We touched glasses and I asked: "I understand all about dinero y amor but what was that last part?"

"And the time to enjoy it!"

"Oh, I'll drink to that!"

We talked endlessly about where we could possibly live, where was the best climate in the country and what would she want, a girl or a boy. "Oh, a boy first of course."

"A boy first? How many are we gonna have?" She laughed uproariously at the thought. I was so happy, I nearly forgot the seriousness of our mission.

"I'll call my office in the morning and pass on that thought and see what they say. Okay?"

"Okay!"

The next morning, I indeed called Bongers and while we were sitting at the breakfast table, she smiled at me from behind her cereal bowl. I felt rather weird, because my boss might already have gotten a transcript of our conversation about babies, but I couldn't let on that we were bugged, so I called. Bruce listened as I explained about her acceptance of the protection plan and our proposal to live together.

"Will she work with us? Will she give us information we need?"

I tried to look shocked, paused and told her: "Mr. Bongers wants to know, are you going to work with us? Will you give us all the information we ask for?"

She stopped eating and her face dropped. "What kind of information? Can I talk to him a minute?"

"Sure!" Then into the phone: "Mr. Bongers, Julia wants to talk to you. Okay?"

"Of course!" I handed her the phone.
""Good morning sir, I'm Julia. What kind of information?"
"All you know about your father's drug operation."
"My brothers too?"
"Probably!"
"Oh, I don't know." She handed back the phone.
"Sorry, Mr. Bongers, she got off the phone."
"That's okay, Call me again tomorrow." Click.
She had gotten up from the table and walked out on the balcony.

I walked up behind her and put my arms around her, but she turned around sharply: "Were you aware of that?"
"Of what?"
"He wants me to sacrifice my brothers, I can't do that." She walked away from me.

Something had snapped. Something clicked in her mind. She added two and two together and figured out that I was part of a set-up. She never said so, but I could feel it. She didn't talk or smile any more and I didn't know how to handle it. When I started to talk or tried to warm up to her, she waved me off. "I have to think," was all she said. She put on her bathing suit and walked out. I was stunned, but figured that she was entitled to her privacy and she had to sort things out in her own mind at her own pace.

I didn't know what to do. I considered calling Bongers and telling him, he had been too blunt. He could have used more diplomacy, but I decided he was more experienced in these areas than I, so I didn't make the call. I watched T.V., tried reading a book, none of it worked. Finally I put on my bathing suit and went looking for her at the pool. No such luck. She wasn't there. The beach maybe? She couldn't have gone far, without money and nothing but a bikini. I walked the beach from one end to the other, but there was no sign of her. She didn't have the keys to the scooter, I had those, so where could she be? Come to think of it, I really didn't know her all that well. I only knew her when she was in good spirits and at the time of panic, me being shot, she was in full control of herself. I didn't know what to think and I was starting to panic. I ran back to the pool, raced around it and for some reason looked up at our balcony and there she was! My heart nearly stopped. I was up in our suite so fast, I must have broken some records.

"Honey! Honey! Where were you?"

"Where was I? Where were **you**?"

"I looked all over for you, ran up and down the beach, around the pool and I was going crazy. Where were you?"

"I was in the pool. I had to think...I..."

I gasped: "You were IN the pool?"

"What's wrong with that?"

"That's the only place I didn't look. Oh, honey, are you alright?"

"Not really. I'm a little shook up and I think it is best that we go home."

"Home? Why? You can't go back to Opa Locka and why? We're here in paradise, so why..."

"I don't feel in paradise any more. I feel deflated. I don't want to say: 'betrayed', but I don't feel good about this trip any more. I think we should pack..."

"But Julia, listen, please listen... please. Let's stay just one day. I'll trade the boat tickets for airplane tickets and we'll fly out tomorrow. Where do you want to go back to? Naples? Don't you want to stay with me in New York for a few more days? Oh, Julia!" I nearly cried. I kneeled next to her on the concrete slab that was the balcony floor and I didn't care if it hurt my knees, nothing mattered. I put my arms around her and just held her. "One more day." I whispered. "Just one more day."

As it turned out, it was senseless to trade our tickets, the boat would stop on it's way back from the Bahamas and all we had to do was board right on schedule, as planned.

It wasn't the same. The fire had gone out of the affair. She didn't smile much, didn't say much and when she did she would insist on needing more time to think.

I was as attentive as ever, but I started checking myself. Whatever I was doing, was that the sincere thing to do or was I over reacting? It drove me nuts. I had never realized how much I did care for this young beauty from Colombia. Oh, we still made love, but only at night when it was time for bed, like married couples do. It seemed more like a duty, fulfilling a need like eating or going to the bathroom.

When we parted in New York, I held her very tight before depositing her in a cab and whispered: "Julia, I love you. Don't forget that." She didn't look back. This was the first time that I had told her I loved her and believe me, at that point I loved her more than my own children and that's something. It was the last time I saw her.

Life was rotten thereafter. I worked a lot, was assigned to the investigation, rehashed all the testimony that was recorded when I was in the hospital and with that information, the wheels were set in motion. A nation wide operation was going to clamp down on all the money launderers, the in-between contacts, the harbor and airport smuggling activities and that included Julia's brothers and cousins.

I was not really in the midst of the fray, I worked indoors at the planning and logistics. When it came off at three o'clock one morning, in seven different states, FBI, Federal Marshals, local police and sheriff's departments, the CIA and Homeland Security all swarmed down on offices, homes and warehouses and arrested dozens of people, confiscated hundreds of kilos of contraband and killed only one. It was labeled a huge success. Julia's brothers were not amongst the captured. They had vanished.

Chapter Sixteen

Lucky's Wrath

This time I was hauled into Washington. Summoned to come to Secaucus, our New Jersey Headquarters, from where I had the honor of personally being escorted by Bruce Bongers to the J. Edgar Hoover Building in D.C..

Bruce himself was alright. He didn't say much, but he also didn't harass me.

Washington did. You can't imagine how these minds run and how things get twisted in these *'intelligence'* brains. The drug raid whole operation seemed like a smashing success, with one exception: *They had severely smashed Lucky's competition!*

Yes, all of Lucky Vargas' lieutenants had escaped unscathed. As if they had been forewarned! Their financial assets had been removed to overseas banks, their accounts had been cleaned out and their real estate holdings had been sold in the nick of time. A clean, very clean operation and I was suspected of having been involved in alerting them to the impending action against them.

I was stunned! I was flabbergasted! How could they even insinuate it? Well, they had replayed the tapes from Bermuda a million times and tried to figure out how and where I told Julia that they were on her father's trail and about to close in on him.

I didn't say a word of the sort. Yet they spliced a few sentences together that made it sound like that, but they were not very conclusive. So, they tried another tack. They tried to nail me for having talked to Julia from a remote phone that they couldn't track, although they had no recorded proof of any of that.

I was in the hot seat for hours. I was virtually accused of treason. It was sooo off the wall that at one point I stood up and screamed: *NO, NO, NO! I had no contact with her since we split in New York! NONE, Why can't you believe me?"*

They finally let me go. Back to Secaucus, back to my car and there I invited some of my colleagues for a drink at Mario's, a local watering hole. Two of them came with me. One of them Bruno Garcia, Bongers' immediate assistant. I was grateful for their company and I spilled my heart out. Initially I had decided to get drunk, but at their insistence, I had just a few beers while I poured my sad story all over the bar. I even told them how we had wanted to start a life together and have babies. A boy first. By the third beer, I started losing it and I broke down. They led me to a booth and I cried like I hadn't since my family's breakup. They were most sympathetic and Bruno volunteered to drive me to the condo in Piermont and continue to have a drink when we got there. I declined. I had some coffee, dried my tears and decided to say hello to my kids while I was within fifteen miles from them. We said goodbye and I thanked them profusely for lending me an ear when I needed it.

The kids were very happily surprised to see me in the middle of the week, although they both had homework to complete, so I talked some to my ex, who was having a drink, but still remarkably sober. I must have looked a mess, because she asked: "Do you need a drink?" Not: "Do you want a drink?" or : "Would you like a drink?", no she specifically asked me: "Do you need a drink?" I must've looked it. I had a scotch and a second one and little by little I told her about my problems without ever mentioning Julia. I had her believe, that the ambush in Bogota and the bullet in my shoulder had gotten me in hot water with the company and that I somehow had botched the operation in Colombia. Of course, she had read about the giant drug raid and all the arrests and couldn't understand why I was not the hero of the day and poured another scotch. The kids joined us for a bit, my son kissed me goodnight and I just melted. I started crying and they all wanted to know what was wrong and how they could help.

All I told them, that I was probably going to be retired. Medical retirement because of my shoulder and being kids, they thought that was great. More time for them. Another scotch. By the time my daughter got ready for bed, they convinced me to sleep in her bed and she would sleep with her mom and I agreed and nearly passed out. I slept within a minute.

An early breakfast arrived at the same time as my hangover and after they left for work and school, I read the paper and promised to lock the door behind me when I left. I laid back on the couch and fell sound asleep. An insistent ringing of my cell phone woke me up and I was so disoriented, I didn't know where I was. The ringing stopped, but I did find the phone on my daughter's nightstand and I looked through the *recent calls* to see who wanted me. Bongers! He picked up on the second ring: "Where are you?" No "Good morning," no "Hello!", no, just "Where are you?" When I told him where I was he asked: "Are you alright?" I thought Bruno might have told them that I was suicidal or something. I told him I was great, except I had more drinks last night than I needed.

"Were you near your condo in Piermont at all?"

"No! Why?"

"You better head over there. I'll meet you in a half hour."

Half hour? I hadn't shaved, hadn't showered and the trip was at least thirty-five minutes! Well, I zipped up my pants and ran out of the place to my car and careened through the complex to the street. I put my red flashing light on top and raced through the city streets to the interstate. I made it in thirty-three minutes. Bongers wasn't there yet, but there were two fire trucks, a half dozen police cars with flashing lights and an ambulance that was just pulling out of the parking lot. As I ran up to my door I was stopped three times, but my badge earned quick admission to the crime scene. Crime scene? Accident scene? I didn't know at first, but when the police captain in charge finally believed that I lived there, he told me it was a crime scene alright. The door had been booby-trapped and someone had been blown to bits. "Who?" I didn't know 'who'! Not me, that was for sure and then it dawned on me, the booby-trap had been meant for me. I sat down on the steps, my head spinning. If I had gone home last night, I would be the 'bits and pieces' in the ambulance. That's how Bongers found me. He wanted me to visit a doctor. When I said NO, he wanted to know why I hadn't come home. I told him. The puzzled look on his face told me that he was glad I was alive, mixed with doubts about me having known that I might be in danger. I left him puzzled.

I must have been real dense, because it took me a half hour before I realized that I had a cleaning lady come in once a week and that she had to be the one that got massacred. The hospital confirmed it was a woman, young woman, about twenty. That was her. Poor thing! Miserable rotten bastards! I told Bruce I wanted to go after the S.O.B.'s but he told me: "Nothing doing! You're going across the bridge."

I was escorted to my protection home. I didn't know what to think or do, so I went with them. When we got to escape house, I talked for hours, they recorded everything I said and finally left me alone with the assurance that I was under guard and not to leave the house. For no reason whatsoever!

This was probably the lowest point in my life. I was an intelligent person with an above average I.Q. and yet I was being treated as if I had lost half of my marbles. Well? Did I? Was running around with a beautiful young sex maniac a sign of going crazy? I didn't think so. Did it impair my common sense? Possibly! At that point I could have turned to the bottle and become an alcoholic, but I didn't. I turned to the computer and started to write. Every little detail I could remember. I drank a gallon of chocolate milk as I typed. Made three bathroom trips and typed some more. At six I decided to chuck it for a while and check the news. First the local stuff. Same robberies, same murders, same politician in hot water. I had seen it all ten thousand times before. Then the phone rang.

"Check channel seven." It was Bongers. I switched to seven and waited. He hadn't said anything but: "Check channel seven." And nothing of interest happened till suddenly: *"In Bonita Springs, a vehicle blew up in a supermarket parking lot. The driver and two passengers were killed, all female and four other people were hurt. The police suspects terrorists or a cartel type execution."* I jumped a foot in the air. "Julia!" I screamed, although there was no mention of her name, nor were there any identifiable body parts shown on the tube.

I knew it was Julia! I could feel it in my bones! "Oh God, oh, God!" I screamed in the empty house. I didn't know what to do, but then I thought about Bongers and pushed his number.

"Was that Julia?" I literally screamed into the phone.

"I'm afraid so. We're not sure, but I'm afraid it was."

"Why? Why? If she worked with them, why would they blow her to Kingdom come?"

"We don't know. It may have been the other cartel, trying to get even."

"Oh God, oh God!" I sobbed and clicked the phone shut.

Within seconds, it rang again: "We're sending someone over to stay with you. Remain calm. There is a chance it wasn't her."

"There is?" Click.

They sent a psychologist. A young female, about thirty-two, maybe thirty-five.

She wore a wedding band/engagement ring combination, so I knew she wasn't there to sexually relieve me. I wouldn't have been up to it anyway. She asked if she could fix me a drink and that surprised the hell out of me. But it helped. She had a soda. We talked. She had two children, four and sixteen months.

"Shouldn't you be home with the kids right now?"

"My husband's there. They're fine."

She had been an Army Doctor in Iraq and as part of her training, she learned to march in the desert, shoot a rifle and launch a rocket. I was impressed. She did that for six years. Help soldiers, I mean. No, she did not shoot rockets for six years. Paid off her student loans and learned a lot. Wounded soldiers, who gave up on life, paralyzed soldiers who couldn't function in society anymore were her main patients. I was stunned.

My problems seemed sooo small all of a sudden, that I nearly felt ashamed. She was prepared to stay the night, presumably so I wouldn't commit suicide, (She didn't say that, but I could figure that out) so I sent her home after midnight. Strange but true. I felt a lot better. Somehow I felt I could still take on the world and live for my children. At that point I made a decision. I was going to take flying lessons. The flight over Bermuda with Julia was something I would cherish all my life and taking lessons would help me relive all that. I fell asleep on the couch.

I woke up with a new determination, but I was shot down twice before the day was half over. First Bongers dropped by personally. It was Julia! She was four months pregnant. I collapsed.

A Company doctor came and examined me and a deputy director who came along informed me, that I was on medical leave from here in and that my retirement papers with all the benefits would arrive soon. I would live under witness protection for the rest of my life, so I had nothing to worry about.

"Oh yeah?" I shouted after they left. "Oh, yeah? I'm gonna buy a pool table and I'm gonna take flying lessons, you creeps. Do you hear me, you creeps?"

"That's my story. My FBI story. I hope you can write a book about it. Don't use my name."

Chapter Seventeen

Fred's Turn

Pensacola Beach, Florida
Wednesday, 10 AM

Fred turned off the recorder. The story had him stunned. It made him realize that he had been totally oblivious of one of the other facets of life: DRUGS.

He had received the tape in yesterday's mail and listened to it at night and again this morning. He was still shaking his head. This was like a science fiction movie, something that happened in another world.

"Can you write a book about it?" had been the last question.

"Damn tootin!" Fred said to himself.

"What did you say honey?" his wife called from the kitchen.

"Nothing." He murmured, "nothing."

He walked onto his balcony overlooking the pale teal and dark blue waters of the Gulf in front of him. There was hardly any surf. He pictured himself on a similar balcony in Bermuda and two people, obviously in love and now totally destroyed. One physically and the other mentally. "What a shame." He thought to himself and right then and there he made up his mind.

He would have the tape transcribed. He knew just the person for that. The part-time church secretary sometimes did work for him and she had his complete confidence.

Then he would destroy the tape as he had promised. His mind was made up…..

He would write that book!

On his way to the bathroom, he checked the phone book for the nearest FBI office. He was going to expound on this story. After a quick shave and shower, he was off. His wife was going to a Woman's Club meeting, so he had time to himself.

Pensacola
The Gen. "Chappy" James Building
2nd Floor. FBI

Well, that was the first step and the first disappointment. He didn't get to talk to anybody. They operated behind a locked door with a numbers lock on it and he never got beyond that. Through her little window, the woman insisted that there was nobody who would talk to him.

"Do you realize, lady that I might have some very pertinent information that you folks would like to have?" (He knew he didn't.)

"Here's our card, you can fax or e-mail us and we'll be in touch if need be."

"This is harder than getting on the Oprah show." The woman grinned politely.

"I'm writing a book about the FBI and I'd hate to print misleading facts, so I need to talk to someone." He decided on a different tack.

"On the card you see our information number in Jacksonville. A Mr. Sullivan is our Public Relations director. He can help, I hope."

"I wish I could say thanks. Good day!"

He couldn't even slam the door behind him, because it had an automatic closer that closed the door ever so gently. He thought of kicking it.

"These bums are paid good money through my tax dollars and I can't even get the time of day out of them." He was utterly frustrated.

Pensacola Beach

The visit at the church was a little more productive. The young secretary was eager to do some work at home and once her little one went to sleep in the afternoon, she could really get at it. No price was mentioned, because he was always satisfied with what she charged and she was always happy with what Fred paid.

At his computer in the bedroom overlooking the Gulf, he typed out a letter assuring his FBI hero in New York, that the tape would be destroyed as promised. He also extended his condolences and assured him that the book might eventually clear him. He wrote that he would send the manuscript to him for approval, prior to publication.
ps. *WHAT A STORY!*

Mr. Sullivan in Jacksonville was not available, but would call back ASAP.
"Damn." Here he was: full of energy and ideas and not going anywhere.
Fred called Bongers in New Jersey. He wasn't in but would also return his call.
Finally, he called Ted.
" Ted, have you ever been in Colombia?"
"I'm on the road. I can hardly hear you."
"Have you ever been in Colombia?"
"No."
"Wanna go?"
"Why?"
"Because we haven't been there yet."
"I'll call you back." Brother Ted broke the connection.

The Golden Pig

A plan was starting to formulate in his mind. He got out a yellow pad and started outlining his next book and a trip to Cartagena was part of the plot. By the time his wife walked in at 2:30, "Honey? Have you eaten yet?" he had thirty five chapters in his mind and on the pad. All he had to do now was go traveling and go snooping a lot and the chapters would grow into a real book. Probably a realistic book.

He wished he had the tape in hand again, so he could write down some more details, but that had to wait. The church girl could maybe finish it today.

His wife brought him a take-out box with leftover grouper from her lunch and along with a beer, that made for a perfect lunch. He fell asleep in his recliner.

He woke up when his wife nudged him: "Honey, someone from the FBI. Are you in trouble?"

He grinned at her: "Not yet!" Into the phone he said: "Van Dyke here!"

It was O'Sullivan, not Sullivan as the woman had suggested, and he was less than helpful. NO, nobody would do an interview with a reporter.

"I'm not a reporter, I'm an author. I write books."

It didn't matter, no interviews with authors either. There was just no need for that type of thing and there was no department with that sort of job assignment.

"Well, I'll see how much dirt and scum I can dig up about you people and I'll smear it all over the headlines!"

"If that's what you want, Mr. Van Dyke, that's fine. We're enforcing the law, we're not in a popularity contest…"

"Drop dead!" He hung up. Fred rarely lost his temper, but the FBI attitude had gotten to him. "Drop dead!" he said again. This time to a dead phone.

It was too early for a drink, so he did the next best thing. He went for a walk on the beach. That was his favorite way of getting the gray matter in his head back in line.

"Honey? You wanna come and walk with me?"
"Just a second!"

Walking the beach was Fred's favorite way of cleansing his brain. It was as if the clean air renovated some of his dead cells. Whenever he had writers' block, the soaring birds or the little sandpipers stirred up his thinking powers and inspiration would again overwhelm him. In this case, it settled his mood and while he picked up some empty cans and bottles left by unconcerned beach bums, a pattern started to form in his mind. He would do some of his own research. He would do some of his own investigating and maybe get in the middle of the fray, so he could really put an exciting novel together. Maybe a murder/mystery. Maybe an espionage story. A cartel war? Whatever? He could feel it in his bones, This was going to be an adventure. He was whistling by the time they trudged back to the condo.

Unfortunately, he missed out on two calls. The New Jersey FBI chief, Bongers, had called back and left a message to try again. The other one was Ted and he said, he might be home the remainder of the day.

Bongers was out of the office, but Ted was available and talked a mile a minute before Fred could get to the reason for his call. Ted remembered the shy man in Ray's basement, who sat in the corner all night while he was singing at the bar.

"What about him? Are you taking him to South America?" Ted was always full of it. Funny? Sometimes! Full of it? All the time.

"What would you say if we book a little cruise, from Caracas to Cartagena, then on to Barranquilla, with an overnight stop in Bogota and on to Martinique before we fly home?"

"What's the reason? What's our excuse this time?" Ted remembered the last barefoot cruise they'd been on to celebrate their sister's birthday.

"Good thinking. Let's think of a good excuse." Fred laughed out loud. "How about: We missed your company?"

"Sounds good to me. E-Mail me details. Ciao!"

The tape had been partially transcribed. Fred ran over to the girls' apartment and retrieved the transcript. It would get him started that night. He was as excited as a young heifer in spring.

In the morning, he got through to Bongers in New Jersey and to his surprise he didn't seem like the Florida G-men at all. He asked if there was ever an occasion for Fred to be in New Jersey and when Fred told him: "Half of my relatives live there. That's where we got off the boat, in Hoboken."

"From where?"

"Holland."

"That's where my dad came from and my mom arrived in Hoboken as well. My dad was already here….. " and from there on in they talked about : "Where in Holland?" and "When?" and "by gosh, we might originate from the same area."

Anyway, Fred had an open invitation to see Bongers when he got to Jersey.

Now he was getting someplace.

Chapter Eighteen

Jersey, here we come!

Fred needed an excuse to go see his nephews and nieces in New Jersey and visiting the FBI in Secaucus was as good as any. With his laptop and his recorder he could work on the road and with his new camcorder he could film any evidence they might stagger upon. He had gotten a new little digital Sony for Christmas and he loved it. He didn't quite understand all the workings, but he loved it just the same. Not having to deal with cassettes and tapes was such an improvement over his old recorder. This one had a disk, just a little smaller than the ones he used in his computer.

The transcript had been completed, the tape destroyed and the mini-van was loaded. Both the wife, Kathryn, and Fred loved to travel. They would hit the road early, three or four in the morning and travel till six or seven in the evening and make real progress. Fred would drive while it was still dark, and after about three hours, they'd gas up and switch seats. That way, either one of them could doze if they wanted to and be refreshed for their next turn behind the wheel. Kathryn was barely five feet, but in the mini-van she could sit up high and have a real good view of the road ahead of her. When it was Fred's turn to drive, she would do one crossword puzzle after the other, or devour a book in just hours. Amazing brain in that little body.

Fred would try to type if the road was not too bumpy, but if it was, he would get his scratch pad and jot down his thoughts. Either way, the time and the miles just flew by and at six o'clock Fred announced: "Cocktail time" and they started looking for a suitable motel with a good steakhouse built in or nearby. They got close to Fredericksburg Virginia on their first leg. Not bad!

When they passed Baltimore the next morning, Fred contacted Bongers and after playing musical phones for a while, he got through to him and they agreed to a drink after work on the following day. T.G.I. Fridays was their choice at 5:30 on Route 3, near Passaic.

"Great going." Fred said to Kathryn, who was keeping her eyes on the road and the cruise control at 72 MPH.

He started to outline the questions he was going to ask the G-man, without letting on that he was familiar with the tragic events involving 'Ralph' and 'Julia'. It wouldn't be easy to ask intelligent questions and not make any slip that he had some inside knowledge. As a cover, he would make a remark about some FBI agents that he palled around with in Tampa and then Bongers might conclude that this could be the source of his inside information. "Yeah, that might work." He murmured.

"Huh?" Kathryn thought he was talking to her.

"No, nothing. Just thinking out loud."

Friday's
5:15PM

Fred had found a fairly remote booth in the corner of the restaurant and reflected on the events of the last two days, while waiting for Bongers. The visit with his Godson and his young family had been fabulous. It was amazing how well these young folks were doing financially and how tall their children had gotten to be. Their son was already six foot one and he was only fifteen. Their daughter, at age eleven was at least five foot five and still growing. Both of them were doing well academically as well as being great in sports. Logically, the parents were bursting with pride and Fred glowed right along with them, because he was the original pioneer who had brought over his siblings in the late fifties. If it weren't for him, he and his descendants might still be digging tulip bulbs in Holland. What a thought!

Bongers was one minute late, but that might have been because the hostess couldn't figure out who he was looking for. Fred had told her he'd be looking for :"Fred, the Dutchman" and Bongers asked for: "Mr. Van Dyke." The hostess didn't see the connection.

Bongers was much taller than Fred had expected. At least five inches taller than himself. Other than that, he looked like a Dutchman, a real Hollander. Deep blue eyes and a shock of blond, curly hair on top of his head, not quite a military haircut. He could be related, that's how familiar he looked. After some brief introductions, Bongers ordered a Heineken and Fred another Bud.

"Got used to the taste," he explained. "That's all my daughter and son-in-law drink, so I had to have it in the house at all times and eventually I developed a taste for it."

For a few minutes they talked about their backgrounds and the similarities of coming to America by means of Hoboken. Bongers told him that his dad had fought against the Germans in the underground after escaping from a labor camp when he was only seventeen. During the *"Market-Garden"* operation in September of '44 that resulted in *"A Bridge Too Far"*, his dad had joined up with the American Forces and became an interpreter and translator because of his knowledge of German. After Germany capitulated, his dad was assigned to the Intelligence department of the Army that concentrated on finding and prosecuting Nazi criminals. In '46 he was given a field commission and a year later, he married his hometown sweetheart and they lived in Germany for two years before his transfer to the U.S. His mom followed by boat and they settled in Northern New Jersey where he, Bruce, was born..

"Made in Germany, born in America," he joked while he held up his glass in a toast.

"I'll drink to that." Fred would drink to anything as they touched glasses.

The Golden Pig

"What is it that you're looking for, Fred? What's your interest in the FBI?"

"Well, in the first place, I write books and…."

"What kinda books?"

"My first one is about growing up in Holland during World War Two and I brought you a signed copy, so you can read what it was like during the Nazi occupation although I'm sure your dad…."

"How much is it?"

"No, no, that's my gift to you for…"

"No such thing. I can not and will not accept any gifts from anybody, as a matter of fact I'm going to pay for my own beer."

"Aw, come on!"

"That's the way it is Fred. So how much is it.?

"In Barnes & Noble it would cost you $19.95, but direct from…"

"Here's a twenty and tell me, how old were you during that time?"

"I was about nine when it started and about fourteen when it was all over."

"Wow, my dad is gonna love this. Thanks! Now back to the FBI, what have we got to do with WWII?"

"Nothing really, I'm interested in your involvement in the war on drugs."

"Why drugs?" Bongers wrinkled his eyebrows in question.

"Three reasons." Fred told him briefly about the adventure in Spanish Harlem and what the cops had told him about their frustrating war against the drug trade. When Fred mentioned 'Lucky Vargas', Bongers stopped him.

"What do you know about Lucky Vargas?"

"Well, sergeant in the Fifty-First said that they didn't know what he looked like and that we were even suspect for a while, because we didn't fit in with the local gentry"

"He thought that Lucky might walk into a local bar himself?"

"That's what he said. He said there was a real cartel war going on and that Vargas was trying to muscle in on their turf. Is that true?"

"I have no idea, but I doubt it. What are your other reasons?"

"When my daughter was in High School in Tampa, I received a phone call at the office one morning to come to the school, because my daughter and two other cute little blond fifteen year olds had been arrested for smoking pot on the school grounds. Can you believe that?" Fred stopped and rubbed his eyes a moment as if he was trying to rub away some bad memories. "I didn't think the girl would ever smoke. She hated it when her mother smoked and here she was smoking dope! And on the school grounds! Had she gone crazy? And when did that start? I never had an inkling! She'd been fooling around with that stuff for a while already. What a mess. The cops must have thought I was real stupid and I guess I was. She didn't stop. In spite of all the promises and tears, she didn't stop. I learned to tell by the oversized pupils when she came home and one night I grilled her and grilled her for hours. I wouldn't let her go to sleep until I found out the truth. One of her classmates stole it from her older sister, a senior in the same school. Well I visited the parents to see how we could put a stop to this. The father was Minister in a local church and when I told them all about pot and the source, I thought they were going to strangle me at their kitchen table. *"OUR DAUGHTERS WOULD NEVER DO A THING LIKE THAT AND WAS I CRAZY?"* They threw me out of the house. Two years later, the oldest daughter was found in a crack house in Ybor City, naked and dead, with a dozen junkies passed out all around her. She'd O.D.'ed. I guess the Minister and his wife believed by then.

On another occasion I nearly killed somebody. Around the corner in the Town and Country section of Tampa, friends of ours ran a 'teen' club. Foosball machines, pinball, a little dance floor, all nice and above board. A great place for teenagers to congregate over the weekends. No alcohol, well supervised, with just one problem. Rumors kept reaching us that drugs were being sold outside the place. The police checked a few times without results. From my daughter I learned that a kid from the other side of town would come in and sell 'stuff'. I asked her to identify him, all she could tell me was that he drove the longest old car she had ever seen.

The Golden Pig

Well, one Saturday, I was poking around in my front yard and an old Chrysler Imperial pulled into my driveway. The longest old car I have ever seen. I guess it was gold colored at one time, but by now it was dirty brown. My heart stopped momentarily. I had a hard time breathing, but I controlled myself as I walked around the car to the driver side. A scrawny, longhaired teenager sat behind the wheel and when I asked, 'How can I help you?' he asked for my daughter. I said: 'Just a minute' and walked into the house. I got my colt 38, tucked it in my belt on my butt and walked back to his window.

I said: "I understand you're the guy who sells drugs around here, right?"

"No man! No way!"

"Don't lie to me, you little bastard!" I was screaming by then and I pulled out my gun. My heart was racing at a hundred miles a minute, I was so mad. I put the gun to his head and hollered: "If I see you in this part of town again, I'm gonna blow your goddamn brains out! Do ya hear?" and I cocked the gun. If he had said one wrong word, I would have pulled the trigger. He nodded: "Yessir, yessir," cranked the car and took off. I went in the house, grabbed a cold one and collapsed. *I had nearly murdered somebody in cold blood.*

I was within one hundredth of a second away from pulling that trigger. I would have spent the rest of my life in prison for pre-meditated murder. All because of drugs.

Fred finished his Bud and signaled for another one. Bruce was fine. Fred had gotten himself all worked up again and rested a bit, regaining his composure.

"And third?" Bongers wanted to know.

"Third?"

"You said you had three reasons."

"Oh, ya. I had befriended a musician in the Tampa Bay area. A piano/player/singer who played clubs all over the area. I love to sing, so many a time I hung around the piano bar and sang my heart out. I had a little Cessna at the time and he asked me to take him up sometime and I did. Then one day he called and wanted to talk to me in the middle of the day. Because of his trade, I only saw him at night, normally. We met over a beer and he told me about his brother-in law in Saint Pete who had loads of money, a big house on the water and a huge yacht. I should come party with them sometime. Fun people. Rich people. Then came the kicker: He had a proposal for me. I should climb in my little plane some Wednesday, fly to the Bahamas, park the plane for a while and fly back to Tampa. This would pay me $3,000 and I wouldn't have to do anything but fly over and back.

"Three thousand dollars? There are many times when I don't make that kinda money in the whole month. Three thousand clams each Wednesday? Come on! What's the catch?"

"99 pounds of marijuana."

"Ninety-nine pounds of pot? Where would I get that?"

"You do nothing. You park the plane, somebody sticks it in there and you fly back. You leave the plane and walk away and someone will bring you three thousand dollars in small bills."

"Bruce. I was furious! I controlled myself, but I was steaming. For them to think that I would stoop so low as to get involved in smuggling drugs and stupid enough to risk getting caught?" Fred shook his head, just thinking about it. He took another swig of his Bud and continued: "I told them, I'd let him know. I called TOBACCO, ALCOHOL AND FIREARMS in Tampa. I didn't call from my own phone in case it was bugged by the druggies. Would you say I was getting paranoid? I tried to get in touch with the head honcho and propose a sting operation, where I would seem to cooperate with the dealers and meanwhile help the department identify the people involved and get evidence against them. Sounds great so far?" He took another long swig. "Guess what? I never got in their door. In the hall of their Tampa office, an agent came out and insisted on knowing why I wanted to talk to the boss and I had no choice but tell'em what I had up my sleeve. When he asked: "How much is involved?" and I told him 99 pounds and $3,000 he said they were not interested in small fry and I was excused. Can you believe that? I guess, and I'm still guessing that 100 pounds is a

The Golden Pig

felony crime and anything under is a misdemeanor, but I've never been able to verify that. What do you think?"

"You may be right Fred. So what did you do?"

"Nothing. I never called him back. I wasn't about to get involved in something illegal, not for any kinda money. Now you know the source of my interest and now I'd like to ask you some questions."

"Okay. I'll see what I can answer."

Fred wanted to know how much pot, how much heroin and how much coke was consumed in a city the size of Newark and how that translated into dollars.

Bruce promised to send him a government publication that outlined all that.

"How many deaths are associated with that trade, annually?"

"It's in the pamphlet."

"Does it break down overdoses and murders? Killings of other dealers and killings during robberies trying to get money for drugs?"

"In the pamphlet."

"You're not very talkative."

"You see Fred, I might make mistakes or be unsure. The brochure is right on target."

"Okay, let me give you my address or can I swing by and pick it up?"

"I'll be at the reception desk by 8:30 in the morning."

"Alright! Now something else. If in my research I stumble on something, how do I relate that to you?"

"Like what?"

"Like, I stumble on a boatload of coke, destined for the U.S.. What do I do?"

"From where?"

"You're not answering my question. How do I get an important message to you?"

Bruce had to laugh at that. "You are persistent, aren't you?"

"Aren't you? How else do you get anything done?"

"Touché! Here's my card with all the data you need, including my cell and now I must head home or dinner will get cold."

"We'll do this again sometime? Ya?"

"Ya! We will. Thanks for the book."

Chapter Nineteen

Cruising the Caribbean

Caracas Venezuela

The way the brothers had finally figured it out, they boarded the ship in Curaçao after spending two days there, then sailed on to Caracas. From Venezuela they would hit Cartagena and they'd leave the ship in Barranquilla. After two days in the harbor town, they'd take a train ride to Bogota, spend four days touring the city and surroundings and then fly home. It wasn't exactly the way Fred would have liked to plan it, but they had to look like tourists after all, so they went the tourist way.

Caracas didn't show them much, compared to the many Caribbean resorts they had visited in the past, but the flight by Angel Falls was impressive. What an unbelievable waterfall. Even Ted was impressed. He never once joked about it, so that meant he was in awe!

While having a last *'Carib'* beer at the docks, Ted finally got around to asking: "What is your real fascination with Colombia? Are you considering going in the drug trade?"

Fred couldn't help but laugh. "For what? I don't need the extra money. If I made more money, all my relatives would come begging and you know how I hate to cry."

"Why would you wanna cry? Money never made you cry before?"

"No dear brother, just the thought of all my dear relatives and friends wasting my money on frivolous things like cruises and speed boats. It would break my heart."

"You're so full of shit, Fred, that your pupils are turning brown. I can see it from here." He had to laugh at his own jokes and the ladies, sipping margaritas, turned and asked: "What's so funny?"

"Fred is being comical. He's not good at it though. He'll never make it as a stand-up comedian. Hahahaha!" Turning back to Fred: "Tell me the truth. You've got something up your sleeve, right?"

""You're right. I wanna be like Michener and Hemingway and I want to write my great novel, called: *"Bogota, The City Of Angels."*

"Now I know you're full of it. Let's drink up and start drinking on board. It's cheaper."

Cartagena

The ship arrived early in the morning and all four were manning the railing to watch the beautiful scenery. Like many of the Caribbean ports, the city was built against the mountain slopes and from a distance it looked like a giant hand had brushed some bright streaks of paint along the lower edges of the hills. The early morning sun bathed it all in brilliant shades of green, white and red. It seemed all the white houses had red roofs and they dazzled before their eyes.

The closer they got into the harbor, the duller the colors became as the city buildings and the warehouse along the docks started to obstruct their view. Fred had studied the layout of the harbor on the computer and wondered how far from Lucky's domain they would be docking. Next, he had to find an excuse to go strolling by there. Two middle aged tourist couples might not be a familiar sight in that part of town. He'd work on something. Ted always liked to hang out with the locals, so a local pub should make for a good bait. The only problem was, on the internet, it showed no bars around the docks that Fred wanted to visit. Well, they certainly could try to find one.

The ladies were always good sports. They had to be otherwise they would never have married the kookie brothers or stayed married to them and that's the way it was this time. While all the other passengers headed toward busses or walked in the direction of town, the happy foursome walked the opposite way to the more shabby part of the harbor.

Within a quarter mile, they found the first rinky-dink bar and they joined a dozen foreign sailors for a beer.

"The first beer of the day, keeps your kidneys at bay!" Ted had invented another new toast. He struck up a conversation in Spanish with several scruffy seamen. But to his surprise, none of them spoke much Spanish. Only the bartender in fact and a withered lady at the end of the bar. Apparently, they came from all over the world although the majority looked Philipino or Indonesian. That was no problem for Ted who started in on them in Malayan. Something he had learned while stationed in New Guinea. Another beer and they were off again.

"We could be drunk by noon." Kathryn commented and Ted countered: "That's okay, we'll put you in a cab and then they can roll you aboard."

The walk did them good. It must have taken them twenty minutes before they encountered another bar and of course, that made them thirsty again. Meanwhile, Fred had filmed them in and out of the bar and filmed some of the ships and warehouses while trying to identify which ones belonged to Vargas. Fred had read and re-read the transcript, but for the life of him, he couldn't remember if it mentioned a name on Vargas' properties. All he could remember that it said: "Shabby looking buildings and a big Mercedes and air conditioning in the office." There were plenty of shabby buildings and Fred zoomed in on all of them and the names of the ships at the docks. Many nations were represented and many were registered in the Bahamas and Panama. Fred knew that didn't mean much. Anyone could get registered there and mostly shady companies took advantage of that. He wondered if his information would have much value for the FBI or the other U.S. agencies. The second bar had more of a crowd. There was a little dining nook in the back and a smell of *'arroz con pollo'* greeted them as they walked in the door. Again, Ted did most of the talking while the ladies wondered if the bathrooms would be clean.

"Hey, Fred! The barmaid says you should drink beer with tomato juice. It's better for you," Ted hollered in Dutch.

"Okay, sounds healthy to me." Fred answered in the same language.

Ted had hollered that statement across the room and invariably, someone asked: "What are you speaking? German?" and that was always followed up with a conversation in that language, because after all, the boys had lived through five years of German occupation and they spoke the language beautifully.

"That's it!" Flashed through Fred's mind. "Lucky is a Kraut by birth, so maybe some of these folks in here work with him or associate with him and maybe he even eats in this joint. There's not much else around."

He decided to strike up a conversation with a bearded fellow who had addressed Ted in German. He was maybe seventy and looked weather worn, like an old fisherman who had spent a lot of time at sea.

"Prost! Wo wohnen Sie in Deutsland?" (Where do you live in Germany?) Fred decided to act as if he was talking to a fellow tourist.

"Nein, nein, ich wohne hier." (No, no, I live here.)

"Aber sie sprechen gut Deutsch." (But you speak good German)

The conversation went on and on in German, spoken by an American from Holland in a bar in Colombia. Small world. Fred bought a drink for his new friend who introduced himself as Enrico. (Probably Heinrich by birth, Fred thought.) When he received his second glass of beer and tomato juice, he raised his glass to the light and looked at it while asking Enrico if both the juice and beer came out of a can or a bottle, because he had been warned to drink nothing that came out of a tap. He was put at ease. Both came out of a bottle. His new buddy drank Cuba Libres and the conversation shifted from: "How long have you lived here?" to "Are there many Germans around here?"

According to Enrico, many Germans had come to South America right after the war, because there was very little work in Germany, unless you wanted to clear rubble all day and there was little hope for improvement at the time. He had been drafted at age seventeen and the only skill he had was killing. With a rifle, grenades, bayonet or a pistol, it didn't make any difference. His job was killing as many Russians as possible and he had barely made it across the Elbe to the Allied sector, so he surrendered to the Americans. He said he still shuddered at the thought of what the Russians would have done to him. In Hamburg he had mustered aboard a freighter and after two years of that, he jumped ship in Cartagena and went to work for another German, who had an export business.

"I didn't have any skills. I couldn't even drive a car, but I could work hard, so I've been working on the loading dock for all these years." It was remarkable that he spoke his native tongue so well after all these years, with just a trace of a Spanish accent.

"Still?"

"At my age? You're kidding, no? I oversee the loading and I still make enough to live. My wife died five years ago and….."

"A German wife?" Fred interrupted him.

"No, a local girl and we have three beautiful daughters, right here in town. How about you?"

Fred told him briefly how he had ended up in the U.S. and how they were now on a cruise.

"So that loudmouth is your brother?" Ted was singing an old wartime marching song and two of the customers were singing right along with him.

"Just a minute." Fred took out his camcorder and recorded the future opera singers for posterity. Enrico and the wives also ended up in the picture, as did many of the customers.

The women had been involved in animated conversation with a few rugged looking seamen, but were now ready to mosey on.

Ted had different ideas: At the top of his voice he was singing: "Wer soll dasz bezahlen? Wer hat so viel Gelt?" (Who's gonna pay for this? Who has so much money?") Somebody turned on the jukebox and blared him out. End of song.

"Just one more! Just one for the road." One thing was sure about Ted: He didn't know how to quit.

"No more for me."

"Me neither." The women had seen and heard enough. "We're gonna call a cab. We've been told what we need to see, so let's go."

Fred could have stayed another hour, trying to find out more about Enrico's German boss and if that was indeed THE Lucky Vargas. He got just one more question in: "Where's the place where you work? Near here?"

"Just four warehouses that way." He pointed in the direction from which they had come. In other words, Fred had already recorded it without knowing it. He wondered if they could film it again while looking for a cab. It didn't work out that way. The barmaid had called a cab and when they waived goodbye at the crowd, it felt like they had known them for ten years. No wonder! Ted had bought half of them a drink.

The cab retraced their steps and all Fred could do was count the buildings they passed and look at the ship that was docked directly across from it. The *"Santa Teresa"*, registration 'Bahamas'.

He didn't quite know what to do with his information, but he figured as soon as he was back on board, he'd e-mail Bongers the following message: "Santa Teresa being loaded at Lucky's dock." And wait for results. For now, he'd enjoy seeing the sights and the company of his fellow travelers.

Chapter Twenty

Colombia, South America

Barranquilla

The ship had left Cartagena in the early evening and turned north again in order to moor in Barranquilla and thereafter stop at the port of Maracaibo before going back to the Netherlands Antilles and start their circle all over again.

The Van Dykes were celebrating their last night aboard and the piano bar resounded with song and laughter. They'd made a number of friends aboard and of course 'good wishes' and 'Bon Voyage' were heard regularly as people retreated to their cabins.

Barranquilla was beautiful with many more cathedrals and palaces than Cartagena or Caracas had to offer. Their flight was not till the next morning and they found lodging in an old Cloister that had been converted into a hotel. The walls were a foot and a half thick and even the rooms that had no air conditioning felt cool and comfortable. The ceilings were high and the sculptures magnificent. Statues of saints and angels lined the galleries and the dining room. According to Ted, they could be canonized if they stayed for two weeks. Overnight was not a guarantee to Sainthood. Two weeks was the minimum. The other three suggested that he'd stay two weeks by himself, because they felt saintly enough already and didn't need any additional blessing. The old elegant building also featured a wine cellar and they had a complete education in Colombian and Chilean wines. Ted insisted on buying a case of each in spite of his wife Annabella's objections that he could buy the same wines back home for half the price. "These labels are printed in Spanish. That makes them more authentic." he explained, but his wife wanted to know: "Does that improve the taste?" It didn't matter what anybody said, the wine was bought and would be shipped. Fred was more practical. "You paid for the wine and now you hope that they'll really ship it?"

"Sshhh. You're in a Holy place."

The planned train ride to Bogota was going to take too long, so they bought airline tickets instead. The flight on the twin propeller plane was just an hour and a half, but they were able to admire the beautiful countryside under a cloudless sky. The foothills of the Andes stretched in a long string toward the center of the country. When they consulted a map, they realized that Colombia was a lot larger than either one of them had anticipated.

"We'll just have to come back some other time." Fred suggested.

"How much further is it to Machu Pitchu?" Ted wanted to know.

"Forget that. That's a separate trip altogether. Maybe next year."

Fred made sure that they were going to stay in the same hotel, where Julia and Ralph had stayed, with the exception that he was not looking forward to being shot outside the front door. Maybe he would use side doors instead. Of course, nobody should be gunning for him, 'cause nobody knew he was there and no one had reason to suspect 'his self-imposed secret mission. His plan was to over-fly the country and see if he could see coke plantations from the air and film them. Other than that, he had no real plan.

The Golden Pig

That changed that night. In the hotel lounge, he befriended an American Pilot. Ted was singing 'Guantanamera' with a strolling guitar player and the lone pilot sipped straight whiskey at the bar and smiled at the entertainment.

"I deny all knowledge of that individual." Fred told the American, "Don't believe rumors that he's my brother. By the way, I'm Fred."

The lanky pilot shook his hand and said: "Hi, I'm Leroy."

"Nice to know you, You come all the way to South America and drink whiskey? Don't you like their stuff?"

"No, I'm not here long enough to learn to respect their drinks, so I stick with what I know."

"Why don't you stay a little longer?"

"Hahaha, good thinking. No, I flew in this afternoon and I'm flying out again tomorrow afternoon."

"Boy, that barely allows you time for a swim and no time to go sightseeing. Why the hurry?"

"I fly cargo. I fly in and out and sometimes I have a stopover like this."

Fred was elated. "A fellow pilot? Whaddaya know? I've been flying for nearly fifty years, but I'm about to hang it up. What do you fly?"

"I fly mostly Falcon and Lear jets. But I'm here in a Gulfstream."

"Ah, Grumman Gulfstream?" Where's your crew? In bed already?"

"No, no, no. I fly alone."

"No co-pilot?"

"Nope, all alone."

"Why don't you wait a few days and we'll all fly back with you and I'll be your co-pilot. No charge."

Leroy grinned at the offer and signaled for another drink.

"Thanks for the offer, but I have to head out tomorrow. When are you leaving?"

"In about four days. We cruised the Caribbean and decided to see something inland instead of all the tourist ports, so we'll stay here and do the town and maybe some of the surrounding cities and then we fly home."

"Where's home Fred?"

"Pensacola Beach and my brother is up near ..."

"I learned to fly in Pensacola."

"Navy?"

"Marines."

"Wow. I'm Air Force myself. Royal Netherlands Airforce actually. I flew F-84's."

"Korea?"

"No I got my wings when the conflict was over, so I never got there. How about you?"

"I flew A-4's and then T-1's and some transports."

"You're a lot younger than I so you must have enjoyed Vietnam."

"Enjoyed? Well, in a way. A lot of behind-the-scene stuff. Working with the CIA and the Green Berets, secret stuff. Some of it fun, some of it dangerous, but all of it exhilarating!"

"Wow! I read some books about those missions. Did you ever read a book called '*Bonnie Sue*'?"

"No. Bonnie Sue?"

"About a Marine helicopter squadron in Nam. That was their call-sign. I still can't believe what these guys went through. You might wanna read it sometime."

"I'll try to remember that." He ordered another whiskey. He was drinking Jack Daniels and he drank it straight. Fred wondered if he could fly straight the next day.

"Who do you fly for now? Fedex?"

"No, no. A private carrier company. No hassles."

"I never did want to fly commercially after I got out of the service. I didn't wanna wear a uniform any more and say: 'yes sir' and 'no sir' any more in my life."

"Didn't you say you'd been flying for fifty years a moment ago? By the way, another beer?"

"Yes! Dos Equis. Por favor. Yeah, I got my commercial and became a flight instructor, then in business I needed a plane sometimes, so I bought a Cessna and I leased it back to a flight school, so I could fly for practically nothing. Taught my son how to fly from the time he was nine years old and he's an Air Force pilot now. The U.S. Air Force." He added.

"Why are you giving it up?"

"My wife and I fly sometimes and she loves it. I belong to a flying club, you see and I have a choice of eight planes, but she never wants to hold the controls, doesn't ever want to talk on the radio and recently a friend of mine had a stroke, his wife attempted to get the plane down while the tower tried to tell her how and she killed them both. You probably read about it. Anyway when my bi-annual is due and my physical, I'm just gonna let it lapse. That'll be it."

"How are you drunks?" Ted gave up his singing lessons and had meandered over to the bar.

"Leroy, this individual sometimes claims to be my brother. Ted, meet Leroy. What's your last name?"

"Anders." They shook hands. "Ted Van Dyke. Great-great-grandson of the famous painter." Ted was already slurring his words.

"What have you been drinking?" Fred sounded like a concerned older brother.

"Pisco sours."

"What?"

"Pisco sours. You oughta try some." He turned to the bartender: "Tres pisco-sours, por favor."

"What the hell is that?"

"You'll like it. Don't worry.'

"If it gets you this high this fast, I'd better worry. How many have you had?"

" Only four or five, but man, they're good."

The barman set three glasses in front of them that looked suspiciously close to whiskey sour glasses filled with a white substance and a light layer of foam on top, sprinkled with a brown powder.

Ted handled the distributing of the drinks and said: "Salud", clinked the glasses and took a long sip as if he was savoring it right down to his toes.

Leroy and Fred sipped the frosting off the glass.

"Man, that's pretty good," said the pilot and brought it back up to his lips.

"What's in it?" Fred wanted to know.

"First quality tequila and sour mix, sprinkled with cinnamon." Ted was already an expert apparently.

"Is there crushed ice in it?" Fred wasn't going to touch anything that had to do with water or ice.

"Do you see crushed ice? This isn't a margarita. This is genuine stuff. Stuff made for gentlemen."

"Then why are you drinking it?"

"Because I'm a caballero, a gentleman. And you Leroy? What gives us the pleasure of your company?"

Fred answered for him. "He's here on a mission, flew in today and is flying out tomorrow."

"Oh good. I'm sick of my wise old brother already and I'm flying back with you. How far are you going? Are you going to Boston?"

"No," Leroy chuckled and drank down the rest of his pisco. "No I don't go any further than Florida."

"Forget that. Been there, done that. We had a reunion at Disney one year and my little darling brother lives there and that's enough reason never to go back there again. Tres mas piscos." (three more piscos) He waved at the barman and held up three fingers.

"No, Señor, dos! Solemente dos." (Only two.) Fred felt he was onto something and needed to keep his mind clear.

The pilot seemed to like the sours as much as brother Ted and sipped heartily from the new drink.

"Did my brother say he was a pilot too?" Ted was on a roll. "Well let me tell you something. He's a pretty lousy pilot. I know. I've flown with him. One day we were flying to Washington and he couldn't even find Washington National. Do you know how big that place is? Well, we landed at College Station instead. Do you know

The Golden Pig

how small that place is? How can you confuse those two airports? And on the way back we landed at Fort Meade, tied the plane down and when we got in the taxi we found out we were at Laurel Airport You know Laurel? Where they race horses?" He turned to the bar again: "Tres mas!"

"No, no! Dos!" Fred wasn't going to get loaded tonight.

"Here's to you and all the pilots in the world. You have an amazing record you know?"

"We do?" Leroy was starting to smile more and more. He seemed no longer in the dumps. "Like what?"

"You know that the navies of the world have left thousands of ships down on the bottom of the sea, but you flyers have never left one plane up there. Not one! Hahahahaha." He doubled up at his own joke.

Ted and Leroy continued to get sloshed and Fred was making mental notes about the pilot, his mission and his destination. The Gulfstream was returning to a rather small airport. Not Tampa International, Orlando or Sarasota. No, he was flying into Zephyrhills. An airport that didn't even have a control tower and was mainly known for its sky-divers, not for international cargo. Fred's mind was racing. He felt he was on to something. He would call Bongers. If Leroy left in the afternoon, he would arrive in Central Florida after dark. Why? There was no legitimate reason to plan a flight that way. Soooo, it *had* to be illegitimate.

After calling New Jersey in the morning, the women found a taxi to the center of town and the boys headed for the airport to rent a little plane. That was easier said than done. Fred's Commercial license did not impress anybody at the flight school and the only way they would rent them anything was with an instructor, which added sixty dollars an hour to the bill.

"It's only money!" was Ted's comment, but it screwed up Fred's plan of circling and filming the countryside. The next best plan was to fly to Medellin and back and hope for the best.

With their instructor Angelo in the right seat and Fred in the command pilot's seat, they taxied out.

"Angelo means Angel, right?" Ted never stopped. "Great. I always wanted to fly with the angels. Hahahahaha!" Even Fred had to chuckle until they taxied past a Grumman Gulfstream with the logo of James Waters Inc. on the vertical stabilizer. He had seen that logo plenty of times, flying in and out of Tampa Airport.

"James Waters? Flying cargo? No way! I know Jim died a few years ago, but his business is still flourishing. I need to get to a phone again."

Chapter Twenty-one

The Pilot

Andrew Leroy Anders first fell in love with planes when he was only five years old. MacDill Air Force Base in Tampa was having its annual open base. That meant that dozens of planes would be displayed in a so called *Static Show* and dozens more would participate in a gigantic air show, headlining the U.S. Air Force demonstration team, the *THUNDERBIRDS*. In order to take it all in, he and his Dad had left early and he got to climb in and out of many aircraft before the actual show started. The small planes that trailed smoke as they gyrated over the field fascinated him the most. The jets with their earsplitting noise were interesting, but frightening. He didn't like thunder either. All in all, it was a good day. He had two hotdogs and plenty of potato chips, which was more than he had ever had during any event and he was convinced he wanted to be a pilot.

The love never left him. When he was only twelve, he became a Civil Air Patrol cadet and got to fly for the first time in his life in a Cessna 172 at Vandenberg airport, between Tampa and his home in Brandon. Throughout High School, he continued in that Air Force Auxiliary and when he was admitted to the University of Florida, he joined the Air Force R.O.T.C. program. He was tested, physically and mentally, including a turn in the altitude decompression chamber and was assured a *'Pilot Slot'*. That meant, upon graduation he would automatically go into pilot training, but besides that, he got to wear a little silver pilot's wing, indicating his selection. He was proud as the dickens. As a student, he was never near the top, but as a cadet he was outstanding. All the drills, the discipline, the dedication to his country and the Air Force were things he simply thrived on. One hitch developed. Korea was not a threat any more, the Russians seemed to be settling down and in his junior year the Air Force was cutting back some of their programs and Leroy's (he preferred Leroy over Andrew) pilot slot was eliminated. That didn't mean that he might never get into flight training, but it wouldn't be automatic nor immediate. He hit the panic button. He called his Dad and told him he was quitting school and joining the Army, where he would get accepted in helicopter training without any reservations or conditions. His Dad flipped! He told Leroy: "You can do anything you want. You can join any branch of the service you like, but you can't quit school. First you graduate and then you choose. No son of mine is going through a military career as an enlisted man. I did enough of that. You want a military career, it's gonna be as an officer, you hear?"

Well, that settled something and after a few days of talking to recruiters, Leroy called back and told his dad that the Marines would accept him upon graduation and put him into flight training immediately. After he hung up the phone, his Dad said to himself: "Great Scott. Not the Marines! I used to hate the bastards, but at least he's staying in school."

Three months after graduation he began training at Whiting Field near Pensacola as a brand new second lieutenant. He couldn't believe his good fortune. This was what he had always dreamed of. After flying in the T-34 trainer for more than 130 hours, he was transferred to Corpus Christi where he eventually earned his golden wings as a Naval Aviator. He married his college sweetheart the day after graduation and since the whole family had traveled to Corpus for his graduation, they were present for the wedding as well. No one in the whole world was happier than Andrew Leroy Anders.

Their first assignment was to Beaufort, South Carolina, where

Leroy was checked out on the A-4, a real first line jet-fighter. Life was a ball. Love was overwhelming and he could have gone on living like that forever. Within a year, they produced a bouncing baby boy and he arrived just in time for a transfer to El Toro Marine Station in San Diego. Vietnam had become a problem and Marines were already over there, training the South Vietnamese. Leroy was anxious to go and get in the fray. This is what he was trained for and this was something he was looking forward to. Leaving his (again) pregnant wife and his young son was not something he cherished, but being a Marine, that was inevitable. Being away from home was just part of the job.

After a one year tour in 'Nam, he came home to his family of three, one wife, two sons. He was ecstatic. A few things occurred that changed his life forever. First of all, he was checked out on a T-1, a little passenger jet. It didn't offer the kind of excitement that the fighter had provided, but it was a fun plane to fly and it would not be involved in combat. His wife was happy and pregnant again. This time they were hoping for a little girl.

The other thing that happened was: He was approached by the CIA. His contract with the Marines was coming to an end and although he had every intention to sign up again, the CIA offered better prospects. For one thing: a LOT more money. Inasmuch as the CIA was a branch of the government, his years in the Corps and the years he would spend with the CIA would all add up to retirement and after much deliberation he decided to leave the Marine Corps. The main concern was money. With three children to raise and to put through college, there was no doubt that it would take a lot of dough. Another important factor was that his wife and children would get away from base housing and return to Brandon and the benefit of having all their relatives around them. His and Hers.

Part of the deal worked out well. They bought a nice four bedroom split level near the center of town and within walking distance from schools, because that was becoming a concern, the oldest was ready for kindergarten.

The deal that did not work so well was his flying assignment.

He was sent to Vietnam and later to Laos as part of Air America, a secret U.S. Government organization, that didn't exist. At least, the government denied its existence. If they were ever captured, they would be identified as *mercenaries* not as *employees* of the U.S. It was a strange setup, but the missions were exciting and the money was great. A little girl was born back home and Leroy was dying to get home and embrace his brand new daughter.

He did get to see her for two weeks when she was four months old and when he was back in Laos, flying around with Green Berets, he was informed that his darling wife was expecting another one.

By the time, he had spent twenty years in government service, he quit and Nixon cut back on the retirement package that they had expected. No big deal, except that Eastern Airlines, where Leroy had found a job, went out of business and Leroy flunked his next flight-physical. One of his eyes was giving him problems and even though the airlines allowed pilots to wear corrective lenses, no other airline wanted to hire him. Their children now totaled five with one on the way. An addition had been added to the house and even though it cost a bundle of money, it was cheaper than trying to buy a bigger house.

Things didn't go so well. Leroy obtained a teaching certificate and did a lot of substituting while waiting for a permanent position within the Hillsborough County school district. Then tragedy hit. Andrew Leroy Junior was involved in a car accident, a serious one. He had been allowed to use mother's minivan to go to a school basketball game, but on the way back, they stopped at a party, had some beer and with three more buddies in the car, Leroy hit a parked truck, killed one of his passengers and was pretty mangled himself.

The hospital bills were outrageous, but the government picked up a lot of it.

The lawsuit by the parents of the dead boy was also outrageous, but the jury agreed with the plaintiff and awarded a huge sum of money. Bankruptcy laws protected their home and cars, but the lawsuit cleaned out all their other assets. Just when they were ready to start preparing the oldest ones for college, there was no more money.

Junior had been pretty well patched up by many surgeries, but sports scholarships were out the window. He would never get back to his former athletic level.

The beautiful, happy life of Andrew Leroy Anders was shattered.

There was just one ray of hope.

Years before, a flight buddy from the Air America days had visited him and offered the most off-the-wall deal that Leroy had ever dreamed off: "Fly drugs."

Just one flight in a little twin jet, out one day, back the next, would pay $100,000.

"One hundred thousand dollars?" Leroy was astounded. "For one flight?"

Of course, there were some drawbacks. Some severe drawbacks! Get caught and you spend time in prison. You fly low, by yourself. You stay below the radar and you only fly at night and into small airports. You park the plane, walk away and someone delivers one hundred big ones in small bills, Directly to the house.

Leroy told his buddy he was crazy.

This time he called him.

A package of flight manuals for a Falcon jet was delivered and Leroy studied hard. He had never flown a Falcon, but what he had flown was very similar. His wife believed that he had an opportunity to fly for an air line or cargo company again.

He was given instructions, where and when to find the plane and the flight plan he was to file. All very professional. With lead in his shoes and a heavy heart, he packed an overnight bag and said goodbye. It had been a long time since he left home for a few days and he was scared stiff. He found the plane, the keys and the flight instructions as planned and although this would be the first time ever that he would fly that type of plane without a co-pilot, he felt pretty competent once he was sitting in the left seat again.

Everything worked fairly well. He climbed out according to his clearances, but once over the Gulf, way out over the Gulf, he went on the deck and changed course, South-West. At such a low altitude, the plane sucked fuel, but he had plenty and when he approached the coast of South America, he climbed back to 20,000 feet and asked for clearance to land at Bogota International. The following afternoon he took off, reversed the whole routine and roared back over the Florida coast at 300 feet in the dark and landed at a remote field in Hernando County. A car was waiting for him and delivered him to his car at the take-off airport. He arrived home without an incident and one hundred thousand dollars was delivered the next day. WOW! He found it hard to believe that it all had happened so easily and from thereon in he concentrated on teaching and getting his kids in college.

The money ran out in two years. He called again.
This time it was different. He had to steal the plane.
"NO WAY!" There was no way he was going to get involved in anything of that sort. No Way!.

Two months later he called again. "Where and how are we gonna manage this?"
"No problem, man." This time he received instruction manuals of a Grumman Gulfstream, very similar to the Falcon. He studied hard. This would be the last time. This would cover all the expenses from now on and he would never have to pull this again.

His wife dropped him off at Tampa International, at the far side of the field and she was to pick him up the next evening at Zephyrhills.

The instructions were again immaculate. He walked to a hangar, found the doors open, the keys in the plane and the flight plan, already logged. He started to relax a little, and when the engine had been cranked and he received taxi instructions, he was his old self again, a confident pilot.

All went well. Just like the last time. Just one difference. He met some crazy Dutchmen in the bar at night and had a ball. He got a little drunk, but he had plenty of time to sleep it off. Everything was going to be just honky-dory.

Chapter Twenty-Two

The Chase

Secaucus, N.J.
FBI office.

Bongers had smiled when he had gotten Fred's E-mail about the Santa Teresa and passed it on to the Florida bureau. They promptly wanted to know about the cargo, ownership and sailing dates, but Bruce had none of that available, so he advised them: "Check it out and keep me posted. It comes from a reliable source."

When he found the phone message that Fred had left, he called Tampa. The head of the Tampa office, Brett Gipson, was familiar with the Zephyrhills Airport and said he would set up an operation in conjunction with NARC and attempt to capture the incoming jet. Bruce said to himself: "That might be an interesting operation. Too bad it's out of my territory and I don't have a real excuse to go out there. I better stay here and stay informed."

When Fred's phone call came in from the Medellin airport, he was there to take it personally and was astonished when Fred told him about a Tampa based corporate jet, sitting on the ramp in Bogota. "You may have something there Fred. Be careful, though. These folks are ruthless. Where are you calling from? Medellin? You're in the middle of the cartel battle fields. What are you doing there?"

When Fred told him he was trying to film the coca fields, Bruce told him: "You better get out of there if you value your life. Call me later."

Within minutes he was on the cell to Brett who was on the road to Zephyrhills already .

"What are you saying Bruce? The James Waters Corporation? That's odd."

"What's odd?"

"I heard on the early news that a mechanic was missing from his assigned hangar. He didn't arrive home last night. I'll check that out and get back with you."

Gipson called his office as his blue Ford sped north along I-75.

"Shirley? Get hold of the head of the James Waters' aircraft division and have him call me on my cell immediately. Thanks."

As they turned off on State road 54, the phone rang again. A mister Paul Brevelt.

"Paul, thanks for calling, what's your function within the company?"

"Officially? The V.P. in charge of community affairs, but in reality, I run the rolling part of the company, trucks, cars and planes. Why?"

"Do you know where your planes are? "

"Sure, one's at 30,000 feet from Nashville to Tampa. One is in France and the little one, the Gulfstream is at Tampa International."

"You better check. You may have an empty hangar at Tampa."

"What are you saying? We have a mechanic missing, but a whole airplane?"

"Check it out and call me back."

Just as the Zephyrhills airport came in view, the phone went off again. "Brevelt here. The plane's gone. How did you know?"

"One of my men will be over momentarily and hit Tampa International with you to see what we can learn. Talk to you in a while."

On the field they found the little F.B.O. (Field Business Office) and located the manager behind his desk in his crowded, cramped office. The desk clerk hadn't questioned them and that was good because they wanted no notoriety at this point in order not to scare off the potential drug dealers. They wanted to catch as many as possible when the plane came in. The airport manager, a young dark haired man with a broad face and huge shoulders couldn't have been more than thirty years old. He introduced himself as "Marvy" with a broad British accent. When asked about that he explained: "Actually, I'm from New Zealand. Came here to sky-dive as a teenager and never left. How can I help you?"

Gipson introduced his partner as John Cockran and started off by telling Marvy: "This is top secret. Not a word leaves this office, understood?"

The smile died on Marvy's face and all he said was: "Find a seat, will you?"

Since there was only one chair in the room, another one had to be brought in and when the door closed, there was barely breathing room for all three.

Gipson had the posture and the bearing of an Army general and his deeply lined face spoke volumes about experience and authority. His voice sounded a lot like Robert Mitchum, but the face didn't match.

"Marvy, tonight we're expecting a jet to land here loaded with coke." Marvy flinched and the G-man continued. "We aim to confiscate the plane, it was stolen by the way, and all the goods. We also want to catch the smugglers. More than likely, someone will meet the pilot here, because we don't believe he has a car here. Right then or maybe later, maybe much later, we expect a crew to appear and unload the plane. We want to catch all of them and all of the dope. What that entails is that this has to be a very hush-hush operation. You, nor your personnel, can let on that anything is in progress, because if the smugglers get wind of it, they may radio the plane and he might land somewhere else. That would be a disaster. So all throughout the day, you'll see strange mechanics and painters working all over your field, checking aircraft and vehicles and when anyone objects or reports something, tell'em they're under your orders, conducting inspections. The important thing is that no one becomes suspicious." He took a breath and looked Marvy deep into his blue eyes. "Is that pretty clear?" Marvy nodded. "If you should get a call from any official agency, like the CIA, the U.S. Marshalls, the Homeland Security, anybody, just take messages and call me immediately. This is my cell number."

As if by command, his phone rang right then and there. "Gipson. Yes… Yes… Dead?... Yes." He closed the cell. "They found the mechanic behind the hangar between some airplane parts."

"Murdered?" John asked. His pale face had turned white.

"Yep! It gets murkier by the minute." He stood up, "Stiff upper lip and all that rot, Marv." and reached for his hand. "We'll be in touch. What time do you get off?"

"Hopefully at six. By then I'm ready for a bloody beer."

"I know how you feel. See ya."

All day long the Feds and the local Sheriff's department worked together to get as many undercover people on and around the field. There was no sign of a getaway car, so it was safe to assume that someone would come out to meet the plane after touchdown. At night the entrance gate was lowered as a rule, so that part should be easy to control.

After another conversation with Bongers and a closer take-off time, they estimated that the plane would land at about nine, maybe nine-thirty. There was little else to do until then, so Gipson and his partner took a personal look at the company hanger at T.I.A. and where the body had been found. The murder weapon was right there among the scrap, but didn't have any useful fingerprints. The mechanic was killed by a severe blow to the skull with a plumber's wrench.

"Probably teamwork, " John observed, "one walked up to him from the front, while the other one clobbered him from behind. The bastards. All for money. Yech!"

Gipson went home for an hour's rest and was back on the road by seven. The walkie-talkies around the field reported nothing unusual, so all they could do was wait. In the little F.B.O. building, just one person handled the Unicom radio and incoming phone calls.

Brett was lounging in a lazy chair, skimming through flight magazines, killing time and waiting for a radar report. The jet was expected to come ashore north of Clearwater and rise up from 300 to 1,000 feet to set up a traffic pattern for landing. The wind was light from the east, so the jet could use the longest of the three runways and that would put it in the middle of a spider web of hidden pick-up trucks and armed lawmen.

Nothing happened for a while and John Cockran, who was on guard duty at the gate, stretched his long legs inside his car, when a light approached the gate. He got out and walked to the passenger side of the shiny Lexus and asked the nice looking lady: "Can I help direct you ma'am?"

"I'm picking up my husband."

"From the office?"

"No, he's flying in in a jet, but I don't think he's here yet."

"What time is he expected here?"

"Right about now, I think."

"Well, if he's in a jet, he'll be using the long runway and he'll probably park at hangar "B". Do you know where that is? Could you find it in the dark?"

"I don't have a clue. It's all so dark."

"Well, once you get used to the little blue and yellow lights along the runways and taxiways, it isn't so difficult. Just a minute." He talked into his shoulder mike. "Can someone cover me at the gate for a few minutes? I'm guiding this lady, Mrs…." He leaned over to the car, "Mrs…?"

"Anders."

"I'm taking Mrs. Anders to hangar "B", I'll be right back." In his airport security uniform he stepped back to her window: "Follow me ma'am, stay close so you won't get lost." He opened the gate and got into his white and black 'security' car and blinked his lights. She followed closely while they zigzagged through an endless array of taxiways and roads and stopped in front of a dark hanger with a huge white "B" over the giant doors. John got out and walked over to the little white vehicle and opened the door and ordered: "Out!".

"Why? What?" She stammered.

"Just get out. DON'T TOUCH THAT BAG!" By now he had his pistol in his hand and motioned her out. "Put your hands on top of the car!"

"But what?" She leaned forward and obliged.

"Just put one hand behind your back." He clasped a handcuff on her wrist. "Now the other one." She had to shift her feet in order to keep from falling on her face.

John turned her around while talking in his mike; "Suspect in custody. Do you want me to leave her car here?"

"Yes, bring her in." With Mrs. Anders in the passenger seat of his truck, John drove to the FBO where Brett took over. "Did you read the lady her rights?"

"No, I..."

"Come on in ma'am, you have the right to remain silent.... " Gipson completed his required routine and when she finally got word in edgewise, she hollered: "What is this? Who are you? What's going on?"

"Accessory to drug trafficking and an accessory to murder to start." She collapsed in a chair: "What are you saying? I'm here to pick up my husband and you people..."

Just then the radio crackled: "Unknown object crossing the coast. Due east. Speed 440 knots."

"That's him. Number three? Are you in position? Get in the suspect's car. Four? Lie down on the back seat. When the suspect exits the plane, drive up as if you're picking him up. Over."

"Wilco, three."

"Wilco, four."

"Get ready." Brett pointed to the desk clerk, who moved over to the radio.

"I think you people are all.. " Mrs. Anders started again.

"Take her outside.!"

Two pairs of hands grabbed her and took her out. Gipson did not want an incoming pilot to hear a woman's voice when he called in. And call in he did. A long seven minutes later.

"Zephyrhills Unicom, what is your active?'

"We're landing zero eight, right pattern, winds four knots, visibility unlimited. You're number one in the pattern."

"Roger. Zero eight."

The noise of the approaching jet was audible and they saw his lights come on when he turned down wind.

"The S.O.B. doesn't do much talking, does he?" The radio operator commented, because the airplane was supposed to report his position on down wind, base leg and final. The jet didn't report a thing, but they saw it coming in over the runway and heard the screech of the tires as it touched down. It didn't take but five minutes before a call came in: "We got him, he walked right into the car."

Chapter Twenty-Three

The Trap

Over the Gulf of Mexico.

Leroy felt better once he passed over most of the Caribbean Islands and let down to the deck. He woke up a little hung-over, but he was sucking 100% oxygen and it cleared his brain in no time. Just another few hours and it would all be over. No more dope runs and no more money problems. The good life lay ahead of him.

As the sun was going down to his left, he kept navigating by means of his GPS. What an invention! He didn't need radar or traffic control to get anywhere, he knew where he was and where he was going at all times. He had to hit Florida's West Coast somewhere north of Clearwater where a 1,800 foot TV mast was a considerable obstacle and south of Cross City, where the Navy had a balloon flying on top of a 15,000 foot cable. Hitting either one of them would be deadly. No problem! His instruments told him he would be at least fifty miles north of the huge tower. Piece of cake. Once the sun went down in a spectacular sunset, it grew dark pretty rapidly and that was just what he needed. It was pitch black as he hit land and climbed to 1,000 feet by just a little nudge on the wheel and he contacted Zephyrhills. The winds were calm, he could use the long runway and in another twenty minutes he'd be in the car with his wife and the scary adventure would be over. The 100 Grand would be at the house in a few days and life would be a breeze from there on in.

He joined the traffic pattern, went through his pre-landing checklist, turned on his lights, lowered flaps and dropped the wheels. Everything was in the green and he leisurely turned to final and touched down at the end of the runway with just a brief squeal of the tires as they went from zero to one hundred and fifty miles an hour in just seconds. "Grease job", he said to himself as he reversed the engines and started to tap the brakes.

"Plenty of runway." He assured himself and easily turned off at the end in the direction of hangar "B". He already spotted his wife's car and when he stopped in front of the hanger and turned off everything, he saw her moving toward the plane. Leroy unbuckled himself, got out of his seat and lowered the door that also served as exit stairs. He grabbed his overnight bag and walked down the steps. The trunk popped open as he approached the car. He dropped his bag in the trunk and opened the passenger door. He slid in as he said: "Hi Honey!" he felt a sting in his back and a male voice saying: "Put your hands on the dash and don't move. You're under arrest." The G-man had been hiding between the seats and Leroy never noticed him while getting in.

"What the hell is this?"

"Shut up and put your hands on the dash, or you'll get a bullet in your spine." He felt something hard being pushed harder against his vertebrae and hollered again: "What's going on? Where is my wife?"

"Shut up! You have the right to remain silent…"

"Like hell, I'm not gonna be silent! What is going on?"

The lady driver had put the car in gear and they were moving toward the entrance of the field. The Fed in the back seat, Gordy Poole, pushed the nozzle harder against Leroy's back:

"I will pull this trigger and you'll be dead in a second if you don't shut up. You're under arrest for grand theft, smuggling and an accessory to murder. You have the right to…."

"Murder? What do you mean murder? I'm a pilot, I just fly the plane. You got the wrong man and where is my wife? Why are you driving her car?"

"Again, shut up." The car rolled to a stop at the FBO and agents descended on it from four sides. While one of them opened the passenger door, Gipson stepped up with his pistol aiming smack between the pilot's eyes. "Out! Hands up."

While one lawman frisked him, another brought one arm down and clicked a cufflink on his wrist, followed by the other one and Leroy was led into the FBO, where his wife was slumped in a chair. She jumped and screamed at the top of her lungs: "Honey! What are they doing to you? What's happening?"

He attempted to rush to her, but two pairs of strong hands kept him in his place. The wife was held back in the same way and went into a crying frenzy.

"What the hell do you think you're…"

Brett interrupted: " Read him his rights." One of the deputies took a little card from his pocket and standing within inches from Leroy's nose, read the prescribed rights article. All the while Leroy kept hollering, until two deputies forced him onto a seat while a third one secured his cuffs to the back of the chair.

Mrs. Anders was taken out a few minutes later and was transported to the Pasco County Jail. She screamed all the way in. For twenty minutes.

"I have to get to my kids. I gotta get home. I have six kids at home! I'm supposed to be able to use a phone. What's the matter with you people? Are you crazy? Is this Hitler's world all over again? I gotta call my kids. Don't you understand? What kinda heartless bastards are you? Don't you have a wife and kids? What are you? Animals?"

She kept it up all the way, where she was turned over to the Pasco County Sheriff's Department. The deputies sighed sighs of relief. "What a job!" One murmured.

Leroy was grilled by Gipson right there in the FBO building.

"What time are they coming to unload the coke?"

"I don't know what you're talking about, man. I have electronics aboard."

"Colombia exports electronics to the United states? I thought it was the other way around. Quit stalling. When is the plane scheduled for unloading?"

"I don't know. I just fly over and back and that's it."

"How often do you do this?" Gipson changed course.

"How often, This is only my second time and..."

"You expect me to believe that?"

"Yeah, man. I flew for the CIA for years and now I just ..."

"The CIA?" Brent was earnestly surprised.

"Yes, I was in 'Nam and Laos for five years, flying for Air America, so can you now please unbuckle me and let me and my wife go home?"

"Not so fast. You're under arrest for grand theft and.."

"I never stole a thing in my life. Where..."

"What about this plane?"

"I didn't steal it, it was supplied by ..."

"The James Waters Company says it was stolen and a man was murdered in the process, so that adds murder..."

"Come on!!" Leroy was shouting by now. "I was handed the keys to the plane and a flight plan. I had nothing to do with anything else. Come on, you gotta believe me."

"Let's hope the judge believes you." Turning to some deputies: "Put him on ice. I'll talk to him later."

"You can't do that. I've got six kids at home, I gotta get home. And what did you do with my wife?"

"Get him out of here!"

Gipson organized some drinks and sandwiches for the group and for all the agents scattered around the field. "It may be a long night."

He gathered a group of his key people around him and started to plan.

"We have no precedent, so we don't know if the smugglers show up right after touchdown, or if they wait for daylight. A night operation might be too risky for them and draw suspicion, so maybe at dawn or anytime in between. We have no choice. Let's plan on being here all night. You, Joe, being with the Sheriff's department, you know what is best. Should you relieve the men on duty at eleven or keep them on and pay them overtime? What do you think and how would your troops feel about it?"

"It's a mixture, sir. Some have to go home. Kids, you understand and some may be able to stay. I'll call them individually and handle it accordingly. One way or the other, we'll be well represented."

"Thanks, Joe." The sheriff's sergeant left.

The Tampa Special Agent continued. "I know we're only guessing, but I bet you donuts to dollars that they won't show till daylight. They may come with more than one vehicle, but that isn't likely. I see them coming in with a panel truck that they back up to the plane, load within three minutes and are gone." He paused and looked around the room at the tired but determined faces. "Any other or better ideas?" There were none.

"Okay. Now that the plane is in place, relocate the various pickup trucks and cars, so we can surround their vehicle in seconds. Keep them out of sight, but ready to roll at a moments notice. Have your guns out. Have a few snipers on top of a car, ready to take them out. Remember the men we're up against are ruthless and they are professional killers. Don't hesitate to shoot, but we'd like to capture them alive. We need to pump them. Don't take chances, though. When in doubt, kill'em. Any questions?"

When most of the men and the one woman filed out of the room, he said to his aide: "John, I'm gonna sit in this chair and sleep a while. I'm betting I'm right about the morning raid, but wake me at the least disturbance, okay?"

"Right boss. Sweet dreams."

Gibson slept for four hours and when he woke up, he wished he had brought a toothbrush. He had a terrible taste in his mouth and he looked at the young girl behind the counter with sleepy eyes. It took a few seconds before he realized where he was and when he did, he got up and asked the girl: "Who are you and what are you doing here?"

"I'm Diane and I started at midnight. I handle the desk and the radio till eight when Marvy and all the rest come in."

"Oh, yes. Of course. Life goes on and so does business, whether we're here or not. Any news?"

"What kinda news?"

"Forget it." Brett found a bathroom and when he reappeared he fixed himself a cup of coffee and stepped outside. His assistant John was sitting in an unmarked car in front of the building and stepped out, the moment the light from the FBO door flooded the parking lot.

"Anything happening, John?"

"Nothing. Not a thing. People don't fly much at night I guess."

Gipson scanned the area and said: "Good job. Not a car in sight. Who's handling the gate?"

"One of the deputies, dressed as a security guard. The "FOLLOW-ME" truck is parked right next to the gate and we have two agents in it."

"Good. Nothing to arouse suspicion?"

"Doesn't look like it. It's been a long night already and we have four more hours to go before daylight. I instructed the teams to alternate two hour naps, so they should be fairly fresh in the morning."

"Did you get any sleep?" Gipson could see that his aide looked worn out.

"Not yet."

"Who's in the car with you?"

"Gordy. He's sleeping right now."

"Okay, switch. I'll be inside by the radio."

Inside, he approached the desk and asked: "Do you know what's going on?"

"Not really. When I came on at twelve I was stopped at the gate, which was unusual. All the guards know me and flag me right in. Not this time, I had to show my security pass and explain what I was doing here. What's going on?"

"We're expecting some trouble, probably at daybreak, so we're getting ready."

The petite brunette remained curious. "What are you? The cops?"

"FBI. This is a federal operation. I'm Gipson by the way and you have to notify me immediately when that Unicom starts squawking, okay?"

"Sure thing."

Gipson went back to the deep leather chair, checked his cell and his two way radio and made himself comfortable. He dozed again till seven and was surprised that it was broad daylight and nothing had happened.

At quarter to eight, Marvy came in and all over the field activities started up. A fuel truck was motoring up to the flight line, mechanics opened hangar doors and trucks and cars started flowing through the gate.

"Is there another entrance at the far side of the field?" Brett asked Marvy.

"There sure is. It's only open from seven to nine and from four to six to expedite the traffic of the personnel on the base. Didn't you know?"

"Didn't think of it." Gipson called the team closest to the Gulfstream: "Any movement.?"

"Nothing, nada. The door to the plane is still open, but no one has been near it."

"Thanks." He called John, who was still out front. "Do we have someone at the other gate on the other side of the field."

"Affirmative. Henderson and a deputy are out there."

"Thanks." He heaved a deep sigh, all the way up from his midriff. "Whew! For a moment I thought I might have screwed up." He wiped his forehead. "Better call Bruce and keep him up to date."

Instead of using his cell, he used a land line. "Mr. Bongers, please."

"May I say who's calling?" A female voice demanded.

"Tampa."

"Just a moment."

"Bongers."

"Bruce, I don't know who your informer is, but you better keep him." He accentuated 'him'. "The guy was right on the button. We have the plane and the pilot and he came zooming in, right on schedule."

"Great." Bongers was pleased, because they received so many false alarms and people crying 'wolf' that he was relieved that he had provided a solid lead. "Who was the pilot?"

"That's the troubling part. He's a former CIA pilot. Air America."

"You gotta be kidding."

"No, I'm not.... There goes my radio! Panel truck at the gate, this might be it. Talk to you." he unceremoniously hung up the phone and dashed outside.

From inside the car they could not see the gate or the panel truck, but their radio informed them that a white panel truck was proceeding toward the plane.

"Let's go. Keep your distance. Gordy, do you have your rifle?"

The man in the passenger seat lifted the weapon that had rested between his legs and nodded.

"Get it ready." Gordy nodded again. All he had to do was flip the safety and he was ready to fire. "Bring'em on." He murmured.

The car had rounded a corner and now they could see the white van way in front of them. They kept their distance.

"Gordy, roll down your window and get ready to blow out their tires"

Again, Gordy just nodded as the window went down noiselessly. Up ahead, the van stopped at hangar "B" and started to back up to the open airplane door.

"NOW!" Gipson hollered into his mike. "John, turn left and stop."

The driver followed orders and the moment the vehicle came to a halt, Brett ordered: "The tires Gordy."

The sharpshooter had his rifle out the window in a sec and with his left elbow resting on the doorframe, aimed and shot, aimed, pulled the trigger once more and repeated it a third time. Three tires on the vehicle exploded. The driver door opened immediately and a short stubby man spilled out while four vehicles came bearing down on him. From their position, Brett and his team could not hear what was being said, but the stubby man laid down on the tarmac and a shot was heard from the other side of the van.

"Let's go!" Gipson hollered and John had the tires squealing within seconds. When they arrived at the scene, everything was under control. Two men were down and hand cuffed and another one was face down in a puddle of blood.

"Came out with a gun in his hand," a deputy explained. "I hollered 'drop it'. but he raised his gun and I blew him away."

"Good work!" Brett spoke into his mike: "Bring up the SUV and let's see what these clowns brought in."

No one on the team had seen that much cocaine in their life. There were five crates, all loaded with cellophane wrapped packages.

"It looks like they're packages of exactly one kilo. I'm just guessing, but I would say we're looking at two hundred and fifty kilos, about six hundred pounds. What would you say that is worth in street value?" He was talking to no-one in particular. "Ten, twenty million, maybe more?" There were several suggestions, but it didn't make any difference because they had the job of unloading it.

"Fellows, come sit." He pointed to the luxurious interior of the plane. When a dozen lawmen were either sitting or standing, he started, "The SUV is too small for this kinda load, so secure a truck, U-haul or something. Find replacement tires and wheels if they're damaged, we're going to use this truck for bait if we can. Get started on the captives and find out where the delivery was to take place.

Maybe we can catch a few more of them. I'll call Washington and get clearances, because we may be traveling interstate and we'll need the help of the other districts. Get going. And by the way, Thanks. Good work!"

Chapter Twenty-Four

Medellin

12 Noon.

Ted was saying: "If you consider the sixty dollars an hour that we're paying the pilot, this could be a very expensive lunch, unless we eat very fast." They were sitting in the little restaurant on the far side of the field, across from the international terminal with the big passenger jets. Fred had called Bongers with the info about the James Water airplane and was just about to comment after he swallowed the flan he had in his mouth, when two elegantly dressed gentlemen walked up to them.

"Would you come with us please?" Perfect English with a charming Spanish accent.

"Come where? And why?"

"We are with Airport Security and please come quietly."

"No!" Ted exclaimed. "You estoy comiendo y voy a terminar." (I'm eating and I want to finnish.)

"Por favor, Señores. Vengan." (Please, gentlemen, come!) The taller of the two, who had been doing the talking was getting visibly annoyed.

Fred stood up and walked to the counter and asked the cashier: "Are these people with Security?"

She answered: "I don't know."

"Call the police. I don't trust those clowns." He walked back to the table and faced them: "Show me some badges, some ID!" He held out his hand as to receive some form of ID and the shorter man grabbed his hand and with one swing twisted it behind his back. "Ay, Ay, POLICE! CALL THE POLICE!" He hollered across the restaurant and as a few of the other customers got up, including their pilot, the 'gentleman' turned Fred loose and with a bow and: "*Con permiso*", they walked out of the restaurant.

"What the hell was that all about.?" Ted wanted to know.

"Later!" To his pilot he said: "Get the plane, taxi right to this door and we'll jump in. Let's go!" The pilot rushed out leaving the rest of his food.

Someone else walked up, a man in a flight suit. "What was the problem?"

"I don't know, but I know enough that I don't go anywhere with someone who isn't in uniform and doesn't show me a police badge. Not in this country or any other. The fact that they didn't want to face the police was enough evidence that I was right.

Here's our plane. Hasta la vista." They ran out the door and into the little airplane.

The pilot received taxi and take-off clearance while they were taxi-ing and Fred instructed: "Back to Bogota, the fastest way possible."

The return trip was uneventful and Fred tried filming coca fields, but he was never sure what he saw. There were many cultivated fields that they flew over, but they might have been corn or wheat or other vegetables. He figured he could later enlarge the pictures on the computer or his TV. As a precaution, he took out his disk from his camcorder, tucked it inside his shirt and inserted a blank one, just in case.

The incident in Medellin had him on edge. He had a creepy feeling that they might be confronted again in Bogota as soon as they exited the plane.

He was right. The moment they landed two cars, marked POLI-

CIA, pulled up to the plane and a uniformed policeman opened the door for them and said politely: "Would you gentlemen please come with me?" They obliged while they saw the pilot being loaded in the second car.

"Where are you taking us?" Fred was very edgy.

The policeman in the driver seat just raised his index finger and said: "Momentito," (Just a moment.)

They didn't have far to go. The car stopped in front of a door marked SEGURIDAD and they were beckoned inside. After a knock, they were ushered into a nicely furnished office where a greying gentleman with a huge black mustache sat behind a massive desk.

"Gentlemen, come in. Sit!" He stood up and pointed to two overstuffed chairs on the side of the room. He picked up his hat and with an elegant motion positioned it on his head. It was nearly comical. The hat really adorned him. Multiple gold braids crossed over his visor and the hat did make him look very important. Maybe that was the reason he put it on, trying to make an impression.

"Por que estamos aqui?" (Why are we here?) Ted wasn't happy with police forces any more.

"Ja! Ustedes hablan Espanol?" (Ha, you speak Spanish?) The golden trimmed officer looked surprised.

"No, no," Fred interjected. "He does, but I understand just a little."

"How come he speaks?" His English was good, but his accent was thick.

"He was married to una Borinqueña for many years."

"Borinqueñia?" He lifted his eyebrows which lifted his hat as well.

"I can speak for myself and I want to know what the hell we're doing here. I'm ready for a beer and since we're on vacation, it's high time." Ted had a very short fuse.

"You like a beer? You too?" He signaled the police officer who remained standing by the door: *"Tres cervezas frias."* (Three cold beers.) The policeman turned and disappeared.

"I will try to let you understand our position. We checked with the plane rental company and we found out your hotel and your names and we understand you're on vacation for a few days,"

"For a few weeks, but just a few days in Colombia." Fred was clarifying their presence as beers and frosted glasses arrived.

"You got beer in your police station? Boy, Americans can learn a lot from you guys. Doesn't he get any?" Ted pointed to the cop who served as waiter.

"Hahahaha! No, he has to wait till he gets off duty, then he can have one too." He accepted a glass from the polite police server and raised it. *"Salud!"* (health.)

"Salud."

"Salud" They toasted and sipped. Not Ted, he didn't sip, he drank. Must have been thirsty.

"Now let me explain. When we received a call from Medellin that there had been a confrontation in the restaurant, our first thought was: 'fighting cartels.' Not uncommon around here. We found out that you had made a call to the United States and that you were confronted by two men who wanted to take you away. What made you suspicious?"

Fred answered: "They were too nicely dressed. Very expensive clothes. Cops can't afford $200 shoes and they offered no ID. I distrusted them immediately and I figured if they're legitimate, they'll stay when the cops arrive, right?"

"Very good thinking. Are you a law official yourself?"

"No, but I grew up under unusual conditions."

"Like what?"

"We lived under German occupation for five years and since we had a bar, we saw everything, common soldiers, Secret Service, real Nazis, underground agents, we saw them all and we learned a few things. Keep your eyes open and don't talk."

"Really? Germans? In what country?"

"Holland."

"Holanda! Muy bien. May I see your passports? Are you American Citizens now?"

"Yes, we are. For a long time already." Ted answered as both of them handed over their passports.

"Born in Belgica?"

"Yes, my folks lived in Belgium for eight years and three of their children were born there, including Ted and me."

"I'd like to travel to Europe sometime, especially Spain."

"Do it, man. Do it." Ted was all for it.

"Not so simple. Back to our story. What were you doing in Medellin?"

"Doing? Nothing. We stopped for lunch."

"You flew to Medellin for lunch? Isn't that a bit expensive?"

"Well, yes!" Fred had to admit. "Besides we had to pay the pilot $60 an hour, so…" He stopped. … "Wait a minute, we haven't settled our bill yet at the flight school."

"Don't worry. They have your credit card imprint. They're not worried. So why Medellin." He was persistent.

"You see, I'm a pilot, by the way, how should we address you? Major, Colonel?"

"I'm sorry, I'm Captain Quintero."

"Thanks Captain. As I was saying, I'm a pilot, so wherever we go, we rent a little plane and fly around the countryside. Only in Caracas they wouldn't let me fly by Angel Falls, so we went on a tour flight. Well, here they wouldn't rent me a plane either and the only way we could fly around, we had to have an instructor with us. Well, that was okay, but then when we talked about flying around he wanted to know what we wanted to see? He had to file some sort of a flight plan and he suggested that we'd fly somewhere for lunch and back and we did. He did say that we would see some of the most beautiful scenery from the air and he was right. It's a beautiful country."

"How far is Machu Picchu from here?" Ted interrupted.

"Machu Picchu? A thousand miles at least I think."

"Isn't Peru next to Bolivia?"

"Ted, if we ever go to Machu Picchu, we'll go on a two week trip, you can't land anywhere near there."

"Señores, back to the story. You ate at the airport and the two men walked in?"

"Yeah man, and we got out of there in a hurry."

"Did you take many pictures?" The captain pointed at Fred's camcorder?"

"No, most of the country is just plain green, not like flying over the Grand Canyon."

"May we have the film?"

"What for? I have no film."

"Sir, shall we remain friends? Open your camera and give me your film. We'll analyze it and return it to your hotel."

"But I don't have film, I have a disc."

The captain seemed genuinely surprised. "You have a disc in there? No film."

"No film."

"Then give me the disc."

"Why?"

"Let's say, we're playing it safe. We believe you, but we want to make sure. You understand? Don't worry, I'll bring it back."

"You'll bring it back? I don't know if these are available yet in your country. You know our hotel?"

"Sure."

Reluctantly, Fred removed the camcorder from its case and turned on the mechanism. A push of a button and the disc appeared. He pulled it out and handed it to the Colombian Officer: "Don't touch the surface, handle it by the edges."

"How much photos can this hold?"

"Photos? A few thousand. Movies, ninety minutes."

"Maravilloso!" He studied the little disk in his hand, "How much it cost in America?" He pointed at the camcorder in Fred's lap.

"About six hundred dollars."

"Six hundred. That's all? You send me one?"

"Send you one? I guess I could."

"Sell me yours?"

"Mine? I'm not through with my vacation, I need to film some more. For posterity, for my kids and grandkids, you understand?"

"I give you $600 and you'll send me one.?'

"Sure. Give me your address."

"I come by the hotel after dinner. Nine-thirty." He stood up as if the interview was over. "Who did you call in New Jersey?"

"New Jersey? When?"

"From Medellin. An unlisted number?"

"I called my sister on her cell. Her boy is in the hospital."

"Why call from Medellin and not from your hotel?"

"He came out of surgery at eleven local time and I promised I would call immediately, he's my Godson."

"Gentlemen, I see you tonight."

"Thanks for the beer."

A police car delivered them back to the hotel and as they walked up the grand staircase, Fred said to his brother: "Can you believe that?"

Chapter Twenty-Five

Flight from Evil?

Hotel Domani
Bogota
3 PM

"I'll tell you what! I'm getting out of here! You can stay if you want to, but Annabella and I are on the first plane out tomorrow. Just give the hotel a forwarding address, where to ship the body and..."

"Whose body?"

"Yours." Ted's mouth was running a mile a minute in the exotic lounge of the hotel while drinking pisco-sours again. "You don't think you'll get out of here alive, do you? You told me about that Ralph guy that got shot right here, so what makes you think you'll be an exception. From what you told me, that guy was much more of an innocent bystander than you are, so he was lucky that he was just injured. You're involved in this mess, so you'll be killed for sure." He took another sip of that cool sour liquid, licked his lips and continued: "Now I don't mind handling the funeral arrangements back home and I'll tell you what, if you write your will right now and put a sizable amount in for me, I'll even deliver the eulogy. How's that?"

"Can you shut up for just a minute?" Fred was getting tired of the lecture, although he agreed with his brother that it might be healthier in a different locale. "As soon as the women come back, we'll bring it up for a vote and we can call the airline and…"

"I don't give a shit how you vote or if you wanna run for president, I'm outta here tomorrow. We came out here to see beautiful Bogota and all I've seen is two crummy airports and one crummy hotel bar and have been attacked by terrorists and nearly kidnapped and been arrested by the cops. That's enough for me. By the way, where the hell are the women? They couldn't possibly shop this long? Could they?"

"They can't? Where have you been? Don't you pay the credit card bills? They can shop for twenty hours a day and do it all over again tomorrow." Fred ordered another beer. "I'm gonna take a nap and by then, they should be back." He took his beer bottle and got up.

"You don't think the women might be kidnapped?" Ted smiled as he asked that.

"Well…… Is their insurance paid up?" He grinned back at his brother, "Then you have little to worry about. Have fun!" With that he walked out.

At 7:30, they were all back in the bar, waiting for dinner to be served. The women had gotten into pisco-sours as well.

"You visited four castles, a museum and three cathedrals? And you only bought one shawl?"

"Oh, but it's a beauty, it's made from genuine alpaca. Feel how soft that is." Kathryn had the purple and blue garment draped around her shoulders, making her look real elegant. "Real alpaca." She repeated.

"How can you tell? How do you know it didn't come from a cat?" There was no way of stopping Ted. He had stayed at the bar for hours and was already three sheets to the wind. He had promised Fred he wouldn't tell the gals about the incidents at the airports, so they wouldn't worry, but his insistence on flying out in the morning did have them wondering what had happened. Ted's answer was:

"I have already seen so many cathedrals and churches in my life that I don't need to get converted or confirmed any more. So what I wanna see from now on is topless beaches, so let's fly to Martinique. Gorgeous beaches."

"Why do you wanna go there? If you've seen one, you've seen 'em both." Anna was nearly as funny as her husband.

"They're waving us to come and eat." Fred got up and the rest followed.

"I'm selecting the wine tonight." Ted thought he was the expert.

"No, you're not." Kathryn had a mind of her own. "I don't know what I'm gonna eat and once I know that, I'll order my own wine, thank you very much."

During that conversation, they had strolled from the lounge to the dining area, where just one lone individual was sitting at a corner table. He looked American, not Latin.

"Howaryadoing?" Ted greeted him as they seated themselves around their assigned table. The man waved back and nodded, because he had his mouth full.

The meal progressed very pleasantly. The sopa was excellent and the Ropa Vieja was delicious.

"When it comes to food, I could stay here for a month. For my health? No. I'm leaving tomorrow. You can stay if you want to. As soon as we finish eating, I'll call the airlines and change our flights.'

"What if I don't wanna leave yet?" His wife was enjoying the place.

"You can stay forever, as far as I'm concerned, just keep sending me alimony checks."

"*I* send you alimony? No, no, that's not the way it works. *You* send me money. I might wanna live here."

Right at that point the police captain, in civilian clothes, walked up to the table and Fred rose to greet him. "Hey, folks, meet Capitan Quintero."

"No, no, no. Ephrain Quintero. Do you mind if I join you for a minute? Thank you." Fred had lugged over a chair from another table. "*Un poquito de vino, Ephrain?*" (A little wine?)

"*Si, Rojo por favor.* (Yes, red, please) Gracias." The waiter had quickly rushed over a glass.

"Something to eat, Captain?" Ted had obviously already forgotten his name.

" No, gracias, I ate at home. I came to conclude our little business deal. I had to go to the bank and get dollars. You were true? Six hundred dollars and you send me one of your cameras, no?"

"Camcorder?"

"Oh, yes. Camcorder, same as yours? By the way, here's your disk. We couldn't play it. Sorry."

"That's too bad Captain, you should see all the naked girls he filmed." Ted thought he was irresistible.

Fred cut in. "Yes, exact same and where do I send it?"

The policeman reached inside his elegant blue sports coat and extracted an envelope and handed it to Fred. "In here are all the instructions and the money and I hope you can secure instructions in Spanish."

"Okay, I'll take care of that." Fred stuck the item in his shirt and continued eating.

"Where did you find this fine looking man?" Kathryn wanted to know. He was indeed a good looking Latin man with his dark eyes and his very masculine mustache.

Before the captain could answer, Ted cut in: "You don't wanna know, right Capitan?"

"Probably not. How long are you staying here?"

"Funny, you should ask. My brother wants to get out of here in the morning, his wife wants to live here forever and I would like to see more of the city, so we're at an impasse right now."

"You may be at an impasse, but I'm not. I'll wait for you in Martinique. Can I borrow your camcorder? I have a lot of filming to do. Hahahahaha." He had to laugh at his own nonsense. "Señor

Capitan, how difficult would it be to get a flight out of here in the morning?"

"To where?"

"Anywhere, just outta here."

"That shouldn't be a problem. Most flights are not full. I thought you wanted to go to Machu Picchu, and a flight leaves for Cuzco at ten past ten. You should be able to get on. Just remember to take altitude pills. Cuzco is at eleven thousand feet. But ladies and gentlemen, please excuse me, I have business to attend to. *Buenas Noches*." (Good night.) He got up and Fred raised up along with him and asked: "Don't you want a receipt for your money?"

"No, no. I trust you. People from Holland don't steal. Adios!" They shook hands and he was gone. When Fred sat back down at the table he asked: "Do you know what he just told me?" He looked around the table. "He said, 'People from Holland don't steal."

"He obviously doesn't know *you* very well."

Anna choked.

The women went to bed, but Fred came back down and joined his brother at the bar, where he was in a lively conversation with the lone diner. "Hey, Fred. Meet Harry Weaver, he's a pilot too!"

'Good God, not again', flashed through Fred's mind, but he shook the man's hand and commented: "Nice to see another fly boy? Jet Jock?"

"Not since I left the service, last jet I flew was an F-105."

"Ah, the THUD?"

"Yeah, long time ago? What did you fly?"

"Its older brother, the F-84."

"The Thunderjet? Straight wing?"

"Sure thing. Couldn't do but mach point-eight-one, but it was a fine flying machine. What do you fly now?" "Cerveza!" he waived at the barman.

"I fly a twin Beech. Great plane, but not too fast."

Fred was smelling excitement again. "Gracias." He accepted a cold bottle of Dos Equis. "For a company?"

"No", Harry answered. "That's my own plane. I deal in gold and jewelry and some of the antique Inca statues can still be found in this area."

"Aha!" Ted interrupted, "So you're one of the guys who rob the old temples. You may never go to heaven. Their Gods are up there watching you and you'll be punished." By now, Ted was really loaded and Fred suggested: "Let me help you up to bed."

"Like hell you will. I need another Pisco-sour. I may even pee vinegar tomorrow, I had so much lemon juice to drink."

"Sit on the couch here for a moment." Fred grabbed him by the arm and surprisingly Ted followed like a lamb and sat down.

"He'll be out like a light in a minute." Fred sat back down next to the flyboy and reached for his beer bottle.

"Do you still fly?" Weaver wanted to know.

"Oh yes. I still hold a commercial rating, but I only fly for fun. I had my own plane for many years, but business-wise, I couldn't afford it any longer, so now I just rent whenever I want to go someplace. Now I fly out of Pensacola Regional, how about you?"

"I live in Air Park. I keep my plane in my own hangar next to the house. Very convenient. The only thing is we have no gas in the Park, so I have to stop over in Jacksonville to top off my tanks, but that's not a major problem. It's only fifteen minutes."

"So, you're in North Florida, near Orange Park?"

"No I'm actually in Georgia and I wish I could get gas in Georgia, because it would save me twenty cents a gallon."

"Good God, that's a lot of difference. I pay three forty in Pensacola for Avgas."

"That's about right."

"We're debating right now whether we should stay or leave in the morning. My brother wants to see topless beaches. How long are you staying?"

"I'm out tomorrow about eleven. I have to pick up one more load and that way I'll be home just about dark."

"Do you have lighting on your field?"

"Just runway and taxi lights. No ILS or anything, but the weather should be clear tomorrow, so I'll be okay."

"Well, Harry, I'm gonna see if I can get my jolly brother up to bed. Have a good flight."

"Come see us sometime."

"What's the name of your field?"

"Woodridge Park. It's on the map."

"I may just do that." He walked over to the couch and somehow raised his brother and got him in motion.

In his own bedroom, he said to Kathryn. "We're outta here tomorrow."

Chapter Twenty-Six

The Propeller Jock

Harry Weaver smoked pot for the first time in Vietnam. The gal he hung out with in Saigon was not only a beauty, but also very seductive. She did things with him in bed that he had never dreamed of in his life, but she also convinced him that a few puffs of marijuana would enhance his climax. One thing was for sure, it made him more horny than he had ever been in his life. He didn't get too much time to spend with her, because his base was too far away for nightly trips, so he got with her about once a week. She made him feel like he was her only lover, because she was always available when he wanted her and she never rushed him off.

Flying the THUD was an unbelievable experience and the big fighter kept him nearly as excited as Winny. In a different way of course. His main job was bombing and strafing plus keeping MiG fighters and SAM missiles off his leader's tail. They had lost a few men to SAMs already and it was a constant threat when they were up there.

He convinced himself that his exploits with the Vietnamese girl and the occasional reefer helped him relax and do his job that much better. Her name was Nguyn, but she pronounced it WIN, so he called her his Winny, or Winny the Pooh. After a while, he started to take some reefers to the base and would smoke one before going to bed. Made him feel real good. It didn't take long before someone recognized the smell coming from the latrine and one night he was surprised by two M.P.s and even though he managed to flush the one he was smoking down the toilet, he had a few more of them in his shirt pocket and he was nailed. His Commanding Officer had no patience for that kind of conduct and Harry was grounded. It didn't matter how much he assured him that it didn't affect his flying, but potentially endangering his team member's life was unacceptable. He was shipped home.

It didn't come to a court martial, because he was given a choice of getting out or face the court. He got out.

Finding a flying job was not that hard, but finding a flying job he liked was more difficult. For a while he flew as captain on a business jet, but that involved sitting around for hours or sometimes for days while the executives were involved in meetings. It bored the living hell out of him. A small start-up airline turned out to be better. He flew a fairly regular schedule and was off most nights and three weekends a month. The pay was reasonable and the job was based in Savannah. He found a cute little apartment, but couldn't find a good substitute for Winny. He suspected that American women didn't have the sexual imagination as the Orientals. He dated on occasion, smoked a few reefers now and then, but only after working hours and on days off. They didn't cost too much and it provided him with a very pleasant high. Life was pretty good.

On one of his short hops, he brought passengers from Raleigh to Hilton Head and a most charming lady, about five years his senior showed a great deal of interest in him.

She was of average height, but well proportioned. Short, blond, curly hair gave her a boyish flair and her smile and mannerism reminded him of Doris Day. When he strolled through the cockpit before take-off, checking if everyone was happy, she smiled at him broadly and during the brief stopover in Charlotte, she walked up front to chat a minute. She said she had always been interested in flying and considered taking flying lessons, but her husband was dead against it, but now that he had passed away, she might attempt it after all. "Do you give instruction?" She asked.

"I briefly instructed in the Air Force, but not so far in civilian life. I would have to get an instructor's rating first."

"Too bad. I might hire you."

"That might be interesting. It may be worth my while to get a rating. Where do you live?"

"Hilton Head, most of the time."

"Well, Ma'am, I have to crank her up again, so excuse me, go buckle up and we'll talk again on the Island."

Upon arrival, they took time for coffee, while the passengers loaded and unloaded, and they exchanged phone numbers and since he lived within forty five minutes from her home, he promised he would call.

"By the way, I'm Carol and you?"

"Harry. Harry Weaver." He shook her hand. She held it a little longer than necessary and he read a lot of promise into that handshake. "I'll wait for your call."

"Tonight, after eight."

"I'll be home." She left.

The eight o'clock call resulted in a trip to Hilton Head and a few drinks in one of the many cozy nightclubs on the island. When they danced, it started to become a sexual warm up and before midnight, they were in her lavish bed in her palatial home. It was a good thing he had to get up at seven in order to fly out of Savannah by nine fifteen, because if he had stayed in bed with her any longer, he might not have been able to walk straight. She wore him out. She was not as imaginative as Winny, but she sure was insatiable. He promised, he'd be back that night.

It didn't work out that way, because he was weathered in at Raleigh International because of a violent front coming through with a chance for tornados. Well, he needed the rest. A few days later was his day off, so when he arrived two nights after their bedroom introduction, he could stay for a couple of nights in a row. This time they hit the sack before they went out for dinner and a drink and continued where they left off when they got back home. They stayed in bed till ten in the morning and also talked a lot. He had wondered why she was such a young widow and she told him the weirdest story he had ever heard. Her husband was an executive within his company and made loads of money, but a power struggle ensued and one day her man was shot down on a Chicago street in broad daylight. He was only forty-one. He was ten years older than she was and all that happened two years ago. She had inherited a good deal of money and a big insurance settlement and it was all safely invested and she shouldn't have a money worry for the rest of her life. Her only problem was boredom. It seemed that all the eligible men in the area were elderly and most of those couldn't dance. Result: she didn't go out much. Visited her sister in Raleigh on occasion and played tennis at Vandermeer's twice a week with three other gals. That was it.

After a nice swim in her pool, naked, they went for brunch and talked some more.

To his surprise, when they got back, she produced factory made reefers with a golden mouthpiece, rolled and packaged in elegant cardboard boxes. Twenty-five to a pack. He'd never even heard of those and they were excellent quality. "Columbian." She said.

Their affair went on for three months, with only one problem. She wanted him around all the time and even though they had started flying lessons and she had to study a lot, she became increasingly impatient. She just didn't want him to leave any more. In her scheming mind she worked up a plan that would keep him home. She would buy a house on an Air Park, buy him a plane so they could fly an occasional charter and make some money and she guaranteed him a weekly salary that was higher than what the airline was paying. Harry was reluctant.

"Oh, I'm just a gigolo!" he'd sing, imitating Louis Prima's hit from the fifties.

"No, no, no! " She protested. "You'll earn your keep, I promise."

What helped him make his decision was the fact that they got into smoking pot more regularly every week and that he got to be very lethargic about his flying job. Many days, he barely showed up on time and once, he didn't show at all, because he had dozed behind the wheel on I-95, ran off the road and cracked up the car.

He missed his flight altogether and under the pretence that he was hurt, he resigned his job.

They bought the house along the runway and the plane of his choice, a Twin Beechcraft. He loved it. It fit in the hangar next to the house in South Georgia and he could take it up anytime he felt like it and the weather was right. She flew with him all the time and she got to be pretty good at it. From time to time they had a charter, flew into a small airport, loaded a few packages and delivered it to another airport. It was fun.

Exactly one year after they met, they got married and celebrated with a cruise around Hawaii. Somewhere along the line, he couldn't quite remember when exactly, she had introduced him to coke and heroin. A sniff of 'H" up his nose put him on cloud nine. The 'high' was so high, that he felt on cloud nine hundred, not just nine. What he didn't like was the after effect. He felt lousy for two days. He decided to stay away from that and stick with pot. He also started to realize what their 'cargo' was when they had a load to deliver. Either dope or cash! She handled all the business and there was always plenty of money. He wasn't sure, if Georgia law automatically made her property his as well, but he didn't take chances. He invested, without her knowledge, in undeveloped land. He had seen how real estate exploded around Hilton Head in the past few years and he felt that was a safe investment, something that would just grow and grow in value as the years went by.

Physically, their attraction never faded and he felt he really loved her, at least enough not to want to fool around. Her love for him never was a question. She was crazy about him and showed it all the time, in bed and out. She showered him with gifts and money and would hardly ever leave his side. He found out what had killed her first husband. He was knocked off because of a turf war between rival drug gangs and that explained how he had accumulated his wealth. Running dope!

Harry stayed out of the business end of the deal, he just flew and made sure they got to where they wanted to go and get there safely.

Carol started to 'shoot-up' more regularly and she was very loving when she did, but not so great in the morning after. At first he didn't like going on trips by himself, but little by little she begged off from flying with him more and more and he learned to enjoy being alone in the craft and doing what he liked best: Flying!

When Carol came up with a proposal to buy into a casino on the Gulf Coast, he got very enthused and they spent three marvelous days in Biloxi and decided that was a great way to work and live when they grew older. Just one little problem: a little short on hard cash. They checked their many holdings and tried to decide which ones to sacrifice for ready money. It was't easy. They liked what they owned and liked to keep it. There was one other solution: Fly all the way to Colombia or the Bahamas and make a hundred thousand per trip.

Harry wasn't stupid. He knew about radar patrols and surveillance by the Coastguard and what the penalties would be if he got caught. They decided on a trial run. They flew to the Bahamas one weekend and back. He climbed out according to the flight plan he had filed and came back on the deck over the Atlantic. They hit the Georgia coast over the Golden Islands and climbed to a thousand feet and were home safe and sound within a half hour. For two weeks, they sweated it out, waiting for Homeland Security or the FAA to knock on their door and question them about their trip. It never happened.

Next was a trip to Bogota. Same kind of procedure. Out legitimately, back on the deck, this time over the Gulf. They hit the coast just north of Steinhatchee and turned due north to the Georgia border and east toward home. Again, for two weeks, they were on pins and needles and nothing happened.

When it was time for a real profit run, with all the instructions of where to go and what to expect, Carol came down with the flu and Harry decided to go alone. All went as planned and a few days after he returned, a truck appeared, picked up his cargo and delivered $100,000 in small bills.

Two months later he made another trip. He would stay in the Domani Hotel in Bogota. A pleasant place.

Chapter Twenty-Seven

Two in a Row?

N.J. FBI Headquarters
8:15 AM

Bongers couldn't believe his ears. Fred had given him the details of Harry Weaver's impending flight and he had just heard of the results of the successful operation at Zephyrhills. Two in a row? If that were true, Fred would prove to be the most reliable source they had ever had. It would also mean that Fred better get the hell out of there, because it shouldn't take long for anybody to figure out who the source was. Bruce told him so and he was assured that they would be on the 9:15 flight to Saint Martin. Ted was still fussing about going to Martinique, but agreed they could always go there later or even tomorrow. The important thing was: "Get out!"

After getting through to the Atlanta FBI office and providing them with all the available details, Bongers got back in touch with Brett in order to find out where the panel truck was heading. They had replaced the cellophane wrapped packages with similar packages of flour and were still quizzing the two smugglers about their destination. The truck was registered in Biloxi, Mississippi and agents were already staking out the truck dealership that owned the van. The owner, Owen DeLaFarge, had been under surveillance for awhile and was suspected of being the supplier of coke for the casino belt on the Gulf coast.

So far, neither of the drivers had cracked and given out any information, but the chubby one who was the first to tumble out of the van when his tires were shot out was starting to weaken. They were sitting in the local Sheriff's office and Brett had separated them. The roly-poly guy was given some coffee and a donut and his hands stopped shaking a little.

"Your driver's license says that your name is Willard J. Somers. Is that your real name?" Gipson was handling the interrogation.

Willard nodded: "I go by Willy."

"Mississippi State Patrol tells us you've spent some time in prison for armed robbery. Is that correct?"

"I was set up man! I was paid to chauffeur somebody and…"

"I understand. How'd you like prison? They treat you alright?"

"The food stunk and I …"

Gipson interrupted him again. "And you like food, right?"

"Yeah man. My wife is the best Cajun cook there is. She's from right there…"

"Well Willie, unless you cooperate with us, you will see your wife only through bars when she comes to visit you, and you'll lose a few pounds over the next twenty years inside…"

"No, man, no! I don't wanna go back to prison. No way!"

"Okay, then start talking. Who owns the van and where were you going to deliver it?"

Willie started spilling the beans and handed over more information than they could possibly have asked for. The tires and wheels on the delivery van had been replaced. Two of the agents were going to drive it up and Gipson, John, his assistant, and Willy were flying up to meet the Mississippi FBI chief at the Pascagoula airport. The other smuggler was transported to Tampa for further grilling.

In Biloxi, investigators found out that DeLaFarge also had a stake in a grocery wholesale supply house in an industrial park.

Things started to make sense. Food supplies would be intermixed with cocaine supplies and in one case, a little, individual serving package of Rice Krispies had been found at a casino with a residue of coke. The little box had been traced to Blue Bayou Food Supply, the very one that Owen owned. There was not enough evidence yet to invade the place, but a Search Warrant had been requested and granted. The Feds were ready to strike.

It would take the G-men a day and a half to make the trip from Zephyrhills in the van and that was good. It allowed every law enforcement agency to get organized and prepared and it would allow Brett and John a decent night's sleep. The wives had arranged for some clean clothes and toiletries and met them at the unmarked jet at Tampa International. Willie would have to learn to live in the same clothes he was wearing. Too bad.

To everyone's surprise, the smugglers had no cell phones with them and in retrospect that was great, the Biloxi gang could not verify their location.

"They must have an awful lot of confidence that their team would not get caught."

Gipson commented. "It probably indicates that they're all very experienced." He shook his head. "It's really frightening that this kind of operation may have been going on for years, maybe decades, right under our noses. Frightening!"

Complete with clean clothes, they were off to the land of the bayous and the beautiful trees.

At Pascagoula, the Tampa team was met by Special Agents Lefebre and Greeley.

The Mississippi chief, Lefebre, resembled Lafayette, lanky with a full head of dark hair and a thin mustache. Greeley looked more like a Greyhound bus driver; squat and hefty around the middle. What was left of his hair was dark and resembled a ring around his head like a Dominican monk. They were greeted warmly. Rooms at a local Holiday Inn had been provided and in one of the suites, a briefing was to take place. Willie was taken to a local jail for safekeeping.

"You know what you promised." were his last words to Gipson before he was lead away.

"I remember. I won't forget." The Tampa chief assured him.

"We have everyone on our team. The highway patrol will be with us when we attack the warehouse and the truck dealership at the same time. Undercover agents will be in the Casino kitchens, when their panic buttons ring. We fully expect some call to get through to alert the different dealers and they may try to make a break for it. We'd like to catch them all. That would be great. Homeland Security and the Federal Marshals also want to get into the act, because they're afraid we'd hold out on them, but that's alright. We're having a meeting with them at nine in the morning and we're expecting to hit the scene at four o'clock. Are you in touch with your men in the van?" Lefebre wanted to know.

"Of course. They will be here no later than two. They have my cell number and they'll keep me posted. No problem." Gipson nodded as he spoke. "How many people in the dealership and the supply house do you think are involved in this and how many will be carrying weapons?"

"We don't really know. We do know that Owen has a license to carry, so I'm sure he'll be armed. His salesmen and staff? We don't know. We do know that his sales manager owns a big expensive house out of town, a condo on the beach and has an apartment in a casino, so he's making a lot more than the average dealership managers, so we're pretty sure he's in on the deal. The rest of them, we just don't know. At the warehouse, one or two **have** to be in on it in order to have an orderly distribution set up, so we're counting on at least two armed men over there. We'll be ready. We should have a dozen lawmen swarm all over them at both locations. We should have no problems." He sipped some of his cold coffee. "By the way, how'd you get the tip off on the heist in Zephyrhills?"

"I don't know. I got a call from New Jersey. You know Bruce Bongers, don't you?"

"Sure."

"I have no idea where he got the info, but it sure as hell was accurate."

"Great. Now you guys get some rest. I understand you were up half the night?"

"We sure were."

"By the way, the restaurant downstairs has great prime rib. Have a good one." With that he got up and left the two Tampa men on their own.

The meeting the next morning was well organized and Gipson was a mere spectator, rather than a participant. If it had taken place on his home turf in Tampa, he would have run it the same way, but in Biloxi he was just one of the boys and he agreed with the way it was all handled. The operation involved forty lawmen and the local police force on standby, in case they were needed, as well as traffic control. That proved to be a mistake. Someone on the force worked for Owen on the side. They were close hunting and fishing buddies. The only one of the Biloxi police who was at the planning meeting was the chief, but he informed his senior officers later and the news filtered down. Not in detail, but enough rumors to put DeLaFarge on alert. He decided to teach the Feds a lesson.

The van arrived thirty minutes early in Pascagoula and that was the signal for all the troops to proceed. Two FBI men were in the cab, along with a Narc. All of them were wearing bullet proof vests and in the back were four other so called Narcs from the Department of Drug Enforcement, heavily armed and ready to jump out and storm into the building. The Feds had learned from Willy that the vehicle was to report to the food supply, rather than to the truck dealership and that's where they expected Owen to be in order to receive the treasure trove of cocaine.

Brett accompanied Lefebre to the dealership where the main targets would be the owner, if he wasn't in the supply building, and the sales manager. In the kitchens of the casinos, dozens of undercover men were ready to do some handcuffing. The watches were synchronized and all of the excitement was to start at 3:30 sharp. Over the radio, they could tell that everyone was in place and right on the dot, Lefebre called out: "Let's do it."

The van pulled into the industrial park and started to back up to the load-off ramp, when from across the way, an automatic weapon cut loose with a volley, right into the cab, killing all three men with at least four or five bullets in each of them. The truck continued rolling and bumped into the platform with such force that the four men inside fell all over themselves. Before they could get out, the pickup truck from which the automatic weapon was fired squealed out of the street with rubber burning, but was cut down by the agents that had followed the truck at a discreet distance. The truck driver was killed instantly and the out-of-control truck hit a curb and jumped, crashing into a parked Cadillac that burst into flames and the truck rolled over into the parking lot of a manufacturing plant crashing into an overhead door. The car in pursuit screeched to a halt and two G-Men jumped out, guns at ready, in case somebody had survived that spectacular crash.

Meanwhile, the four Narcs in back of the van had stormed into the food factory, backed up by three FBI men who stormed into the front door.

"DOWN! DOWN ON THE FLOOR! THIS IS THE FBI!" they hollered at the work crew that was busy loading pallets with boxes of groceries and cans. Everyone went down. A few women screamed thinking they were being robbed. The office girls were nearly hysterical and it took a few minutes to get them to cooperate. But in five minutes everything was under control and one by one, the prone people were allowed up in order to identify themselves. All of them proved to be laborers. No one in management was in the building. The lawmen excused most of them and sent them home, except for two office girls that they held for questioning and four workers that were suspected of being illegal immigrants.

At the truck dealership, cars converged from four sides on the buildings and men with black baseball jackets, spelling out FBI,

DEA or U.S. Marshall on their backs, rushed into the offices and the maintenance and repair buildings. After questioning everyone, including the ones in the remote body shop, they turned over three potential illegals to the local police.

In the casinos, not a single suspect was caught and there was no trace of heroin or cocaine.

6.50 PM
The Oysterbar

Lefebre looked at Gipson over coffee and shook his head for the fifteenth time: "What a bust. Three of our men dead and two of theirs and no proof of any contraband." He put his head in his hands. Brett said nothing. He swallowed hard and thought about ordering a drink. He could use one by now.

Chapter Twenty-Eight

Georgia On Their Minds.

Atlanta
FBI District Office.

The wheels of the law enforcement agencies started to turn rapidly, once the information had been assimilated. Bongers didn't have to do much convincing when he talked to the Special Agent in charge. They had already heard about the success of the mission in Florida on the previous day and all the necessary forces were assembled and briefed in no time. In order to keep Mrs. Carol Weaver from alerting her husband, an 'Avon Lady' approached her door and promptly arrested her. The FDA and the FBI searched her house all day and questioned her endlessly. They hadn't expected that the lady would actually shoot-up herself, but all the drug paraphernalia and the marks on her arm told a very convincing story. The chief investigator, Andrew (Andy) Sloan, took hours and hours to patiently draw out of her, how much trafficking had taken place out of her home and where the deliveries were made. He found endless files, outlining the routes through which the moneys were received and delivered. One casino seemed to be the top laundering facility. The tape recorders hummed all day and the information mounted to the point that Andy exclaimed to his supervisor: "This is more info in one day, than we normally get in a whole year."

Mrs. Weaver was offered immunity in return for testimony in court against her husband and any other culprits they might capture. She was given assurance that she could keep her Hilton Head home and some revenue producing investment. All other assets would be confiscated. Millions of dollars worth. She cried a lot and begged for an upper because her stomach was all in crunches. A doctor tended to her and calmed her down with some amphetamines. They let her sleep, while cuffed to the brass headboard of the bed.

Since they lived on a private field, there was no radio, no Unicom, to worry about, so the police officers expected to meet Harry with complete surprise. All police cars were moved out of sight and wouldn't return till after dark. Most lawmen were given a break to get some supper and some rest.

Bongers had called back with the information he had received from Fred that Weaver had left the hotel at 7:30 local time and allowing an hour to get to the airport and get the plane ready, they had an approximate departure time. The plane's manufacturer, Beechcraft, provided the average cruising speed, so they expected landing between nine and ten at night, unless he had landed somewhere else. Carol assured them that he wouldn't and that he always flew straight home.

Everything was in readiness; twelve Georgia State Troopers would charge and surround the plane as soon as its velocity was reduced to taxi speed. There was to be no shooting unless the pilot should fire first which was very much in doubt. According to his wife he carried no weapon with him.

Seated around the dinning room table in the sumptuous setting of the Air Park mansion, the last details were being ironed out and another phone call was made to New Jersey, to check if any other details had become available. The top brass of all the services involved had come in from Atlanta, partially to lend their expertise and partially to share in the glory if all went well. Carol was being kept in her bedroom under guard by a female FBI agent. In the midst of their euphoria, they received a terrible letdown: a call from Biloxi and their miserable failure.

Three of their agents dead? What happened?

Were the Georgia officials a little overconfident, thinking that every thing would be peachy? Was it possible that a team of smugglers was to meet the plane in order to take possession of the goods? Could a shoot-out result? All of a sudden decisions had to be made. Troops were called back from their dinner breaks and guards were posted at the entrance to the gated community and every visitor and resident was to be checked when entering the property. Snipers were posted on four sides of the gate, ready to shoot and kill anyone who resisted. The security guard was replaced by an FBI man of about the same size, so they could swap uniforms. The security man got an unexpected night off, but he had to spend it in the Weaver home with all the other G-Men. They couldn't take any chances that he might be in on the deal and forewarn the culprits. The attitude inside the house changed from happy and confident to concerned and edgy.

Waiting now became a drag and time crawled very slowly. Constant checking with the various lawmen by means of their shoulder mounted radios became the norm. A location map was drawn and the positions of the cars and the men on foot were numbered and posted on the handmade chart. The atmosphere became tense.

There was no way to check or overhear any possible conversation between the pilot and another on the ground. Anyone could be reached if they had access to the radio frequency or if they had a cell phone.

The officials had lulled themselves to sleep thinking there wouldn't be any communications, so obviously no problems. Suddenly they had to consider all different angles and prepare for it. With four different agencies involved and no clear cut leader to control and direct the operation, things became somewhat of a shambles. One director would give an order and another one, not knowing what director number one had said would give a different order and before long, it seemed like four different operations were being run at once.

A refreshing change of pace came about when Bongers called from home in New Jersey and asked how things were going and had the plane come in? He asked some very simple questions:

"Are your patrol cars ready to block the runway if he suspects something and attempts a go-around?"

An old truck was readied to become the sacrificial lamb in case the plane accelerated again.

"Make sure no one answers the phone in the house and have a recorder hooked up to it so you can record all incoming calls without alerting anybody."

"Right!"

"Do you know if he was to redistribute the dope by plane tomorrow or is there a crew scheduled to come and collect it like in Zephyrhills?"

"Someone! Get with Andy and have him check his notes to see if Carol indicated anything about a pick-up and when. If not, get the info from her now."

"Are any of the neighbors involved in the operation as well and are your men protected from danger if they are?"

"We think the neighbors are on the up and up, but get a team going to check them out and make sure that nobody radios Weaver of our situation here."

"Have you checked with the FAA, and have they signaled a plane that is not in communication with their traffic control?"

"Someone call the Jacksonville tower and get that info." The Atlanta chief kept barking orders. "Wait! Wait! There's a plane over head and the runway lights came on.

This is it! Bruce, this is it!" He hung up and sighed: "Bongers, I wish you were here."

Into his radio he hollered: "Action, men! Action, Everybody! This is it. Let's nail him."

Chapter Twenty-Nine

Flashing Blue Lights

Domani Hotel.

Harry had to get up fairly early because his aircraft cruised at 340 knots and he had a long flight ahead of him. Once at his prescribed flight level he could take a potty break if he wanted to, because the autopilot kept the plane right on course and at the precise altitude. He had installed a simple septic device, like the ones that are used in small boats and campers. When he let down to sea level over the Gulf of Mexico, he could still fly on autopilot, but he would keep his hands on the controls at all times. He wasn't going to have any surprises.

On the way out of the hotel, he waved briefly at the crazy brothers and their wives, who were piling into the dining room. "What a bunch." he said to himself and busied himself with his luggage and a cab.

The plane was serviced and ready to go. He paid for his gas with a credit card, checked his storage compartment and performed a routine pre-flight check.

Everything was cool and he fired up his starboard engine and after the RPM settled at exactly 1500, he started the other.

All the gauges read normal. Again he glanced over his clearances, his climb-out, his cruise and assured himself that all was well. He loved the hum of his engines and all the instruments indicated that the plane performed like a charm. He took off.

Once he was past the Yucatan Peninsula, he slowly descended till he was only fifty feet above the water and he settled back for the long boring haul across the Gulf. That was the most taxing part of the flight. It was long. It was straight and level, but he could never take his eyes off the horizon or his instruments, because at that speed, all he had to do was blink, push the wheel a little bit and he would hit the water with such force that the plane and his body would be smashed into a thousand little pieces. Hour after hour went by and he was relieved not to have seen any boat traffic, the kind of vessels that might alert the coastguard, which could result in a fast jet getting on his tail and forcing him down somewhere. Finally…, finally, the green coast of Florida came into view and his GPS told him, he was right on course. When he pulled up to three thousand feet, he saw the Steinhachee river under his right wing and he changed his course a little in order to bypass Tallahassee to the east. Once over Georgia, he let down to a thousand and as the sun set behind him he cruised to the Atlantic coast. He finally had a chance to walk back and relieve himself and he munched on some crackers when he got back behind the controls. When he was within a hundred miles from Brunswick, it was pitch dark, but the clouds were a thousand feet above him and that made it just perfect. His instruments told him he was within miles from home base so he slowed down to a hundred and fifty. When he passed over the field, he changed his radio frequency to 122.8 and clicked his mike button five times and as by magic, the yellow runway and the blue taxi way lights came on He set up his pattern as he had done a thousand times in the past and went through his pre-landing procedures. The gear came down and locked, the flaps went down to full on final and within seconds he was over the runway, his tires screeched as they made contact with the runway and he started tapping the brakes. The end of the runway came at him rapidly and he hit his brakes more solidly. He slowed to turnoff speed and when he applied right brake to start his turn onto the taxi strip, all hell broke loose. From every angle, patrol cars with flashing blue lights and bright headlights raced up to him and he had to stand on his brakes to keep from hitting some of them.

"Shut off the engines and come out!" a loudspeaker blared at him. He hesitated, but had no choice. He shut down his plane and didn't have to be told: "Open your door and come out with your hands up." He knew what to expect.

What he didn't expect was, his wife was in the backseat of one of the patrol cars as he was handcuffed and shoved into the back of another. A little tractor was hooked up to the front wheel of his plane and he watched as it was being towed toward his house.

"You have a right to be silent...." a patrolman in the passenger seat started to read off, but Harry paid no attention. He knew his world had come to an end. His beautiful world with his beautiful wife was shot to hell in just a few seconds, surrounded by blue flashing lights.

In Brunswick, in the interrogation room of the county jail, Harry was faced by a middle aged man, who introduced himself as special agent Hoyt. His cuffs had been taken off and he was offered a coffee or a soda. He chose the soda.

"How was the flight?' Hoyt started.

"Shall we cut the crap?" Harry's eyes were shooting darts.

"You mean?"

"Cut the niceties and tell me what I'm up against. You caught me red handed, so give me the scoop."

"Let's understand something, Mr. Weaver: You're in deep trouble. How deep depends on how well you work with us or against us. You can look forward to a long life behind bars or a little time with maybe even a Federal Protection plan if you cooperate with us. It's your choice. Now shall we start from the beginning? How was your flight?"

"Let's get something straight first. I will not do or say anything that will implicate my wife, understand? She had nothing to do with this and..."

"Oh, no? She just shoots up on occasion and uses up the money her first husband made in the drug business? Let's not get cocky, Weaver. We have too much on you. We spent the day in your house going through all the records, so there isn't much you can lie about, so let's start a different approach. Let's see how much time your wife will spend in prison and by how much you can reduce it. You personally."

Weaver slumped over in his chair and put his elbows on the table. He rested his chin in his hands and said nothing. Neither did Hoyt.

Finally, Weaver raised his eyes and said: "Do you know how stupid all of this is? How unnecessary. We have enough money to live comfortably for the rest of our lives. We didn't need this shit, flying back and forth with dope. It's all so stupid." He lowered his eyes again and Hoyt thought for a moment that he was going to cry. Behind the one-way mirror on the wall, four eyes and ears and a camcorder were taking it all in as well.

"Then why?" Hoyt nearly whispered.

"Because," Harry started and stopped. "Let's first get something straight. Talk about facts and figures. How much time would my wife and I face if we didn't cooperate and..."

"A long time..."

"Let me finish. And what would I have to do to see that she gets no time at all and what kinda cooperation do you want from me to cut my time or... even eliminate it with all the protection you mentioned. Give me facts." He sat up. "Details, exact details."

"Of course you understand that I don't make those decisions. This will be decided by a judge and my su..."

"Horseshit! You get me that judge and we'll work out the deal, 'cause do you know something? I don't think that you can do anything but snow me, so let's all get some sleep and present me with stuff in writing! In writing, you hear? Because I'm starting to smell a rat here and I'm not falling for it. Good night," He stood up and two deputies jumped into the room and grabbed him, ready to cuff him again.

Hoyt remained unflappable. "Mr. Weaver, calm down and sit. Let's talk this o…"

"Like hell. In writing! That's it."

"I'll inform your wife that you will not assist her case."

"You miserable sonofabitch!"

"Get him out of here."

As he opened the door he said to the onlookers. "He's right, I should get some sleep."

Chapter Thirty

The Penthouse

Biloxi, MS

Jerry Robinson, nee Geraldo Radowicz, stood on his sixteenth story balcony and whispered into his cell phone. He changed phones three times a day. Never called on a landline, afraid they were bugged, and spoke very softly although nobody within ten feet could have heard him. He was talking to his father, who nowadays went by the name of Vargas instead of Robinson as he had in the last twenty years.

Geraldo was born forty years ago, the second son of a displaced German father and a Colombian mother. He had inherited the height from his dad, but the Latin good looks from his mom. He resembled Ricky Ricardo, except he had a thin mustache, but he could play the drums and sing as well as Ricky ever could. His ambitious, but ruthless father had always provided his offspring with a good education and generally, a good life. Geraldo was no exception. At age twelve he was sent to Switzerland, where he spent five years in an all boys school and received a rigid education. He learned four languages besides his Spanish and became an avid skier. At seventeen he enrolled in Harvard, because his older brother was already there, two years ahead of him. He was a stand-out on the tennis court and by the time he was twenty, he was also a stand-out in the bedroom. Money was never a problem, girls were plentiful and his good looks made him very much in demand. He was accepted in law school and earned his doctorate in Juris Prudence when he was twenty-three, the youngest lawyer in his class.

Against his will, his dad made him join a law firm in Chicago, because in his words: "I need a contact there. Pretty soon I'll set you up in your own firm."

Much to Jerry's (He had become 'Jerry' back in Switzerland) surprise, he liked Chicago and he liked the firm he worked for. It was there that he met a young Assistant District Attorney who gave him quite a hassle in a court case, where he was the defense lawyer.

He won the case, his client went free and he bought Ingrid, the Assistant, a drink after work and within the year married her. She was of Swedish stock, very fair and had a lovely mouth that sent him into space whenever she smiled. He never took her to Cartagena, so she didn't meet his father, but four of his brothers and two of his sisters attended the wedding and she loved them all. Two years later, they had their own law firm. It proved to be somewhat of a struggle to build up their clientele, but money always appeared when they needed it. They were spending a hundred thousand more than they were taking in and although she loved the huge house in the suburb and the cozy apartment on the lake front, Ingrid became more and more suspicious about his source of dough, but he wouldn't talk about it.

One day, the house was sold, the office closed and she was given an ultimatum: "Stay here by yourself and make a life or come with me wherever I go." She hesitated and he was gone the next day. "Radowicz & Radowicz" ceased to exist as a law firm in Chicago.

Ingrid went back to work with the District Attorney and learned that a huge drug cartel had been eliminated by the Feds and that it had ignited a vicious war between rival factions, one blaming the other for selling out to the cops. For weeks, gangland style murders were the news of the day, but Jerry Radowicz was never mentioned. She had her marriage annulled.

The same Jerry was living like an Arab Sheik on the top of a magnificent casino and a harem available if he wanted it. An outsider might think that he had the life of Reilly, but he was under a lot of stress. For years, his dad had operated a successful drug cartel out of Cartagena, but in the last few years, that didn't seem enough for the old man anymore. He wanted to be the biggest of the drug lords and even had this fantastic vision that he was going to be the only one. He called himself *the Golden Boy,* but was soon known as the *the Golden pig, El Cochino de* Oro. Two other Caballeros Grandes were not about to simply play possum and retreat. On the contrary, it set off a drug war, the likes of which the trade had never seen. Vargas ordered assassinations as if he were ordering pizza and even though his sons argued strongly against it, he continued his goals with a vengeance. The result was lots of men killed by opposing cartels and by police. Lots of money and contraband confiscated and a lot of dealers in prison, singing like canaries. The cops had seldom had so much insight into the hierarchy of the cartels as they were now extracting from the dealers in custody. The information that became public blew away the cover of the Radowicz brothers and all the related big shots, who previously ran *respectable* law firms and laundered millions of dollars without a trace.

Now, that was shot to hell and right then and there, Jerry was getting an earful from his dad about the latest fiasco, the loss of the cargo in Zephyrhills. Jerry was lucky that a loyal policeman had tipped him off about the impending raid in Biloxi, so he got all of his key men out of sight and all the contraband hidden before the Feds could get to them.

Lucky Vargas, the irate old man, was calling from his compound in the hills above the harbor and wanted Jerry to tell him who had leaked the information about the flight and he wanted steps taken immediately to eliminate the informer. From Medellin he had received word that a couple of Gringos, probably CIA men, were snooping around and he wanted them found and caught. He was

The Golden Pig

about to teach the Americanos a lesson. (At that point, neither of them had any idea that the next load in a Twin Beech was about to be confiscated as well.)

Geraldo promised to get right on it. He didn't. He had to think. In the last bloodbath, two of his cousins and his sister Julia had been killed and he had never trusted his dad again. The old man insisted that he had nothing to do with it, but he heard from the other siblings that Julia might have become an informer for the FBI and that they could not afford to keep her around. Her death had been a terrible shock to Jerry. She was such a delight, such a happy, carefree soul, that he had considered dropping out of the organization altogether. There were just a few problems: What would he do for money? He couldn't practice law anymore under any name, Radowicz or Robinson. His name was dirt in the U.S. . Besides, his dad would probably have him gunned down, the way he had his sister. So.... he stuck it out as the executive manager of a casino.

His old man worried him. Rumor was that he had worked for Hitler and now he was starting to act like him. Jerry felt it wouldn't hurt if he set aside some money in Honduras or Guatamala or even Switzerland and simply disappear one day. The thought of taking up ski-ing again appealed to him.

He fixed himself a drink and sat down on the porch enjoying the beautiful sunset over the Gulf. He knew he had to do something. His dad would call back looking for results. After he fixed another drink he dialed the number of the Domani Hotel in Bogota and waited for the manager to get on the phone. The resident manager hardly ever left the premises, because he lived in a beautiful suite for his wife and himself and knew of all the comings and goings of his customers. He had nothing unusual to report, except that the security police captain from the airport had been in and visited with some of his customers.

"The Airport Security? Did he talk with Anders, the jet pilot?"
"No. Anders left that morning and the captain came at night."
"Caramba! Any other suspicious visitors?"
"No, Señor, just some tourists and my regulars."

"Carajo! We better check Airport Security. Is anybody paying them off?"

"I can't tell from here, but I'll have my man on it in the morning."

"Bueno." (Good) He hung up.

The police in Colombia and certainly in Bogota knew better than to get involved with the Federal Authorities or other cartels. It was bad for their health. Jerry shook his head and said to himself: "I better check with Weaver if everything went alright. He should be down in an hour, maybe two. I'll call him at ten."

He got up to take in the show downstairs. It was supposed to be a good one, Julio Iglesias and lots of beautiful girls.

Chapter Thirty-One

The Wrath of Lucky Vargas (Again)

Biloxi MS

At first, he wasn't too concerned. Jerry called the Weavers at ten o'clock and got the answer machine. "Probably out celebrating." He said to himself and walked back in to the cavernous hall, where Julio was about to make his entrance for the second time. Jerry owned every record Julio had ever made and knew all of his songs by heart. He was having a ball.

After the second show, Julio and his entourage traveled to the penthouse and enjoyed an hour of laughter, drinking and singing. Jerry wasn't entirely sure, but he seemed to remember that Julio left with three gals draped all over him, but he did remember keeping one dark haired beauty for himself, who was as enthused about sex as he was.

When he woke up at three in the morning, he walked out on his balcony, so he would be out of earshot and dialed the Weaver number once more. Still no answer. "Strange," he thought, and crawled back in bed with the girl with the raven hair. In the morning, after the sex bomb had left and he was still reaching a recorded message, he called one of his operatives in Brunswick and ordered him to the Air Park, to see for himself what was keeping the Weavers.

Owen DeLaFarge reported in, along with his sales manager and they discussed the serious problem that Owen faced. He couldn't return to his dealership, because there was a federal warrant out for his arrest. Jerry arranged for the company lawyer to contact them and advise them if it was wise to turn themselves in and get bonded out. The Feds would have to prove in court that they were indeed guilty of violating any laws and they would have to prove it ' beyond any reasonable doubt.' Jerry assured them that a Biloxi jury would never convict them, so: "Relax until Marvin Cohen talks to you and stay put. Have a drink and get laid. That's the best way to keep from worrying."

"Good advice," Owen said, "If only my wife wasn't watching."

At 9:20, the incoming call was most disturbing: "I didn't try to get inside the gate. The place is crawling with cops and they're checking everybody's ID, coming and going, so I just made a U-turn. I'm surprised they didn't come after me. At the local 7-11 I heard, they had a raid last night and they caught the plane after it landed. It don't look so good, Jerry."

"Caramba!" He yelled as he clicked the phone shut. "Papa is gonna have a stroke." He thought about different ways to postpone the inevitable, calling his dad.

It was to early to have a drink, but he sure felt like it. Finally, he called the "FORT', as he called it, his father's compound in the hills. He had already left for the office. Why the old man insisted on driving himself to his shabby warehouses on the docks, was beyond Jerry's imagination. "My Mercedes is bulletproof. This is my tank. During the War I drove bigger tanks, but this one is less noisy," was his explanation. "Big deal." Geraldo Robinson Radowicz murmered to himself He reached his dad with the bad news at 10:45 and, as expected, Lucky went ballistic.

"Who set him up? Was he in the same hotel? Those bastards. I'll teach them a lesson."

"Wait Pap, wait. I talked to the manager last night. The hotel or

The Golden Pig

the employees are not at fault The Airport Security Captain visited the hotel, but he didn't talk to our pilots, so that's not where the problem lies, he…."

"The name of the captain. I want the name of the captain. Now!" His accent was always worse when he was mad. "Verdammtnochmal" he swore, "Get that name. Did you make any attempts to get our merchandise back? We've lost two million in wholesale cost. Twenty million in street value and I want it back. Get on it. Schnell!"

For about a minute, Jerry did nothing. He just sat there, stumped. How in the hell was he gonna get the contraband back? He didn't even know where it was. Stashed in a vault some place, maybe Fort Knox? It was worth as much as gold, so why not? The longer he thought, the more convinced he was that he needed to get away from this. Get out. Move to a foreign country. He could live in Switzerland as a refugee from Bulgaria or Romania. His dark features weren't necessarily Latin. He could pass as someone from Kosovo. He'd better start working on it.

While Jerry was working harder on his upcoming flight than on his father's orders, Lucky himself was issuing orders by the dozen. He was out for vengeance, but he had to tend to some local business first. The Santa Teresa was loaded and ready to sail with a cargo of mahogany from Brazil covering a ton of pure white coke. Once the ship left, he was back on the phone.

In New Jersey, Bongers was reading the transcripts of last night's action in Georgia and tried to raise Fred on the phone. He didn't answer. "Probably traveling on a boat somewhere." He mused.

After he finally got Brett Gipson on the phone in Mississippi, he heard all the nasty details of the botched operation in Biloxi. "Wow! Do you have any leads on where the dealers fled to?"

"No," the Tampa chief answered, "but we found a possible leak in the police department. One of the sergeants bought a $100,000 fishing trawler, but his salary wouldn't allow him to buy a rowboat.

We're grilling him right now and we have a number of traces of phone calls to a local casino. Either there are a number of drug associates in there or one guy is using multiple phones. We think the latter is the case and we're checking it out without making waves. Are you going to stay in touch, Bruce? You seem to have a direct connection and I wish I had one. It would beat paddling in the dark like we're doing."

"Good point. I'm not there and yet it seems I'm in the middle of it. Did you hear about Georgia?"

"Yeah. That went great. No bodies on either side. I wish I could say that."

"Hang in there. You're doing fine. Talk to you."

The New Jersey chief decided to follow his own advice and called D.C. Up in the penthouse of the J. Edgar Hoover building, FBI chief Lester Jarvis was about to call New Jersey when his speaker phone announced: "Mr. Bongers on three."

"Bruce, good morning. I was just about to call you. A lot of things are happening at the same time and no matter who I talk to, you seem to be in the midst of it all."

"Me? Little ol' me? I'm just sitting here in the Meadowlands chewing on a pencil."

"Sure, and I'm on the golf course, hahahaha! Seriously. I understand that you had the inside scoop on both those operations. Who's your source and is he still available?"

"No, I told him to get the hell out of there, because he was nearly kidnapped by a rival cartel and the police held them for questioning and I don't know who the police work for, one of the cartels or the government."

"Did you say 'them'? Did I understand you right, Bruce? And who are they?" He put the emphasis on 'they'.

"Can't tell you that at this point. Might put them in danger."

"Okay. I want you to do this. Take control of the entire operation without stepping on anyone's toes. Call Colonel Guillermo

Armando of the Bolivian Secret Police, the equivalent of our CIA. Give him all the info you possibly can without endangering anybody. Coordinate our operation with his and maybe together we can bust this thing once and for all. Or at least for the time being." He snickered. "I'll fax you the details about Armando. He's a good man. Graduated Yale, way back. Talk to you later and by the way: good job, Bruce."

"Thanks." He said to a dead phone.

By noon he got through to Bogota. The colonel spoke English beautifully, with just a hint of an accent. He listened attentively to Bongers and asked an occasional question. Like Jarvis, Armando wanted to know the name or names of the informers, but Bruce protected their identity, just as he had promised. It was a good and constructive conversation and the Columbian Secret Service would immediately start investigating the Vargas shipping business. Lucky's name had been mentioned before, but they had not been able to pin something on him yet. Things might change. When it came to the question if Bongers would personally come to Columbia, all he could say was: "Quizas? Who knows?"

By four o'clock, Armando called back. Captain Quintero had been gunned down in his car, leaving the airport. The driver, a security guard was dead and Quintero was gravely wounded, burned over thirty percent of his body and two bullets in his upper torso.

"Good God!" was all Bongers could say. "Si, Madre Mia," the Colonel added.

When Bruce walked into his office the next morning, a memo was already on his desk. It was in Spanish and he called in his assistant Bruno Garcia, to read it to him.

It was a shocker.

In the middle of the night, the Hotel Domani in Bogota was engulfed in flames and burned to the ground. While firefighters were attempting to rescue people out of the inferno, shots rang out and at least one fireman was killed plus two hotel employees that lived on the premises.

Police units chased the potential assassins and riddled the escape vehicle with bullets, but it managed to get away, although it was found later with one body in it. He was identified as a criminal who had escaped during a massive breakout of a federal prison a year ago. The hotel was totally destroyed. Five people perished.

"Good God." Bongers said once more. "This Vargas has got to go!'

A triumphant Lucky called Jerry with the same news at about six in the morning.

Jerry threw up. "I gotta get out and fast. Like now!"

Chapter Thirty-Two

Island Hopping.

Sint Maarten (The Dutch Side.)

The happy vacationers were rolling in the aisles of the dockside restaurant. They were waiting to board a catamaran for Saint Barth., Saint Bartholomew. Ted had told the waiter, he wouldn't pay the bill unless the waiter first told a funny joke. The waiter first looked a little perplexed, but then walked away and returned with the manager and a tall black dude dressed in a chef's uniform, complete with a towering white hat.

"This is Jeremiah," the manager announced, "and he tells the jokes around here."

The group, a total of two groups of four who were total strangers an hour ago, burst out laughing before Jeremiah opened his mouth. This was different than what they had anticipated. This was too funny.

"Give the man a beer!" Ted ordered.

"Not till after the jokes." The manager managed to keep a straight face throughout. What a riot. Jeremiah could indeed tell the funniest jokes and kept them in stitches for twenty minutes. Each time Ted or Fred tried to interrupt with a joke of their own, Jeremiah would say: "Shut up! It's my turn." That cracked them up every time.

It might have gone on for an hour, had it not been for the catamaran ringing a bell, announcing its departure.

As they walked the plank to get aboard, Fred's cell phone rang and he decided to step back onto the dock and check the message. It's a good thing he did, because he might have fallen off the gangway if he had been midway between the boat and the dock. It was Bongers who told him about the fire and the massacre in Bogota.

"Where are you now, Fred?"

"I'm just about to leave Saint Martin for Saint Barth. Why'd you ask?"

Bongers hesitated a moment. "I don't think that they had a chance to interrogate the hotel personnel before they torched the place and by burning it, they probably destroyed all records, so your names may not have gotten into their hands. I'm presuming they suspected the hotel people of being the informers, 'cause otherwise they wouldn't have bothered to shoot them, don't you think? So you may be in the clear and you may not."

"Wow!" was the only thing Fred could think of.

"May I make a suggestion? When you land at Saint Barth, take a plane ride around the island. I'll arrange with the French that the plane will develop a problem,,, a so-called problem and lands in Saint Kitts. You'll be forced to stay overnight. Make the most of it and that gives me a chance to get with the Dutch authorities in Saint Martin in order to check out your hotel and see if it's safe for you to return there. If it comes up clean, fly out to another island somewhere and keep on partying. We'll erase your trail, don't worry about that. What hotel are you staying in?"

Fred was so dumbfounded that he stuttered the name of the hotel and Bongers signed off, saying: "I'll talk to you tonight. Have a good trip." For a moment, he just stood there staring at his phone as if he were seeing ghosts.

"Are you coming aboard or not?" That was Kathryn, decked out in a colorful flowered dress and a wide brimmed sunhat.

"I'm coming, I'm coming." He tried to sound normal. "I hope Captain Quintero lives. I'd hate to send the camcorder to his widow."

The Golden Pig

When the taxi stopped on the hill overlooking the airport, Anna said: "I don't think I wanna fly outta here. Look how steep this is!" She pointed to the side of the steep hill, dropping onto the end of the runway. "And look over there!" She pointed at the teal green water at the far end of the field. "There's no way an airplane can get off the ground without splashing into the water."

"Oh, no? Look, there goes one now. He's already up halfway down the runway and.. oops!" They were surprised by a twin propeller job, that came right over them and seemed to plunge down toward the runway. "See! Nuttin' to it. Come on."

"I don't wanna look when it takes off."

"Annabella, just have your camera ready. You'll be bragging about this for years. Make sure you have diapers on though." Her husband never quit. They had loaded up on beer and cheeseburgers in Buffet's place: "Cheeseburgers in Paradise," and were as happy as could be.

The women spent a half hour in the gift shop before their plane was ready to go and two more tourists joined them in the eight seat airplane. Much to Fred's surprise there were two pilots aboard, so that robbed him of the opportunity to fly in the right seat. Too bad, but the view out of the side windows was well worth the money. They hadn't realized that there were so many other little islands around, many of them deserted with clear white beaches and a few palm trees. Some of the islands had one or a few boats anchored off the shores and on one of them a barbeque was in progress. "What a way to live." Ted announced. "Annabella, how about if we sell the kids and retire here?"

"You retire here and I'll keep the kids. I'll have some peace in my old age. Finally!"

Over Nevis the engine slowed and raced and Fred suspected the pilot of doing that.

"Ladies and Gentlemen" The captain announced; "We have a little oil pressure problem on our port engine and we'll put her down for a minute on Saint Kitt to check out the problem. No cause for alarm. Keep your seatbelts fastened. We'll be down in a few minutes."

"I told them not to put PORT in the engines, " Ted quipped, "They should stick with BRANDY. VSOP if possible. More oomph and fewer hiccups."

Nobody laughed.

Everybody exited the plane and two golf carts brought the passengers to the terminal, where a pretty airline representative in a starched white skirt and a flowered shirt announced that the group could tour the island in a minivan for an hour at the expense of the airline. The engine problem was apparently minor.

Ted agreed immediately. "We're making out like a bandit. Free tour of Saint Kitt. We're saving a hundred dollars. Let's find a place where we can drink it up."

The other couple that had boarded in Saint Bart had no religious objections, so Ted commandeered the driver to find the bar with the best view of the island.

"No problem mahn," His white teeth gleamed in his brown face.

The hotel with the best view of the island was an absolute success. It was at least six hundred feet above sea level and from the porch they could count at least ten islands along the horizon.

"Which way are we watching?" Ted wanted to know when a brown skinned waitress called on them.

"Out!"

"Hahahaha! You had that coming!" Everyone was in the best of moods although some of them had tensed up a little bit when it was announced that they were going to make an emergency landing. It was too early for dinner, but beautiful brown eyes recommended some 'island snacks' and they were delicious. The driver had remained in the car in spite of several invitations to join them. After forty-five minutes he walked up to them and told them: "I'm sorry to report that the repair may take a little longer than expected…"

"Hooray!"

"Shut up, Ted."

"And you're being asked: Would you prefer that another aircraft be flown in and return you to Saint Bart or Saint Martin, or would you prefer to spend the night here at the airlines expense?"

"Here of course."

"Wait a minute Ted. There are more people involved than you alone."

"Where? Where?" He stood up and shaded his eyes and stared in the distance over the Caribbean.

"Sit down, you clown. How many of you say; 'stay here'?" Fred felt he had to use some common sense, even if his brother didn't. All six hands went up. "Driver, what's your name?"

"Christopher."

"Okay Cristoforo, inform the line that we'll stay here if they bring toothbrushes. What time would we fly out in the morning? Not too early, I hope."

"Probably about ten."

Fred was still handling things. "Are you going to come and get us or do we…"

"No, I'm staying with you. I'll take you out on the town tonight."

"Hooray for Christopher. Waitress, what's your name? Bring the man a beer. It'll cheer him up."

"No, no, thank you. I suggest dinner here. It's very good and I'll return at seven to take you nightclubbing. The hotel will check you in now and they'll provide everything you need."

"Again, hooray for Christopher!" The native chauffeur smiled and Fred asked him, "Seriously, may we buy you dinner?"

"No, thank you, I'm going to eat with my wife and children. But thanks."

"A CIA agent with a wife and kids? Why not?" Fred said to himself. He fell from one surprise into another.

Bongers called at the same time as they walked into their rooms. Kathryn was in the bathroom already, but just to be sure, Fred walked out on the porch and looked around. No other human beings in sight anywhere except on the beach six hundred feet below him. He didn't think they could hear him.

"How's it going Fred?"

"Exactly as scheduled. You people are fabulous. How does our hotel look in Saint Martin?"

"No problems so far. Nobody has inquired about you, but we're not taking chances. A travel agent has arranged for your luggage to be brought to the airport in the morning and he settled your account. Your names won't appear on any ledger. At ten, you'll meet a private jet, no markings, at Saint Kitt and you'll be flown to Mozambique for a few days rest. Your brother will love that."

"Mozambique? Ted? He said Martinique."

"So he did. What did I say? Mozambique? Well, I meant Martinique. Enjoy! Call me only if something unusual comes up. Have a good one."

Chapter Thirty-Three

The New Jersey-Bogota Connection.

Secaucus, N.J.
FBI N.J. headquarters
1 PM

"Meester Bongers? Coronel Armando here. How are you today?"

"I'm fine. Please call me Bruce."

"Muy bien, Bruise." He hesitated, making a note. "Bruise, you have much information about the drug operations een our country, no?"

"Not enough. We were fortunate to get two good tips in two days and they were very accurate. I wish we could have that type of input every day."

"Do you still have that source, Meester Bongers?"

"Bruce! No, we don't. It was a very temporary occurrence. It may not happen again in ten years."

"What was their connection with Capitan Quintero? Do they work together?"

"No. As I understand it, the captain arrested them briefly and confiscated their camcorder to see what they had photographed and when it turned out they were just innocent tourists, he returned the recorder and asked them if they would buy one in the United States and send it to him. He gave them the money and they promised they would. That was all."

"So your tourists gave you the information?"

Bongers realized he might have said too much. "Not quite! They just happened to be there on a trip. They toured Colombia and the Caribbean. An ordinary fun trip."

"It's a good thing they left. If they had stayed one more night the fun would have ended in a beeg fireball." The colonel didn't sound like he was quite convinced of the innocence of the tourists. "Other question, Bruise. Your office forwarded information about a possible smuggling operation from the docks in Cartagena, correct?"

"That's correct."

"We checked. Most of that pier and most of the warehouses are owned by an American corporation."

"An American corporation? We understand they're owned by a man called Lucky Vargas and…"

"No, no. They are owned by an American corporation called 'Henry Robinsons and Sons' and Señor Vargas leases some of the warehouses and some of the dock space."

"Ah! Now we're getting somewhere. Enrique Vargas is Henry Robinson and is also known as Johann Radowicz, which may be or may not be his real name. We have no proof as yet, but we believe that he was in Hitler's Waffen SS and came to Cartagena right after the war and decided to assume an American name, Robinson. His children seem to have grown up with two passports: Radowicz and Robinson and most of them were educated in the U.S. Two of them became lawyers, one in Chicago and one in New York and allegedly set up money-laundering businesses. We nearly caught them in a huge raid, but they had been forewarned and escaped our net. We're…"

"Excuse me please Bruise, but why you call him Vargas?"

"I was just coming to that. Some years ago, he decided he wanted to became the number one drug lord in the world and he decided that Vargas would be much more impressive than Robinson. But Colonel,…"

"Guillermo, please!"

"Okay, Guillermo. You're telling me something that I didn't know, namely that they incorporated his company in the U.S. and that may explain how the money was transferred in and out of the country. We may check some of the numbered accounts in the Caribbean and Switzerland. We may have something here. So on paper Vargas leased property from Robinson, while all the while it was all his. Very clever. Where does he live?"

"He has a nice estate outside of Cartagena in the foothills. I will find out more about that."

"He's on his third wife I understand and has twelve or thirteen children, ranging from one year to forty. Isn't that something?"

"Well, that shows at least that he's been very busy. I will get on his case immediately. He must be a very dangerous man, the way he had the hotel personnel shot and burned. He must not have much of a heart."

"We understand he had his own daughter and two of his nieces killed, because he believed his daughter talked to the FBI. Can you fathom that? Having your own daughter blown up with a car bomb?"

"Madre Mia! Like I said, maybe he doesn't have a heart. Thank you for all your help. I will call soon."

"Lucy, get me Mr. Jarvis, please." Bongers leaned back in his chair and looked at the notes he had taken. "We have to do something about that clown." He thought. "He is brutal. Wonder how old he is by now? 'Gotta be at least eighty if he was in Hitler's...'"

The phone interrupted him. "Mr. Jarvis on five."

"Lester? Bruce. Just finished talking with Colonel Armando and the picture is getting somewhat clearer."

"Good. Are your informers safe, Bruce?"

"Yeah, they're fine. The reason I called; you said to me, kinda head up the operation, would that include going to Columbia and working together with their team?"

"I don't see why not. I'll talk to Taylor because the CIA has a permanent presence there and I don't see any reason why you guys couldn't work together again. I'll call you back."

"Wait, Lester, wait. Another question. Is it okay for me to fly to Georgia and Mississippi? I'd like to get in on the interrogation, because that may provide me with some of the pieces of our puzzle."

"Sure! Things under control in Jersey?"

"I'll make sure they are."

"Go!"

Bongers pushed an intercom button and said: "Bruno? Come in here a minute."

When his dashing Latino assistant walked in he pointed to a chair: "Sit. Take a load off your feet."

He watched as Bruno Garcia made himself comfortable and continued: "Ever been to Columbia?"

"Ohio or South America?"

"In Ohio it's called Columbus, not Columbia. I mean South America."

"No. Never been there. We going?"

"Possibly. First run home, kiss your wife goodbye and gather up some underwear while you're at it. We're flying south this afternoon."

"Columbia?"

"Not yet. Georgia first."

"For how long?"

"Maybe one day, maybe seven. Pack for seven. Pack your vest." He was referring to his bulletproof vest.

"Never leave home without it."

"See you back here at three."

"Roger!" He gave a mock salute and left.

3PM

When Bongers returned from his trip back home, a message was on his desk that Coronel Armando had called again. He questioned Garcia if in Spanish it was Coronel with an 'R' or Colonel with an 'L', like in English. The 'R' was correct. It took twelve minutes to get him back on the line but it was worth it.

"Señor Bruise. Your information was very helpful. Meester Lucky Vargas does not have an estate in the hills. He has a fort. You can find it yourself on the computer when you go to Map Quest and look up Cartagena. Trail to the southeast, just past the crossings of the interstate and the railroad…"

"Hold it, hold it. I need to write this down. Okay. Go ahead." Bruce grabbed a pad.

"When you are at that crossing of the railroad and the major highway that comes out of the city, going south, swing east one and a half miles. You'll see a private road that ends. Where it ends is a wall. You won't see that on Map Quest, but a satellite picture will show you a walled compound. That's his estate. The large building at the far end is his house, with a 'copter pad on top. You'll see, he's right up against a cliff, the way your Indians built their Pueblos. Look it up. You'll see it. Okay. We found also that the Banco National de Colombia has accounts for Vargas and Robinson. It is starting to make sense. I call you back."

"Lucy, don't put any calls through to my cell. Take a number and you call me with the message, so I can call them back, okay? Pass this on to Shirley when she comes on at five. Thanks." He was ready to go.

From Teterboro they headed for Brunswick in their shiny Falcon Jet. Bruno was all excited because he loved adventure and this smelled like a fascinating outing. Bruce closed his eyes, telling Bruno that he didn't want to be disturbed and that left him with nothing else to do but read a book.

At five, Bongers got on his cell and called Fred. "Fred! How's Mozambique?"

"It's called Martinique. Mozambique is in Africa. This is a great place. I've never been here before, but it's one of the prettiest islands I've seen and the natives are very friendly. Their French is good, except when they talk to one another, forget it. It's all gobbledygook ."

"I'm sure it's some form of Patois. Most islanders speak it. I wanted to ask you a question. How's your German?"

"Still pretty fluent. Grew up with it as a kid."

"I know. I might need you one day."

"Really? How?"

"I'll tell you when I need you."

"Thanks, I think." But Bruce was gone.

Chapter Thirty-Four

The Deal

Glynn Co. Jail
Georgia

"I'd like to meet the lady first." Bongers and Hoyt were going over their notes and had looked at the tapes twice. "Interesting couple. Makes you wonder why they did it. They had plenty of money according to the records, so why get into the smuggling business. Is she a heavy junkie? Did she want her own stash? Doesn't make sense. Let me see what she has to say." Bruce got up without waiting for an answer from Special Agent Hoyt.

They walked down the clammy halls of the jail house into an annex that had been added on for one purpose: recording confessions.

Hoyt stayed behind the one-way mirror, sat down on a stool and put on a headset.

Bongers walked into the interrogation room and sat down on one side of the table on a cushioned chair, while on the other side a hard plastic chair awaited the arrival of the lady. After a three minute wait, the door opened on the far side of the room and a handcuffed woman walked in, wearing an orange jumpsuit. Bongers got up, greeted her: "Mrs. Weaver!" and waved at the matrons that were holding her arms to undo her bracelets.

When Carol sat, so did the FBI man. He was dressed in a white shirt, no tie and his sleeves rolled up to his elbows, He tapped the table with the back of a pencil and readjusted a yellow legal pad,

"May I call you Carol?" He began. She nodded. "I'm Bruce Bongers, FBI." She flinched, but didn't say a word. "We have an interesting pickle here and I'm trying to understand how you got into it." He paused, but again, she only flinched and kept quiet. "It's quite a change from a luxurious home with a pool to a jail cell with a cot, isn't? I hope they're treating you okay?" He looked down and scribbled something on the pad. "I haven't met your husband yet, but I'll see him shortly. Any message you want me to give him?" That opened the floodgates.

"Tell him, I'm so sorry. This was so unnecessary! This was so stupid!" She started to raise her voice. "This was entirely my fault and he should not be held responsible…" Tears started to roll down her cheeks and Bongers nodded at the matrons who immediately provided a tissue. She was a beautiful gal, about thirty five, Bruce thought, but she could do with some make up to hide the bags under her eyes. She regained her composure and started again: "When I think about it, I get so mad at myself.…"

She stopped and the G-man asked: "So, what prompted it? You had enough money."

"That's just it. We didn't wanna touch any of our assets , so this seemed such an…" She stopped again.

"What did you need the cash for?" She didn't answer. Bruce took a wild guess.

"You got deep in hock at the casinos, right?"

"No, not in hock, I usually win. I… We…. " She blew her nose and looked at her hands.

"You wanted to start your own?"

"No, no, not start one. No, that takes an awful lot of dough. You have no idea. You're talking a billion. No." She sniffled again. "No, it's really so stupid."

"The casino in Biloxi offered a good return on the money, right?

And that must have been most appealing." Bongers hit the nail on the head. She started crying again.

"Jerry said...." She stopped. "You know sir, I was doing coke and I feel pretty rotten right now. They've been giving me amphetamines and I could sure use some right now." She wiped her eyes. "Please?"

"Okay. Get her doctor." He directed his order at the tallest of the two guards and she left.

"Is Jerry hurting for money? I thought they were doing alright." Bongers felt he had just hit a vein.

"Haven't you heard of Katrina? Do you know how much they lost? Billions! Billions! And the insurance? What a laugh! It'll take'em years and years before they're back on top. We thought we'd get in on the ground floor with them. It's all pretty legit, you know? Everybody invests in casinos. Politicians, doctors, lawyers, everybody, so why not us?"

"True, why not?" Bruce didn't take a note. He knew it was all being recorded on the other side of the mirror. "How much of a return did Jerry promise you?"

"Do you know Jerry?"

"Not personally, but we've had dealings in the past."

"He's a pretty sharp cookie. Good looking too. If I didn't have Harry, I might have jumped in bed with him myself." She giggled at the thought. A nurse came in and handed Carol a pill and a glass of water.

"Thanks. I'll tell you one thing. When I get out of this place, I'll never shoot up again. It's stupid. You want more and more of it every day. There's no end to it. Every time, I'd snort or shoot, I'd say: This is the last time, baby, but it isn't. The craving gets soooo bad that you gotta have another snort, just to function." She rubbed her nose, just thinking about it. "The withdrawals? They're the worst. You think you're gonna die!" I'm tellen' ya. It's murder." She inhaled deeply. "Thanks. The stuff is working already. You have no idea how bad I felt."

"How many trips did you figure it would take before you'd have enough cash to buy in?" He had to get her back on track.

"No, no. We weren't gonna get cash. Each trip is worth a hundred thousand dollars, but we would be paid in stock."

"In stock? How many trips had Harry made?"

"This was his first and only one. We made two test flights together, checking things out and timing everything. One by way of the ocean and once over the Gulf. Harry is a super pilot, you know? He flew in Vietnam, did you know that?" She started to nod as if she was getting sleepy. "How's Harry?" The look on her face changed to panic. "How's Harry? I wanna see him. It's all my fault, you know. He's in love, the sucker. He'll do anything I ask him, you know? I shouldn't have done it. I shouldn't..." she forgot the end of the sentence and nodded again, as if she was falling asleep.

"We'll talk again, Carol. Hang tough!" Bongers got up and left.

"Hey!" She hollered after him, "Hey!", but he went out of one door and she went out of the other.

Hoyt, who got off his stool and shed his headset, said: "Well, whadaya know?"

"Let's talk to the pilot. Bring him in. Any coffee here?"

While waiting for Harry to be brought in, they fixed themselves some coffee and waited outside the mirrored room until the smuggler was seated at the far side of the table. He looked around the room, stared at the mirror as if he knew what went on behind it, then looked at his shackled hands and wiggled them a bit, maybe to shift the handcuffs a little and make them more comfortable. When nothing happened, he looked behind him at the guards and said: "What's happening?"

"Be quiet!" Was all one of them said and Harry looked up at the mirror again.

"He's getting antsy. That's good." Bongers remarked and with his coffee in hand, he walked into the room.

"Mr. Weaver, good evening." He put down his cup and picked up the pencil that was still on the table. "Want some coffee too?"

"Yes! I'd love some."

"How do you drink it?"

"Black with sugar. Thanks."

Bongers looked up at the guards and one of them nodded and walked out. To the other one he said: "Can you please take his cuffs off? Thanks."

Weaver massaged his wrists and he had a grateful look on his face.

"Is the food okay in this place? By the way, my name is Bongers, FBI. I was an Army colonel at one time and I understand you were an Air Force officer, right? What rank did you have when you got out?"

"I had just made major. I was a captain for seven long years. It seemed they might never promote me."

"Why didn't you stay for the duration? It sounds like you were pushing twenty."

"Let's not get into that and besides, I'm sure you have access to my records, so if you really wanna know, I'm sure you'll find it. Let's talk about getting out."

"Yeah, let's talk about that. Do you have any idea what you're looking at?"

"Time wise? No. And my wife? No! What's the usual?"

"The usual? First of all, you lose all your assets."

"Whadaya mean?"

"Your plane, your houses, other properties, investments, it all gets confiscated."

"Hot damn! How's she gonna live?" Weaver had a pained look on his face.

"How's she going to live? You mean, after she gets out?" Bruce felt he had uncovered a soft spot.

Harry nearly jumped. "Gets out? How long are you gonna keep her? She didn't do anything!"

"She transported contraband and money. You did the flying, so how can you say she didn't do anything?"

"Damn!" He dropped his head in his hands and sighed. After a full minute he looked up again. "What can I do to make her sentence as short as possible or better yet, get her out immediately?"

"Of course, the final decision will be made by a judge, but I can assure you of one thing: if both of you cooperate with us, she'll get all the breaks we are allowed."

"Like what?" The look on Harry's face became one of hope.

"New identity. Witness protection. Income for life. Maybe some other options."

"Have you talked with her?"

"A few minutes ago."

"How's she look?"

"Haggard. Withdrawal problems."

"Damn. I forgot about that. You mean to say that she was already totally hooked on the stuff? I didn't think she used it all that often."

"Up the nose and in the arm. Pretty steadily." Bongers decided to pull no punches.

"Holy shit. What are they doing for her?" It looked as if he were ready to cry.

"They're easing her off. Gently. She'll be alright. She said you were an innocent bystander and that it was all her fault, not yours."

"Christ Almighty. She did?" This time he did break down and cried. "Can you believe that? What a woman." He dried his eyes. "But it ain't true, you know? I was the one who wanted to get in with the casino and I'm the one who was real greedy. You understand, all the assets are in her name and if we were to ever split for some reason or another, I would end up on the creek without a penny, so I figured, I'd get me some stock that would be mine and that would give me some income in due time. You understand? That was not her doing." He had received his coffee and paused to take a sip, while Bruce waited politely.

"Tell me, Mr.... what's your name again?"

"Bongers. B-o-n-g-e-r-s."

"Okay, Mr. Bongers, tell me exactly what you want from me to spring her free and clear."

"List all of your assets, yours and hers. Give us the names of all the contacts you have made, here in the U.S. and in Colombia. All the details. Don't forget something conveniently, because when we find out you lied, all deals are off." He waited while his words sank in, then continued; "Yours and hers." He put the emphasis on 'hers'.

Weaver slumped in his seat. Obviously in deep thought.

"A secretary will get with you. She'll takes notes and record everything. It won't be easy. You'll be tempted to fudge a little, but just remember your oath as an officer and keep thinking about the time Carol would spend in this hellhole." He got up. "I'll talk to you soon."

"Tell Carol I love her and I'm sorry. Sooo sorry!"

"I will."

Chapter Thirty-Five

Cashing in on Gamblers.

Brunswick, GA

"Hoyt, let's stop for a beer between here and the airport. I gotta think a minute. Where's my man Bruno?" The two agents were walking away from the cellblock on the way to the administrative part of the Glynn County jail.

"The guy that came in with you? He's in the cafeteria, I think. That's where one of my men was taking him."

"Let's find him. Can you get away from here for a night? Maybe two? Or Three?" Bongers had to slow down a little. Hoyt's legs were half the size of his.

"No problem. Whats you got on your mind?" Hoyt was puffing already.

"I'm thinking of going to Biloxi. Do you have Lefebre's number?"

"Shouldn't take me but a minute." He pointed to his right. "That's the cafeteria. I'll catch you there in a minute." and walked on.

Bruno Garcia, Bruce Bongers' right hand man was sitting at a long table, finishing a hamburger and a bunch of French fries and looking content.

"Hungry, boss?" He asked as Bongers walked up. "The burgers

are great or do want something else?" He'd already gotten up to go order.

"Burger's fine and a tall iced tea. Thanks." He sat down next to the Georgia G-men that Bruno had been sharing the table with. After introducing himself he looked around the table and asked: "Did you guys get any sleep?"

There were a few chuckles and: "Not much sir, but we understand that we're about to cut out. Is that correct?"

"If I was your boss, I would say so, but that's up to Mr. Hoyt. Here he comes."

Hoyt and the burger arrived at about the same time. "I've got Lefebre's number. Do you wanna call him now?"

"After I wolf this down. I'm famished." It didn't take but three minutes and all the G-men were on their way out, Bongers with an iced tea in his hand.

Hoyt was again trying to keep pace with Bruce. "I have a car out front and we have the pilot standing by."

"Great!"

The unmarked car stopped outside an elegant looking restaurant and the four of them found a fairly secluded booth in the barroom.

The Jersey chief took the lead after everyone had received their choice of drinks. He took a long swig, nearly finished the bottle of Heineken and began, "Here's my thinking: If we can quickly insert ourselves into the casino operation in Biloxi, we might catch Jerry Robinson and some of his henchmen by surprise. The problem is: there is a leak. They were set up and it cost three of our men their lives. Now they think they fixed the leak, but I'm skeptical. I wanna go in without any local yokels and see if we can't grab them without a shootout. Another thing: Jerry's brother disappeared at the same time as he did when we had that big raid last year and he may be running another casino somewhere. Possibly along the same coast. Vegas is too tight. I doubt they got in there. Besides, Vegas or Tahoe didn't have this hurricane problem, so I'd like to find out if a certain Mr. Robinson or Radowicz is operating a gambling resort somewhere between Florida and Texas. I'll ask Lefebre to jump on that. Do you have his number? Thanks."

Another round was delivered and Bruce dialed Mississippi. "Hiya, Bruce here!" He waited for the other party to stop talking, but finally interrupted: "Wait a sec. We're here in Brunswick, Georgia and are about to fly out to see you. What's our best bet as far as an airport and accommodations are concerned".... "Pascagoula?.... Holiday Inn?....

You'll take care of the reservations?.... We'll need a car at the airport.... Four of us.... We'll meet in the morning.... Great!... Do me a favor. Get with Washington.... Find out if there's a Robinson or Radowicz in charge of any of the casinos along the Gulf Coast.... What?... Jerry?... We know about Jerry... We're looking for his brother... See what you can do. Thanks." He finished his beer and looked around the table,

"Pascagoula, hey? What a beautiful name. Spanish or Indian?" The others looked blank, including Bruno. He raised his eyebrows and asked: "Indian, maybe?"

The landing strip was short, but it presented no problem to the experienced pilots and a car was waiting to take them to their hotel. In the bar, having a nightcap, they heard from Lefebre and the news was interesting. The brother was in New Orleans, working on getting a gambling boat licensed and organized, expecting to sail and do business in ten days.

"Whoopee! Let's see if we can snag'em both. Here's to the brothers Robinson!"

They drank up and hit the sack.

The morning brought sunshine, a hearty breakfast and ten more agents into the Holiday Inn briefing room. Two CIA, eight FBI. While technicians were scanning the room for bugs and cameras, the group was introduced all around. They didn't have the benefit of all the electronic gadgets that an FBI office could have provided,

The Golden Pig

but with an easel and a magic marker, Bongers got the meeting rolling.

"Let's go over what we want to accomplish and then I'll open it to questions and suggestions. I'll list it the way I see it." He started writing.

"Number one, we have to get Jerry Robinson in custody without a shootout or a major uproar in the casino." On the board he noted: "#1) J.R."

"Number two. At the same time we have to grab the other Robinson, what's his name?" Someone answered: "Henry." "Okay. Henry. Do we know exactly where he is and do we have any one we can trust in New Orleans? Can we get a secure line to the bureau chief?" He paused in order for the group to catch up on their notes and he sipped from his coffee as they scribbled. On the board he marked: " # 2, H.R. New O."

"Number three. The owner of the truck dealership… What's his name?"

"Owen DeLaFarge." Someone spoke up.

"Thanks. He and his crony, the sales manager, have to be put on ice, so they can't warn Jerry. I don't care how. Arrested? A bullet through the head? We can't have an occurrence like last time when our guys were set up." On the paper he marked: "#3 Owen, +."

"Before I go any further, is this boy Willy in lock-up nearby? Has he spilled anything worthwhile?" Lefebre shook his head.

"I want to talk to that fellow when we finish here." He drank another sip and consulted his notes. "I'm open for all suggestions, but my feeling is, we hit them when they least expect it. I bet you, these boys come down out of their ivory towers to take in the show at night or to socialize with the up-and-up. That's the time to get into their apartments and meet them when they come back up. That's supposing they don't live in the basement." There were a few polite chuckles around the room.

"You have your notes. Work out some details for me. "John, (he addressed Lefebre, not knowing he preferred Jean, the French way.) Get someone with New Orleans immediately and bring me to this boy Willy. We'll reassemble here at eleven and form a battle plan. Okay?" He paused for a moment. "And don't hesitate to bring your own ideas. As a matter of fact, some may be better than mine. See ya at eleven."

In the local Sheriff's office, they didn't have the advantage of very sophisticated recording equipment, so they made do with what they had. One of the deputies' cars was stripped of a camcorder and brought in and an ordinary tape recorder plus a yellow pad were on the table in a little office. Bruce made himself comfortable on one side of the desk, with a cup of coffee in front of him, although he knew he'd had enough caffeine for one day. Within minutes the smuggler arrived. The Fed didn't seem to notice as he was busy scribbling something on his pad. Willy was seated opposite the desk by the two deputies and no effort was made to uncuff him. Bongers kept writing and never lifted his eyes. The smuggler cleared his throat, readjusted himself somewhat and still, the Fed didn't acknowledge that anyone was there.

"Sir!" Willy finally spoke up.

"Shut up." One of the guards hissed and grabbed him by the shoulder. He bent over to the man's ear and hissed again: "Shut up." The Mississippi man, used to the free and open outdoors, was getting panicky and started to show it.

"What's y'all want?" He screamed and attempted to stand up. Both guards grabbed him and pushed him back in his seat.

Bongers didn't seem to hear him. Finally he looked up and said, while glancing back at his notes: "You did some time in jail and you did some time in prison. You don't seem to learn very well, boy. Now you go around hustling enough dope so you'll spend the rest of your life in the penitentiary. You're not too smart, boy and... "

"The other man said I would go free and..."

"SHUT UP!" Bongers stood up and screamed at him. "I'm looking at the records here." He sat back down. "You were hauling 500 kilos of cocaine. That will kill at least one hundred people in overdoses alone and another hundred people that get killed, selling and stealing the stuff. In other words, Willy, you're an accessory to at least two hundred murders and we should either hang you, or keep you in lock-up for two hundred years, right?"

"No, no, no!" The accused was trying to stand up again and the deputies pushed him right back on his seat. "No, the other man said if I told him things, I would get off and go home!" He started to sniffle. "He did! He did! I told'em stuff an' he never come back, but I cooperated. I swear, I did. I don't wanna go to no prison, all I was trying to do was make a coupla bucks and I ain't interested in no drug business. All I wanna do is get back to my wife and kids and I promise you, I'll never get in with them guys again. They's no good. They got loadsa money, but they ain't no good. Mister. I swear, I won't go back with'em."

"Who're you talking about?"

"Them guys that pay me to get the stuff from the airplane in Florida..."

"What guys?"

"The ones that give me the truck and the credit card for the gas and ..."

"What are their names?" Bongers remained unruffled.

"They names?"

"Yes. What are the names of those men."

"Oh, but you don't unnerstand. They kill me if'n I tell you."

"Okay. In that case, we'll just kill you. Two hundred counts of murder. Take him away!"

The guards grabbed the smugler under his arms while Willie screamed: "No, No! I'll tell you. I tell you."

"Put him down." The deputies released the man and he sank back down.

"They'll kill me. You know that, don't you?"

"They'll be dead or in prison by tomorrow, so don't worry about them. Worry about me, because I can send you up for years or let you go back to your family. So.... The names please. Who gave you the truck?"

"Owen did. He said I could keep it after I got back. He'd give me the title and everything and it was a beautiful truck. Brand spanking new, I never owned no truck like that and I could've hauled ..."

"Who gave you money?"

"Money? Money? That was Al Wiggins. He gave me the credit card and four hundred dollars because the others had no driver's license, but they had guns. You see, I never lost my license, but I didn't wanna carry no gun, so that was a good deal. I just drove and I would keep the truck, you know?"

"Who's Al Wiggins?"

"You don't know? He's the big shot in the dealership. He lives in that big house on the hill. You can see it from the highway. All yellow with a bright green roof. Fancy, man, fancy. And he has this big boat in the downtown marina. He got money, man. Loads of money."

"Does he live at home or on the boat most of the time?" Bruce was getting an earful.

"Most of the time? Most of the time? I would say he spends most of his time in Bayberry Hills with his cute little sweetheart. I betcha, she ain't but sixteen years old, but she's a sweetie alright. Wait till you see her and..."

"Where's Bayberry Hills?"

"You don't know? That's the ritziest Condo tower on the beach. Twenty stories, maybe fifteen, but it's something, you know. It's something."

"Do you know what floor she's on."

"The top floor of course. You gotta have the view, man, you know? If you got the money, you gotta have the view, you unnerstand?" Willy was relaxing more and more.

"Who handles the dope in the casino?"

"In the casino? I don't know. Never been there."

"In the Food Distributership?"

"You know about that too? Oh, that's right. I told that other man in Zepherhills. That's Lucille. She handles everything."

"Lucille who?"

"Lucille. Let me think. She gave me a check once for hauling trash from her house. Lucille LeBlanc. B-e…no, no. l-e-b-l-a-n-c. Lucille Leblanc."

"What's her address?"

"Her address?"

"Yes, where does she live?"

"Oh, she's on the corner of Oak and Anderson. Big house. Big fence around it. Big dogs. I wouldn't go in her yard to clean up until she had 'em all locked up, you know. They looked worse than alligators."

"Willie. You're going to get better quarters and better food. I'll be back in a bit."

"When do I get out? I WANNA GET OUT! " He stood up again and hollered.

"As soon as I find out that you told the truth." With that, Bongers grabbed his pad and walked out.

"But, man!" Willie was still screaming.

Chapter Thirty-Six

Betting on a Long Shot.

Pascagoula
Holiday Inn
11 AM

Fifteen men and three women were seated at the long tables that were set up 'classroom' style. Bongers was at the head of the room.

"Morning! Forgive me if I don't remember all your names as yet, but by the time this operation is completed, I'll know them all. Promise. I'm Bruce Bongers from New Jersey and the reason why I'm here is not because you southerners couldn't run this show without me, but because I set off the firecracker that exploded this whole deal. I happened upon an informer who called two shots and both of them were accurate, as you know. We killed two smugglers, captured seven of them and a thousand kilos of cocaine with a street value of maybe ten million dollars, but we lost three of our men. That's the bad part. We need to get the people responsible, the ones that likely gave the orders to kill. I don't have to emphasize that they are dangerous and unscrupulous. Just assume that they have no conscience. I see we have three lady agents in the group and we're going to need you. Again, it will be danger-

The Golden Pig

ous. You don't have to volunteer. There's no pressure on you, but we'd love to count on you. Is there anyone who wants to bow out now? No hard feelings or repercussions." He picked up his water glass and wet his whistle. "Nobody?" He looked at everyone in the room and continued.

"This is the situation. We have four targets and we need to grab them simultaneously. Number one: Mr. Jerry Robinson at the Lucky Star Casino. Our best bet is to deter him when he's in the lounge or the show and get into his penthouse and grab him there when he comes back in. We need a lady to distract him. We need people who can kill the surveillance cameras in the halls, the stairways and the rooms of his suite without arousing suspicion. At this point we don't know who's on his team and who's not. Even if they're not in on the drug deal, most of his employees may feel sympathetic towards him and warn him if they suspect anything. This is going to be ticklish. We do need to capture him though. Dead or alive. Alive preferred." He took another sip.

"They next one is Owen DeLaFarge. We have his farm under surveillance and we believe he's there. He has not been back at the dealership. He may feel it's still too hot for him. He rarely goes out by himself at night, but when he does, he goes with a chauffeur. An armed chauffeur. We're going to try to get him out of the house, because that way we can ambush him without exposing any of our people needlessly. The way we're going to do that is by means of number three: Al Willis. Al lives in the big yellow house up on the hill on your right as you drive into town, but he's got a sweetie up in the Bayberry towers and she's going to be our bait. We have to get to her first, have her call Al and we'll ambush him when he gets out of the house. Problem is that we don't know if he'll be home with his wife or up in the tower with his girl. We have to prepare for both possibilities. Our biggest problem is: We can't trust the local forces. There was a leak that cost us three good men and we don't know if the leak has been plugged completely. Result: We do it all ourselves. We'll have some men from Tobacco, Alcohol, et cetera, plus some U.S. Marshalls, but they'll be here too late for the planning, so they'll help with the manpower." He looked around the room, "Any questions so far?"

"You mentioned four?" One of the ladies spoke up.

"Right on! Number four is a lady named Lucille LeBlanc. She runs, or ran, the food distribution company, which included distributing coke in little individual cereal boxes. We have not determined if she left town or if we can apprehend her and use her as bait in order to draw out Robinson, if need be. These are the four separate operations that are going to take place and at the exact same time. You already know who your team leader is, so we'll break right now. We have twenty minutes before lunch will be brought in, so let's get organized." He walked from the room.

Back up in his own suite, he got through to Washington. He briefed the director on the impending plans and asked him to inform New Orleans and to urge the utmost discretion. They couldn't afford to have anybody blow a whistle and goof up the whole operation. Jarvis also promised to get in touch with the head of CIA, Jed Taylor, and engage his cooperation. Bruce went to lunch.

Holiday Inn
1:30 PM

The teams were being divvied up. Two women in swim gear and robes would enter the Bayberry towers and ride to the top. Two maintenance men would ride up in the same elevator and if the top floor was not accessible without a special elevator key, the team would get off one floor lower and pick the stairway locks in order to get up into the penthouse. The expectation was that Al would visit with his sweetie and leave to go home to have supper with his wife and children like any good husband would. Hopefully, the sixteen-year old girlfriend would be alone, because that would avoid complications.

After securing her, she would be coaxed to call Al with an emergency message at 7:30 and that should get him to run out of his

The Golden Pig

house, right into the FBI trap. He would either be captured or sent to heaven or hell. That was between him and his Maker.

Owen would receive a call from Tweetie-Pie as well. (They hadn't figured out a name for her yet.) Not till after Al was secured and the expectation was that DeLaFarge would run out to help. Outside his gated property, a roadblock would put an end to his illustrious career as a truck dealer and drug smuggler.

Lucille's arrest might be the simplest. A team, man and woman, would approach her house and with any luck, they should be welcomed in as members of the 'home-owners-association'. They would simply arrest her and take her away. A big unknown was: who else was in the house? A maid? No problem! A man? She had no husband, but she might have a butler, a bodyguard or a lover inside her home and that would have to be dealt with. A team would be at her back gate, prepared to neutralize the dogs and stop any attempt to flee by car.

The most complicated situation would be apprehending Jerry Robinson. All the security cameras in the casino, the lounge, the dining room, the halls and the garage could set off an alarm in no time. If Jerry was alerted somehow and tried to make a break for it, the garage might become a battle ground. Half a dozen men and women would act as ordinary tourists or local gamblers and be stationed in vital areas. Two glamour gals would ride to the penthouse if that were possible and if not, someone would have to coax Jerry out of his swank apartment and down into the lobby. It could get complicated, especially if one of the other three should manage to get a message to Mr. Robinson. Owen, Al and Lucille all had to be apprehended without the chance of using a phone. It could all work. Bongers had run operations like that before and everyone had a two way radio. That was a plus and a hindrance at the same time. It was a plus when it came to issuing and receiving orders, it was a negative if it started squawking at the wrong time. Bongers used an example: "Suppose one of you lovely ladies is about to nuzzle up to Jerry, he is good looking by the way, and everything is going well until out of your pocketbook this metallic voice is heard, saying: "team four, are you in place?"

He got a hearty laugh out of that, but it hammered down the seriousness of that possibility. The group broke up in teams again and started working out the details. City maps, casino floor plans, county road charts were examined and highlighted. Bikinis and robes were obtained and radio communication codes were rehearsed and remembered.

Bruce would be in the garage in an SUV with dark windows. He would have to find a spot where he would be inconspicuous. Possibly amid dozens of visiting gamblers' cars. Some had to start out early in order to get into position and others had time for an early supper before the action started.

Up in his room, surrounded by Hoyt, Garcia and Lefebre, he contacted Washington again and was directed to Andy Gneuff, (pronounced "nuff") special agent in charge of the New Orleans CIA office. The two had never met, but they were on the same wavelength: "Capture or kill the bastards." The N.O. team was all set and primed. Their biggest question was; Is Henry Radowicz, Robinson on the boat? There were a lot of workers on the gambling ship as it lay docked in the harbor, but no one had been able to establish if Henry was there or in his home. That presented another problem: Nobody knew where he lived. He had been seen in a local hotel, but he wasn't registered there. It would be logical if he had a condo or apartment right on the waterfront, but so far, they hadn't located any such place yet. At the urging of their director, Jeb Taylor, they had not included or consulted the local police force because of the possibility of corruption within the department and a possible leak that might forewarn the smuggler of the government's intention. As they were speaking, automobile registrations were being checked and if they found one in Robinson's name, they could canvas the nearby garages and see if they could find it. If they did, they would simply post a few agents nearby and capture the culprit when he tried to escape.

The agents on both ends of the line agreed to hold off the New

Orleans attack until after the Biloxi operation was completed, so Henry could not spook his brother Jerry in the Lucky Star.

Everything seemed under control and the G-men ordered up some food. It might be a long night.

Chapter Thirty-Seven

The Dragnet.

At 7PM, two bikini clad ladies got up from their beach chairs at the pool, donned robes, picked up their large beach bags and started for the elevator.

The mission was underway.

A maintenance truck rolled up in front of the building and parked in the 'NO PARKING' area. A pair of men in blue coveralls got out and walked into the big hallway, just in time to catch the same ride up. They didn't even smile at any of the other passengers and pushed the penthouse button. People exited at different levels until just four people eased up onto the top floor. No problems occurred, no special key was needed and the team walked west toward number 1607, ladies first. The men stayed back about twenty feet while the one of the ladies rang the bell. The other stood behind her and to the left, her hand in her bag, fingers firmly around her pistol grip. The peephole flickered momentary and the lady up front waved at it: "Hi!" The door opened. Slowly at first, while a young blond with very blue eyes peered through the slit. "Hi! Remember me? Shirley?" The door opened wider and the first lady stepped in, number two right on her heels, but now with the pistol out and aiming smack at those blue eyes.

"Put up your hands and turn around." Number one agent ordered and spun the blond around so fast, that she nearly tumbled. By then the men were in the room and had cuffs on her in seconds and a hand over her mouth. She was forced down on a couch, face down and only then did the G-Man remove his hand. The two ladies had sprinted around the apartment to assure that no one else was present and the second man had closed the door. So far, so good. Now came the hard part. Lady agent number one reappeared from another room wearing white slacks and a pink blouse, looking like a tourist. She walked to the couch, signaled the G-Man to turn the pretty blond around and when he did, she moved her face close to the teenager and hissed: "If you make a sound, we'll tape your mouth, you hear?" The girl nodded. "Let her sit up." She ordered and the Fed obliged.

"Now, let me tell you why we're here. Your friend Al is wanted for murder and drug dealing and we're with the FBI."

"Oh, no!" She gasped.

"Oh yes. He'll get the electric chair, I'm sure, and you may spend your young life in prison as an accessory, unless you cooperate with us, do you…"

"Oh. no!" She gasped again and tears started rolling from her pretty blue eyes that were wide with fear.

"Oh, yes. Depending on how well you work with us, you may go free. First: What is your name and where are you from?"

"I'm Cindy Mae Monville," Her lips quivered and tears kept coming down. "I'm from Troy. Alabama and I ain't done nothing…"

"How old are you Cindy?"

"Cindy Mae. I'm sixteen and a half and I'll be seventeen…"

"Do your folks know you're here?"

"Oh, no. You're not gonna tell'em, are you?"

"That depends. In a little while, you're going to call Al. Do you have his cell number?" Cindy Mae just nodded. "You're gonna call him and say only ' Al, I'm so sick!' and hang up. You understand? And make it believable as if you're really sick."

The young blond wouldn't look her in the eye and the dark haired FBI woman picked up her chin and said: "Look at me! Look me in the eyes. You will do that won't you, or do you want us to show you the inside of a prison cell first with a bunch of hard nosed lesbian women, who'd love to get a hold of a beautiful thing like you?"

The girl gagged at the thought or maybe because the lady had such a tight grip on her chin. "You will do that, right?"

The blond head bopped up and down and the FBI woman released her grip.

"Let's hear you say it. 'Al, I'm sick!" The girl hesitated. "Say it!" Dammit, say it."

"Al, I'm sick."

"Again, this time with conviction, like you're feeling real bad. Go!"

"Al, I'm sick." It was barely a whisper."

"Okay, give me the phone." One of the men brought a phone and the female Fed said: "What's the number? Listen in on the other phone." She pointed to the other female agent. "Here goes. You say one thing wrong and we'll throw you off the balcony." She dialed, waited for a ring and held the phone in front of Cindy Mae's mouth.

A male voice came on: "What's up?"

"Al, I'm sick." Click. The agent shut off the connection immediately and dug her cell out of her bag, pushed a button and said: "The ball is rolling."

The lady in charge leaned over to Cindy Mae again and whispered:

"Just one more thing. We have here Mr. Owen DeLaFarge's number. In a few more minutes we're going to call him and you'll say: 'Al needs you.' No more. Do you understand?"

"But why?"

"Because prison is a rotten place and believe me, you don't wanna go there. So let me hear you say: 'Al needs you'."

"Just like that? Al needs you?"

"Right. Just like that. Got it? Say it once more!"

"Al needs you."

"Good. Let's wait for the signal." Five minutes went by during which, not a word was spoken. Then.... A crackle from the radio in the bag and: "Got'em. Number two next."

"Here we go. Remember: Al needs you." The lady Fed punched a number and waited..... Suddenly she shoved the phone into Cindy Mae's face and Cindy whispered: "Al needs you." and the line went dead.

Again the cell phone was engaged: "Ball two." Was all she said.

All five made for the door as the house phone started ringing. And ringing, and ringing.

The team outside of Al's hilltop house consisted of three cars and an old pickup. The moment the word came: "The ball is rolling." All engines were started. The pickup was closest to the gate of the estate and backed in between some trees. The cars were just fifty feet back, on both sides of the road on the shoulders, lights out. From their angle, they could see the garage door open and a car backing out.

"One, get ready."

"Roger." The pickup driver had the car in gear and the handbrake on so his brake lights wouldn't come on. Al's car came running down his drive and the automatic wrought iron gate started to roll back. The moment the drug dealers car cleared the gate, the pickup shot onto the road, causing Al to swerve violently and crash into the shrubs on the side of the road. Two cars, lights blazing were on the scene in seconds and the driver of the pickup already had a pistol pointing at Al's head. "Out!" He hollered and yanked at the door at the same time. The door was locked and Al reached for a phone. That proved to be a mistake. The bullet from the agent's pistol went right into the smuggler's eyeball and blew off the back of his head. The door window shattered in a thousand pieces and decorated the dead man's body with a thousand diamond like crystals.

The agents from the other cars had rushed over, pistols drawn, but things were under control already, except for one thing to do.

One of the men opened his cell, pushed a few buttons and said: "Ball one stopped rolling."

Owens case was very similar, but worked out differently. As expected, Mr. DeLaFarge was startled by the phone call, but decided to get some clarification. He called the penthouse, expecting the young lover girl to pick up the phone. His caller I.D. told him that the call originated from the Bayberry Towers, but she didn't answer. He wondered if it was wise to call Al's house, because he sure didn't want to discuss a distress call from Al's girlfriend with Al's wife. He dialed the penthouse again. Same result, no answer. Finally, he decided to call his sales managers' house. After all, he didn't need an excuse to call his employees. The wife answered. As calmly as he could, he said: "Oh, hi Marion, Al please."

"Al's not here. He got a call and ran out."

"When?"

"When? Fifteen minutes ago, maybe." She didn't seem perturbed. Maybe there was nothing to worry about.

"Thanks, Marion. How are the kids?" Owen remained as cold as a cucumber.

"Fine, now that they've got an iPod."

"A what? Never mind. Tell Al to call me when he comes in. Thanks."

He felt that Al expected him to run out to the Bayberry, but somehow, it didn't smell right. He decided to call Jerry. He tried four different numbers before he reached him. He was familiar with Jerry's method of switching phones, so it would be hard to trace him. "Jerry? Owen. Have you heard from Al?... No?... His girl called. She only said: 'Al needs you' and hung up. I called his house and his wife said he ran out after he got a call. Anything unusual happening?... Okay, I'll go see what's cooking. See ya."

Owen buzzed his chauffeur who was playing cards with his wife in their garage apartment. "Damn, just as I was winning." He grabbed his coat and pistol and walked down to the garage. Owen was already outside his front door and got in. "Bayberry" was all he said. The drive from his ranch to the gate was nearly a mile and the Lincoln hummed along at a nice pace. Right after they crossed the cattle guard in the road, a pickup ran in their path and two other cars converged on him from behind.

"What the hell?" he screamed as his face smashed into his dash. He hadn't worn his seatbelt and his driver hit the brakes so hard that Owen flew forward like a bullet. In seconds, the doors swung open and a muzzle was pushed to his neck. "Hands on your head," a voice ordered as two pairs of hands pulled him out of his door onto the concrete. Cuffs were snapped on his wrists behind his back. "What the hell do think you're doing?" he screamed, but the only answer he received was a face in his face that said while pulling his head up from the road by his hair: "You have the right to remain silent. Any thing you say……"

"Oh, shut up!" he screamed. "I want my lawyer and I want him now!" The voice in his face answered. "Don't worry, you'll be needing your lawyer till you fry in the electric chair. He'll love it. He'll get all your money and you die anyway."

"Aw, screw you!" While he was pulled up and pushed into the backseat of one of the cars, someone spoke into a cell phone" "Two out."

Lucille must have been feeling no pain. She was dressed in a silk housecoat that she had brought back from Japan. She loved the feel of the soft material against her bare body and with a sherry at her side she was enjoying an old Doris Day-Rock Hudson movie on TV. The doorbell annoyed her. Mary Jane answered it and came back to Lucille's lounge chair and whispered: "A couple from the home-owners association."

"Oh, balls. What do they want now?" She got up and smoothed her robe around her. At the door, the handsome couple smiled at her and the man spoke up: "May we come in a minute?" With that, he already stepped forward and Lucille was about to say: "Sure", when he grabbed her arm, spun her around and snapped a cuff on her left wrist while the woman grabbed her other arm and twisted around to her back, where the hand cuffs united them.

"What do you think you're doing?" She screamed at the top of her lungs and Mary Jane lunged at the arresting duo, which led to a quick grab of her arm by the G-Man and the maid landed face down on the floor with a shoulder separation.

"You're under arrest. You have the right to remain…"

While the lady Fed was reading their rights, her male counterpart spoke into his phone: "Three down, nobody out."

Chapter Thirty-Eight

Ambush

Lucky Star
Penthouse.
7:35 PM

Jerry was upset by Owen's call. Why would he call him about Al, unless something was wrong with Al. Or maybe it was just a peculiar suspicion about his cute little girlfriend. Jerry had never seen her, but heard about the affair. He thought it was stupid. With all the broads in the world that were anxious to jump in bed with a healthy man, why would anyone want to put up large amounts of money to put up a chick in an expensive flat someplace? So the whole world would know? And to make it worse: an underage kid? "Some guys have their brains in their pecker," he thought, "and they can't see out of it." He put on his gun holster. "Stupid jerks." Normally he would not carry a gun inside the casino. No need for it, but the phone call set him on edge somewhat. He couldn't escape the feeling that something wasn't right.

"Well, it's Julio's last night, I might as well enjoy it." He put on his blue suede jacket and made for the door. As he turned the handle, one of his cell phones rang. He walked back in, looked at all four of them in a neat row on the bar and picked up the one that rang and vibrated. "Hello?"... Hiya, Henry.... Just going down to hear Julio one last time... Everything okay?... The Motor Vehicle Bureau is tracking your car? Was it stolen?... Then what are they tracking it for?... Screw'em, take a cab... Yeah, I know what you mean... I'm nervous too.... No, not my car... Got a call about one of my men... missing... You're right.... Yeah... on a drunk... Yeah... Okay... I'll carry this number with me... Okay..." He clicked the phone shut. "Why would my brother worry about his car? Just because he drives a Masarati, he's got to worry? Do I worry about my car?" He was talking to himself as he closed the door and got into the elevator. "Why is the elevator at this level?" He looked around. "Nobody came to see me. Oh, well."

The casino boss pushed the lobby button. While riding down, he changed his mind and pushed Mezzanine. From that level, they controlled all the cameras in the place. The casino floor below, the garage, the hallways, everything. At the far end of the humongous room with a hundred TV's, a middle aged man was staring at a dozen black and white screens that constantly flicked from one scene to another.

"Joe!" He tapped the man on his shoulder. The operator nearly jumped. "Mr. Robinson! You startled me!"

"That's alright. That means you were concentrating. Which screen covers the top floor? That one?" Joe had pointed to the top right of his panel. "Anything up there?"

"Give it a second. It screens it from four directions. Ten seconds per camera."

The manager stood and watched. Ten seconds: his door. Another ten: the elevator, then the stairwell door and afterward the whole length of the hall. Back to his door, etc. Nothing moved on the penthouse floor. He handed Joe a slip. "This is the cell number I'm carrying. If you see anything unusual call me immediately."

"Sure thing. By the way, Mr. Robinson, is you car a little Jaguar convertible?"

`"Yeah, it is. Why?"

"Maybe nothing, but a few people were admiring it. Maybe a

little longer than usual."

"Really? Show me." A lower screen, that carried a label: "GARAGE 2" changed images every ten seconds as well and it lingered on Jerry's car for a few moments and slipped on to a different sight.

"Nothing now!" Joe said.

"Okay, thanks. Call me if something happens."

"Sure thing, boss."

"What's the sudden interest in our cars? That doesn't smell right. He was still talking to himself as he descended the magnificent staircase to the lobby level. In the lounge the barman poured him a Sherry, Portugal's finest. He sipped with deep satisfaction. "There is no way that California can ever imitate this." He took another sip and nearly spilled it as a lady bumped into him. "Sorry Ma'am!" He said with a slight bow, although he felt that the woman should be the one to apologize.

"Oh, John, do you see what you did? You made me spill this gentleman's drink."

She was talking to her companion, who apparently couldn't care less. Didn't even hear her. "That oaf!" She turned back to Jerry. "Let me buy you a drink. I don't know why I get involved in these things."

"No thanks, I didn't spill any. What things?" He took a better look at her, now that she was facing him. Not bad, maybe thirty, trim and elegant in a modest fashion. White silk blouse under a grey pants suit jacket. Blond, but not bleached. "Not bad.!" He said to himself.

"What thing?" She looked up at him and he noticed she had very pale blue eyes. "Finnish" He thought. "Maybe Swedish."

"You said you got involved in things."

"Oh? Right. We are a dance group in Pensacola and on occasion they sponsor a trip to Biloxi and that's why I'm standing here with oaf and some other dancers. We wanna hear Julio sing. I'm not much of a gambler. When I lose twenty dollars in the slots, I quit. You sure I can't buy you a drink? I'm sure I knocked you all over the place."

"No, on the contrary, what do you drink?" He signaled the barman, "Mario, two please." Mario looked at the blond and she said: "Vodka tonic, please."

"My name is Jerry, what's yours?"

"Deana, Dee-ana. Not Di-ana."

"Do you have reserved seats for the show already?"

"Yes, I believe so. Georgia, our president bought a whole block of tickets, does that mean we're all sitting together or do we just sit any ol' where?"

"I have a better location for you, unless you feel you have to sit with them." Jerry liked the pretty blond. Reminded him of Ingrid, back in Chicago.

"Waddaya mean, better location? Right up front?"

"Right. And maybe you'll get to meet Julio after the show."

"Really?" Her eyes sparkled at the thought and her smile showed off a perfect set of beautiful teeth. "How can you arrange that?"

"I work here."

"You do?" She smiled up at him. Even with heels she was four inches shorter than Jerry. "Great." She hesitated. "No obligations, I hope."

"Of course not. Lets go find our seats."

"All right!" She took his arm and they walked out of the lounge.

Two drinks later and halfway through the warm-up show, Jerry's phone vibrated.

"Yeah?"

"Mr. Robinson, somebody just entered your apartment."

"Send security. I'll be right there." He got up and whispered in Deanna's ear: "A little problem. I'll be back." He disappeared.

The comedian on the stage finished a joke and while the whole audience roared, Deana whispered into her cell: "He's on his way."

At the top of the stairs, Jerry raced to his left to the security room and was stopped in his tracks by two men who looked like fishermen on a gambling junket. A gun was propped in his back and one was pushing into his ribcage. "You're under arrest. Raise your hands…"

Things happened so fast that the G-Men didn't know what happened. Jerry swung at the gun at his chest, knocking it away and turned at the same time, pulling his own pistol and firing a shot into the man's mouth. The pistol in the small of his back fired, but because the smuggler moved so rapidly, it only nicked his hip and at the same time Jerry's gun fired right into the man's groin. Both the G-Men dropped to the floor and Jerry sprinted back down the stairs and the length of a corridor, through a door marked EMERGENCY EXIT ONLY and down two flights of stairs. He suspected that the fuzz had spotted his car, but he didn't have many choices. He had to get out! The emergency door had set off an alarm and a screeching sound filled the basement, where his Jag was parked. It was his only chance. He reached it within seconds, but a window opened in a black SUV and a metallic voice beamed out: "Stop. Raise your hands."

Instead, Jerry kept on running while he turned in the direction of the sound and fired. He didn't know at what. A blast of pain erupted in his groin and he went down on his knees, screaming: "You bastards!" raising his gun again, but not knowing what to shoot at. "Blam." Another shot. This one hit his hand and his pistol went flying.

"Get the ambulance in here. We wanna keep him alive." Bongers pocketed his pistol as he watched three men approaching the bleeding figure on the concrete floor, guns at ready. He got out of the vehicle and joined the rest of his crew, who were busy, searching the smuggler for other weapons and stopping the bleeding. His phone went off.

"Damn! He got two of our men upstairs. Damn! How could that happen?"

Lights blazing and sirens blaring, the ambulance raced in,

screeched to a halt and after applying a tourniquet, strapped the wounded man to a stretcher and shoved him in the back of the vehicle and took off.

Deanna joined them downstairs just as the ambulance turned the corner and asked: "You got him, right?"
"Yep. Nailed him, but he should live."
"Darn! I never did get to see Julio. I better get back upstairs and help control the panic. The hotel security and our guys nearly started a shoot-out, because they're all undercover without badges and nobody knows who's a good guy or a bad guy. What a mess! The customers are screaming! I'll catch ya later." She was gone.

Chapter Thirty-Nine

Way Down Yonder....

New Orleans
The Waterfront.

On the fourth floor of the waterfront hotel, the local director, Gneuff, checked his notes. "Does everyone have a picture of the dude?" All five heads nodded. "Including the guys on the roof?" More nods. "In the cars?" Satisfied, he looked back at his pad.

"How many people are around the Masarati?"

"Four, sir." A grey haired agent answered him.

At fifty-four, ……. Gneuff had seen all sorts of action. In Vietnam, in Laos, in the aftermath of Katrina, helping to control the looting, but he had never been faced with a problem like this. Going after somebody of whom they were not sure what he looked like, and invading a floating casino looking for a man who might not be there.

His hope was that they might spook him and that he would flee down one of the two gangplanks. That way, he should be easy to stop and if they didn't, they might catch him when he was trying to get into his fancy red sports car. A $300.000 car. That was more than Gneuff spent on his whole house. Sometimes he wondered if crime really paid? In the case of Mr. Henry Robinson, it didn't only pay, it paid big.

While organizing and checking the whole ambush operation, a nagging thought kept haunting him. He didn't have anything definite. He hoped the police artist' drawing of Henry's face was close. He hoped that the man was aboard. He hoped that his men would subdue him without the loss of life on their own behalf. He hoped and hoped and that's what had him worried. His dad used to say : *"Hoping you do in church. Here you gotta know for sure."* That was the problem: He didn't know anything for sure.

He was waiting for a call from Bongers in Biloxi and as soon as that came in, a few painters and electricians would enter the boat from the two gangplanks and start in the direction of the executive offices in the bow. Nobody knew where their target might be at any given time. No gamblers were allowed on the gambling boat as yet, so they were restricted to workmen. Men! No women!

Bongers called at 8:10. "We got'em all. Good hunting!"

"Thanks," Gneuff picked up his two way radio and spoke just one word: "Affirmative." He walked over to the window and opened it. While he adjusted his binoculars to the gambling boat across the street, a sharpshooter next to him calibrated the scoop on his sniper rifle. He could pick off a flea if it came hopping down the gangplank. Two men with baseball caps and coveralls walked up the walkway on the far right and the moment they disappeared into the bowels of the ship, another pair ascended the gangplank on the left. The first pair looked like plasterers and the second twosome like electricians, bundles of wiring slung across their shoulders.

Henry was up in his office in the bow with his confidant, Serge Jaoquim, lovingly known as Sarge. Henry was only two years older than Jerry, but he looked ten years beyond that age. His features were more like his father's. More Germanic than Latin. Besides, grey specks were evident in his mustache and sideburns, adding to the difference in looks. He was also the more serious one of the two and the deep lines in his face hinted that he also worried more.

"Sarge. I have called all of Jerry's phones and he doesn't answer any one of them. He assured me just an hour ago that he would keep one in his pocket, even when he went in to watch Julio Iglesias once more." His worried face looked more haggard. "I don't like it. They caught Harry and the guy from Tampa and I have this feeling that they're closing in on us. Has anyone come aboard, that we haven't checked out?"

Sarge, a little man with sharp Indian features, picked up a phone: "Security? Do we show anyone coming aboard lately that we don't know?" His Inca like face set into a frown while his black eyes opened wide. "Two? Where? Two more? Where?"

"Boss, this may not mean anything but two sets of workmen entered on both gangplanks."

"Stop them and have them questioned. I'm going to the control room."

Sarge picked up the phone again while Henry rushed out the door. Within ten seconds he was staring at the black and white screens in the darkened security cubbyhole.

One screen showed two men walking into the front hall of the boat and another showed a pair of men being stopped by a third one. It seemed that the invaders were reaching in their pockets for identification, but instead, a pistol came out and a pair of handcuffs and within seconds, the security man was cuffed and flat on his face on the floor.

Henry had seen enough. He raced back to his office where Sarge was shouting orders on the phone. He ignored Sarge, grabbed a briefcase, loaded some papers and turned the knobs on the wall safe that appeared from behind a painting. The magnificent landscape swung on its hinges and blocked Sarge's view. He couldn't see that Mr. H. Robinson-Radowisz was loading thick stacks of currency into the leather attaché case. The steel door was slammed shut, some wheels twisted a few times, and the landscape was back in place. A black leather jacket and a small caliber pistol appeared out of a closet and Henry was on his way out.

"Hold them off at all costs!" Were the last words he shouted at Sarge and he was gone.

The two agents who were confronted in the stern, called the temporary headquarters on their radio with just a few words. "We've been discovered." The men in the front hall heard the same message and ducked into a side door. It turned out to be the Ladies Room and they kept the door cracked at an inch so they immediately spotted three men storming into the empty hall from the far door.

Gneuff, on hearing the message, ordered: "Storm the place."

The sound of the message reached the ladies' room as well and both men eased out, back to back.

Of the three men that had come storming in, two kept right on running out the doors onto the gangplank. The third one halted inside the door, with his back to the G-men.

"Drop the gun!" One of them ordered, but the security man made no move to drop it. Instead, he twisted around slowly, but before he could point the gun, a bullet ripped the gun right out of his hand.

"Hot damn!" He screamed and with his left hand, he grabbed his bleeding right one.

"Down!" The Fed had his pistol leveled right at his eyes, while his partner was still standing back to back guarding the opposite door, ready to welcome any additional armed men. The wounded man at the front door laid down gingerly. "On your face!"

He rolled over while screaming: "Man, don't you see, I'm bleeding? You bastards?"

"Shut up or I'll stop the bleeding with a bullet in your head. Crawl away from that door."

The two men that had raced out of the hall door heard a shot from inside and decided to go back in and assist, when a bullhorn sounded: "Freeze and drop those guns."

A spotlight caught them in its beam and they lowered their arms and the guns rattled loudly on the aluminum walkway. "Walk forward. One by one. Slowly."

The Golden Pig

Within a minute, they were in the back of a paddy wagon, well secured.

In the other entrance, no confrontation had taken place as yet and two 'electricians' took out their pistols and opened one of the doors leading inside the casino hall. Gingerly at first, then open all the way, both of them. There was no one in sight.

Hidden by the doors, they held their positions, guns at ready. They had heard the message: "Storm the place." So they kept an eye on the door through which they had entered a moment ago, expecting their colleagues to come charging through momentarily, while making sure that no one from the casino side would come out to take pot shots at them. Indeed, within a minute, four men rushed in, spread out and disappeared to the upper deck and into the gaudy room with all the one armed bandits.

Sarge had run back into the security hub and spotted the invasion on both ends. He turned and split. On the far side of the boat, he slipped over the railing and dropped in the dark waters of the Mississippi and let the current take him away.

Ten minutes later, Gneuff had all the security men that had remained on the boat, sitting on the floor of the entrance hall. His men were still searching every nook and cranny of the ship and the CIA man was getting impatient.

"You better talk now and talk fast or you'll be implicated in murder and contraband and your sorry asses will die in prison. Where is Henry Robinson." He looked around at the faces against the walls. Some looked defiant, some looked scared.

"Where is he?" He turned to one of them who was barely a kid. Eighteen, maybe. "He was in the control room and saw the men come in. Then he ran."

"Damn. Where is he now? Where could he hide?"

"Did you check his dinghy?" Someone whispered.

"Who said that? Dinghy? Oh shit. He had a boat? Did anyone

hear an engine start?" He ran from the room, back onto the street.

" Call the local police. Have them run downstream and check all docks for a small boat coming in, probably without an engine. Car one and two, get on it immediately. Get the police chopper up with lights. We gotta find that bastard."

Henry had drifted at least a hundred yards before he started his engine. He steered the little rubber craft across the current and called his wife.

She was at the pier on the west side of the river when he arrived thirty-five minutes later.

He picked up his attaché case and kicked the dinghy back onto the muddy river.

Chapter Forty

The Prison Ward.

Mississippi State Prison
9:15 AM

The warden's office was about as bare as a prison cell. Grey metal desk, a dozen chairs and a twelve foot folding table. Two file cabinets of the same color were standing in the corner, next to the door of a private bathroom. That was about all the luxury the warden allowed himself, a little privy. Two plastic thermal pots were on the table, one marked Regular and the other Decaf. A half dozen mugs of different description decorated the table and sugar and cream packets were strewn all over, some full, some empty. Five men were sitting around the table, ready to compare notes.

Jerry Robinson had been moved to the prison after emergency surgery in the Biloxi General Hospital. According to the reports, he was resting comfortably.

Bongers had been on the phone with Washington, Langley and Jersey for the last half hour and had updated them as best as possible. He and his team hadn't gotten back to their motel until one in the morning and the phone rang already at seven. Langley on the phone. CIA headquarters and the boss himself, Jed Taylor.

He had forgotten that there was an hour time difference between Virginia and Mississippi. Bruce was really not in the mood to talk to anybody, let alone the head honcho, besides that, he was still groggy with sleep. As usual, Taylor did most of the talking and the least of the listening and what it really came down to was that he was trying to lay the blame of Henry's escape on Bongers and the FBI, rather than the CIA, which had handled the situation in New Orleans. The man really did irritate the New Jersey chief and after listening for fifteen minutes, he simply hung up and didn't answer his phone any more. After a good shower and a hearty breakfast, he felt better and he called Langley back with a message that the phones had been repaired.

Two hours later the group was going through a gallon of coffee and getting their notes synchronized.

"We'll see if we can find out from Jerry where his brother may be hiding out." Bruce began. "It's hard to believe that our boys hadn't considered an escape by means of the river. We now understand that at least one more henchman escaped that way, but we may never know if they took off together or solo. Gneuff is so ticked off, he's talking about resigning and retiring. Maybe that is for the best. Does anyone know how old he is or how long he's been on the force? Nobody?" Everyone shook their heads. "Oh, well, it really does not concern us, so let's look at what is up next." He held out his mug and Lefebre refilled it.

"Jarvis wants me to go to Colombia to wrap up Lucky's operation. For those who don't know, Lucky's the father of these two illustrious brothers and he heads up the whole operation." He sipped gingerly. The coffee was hot. "Allegedly," he added as an afterthought. "Taylor feels that his men in South America, in conjunction with the local forces, can handle it without any 'interference' from the FBI, as he called it." He snickered for a moment. "Maybe if we had interfered in New Orleans last night, Henry might be either dead or in custody. Any way, I'll let Jarvis and Taylor fight it out and I'll just do what I'm told. I'd like to get that S.O.B. Vargas personally, because my father used to chase and capture former SS men in Germany and helped bring them to justice. This guy slipped through the net and I'd like to put some finishing touches on my father's handy work. We'll see. At this point I don't think Owen and Lucille know much about the operation in Cartagena, because I don't think they ever had any direct dealings with Lucky. They must have done all their dealing through the brothers Robinson. By the way, we don't have an official count yet, but Owens' ranch yielded another batch of coke, maybe three hundred pounds and twelve million in small bills. Can you believe that kinda money? The casino is more complicated. Some of that money is 'clean' gambling money, if you can call that clean, and it belongs to the stockholders. It'll take a while to sort that out." He drank some more of his coffee and turned to the warden, Jerome DeLisle: "Is the room all set up?"

DeLisle got up and said, "I'm pretty sure, but let me check." He picked up the phone on his desk, pushed a few buttons and asked: "All set?" He walked back to the table: "Five minutes. They're testing the volume and then they'll roll him in."

"Okay, let's meander over there." The chairs were pushed back and the team strolled behind the warden to the hospital building of the prison. Once outside, they had a good look at the expanse of the prison yard with hundreds of blue-clad individuals walking between dozens of concrete block buildings. Bruno Garcia shivered, just thinking what it would be like to spend time behind these fences. "Madre Mia." He murmured.

The hospital was spotlessly white inside. The walls, the ceilings, the floor, everything sparkled. The antiseptic smell was the same as any other hospital and the only difference was that half of the personnel who moved through the corridors were dressed in prison garb. On the right, they entered through some double doors, again brilliant white, and stood inside a bare room with just a few high-chairs, like bar stools, lined up in front of a window, A camcorder was mounted on a tripod in front of the window and on the only table in the room were a few tape recorders and a lot of wiring.

Looking through the window, they could see Jerry strapped on a stretcher, with an I.V. dripping in his left arm. The arm was belted to the frame and an armed guard was standing at the foot of the bed while a nurse worked a clamp on the I.V. line. Bongers nodded at the warden and walked in, carrying a folding chair.

As he unfolded the chair, he looked at the prisoner and tried to control his feelings. That man in front of him had killed one of his men last night by shooting him in the mouth and had wounded another. The dead man was a father of four, two in college. Bruce felt, he could easily throttle the guy and have no compunction about it whatsoever. The man on the stretcher looked at the G-man, but didn't say a word. Neither did Bongers.

He put the chair real close, sat down and with his face about twenty inches away from the killer, he said: "I'm the man that shot you last night. How do you feel?"

"You bastard! I'll never be able to use my hand again."

"That's good. You'll never be able to kill again with that hand."

The look on the criminals face changed somewhat. "Are they dead?" He whispered.

"One, the one you shot in the mouth. The other will live."

"They shouldn't have startled me like that, I thought they were trying to rob me and,.."

"Sure! After they said: 'You are under arrest'. Robbers say that? And then you tried to escape, while the robbers were both down? Let's cut the crap. You're going to fry for first degree murder and the sooner the better. The man you dropped had a wife and four children. I should invite them in here and torture you to death over a three months period. Maybe six." He stopped for a moment, letting the thought sink in. "You'll be glad to know that Owen, Lucille and Al are all in the can. Al may not live. Did you know that Owen had twelve million in small bills stashed at his ranch? Shouldn't that be your father's money?"

"That bastard! That S.O.B. held on to that money and claimed that it had been flown out? That miserable conniving bastard! If I ever get my hands on him, I'll strangle that sonofabitch. That miserable crumb! That lying bastard!"

"Well you may get your chance. You'll be on death row together. Maybe you'll be sharing bunks." Bongers was starting to enjoy himself. "If Al survives, you'll make an excellent death row trio. Maybe you can sing something together. Are you religious? Maybe you could sing: *'Nobody Knows The Trouble I've Seen.'* That would be appropriate. We could cut a record and send it to Henry. He'd love that!"

"Henry? What do you know about Henry?" If he could have, Jerry would have jumped off the bed. His restraints kept him right in place, flat on his back, except for his head that bopped up and down, while his eyes were trying to pop out of his head.

"Henry? Oh, Henry? You don't know. He turned over the whole riverboat operation to us last night. He didn't tell you?"

"Que maricón!" (That faggot.) Jerry screamed. "He talked to me last night an…"

"And you believed him? How dumb…"

"Where is he? Where is that scumbag?" Jerry was shouting and straining against his straps.

"Across the river, comfortably at home. He has enough money and he didn't really want the hassles anymore. He…"

"He's sitting in that big home with the seaplane and the yacht and that bitchy broad of his? He's as guilty as I am and of course my father is gonna favor him anyway, he always has and they think I should take all the blame and rot in prison? Those bastards. Dad always favored him because he was the firstborn and had the same Arian looks. I looked like my mother and I guess my father resented that from the day I was born, those sonsabitches. Well, they're wrong. If I'm gonna fry, they're gonna fry right along with me, do you hear? What's your name?"

"Bongers."

"Huh?"

"Bongers. B-O-N-G-E-R-S. Bongers."

"Okay Bongers. What is Henry getting away with?"

"Away with? Well, he lost the boat of course and all the money that was in it. We estimate that he has at least twenty mil in his house or in safe deposit boxes here and overseas. That's okay. He will provide us with records, but I forgot if I should go down stream from New Orleans or upstream to his house when I get there later today, He..."

"Oh you can't miss it. Thirty miles upstream, the Peligro Plantation? You never seen it? You're in for a treat. Gorgeous. Built by one of the first Italian slave traders of the South. You'd love it, Now something else. What's gonna happen to me?"

"Prepare yourself. You're going to hell!" With that Bruce got up and took the chair with him.

On the other side of the mirror, he flipped open his cell phone and after a few seconds, he asked: "Lester, do you want me to go to Louisiana and try to corral Henry Robinson or should we leave that to Jarvis and his team?"

"I'll call you back."

The warden shook his head and said: "I don't believe what I've just witnessed."

Bruno answered: "Stick around. You may learn something."

Chapter Forty-One

Dog Fight On The Bayou

1500 feet over Biloxi, Miss.
11: 00 AM

"Sir, we have clearance to over fly Keesler Air Force Base and we'll be landing at Biloxi Regional in fifteen minutes. Two sharpshooters should be standing by."

"Great! Thanks." The helicopter pilot was talking to Bongers on the intercom as they sped their way to New Orleans. The FBI Director Lester Jarvis had given a very simple order: "Do it now before anyone flies the coop."

That was in answer to Bruce's question: "Do we get on it immediately or do we try to coordinate a massive effort involving the CIA and local authorities?"

It had taken only twenty minutes to round up a helicopter that picked them up at the prison and was to take them upriver from the Big Easy. The aerial map that the pilot provided did show a little anchor on the west side of the big river, just south of Saint James, Louisiana. That little anchor meant there was a seaplane base, private, with no facilities. In other words there was no gas available or any kind of service. A typical private landing spot.

"That's gotta be it." Bongers pointed out to his sidekick, Garcia. He pushed the intercom button. How far is Saint James from here?"

"Saint James?" The pilot had never even heard of the place.

"Look on your map, thirty miles north of New Orleans, where the river makes a sharp bend. See it?"

"Got it."

"See the little anchor? That's our probable target. How far from here?"

"About eighty-five miles. Approximately fifty minutes including our stop."

"Okay." Bruce switched off the intercom and turned to Bruno: "Let's hope that our guys from Baton Rouge can get there at the same time. If they left immediately after I called, they should be able to make it. There's no highway straight south, so they'll have to follow the levee and work their way through the little towns. It's gonna be close. If we spook Henry and he takes off by car, we'll simply stay overhead and direct traffic till they corner him. Piece a' cake."

"Famous last words." Bruno grinned. "Here we go." The copter was going down toward the Biloxi Airport fire department building, where two men with baseball caps and rifle cases were waiting for them to land.

"Welcome aboard, gents." and as the chopper started to rise: "I'm Bongers. It's going to be a little crowded in here. The chopper was built for six, but it won't leave you much room to maneuver with your rifles. Let me tell you what we're anticipating. There is a nice plantation home on the west bank of the Mississippi. I haven't seen it, but if it's typical, it'll have a great lawn sloping toward the river with some big moss-laden trees. So there should be plenty of space to land. There's also a dock, with a seaplane and possibly a speed boat. Your job will probably be shooting a hole in the boat and in the floats of the plane, so that our suspect cannot escape that way."

"What has he done?" One of the shooters asked.

"Big time drug dealings, accessory to murder, including some of our own. He should fry or spend his life in the can. He's smart and dangerous and we hope he's still there. He outsmarted our people in the city and we suspect he went home. We have very little info and very little time. If he's smart, he'll take all his money and get out of the country fast. His plane may be his best bet. Let's see what happens."

The copter maintained 1,500 feet and the bayou country with all its canals and wetlands sped underneath them with a flurry. It was a beautiful ride. The flocks of birds created moving white blotches against the green and grey back ground below them and seemed to paint streaks across the ground. The noise in the chopper made it nearly impossible to communicate by cell phone, but the pilot could hook up Bongers with a radio transmitter that enabled him to get through to someone else with a radio. That was not so simple. What it came down to was the following: Bongers would reach a radio controller at Biloxi, leave a message with him and wait till the operator called back with a response. For example:

"Biloxi? Bongers, over."

"Go ahead, Bongers."

"Call Jarvis. Pass a message to Baton Rouge."

"Roger. Jarvis to Baton Rouge. Message? Over"

"We're forty minutes from target. Do not contact suspect until we're overhead. Over."

"Roger. Forty minutes, do not contact. Over."

"Roger, Out." To his fellow passengers he said: "Would be easier if I could talk to them directly, wouldn't it?" They all nodded. Too loud to talk much.

The sharpshooters unpacked their rifles, mounted their scopes and loaded the magazines. One shot with a Remington 30 odd 6 and the other had an H&H 222. Bongers admired the weapons and after putting on the safety, the shooter handed him the H&H and Bruce balanced the weapon in his hand as if he were guessing the weight. He shouldered it, pointing out the window and said: "Nice weapon, very light."

"Love it. Very flat trajectory. I bag groundhogs at three hundred yards."

"Really? That's great." He handed back the rifle. Ten more minutes and they should be there. The silver snake in the distance grew larger by the minute and soon became a brownish band of muddy water.

"Target to our right at one o'clock," the pilot announced on the intercom, turning about ten degrees. He was looking directly at the mansion, but his passengers couldn't see it from the passenger compartment. Bongers undid his safety belt and got up in order to look over the pilot's shoulder. The captain in the left seat pointed straight ahead with his left hand while keeping his right on the joystick.

"Got it." He stared at the beautiful layout of an antebellum plantation with a massive lawn in front of the two-story colonial. "The plane's moving!" he shouted suddenly and indeed, although it was barely as big as a flea from this far out, they could detect movement. The yellow and black flea was drifting away from the dock.

"Get'em". Bongers ordered.

"Sir, please sit down and buckle in." The pilot spoke without looking up, both hands busy on his throttle and his control stick.

"Right." But he didn't budge. "They're gonna take off down river." He turned around and hollered: "Get ready. Secure that window. Hand me the hailer." That last order was directed to the co-pilot who handed him a mike that was connected to a bullhorn. The chopper nosed down and the throttle had the engine screaming. Their speed went up by forty knots.

Below and ahead, the yellow and black bug had turned with the bend of the river and after it passed two tugs with multiple barges in front of them, its wake became longer and wider, leaving two silver streaks in the water behind it.

"Get next to them." Bongers remained upright, holding on for dear life.

At that point the chopper was doing at least one hundred and thirty knots, while the little seaplane was struggling to pick up a take-off speed of sixty, so they closed fast. The helicopter pilot had to bank steeply to the left in order to end up in the same direction of the seaplane and Bongers was thrown into the side of the craft.

"Told you to buckle." The pilot said calmly as the G-man struggled to get back up. It didn't take long. "Fly alongside him, same speed."

The copter lurched back, its nose pitching up fast, but this time Bongers held on. Their speed bled off from 140 to 70 in no time, but Bruce lost sight of the plane. Thank God, the pilot didn't because all of a sudden, the little seaplane and the helicopter were flying formation, just fifty feet apart.

The man in the little bug wasn't aware of anything except his rate of climb and his speed. He was doing a good job. The plane was climbing at 400 feet a minute and his speed was slowly creeping up to ninety. Then, all of a sudden, he had the shock of his life. Over the noise of his engine, he could hear the drone of another motor, much bigger and louder than his. He looked to his left and there was a copter, fifty feet back and a loudspeaker bellowed: "Throttle back and land. This is the FBI."

His reaction was instinctive. In a second, he turned the plane on its right wing, dove to the ground and gave it full throttle. It was a case of desperation of the worst kind. There was no way he could outrun a helicopter that size, but his nerves were shot by the events of the last twenty four hours. He realized that his maneuver didn't work very well. Within minutes the helicopter was back in position off his left wing. By now, he was skimming the sea grass and flying between the cypress trees. He figured if he could stay on this heading and at this altitude, he'd be over the swamps of Texas and before long he'd be over the Gulf of Mexico, where he would have an advantage. He'd have more fuel than the chopper and they would have to land somewhere and he could possibly make Mexico without refueling. He concentrated on staying as low as he dared and he even throttled back a little in order to conserve gas. He was cruising at 110 and that was not bad. The annoying loudspeaker came on again: "Throttle back and land or we'll shoot you down."

Henry was gaining more confidence. He said to his wife, who was crying:

"Shoot me down with what? They don't have rockets or a Gatlin gun. Who are they kidding? Mow me down with a pea-shooter?"

At that same moment, his side window shattered. "What the hell was that?"

Inside the copter, the window of the passenger compartment was lowered and two rifles were sticking out in the slipstream.

"Can you hit the gas tank or the engine?" Bongers was still very much in control, but also buckled in. Flying formation on the left of the plane gave him a front row view. Both guns fired. Both gunners aimed again. "Go.!"

This time, fuel streamed from the left wing and the cockpit disappeared in a fog of vapor. Henry banked sharp right, but he didn't have a chance of losing the chopper. It was nearly too easy. When the plane leveled without any attempt to slow down or land, the Jersey director ordered: "Take him out."

The shooters aimed for his head, but the buffeting of the chopper as well as the aircraft made them miss the pilot's head, yet the 30-06 hit Robinson in the left shoulder and he inadvertently pulled on the stick with his right hand and the plane went straight up.

"Watch it!" Bruce hollered, because for a moment it seemed that the seaplane would land on top of the helicopter. The captain banked sharply and threw the coal to the engine and in seconds they were at three hundred feet, making a steep right turn and looking down on a spectacular sight. The seaplane had been yanked up so steeply, that it stalled and slid back momentarily, then it nosed over and glided down toward the swamp below it as if it were going to dive into the murky waters. The plane behaved as if someone was still at the controls, but Henry's body was slumped backwards and against the door, so the plane handled itself and just before hitting the water and sea grass, it nosed up again while the floats hit the surface and the plane glided along.

Up in the helicopter, they wondered if Mrs. Robinson was an accomplished pilot, but Bongers wasn't taking any chances. "Hit the pontoons. Shatter them if you can." Below them the throttle was still wide open and it looked as if it could take off again. Four shots apiece rang out and the floats started to settle a little deeper in the water, while the gas from the left wing still made for an impressive spray. From up above they watched a scene, reminiscent of a movie. With the motor running full blast, the plane sank deeper into the water until the propeller hit and at first just churned, but then seemed to be grabbed by a magic hand that pulled it under water and the plane dove, rolled on it's back, went under momentarily and floated back to the surface, upside down, the floats sticking up out of the water.

"What a way to go!" Was all Bruce could think of. "Call the Coast Guard. Give them the coordinates. We can't land around here any place, so take us home. Well done, Captain."

Chapter Forty-Two

Target Practice, Anyone?

Pascagoula, Miss.
4PM EST
The Holiday Inn Lounge

In the mahogany paneled lounge, seven men and two women were enjoying an early cocktail hour. Everyone was sipping, but only one was talking: Bruce Bongers.

He held up his glass and said: "It's five o'clock in D.C., so let's toast." He waited till all the glasses were facing skyward: "Here's to a big dent in the drug world."

"Hear, hear!" everyone sounded off and drank to the outcome of their operation.

"I'm not sure if this place is soundproof or bugged, so I'll keep my remarks within the limits of what's gonna be in the papers tomorrow anyway, agreed?"

Some people nodded, some raised their glasses and shouted: "Hear, hear!"

"Okay, you clowns. First of all: Great job! All of you!" He raised his glass and again: "Hear! Hear!" sounded all around the table. "Without your quick and efficient cooperation, we could never have pulled this off. There's a lesson in this though: Stay alert at all times.

We shouldn't have lost our man in the casino. When dealing with arch criminals we better be on our toes. A lot of times, they're better trained than we are." He took a long drag from his Heineken and continued. "One of the reasons we're drinking this early is because we're hitting the sack early tonight and…" He was interrupted again by: "Hear! Hear!"

"Come on, you clowns. We need to get some sleep and we have a lot more work to do. We need to roll up the entire Lucky operation in this country and that'll involve a lot of work, including paper work." He held up his hand. "I know. Boring, boring, but that's how we clean things up. Our illustrious director, Mister Lester Jarvis now wants me to go to Colombia and show those folks, how to roll up a drug operation. I'm not sure I'm excited about that." He held up an empty beer bottle and asked: "Can anyone help out a parched, elderly man, who's about to die of thirst?"

Someone hailed a waiter and the parched elderly man seemed less dehydrated after a few minutes.

"For some of the good news. We have been hearing for years about antiquated equipment and lack of training for up and coming agents in our profession, right?" He looked around the table at his audience. "Well, we have confiscated over twenty-five million dollars in cash that will be funneled to training and state of the art equipment."

"Hear. Hear!" Again all the glasses were raised and smiles were exchanged all around the table.

"Plus!" He hesitated and drank heartily from his green bottle. "Plus…. Five million will go in our widows' retirement fund."

"Hear!, Hear!"

"Come on, you guys, let me finish. Five million will go into our scholarship funds, so our kids will have a shot at college!"

"Hear, Hear! Where did all this money come from?" Someone wanted to know.

"Everyone of the culprits, Owen, Al, Jerry and Henry had been skimming the profits and old man Vargas was getting pretty P.O.ed about it, but he couldn't put his finger on it. He didn't know if everyone was raking off profits or just one. Henry had more than ten million in cash with him when he drowned in his plane in the bayou. Owen had twelve million at his ranch. Al and his assets are still being investigated and of course, Jerry's and his brothers' share in the casinos may up that figure when it's all sorted out. Lucille was the pauper in the crowd. Her estate and cash add up to only seven mill, the poor thing. If we could sell the dope we've captured on the open market, we'd have another ten million, but I don't think that's legit." Everyone cracked up and a few more agents around the table shouted: "Hear, Hear!"

"Now for the serious part, before we start slurring, I may be off to South America tomorrow, I don't know what we're up against and I don't mind telling you, I'd rather be going home."

"Hear! Hear!"

"Okay. We have an opportunity to break the back of the drug operation in America. Daily, even hourly, little ol' ladies are being knocked off by some crack head who needs money for his addiction. Daily, people overdose on drugs. Just think of our celebrities that we've lost because of dope. Paul Newman's son, Elvis, Janet Joplin, I could go on for a half hour or more. The point is: we're putting a crimp in the line and we need to finish it. This should be everyone's first priority. Thanks again for all your help and the time you've put into this cleanup, so let's have one more toast and get some rest. Okay?"

"Here's to the hero of the Jersey swamps!"

"Aw, come on!"

7 PM

Up in his suite, Bongers fixed himself a scotch on the rocks and a Cuba Libre for his right hand man, Garcia.

"It's not confirmed yet, but it looks like we might be winging our way to Columbia, or Colombia as you would pronounce it. I really hate to get involved in an operation like that, because I wouldn't have control and when I don't, invariably things go wrong. Besides that, I don't speak Spanish all that well and I might say: "Hands Up." and they might think I'm saying: 'Have a drink'. Anyway, whatever I think, we may be on our way. Any thoughts?"

"Boss, you're doing great. You're on a roll, so keep it rolling."

"Okay. Let me call my Dutch friend and see if he's game. We may need somebody who can speak German."

"Fred? How's Mozambique?" The phone rang about twenty times before Fred answered.

"Oh, Hi! It's Martinique. I couldn't find the phone. They were in yesterdays shorts in the laundry bag. I had to buy new shorts. Do you know why? Because the saleslady said so. Who's this?"

"This is Bruce. How's Mozambique?"

"It's Martinique. Oh, it was great, but now we're in Saint Lucia."

"Boy, you guys don't sit still very long, do you?"

"Ted read somewhere that the girls in Saint Lucia are more beautiful than any ones in the Caribbean, so we sailed over."

"Sailed over?"

"Oh? Right! I didn't tell you that yet. We were at a party on a yacht in the harbor and the host, the captain, said: Let's go for a drink in Saint Lucie and that's what we did because Ted wanted to take pictures of the most beautiful brown eyes in the world. Now we've gotta go back to Mozambique, now you got me saying it. Martinique! because all our luggage is there. No big deal, so we'll get back there tomorrow or maybe the day thereafter. Who is this?"

Obviously, Fred was a little under the weather.

"This is Bruce Bongers, remember?"

"Of course I remember Brucie. How could I ever forget a fellow Dutchman with a drinking problem?"

"A drinking problem? Who's got a drinking problem?"

"You do, Brucie baby. You don't drink enough. That could be a real problem, right?"

"Right. I gotta work on that. Hey Fred, how would you like to go to Cartagena and chase Lucky down a canal?"

"Any time, buddy, any time. When do you wanna go?"

"What time is it out your way?"

"What time? Who gives a shit? I would say, it's time to have a drink. Do you know that these Frenchies on these islands really know how to fix a wicked drink? Have you ever had a B & B? Man that's sooooo smooth and it clears your sinuses at the same time. Why'd you ask?"

"I'll call you in the morning and we'll pick you up at noon at the airport, okay?"

"Whatever you say, Brucie. Whatever you say."

"Bruno, I hope he remembers some of this conversation in the morning. I must say one thing about those guys. They party better than anyone I've ever met, but they always seem to have their wits about them. That must be a talent. I have to check with my dad sometimes and find out if that's hereditary. I may have powers I'm not aware of." He enjoyed the flavor of his Dewars as its aroma tickled his nostrils and his tonsils at the same time.

"We're scheduled for a nine o'clock take-off and we'll fly by whatever island Fred's on and arrive in Cartagena late in the day. Let's just hope that they don't have hand held missiles aiming at us when we're coming in for landing. It'll probably get worse when we try to corner those monkeys once we're on the ground. At last report, they were still shooting people as if it was some sort of target practice. I hope we won't pass in front of their 'scopes. How do you feel about this whole deal?"

Bruno grinned: "It sounds like our kinda deal, boss. We'll have a blast, I'm sure. Besides, I really have to work on my Colombian accent.

Chapter Forty-Three

Harbor Patrol

Saint Lucie, Caribbean Sea
International Airport
6 PM Local time.

"Well, Fred, you look like you belong." Bruce admired Fred's multi-colored shorts and the even more bizarre shirt Fred was wearing as he boarded the sleek white jet without any markings.

"Oh, hell, when you're homeless, you'll wear anything, won't you?"

Fred was as tan as any of the islanders and at least as colorful. He appeared to be far from sober, but he didn't slur his speech. "You interrupted a hell of a party. Are you sure you and your crew don't wanna spend the night here? This is one of the friendliest islands, you've ever been on. They have the greatest bus system. They only seat twelve people, but they'll take you anywhere. Sometimes you have to hang outside, hanging on for dear life and sometimes you ride on top with the chickens and the pigs. They're all very polite though. Not one of them shit on my shoes. My brother Ted wasn't so lucky. He was ready to kill…"

"Fred!" Bruce interrupted him. "Are you sure you're ready to travel?"

"Sure, I'm ready. Got my American Express Card. Never leave home without it." He dug in his shorts and came up with a money clip that probably included his American Express Card. "See? Ready to go. Where are we going Brucie? Not back to the cold country, I hope?"

"No cold country, I promise. Come here and sit down. First class for you all the way." He helped Fred to a seat, reclined it for him and strapped him in. Fred was asleep the moment he sat down.

"What are we gonna do with him?" Bruno pointed at the sleeping figure. "With that kinda outfit, the drug dealers may use him for target practice."

"Don't worry," Bruce countered. "we'll borrow a camouflaged outfit from the locals. I wanna see if we can get this Radowicz/Robinson/Vargas to talk if we catch him alive and Fred here," he pointed at the colorful man in the seat, "supposedly speaks perfect German and can maybe get some things out of the old man, that we can't." Turning to the pilot: "We're ready if you are."

The door was closed, engines were started and the plane commenced rolling down the tarmac. Next stop Barranquilla.

A plain police van was waiting for them and transported the Americans to an outlying hotel. Food and wine was already waiting in the private dining room and the five of them attacked the meal with gusto. Fred was wide awake, but not as talkative. He called his condition: 'an early evening hangover', Besides Fred, Bruno and Bruce, the FBI men, they had two CIA agents with them, Hank Whittaker, a sharpshooter, and William, 'Bill' Grossmann, the CIA chief for Central America. Bill was to be the liaison between the CIA group working in Colombia and the local authorities. He was a middle-aged man in excellent condition. Six feet tall, with a trim waistline and full head of brown hair. His eyes were steel grey and seemed expressionless during most of the conversation that was taking place. When he spoke about drug dealers though, his eyes clouded over and the lines in his face became hard and straight. He could probably do a good Kirk Douglass imitation.

In contrast, the gunman looked like a twenty year old marine. Muscular build and just a flat layer of blond hair on top his head. Pleasant fellow with an easy smile.

Halfway through the meal. the Colombian force arrived, led by Colonel Guillermo Armando. Four of them, two in camouflage outfits as if they just came out of the jungle and two in regular khaki uniforms. The colonel was tall, but the rest of them were rather short, five-five maybe. The colonel had an aristocratic Spanish face, with silver hair and mustache, but the other three could have descended straight from Inca himself. Broad shoulders, short stocky legs and pitch black hair over very tan faces. After introductions all around and a toast with good local wine, the whole group moved into a meeting room that was ready with a projector and a portable screen. Glasses were at every seat, but no wine this time. Pitchers of ice water were waiting for them. Bongers asked if they could have bottled water instead and even though the colonel protested that the water in his country was really good, one of the uniformed men left and returned with a dozen bottles of Perrier. The meeting could begin.

Slides were shown of the harbor of Cartagena and the 'fort' of Lucky Vargas. The decision to be made was: 'where will we try to capture Vargas'? His routine seemed to be: at 8:30 AM, he would drive his bulletproof Mercedes out of his gate and down to the interstate highway. At that time of day, rush hour was nearly over and he'd make it to his dockside office by nine.

The easiest approach seemed to be, corral him right after he exits his gate. He would probably be most vulnerable at that point. Inside his residence complex, the 'fort', it would certainly become a shoot-out. Waiting till he got to his office wouldn't be a bad idea either, because there were many places for lawmen to hide, whereas outside his gate, it was mostly wide open and easy to be spotted. Once they had Lucky in custody, it should be simple to enter his compound without much resistance. So...., the plan was for everyone to be in position at the harbor by eight o'clock. Once Vargas got out of his car, it shouldn't be hard to block his exit, and nobody expected a heavily armed force to be in or around the warehouses. A speed boat would be standing by at the tour boat terminal and could be on the scene in thirty seconds. A covered commercial truck, with ten armed soldiers inside would park a block beyond Lucky's warehouse and be ready to pounce when needed. Another truck would be unloading goods at a warehouse, a block before Lucky's place. A helicopter with two sharpshooters, Bill and a Colombiano, would be warmed up and ready to go, just three blocks inland. Bongers and the colonel would be in a black Toyota SUV with dark windows, parked right off the highway exit, ready to follow Vargas the moment he passed. It should be a piece of cake.

Breakfast would be served at 6 AM, the plane would leave at seven and touchdown at Cartagena was expected thirty minutes later. Plenty of time to get in position, then check and counter-check all the preparations. Copies of aerial photographs and local maps were distributed and studied. Nothing could go wrong, according to the exuberant colonel.

In the hotel lounge, another glass of wine was raised in a toast to their success before everyone retreated to their assigned bedrooms. Fred had bought a toothbrush and a razor and someone promised him a coverall the next morning. "What could go wrong?" he quipped, "I may even be able to get clean underwear. Here's to the girl, that I never did find..." He started singing in a falsetto kind of voice and everyone left him with the bartender. *"Solamente una vez!"* he started and the barman joined in: *"ame en la vida."*

Bongers came back down and hauled Fred out of the bar, "It's gonna be a long day, brother, and a very short night."

"Right. Like the colonel said: What could go wrong?" Fred was again in the jolliest of moods. He sounded like his brother. Once Bruce closed the bedroom door behind Fred, he found his own and murmured: "Right. What could go wrong?"

Everything went right. Great breakfast, smooth flight, perfect landing, clean Toyota, new rifle with a scope, secured on the dash, two uniformed policemen in the front and Fred way in the back. Colonel Armando sat behind the driver and Bongers behind the passenger. He would have preferred to sit up front, but this was not his country. He had little choice.

The Spanish chatter on the two-way radio was incessant. Not at all like the crisp, abbreviated communication that he was accustomed to in the U.S. In spite of all the noise, the colonel seemed happy with the proceedings and reported: "Eberyting es een place."

"Great!"

The waiting began. It was only ten past eight and it would be another twenty minutes before Vargas would leave the house. Bongers looked around him and had to admit, their location was excellent. Nobody would spot them after coming off the cloverleaf and it would be easy to slip behind the Mercedes at a respectful distance. The minutes dragged. It seemed like two hours instead of twenty minutes and twice Bruce had to remind Fred to shut up and wait. He didn't need Fred's advice and certainly not his comments. Too bad the guy spoke a good handful of Spanish and he would strike up a conversation with the Columbians until Bongers finally said: "Now shut up or I'll have your mouth taped." That did it!

Eight-thirty came and went. So did eight-forty and eight-fifty. At nine, the colonel contacted the traffic helicopter that was to announce when Vargas came through the gate. "Nobody come, nobody go." was all he had to report.

"Caramba!"

"Beg your pardon?"

"Ees wrong. He late. Maybe he not come."

Bruce had more patience. It wouldn't be the first time that he sat at a stake-out and waited for three or four hours. "It's only nine-ten. Maybe he got an important phone call."

"Maybe."

At ten o'clock, they pulled up stakes and planned to gather at the local Army post.

"Wait! Wait!" Fred had a different kind of answer. "I know people in the little bar on the docks. One of them is a German who works for Vargas. I'm gonna buy him a drink and see what I can find out. Take me to a place where I can catch a cab." He was already stripping off his coveralls and reappeared like a colorful cockatoo.

""You may put yourself right in the line of fire and get your ass blown off." The FBI man was not at all in favor of letting the Dutchman go smack into the lion's den."

"You worry too much. Get me a taxi and I'll call you when the cab takes me away from there again. No problem, man." He pronounced it MAHN, like the islanders do.

The Columbian in charge and the G-man mulled it over and seemed to agree that it couldn't hurt. Nobody but Fred. They said so.

"Man, I used to steal from the Germans when I was only ten years old and I wasn't scared then and I'm not scared now, so where's my taxi?"

"Do you have Columbian money?"

"I have dollars. The almighty dollahr! Everybody loves the dollahr!"

The van moved out after the colonel confirmed that Vargas had not budged. Two blocks from their waiting post, Fred emerged, looking absolutely silly in his colorful outfit. "I'll call you when I need you." and he was gone.

The cabdriver understood exactly where the foreigner wanted to go and dropped him off seven minutes later. Like the last time, the place was already packed with beer drinking seamen and it smelled again of *Arroz con Pollo.* (rice and chicken.) Smelled great.

Fred tried not to be too obvious, but with his outfit, he stood out like a sore thumb. He decided not to look for Enrico or Heinrich and hoped that the German would find him. He worked his way to the bar, extracted a twenty and ordered Dos Equis, which the bartender didn't have. He had Corona and that was okay too. As long as it was cold and came out of a bottle. He conversed in his best Spanish, which wasn't as good as his brothers, but it helped him along. The biggest problem was: when he said two words in Spanish, the others assumed that he knew the language and started rattling in such rapid Spanish, that he couldn't understand a word. "*Cuidado, cuidado.*" He would say, but that didn't mean 'slowly', it meant 'careful, careful'. It worked though. Not all the time, just some of the time. He seemed to understand: "How are you? and What are you doing here?" And he answered: "*Mi mujer.* Shopping. *Mi? Tengo sed.*" (I'm thirsty.)

He tried to make the bartender believe that he was thirsty and that his wife was shopping. When he said that he was on a cruise ship, he apparently screwed up, because there was no such thing in town on that particular day. While he tried to appear carefree and happy, a chill was crawling up his spine. Something was wrong. He could smell it. The conversation around him didn't flow the way it did before and the barman disappeared into the kitchen. "Probably to get food." Fred convinced himself.

At the same time that his second beer arrived, little Heinrich tapped him on the shoulder: "*Wie gehts den Käsekopf?*" (How is the cheesehead?)

"Ha, der Heinrich! *Wie gehst? Alles gut?*" (How are you? Everything okay?)

"*Nah, gibst keine arbeit.*" (No, there's no work.)

"*Keine arbeit? Wieso nicht?*" (No work? How come?)

Enrico explained that his boss had closed shop yesterday and might not open again. No big deal. He didn't make all that much, but it was an easy job and it helped supplement his social security.

"Well, have a beer on me. I still work, so let me buy this time. *Un cervesa por Enrico, por favor.*" (A beer for Enrico, please.) He turned to the bartender who had overheard the conversation and seemed to understand at least some of it. Two more beers arrived and Fred asked: "I forgot. What kind of work did you do and can't you find another job?"

The five foot five German with his white beard and silver crown shook his head: "No, no. Nobody would hire me at my age. The only reason my boss kept me on is because I've been with him so long and we can practice our German together."

"You had a German boss? Here in Cartagena?"

"Didn't I tell you the last time when you were in here with your singing brother and your wives? Didn't I tell you then?"

"Probably. I forgot. *Verzeihen Sie mir.*" (Beg your pardon.)

Heinrich didn't seem too disturbed. "Come, drink up. I'll show you where I worked." He started guzzling his beer down and Fred followed suit. They banged their bottles on the bar and Fred waited to get his change. All in very colorful Columbian money. He left the coins, tucked the bills in his pocket and followed the white haired figure out of the bar.

He received a personal guided tour of the dockside, listening to the explanations of shipping and loading as well as the names of the various companies and the many countries they traveled to. All very interesting. After two blocks they crossed the street and walked up to a building that proclaimed in golden letters: "VARGAS & CIE".

On the side was a door marked: "*Oficina*" and Heinrich led the way into a surprisingly well adorned office. An air conditioner hummed softly and a Latin beauty behind the desk said softly: "*Hola!*" while Fred was hit hard on the base of his skull. All the lights went out in his head.

Chapter Forty-Four

How Lucky Can You Get?

Cartagena, Columbia.
Bouncing on a highway.

The first things Fred felt when his senses returned were his shoulders. It felt like his arms were being torn out of their sockets. For a while he couldn't remember a thing and he certainly had no idea where he was. The pain brought him back to reality pretty darn fast and he realized that he was face down on the floor of a moving vehicle. His arms were tied behind his back and that's what caused the strain on his rotor cuffs. It hurt like hell. His head wasn't too comfortable either. His right cheek bounced up and down on the metal floor of a moving vehicle and the best he could accomplish was to try to raise his head, so it wouldn't slam down on the hard surface constantly. By trying to keep his head up while lying down, he got an enormous cramp in his neck and consequently, he let his head down again and the pounding started all over again. He twitched and turned and finally was on his right side, so it was a little easier to keep his head off the floor, but it hurt his shoulders and neck even worse. He couldn't think straight. He tried to figure out where he was and how he got there. For a while, nothing made sense, but little by little, his brain got back into gear. Someone must have knocked him out in Vargas' office, because that was the last he remembered. A crushing pain in his neck and then... nothing. "Ah, someone had gotten wise to me." He thought. In the little bar, he already had the feeling that something wasn't kosher and that Lucky had closed shop the day before. Vargas must have figured out why he lost two plane loads of contraband and that somehow, Fred was in on it.

When his eyes started functioning again, he couldn't see much, but he figured out that he was in the back of a pickup truck with some sort of tarp or blanket over him. As the cover flapped in the wind, some light came in around the edges and Fred wondered if he could get on his knees and jump out. Jump out where? On a highway, going sixty miles an hour and then what? Jump off in front of other speeding cars? Not likely.

Getting on his knees didn't seem like such a bad idea, though. He could handle the bouncing better that way. His legs were not tied and by bringing up his legs into the fetal position, he got some leverage and right at the moment that he was giving his body an enormous shove, the pickup slowed and turned off to the right, throwing Fred against the left side of the truck bed. "Damn." He screamed, but when the vehicle straightened out of the turn, the momentum rolled him right on his knees where he wanted to be in the first place.

"Wow! That's better." His face was not on the floor anymore, but his shoulder blades were still being pushed together by the tether around his wrists. He wanted to scream, but he realized that that wouldn't help at all. Now that he had his knees under him, he wondered what would happen if he raised up? Would the tarp blow off? Would the driver notice in his rearview mirror? He was facing forward. What if he turned around and lifted the tarp at the back of the truck bed? That way he could see out and figure where he was going. The pain was becoming excruciating, but the truck was going slower, so they must have gotten off the highway and were now on a country road. Maybe! Things started to come together. In last night's briefing they had shown the 'fort' and the road leading from it and to it. Fred was getting convinced that he was being taken to

The Golden Pig

the Vargas compound and that they had gotten off the highway and onto the country road, leading to the estate. He decided to stick it out. Staying bent over on his knees was the most comfortable position he could think of and he stayed that way. The vehicle slowed and rolled to a stop and Fred decided to play dead. He rolled on his side and didn't move a muscle. The tarp was pulled to the side and a few commands were shouted out and the tarp fell back. Slowly, the pickup moved onto a gravel road. Fred could tell by the noise. It circled to the left and came to a full stop and the engine was turned off. Fred had never in his life been so happy about a ride coming to an end until that moment.

The tailgate was lowered, several voices intermingled and the tarp came off altogether. Someone grabbed his feet and pulled him backwards. Fred remained dead. Three pairs of hands grabbed him and carried him away to a shaded spot and put him down. "Thank God, they didn't just drop me." Fred thought. For about ten minutes nothing happened. He could feel he was in the shade and on a tile or brick floor. A lot of conversation went on all around him and at that point he made up his mind that he was going to learn to speak Spanish fluently. He didn't understand five percent of what was going on. Frustrating, very frustrating!

A hush in the conversations indicated that something was happening or about to happen. It became fairly quiet and he could hear footsteps approaching on the tile floor.

There was a pause and Fred felt that someone was staring down on him. An accented voice spoke softly and two pairs of hands grabbed the prone figure and cut the ropes that held his wrists together. "Whoa!" Fred yelled as his body suddenly sprung back to normal. It had been as tight as a bow string. The release of the pain was so unexpected that he nearly passed out again. For a few seconds, he just laid there, face on the cool tiles, shoulders pressed against the surface and his legs straight out. When he finally lifted his head, he saw a number of legs. Some with boots, some with shoes and some in sandals. He dropped his head and passed out again.

"You are Fred Van Dyke?" He heard the question, but he couldn't focus. He rubbed his forehead and was surprised that his hands weren't tied anymore. He shook his head as if he could get rid of cobwebs inside his cranium. He brought up his other hand and rubbed his eyes and his neck. "Ouch!" He cried when he got to the spot where someone had hit him. The pain cleared his view immediately and he found himself looking at an elderly gentleman of about eighty. 'A Germanic face with thinning grey hair around the edges and a thin straight set of lips'. That had to be Lucky, Fred thought. His mouth was parched and his brain felt like it was afloat inside his head. He concentrated on the face in front of him and suddenly spat out: "Ich habe durst." (I'm thirsty.) The reaction was unexpected. Lucky jumped up and shouted something and Fred collapsed again. He really didn't know how long he was out. Five seconds, five minutes or five hours. He had no concept of time. It probably was more like five seconds, because the scenery before him hadn't changed at all. As a matter of fact, it came into better focus. A soft hand tilted his head back and he greedily drank down a cold mixture of orange and papaya juice. The result was stupendous. All of a sudden his eyes focused, his brain functioned and he immediately wondered why he had spoken German instead of English or Spanish. It had to be a reflex reaction, reminding him of his younger years in Holland, facing a German soldier after stealing his food.

"Sie sind Fred Van Dyke?" Vargas asked again, but this time in German.

"Jawohl, und Sie?" Fred's mind was back in tune.

The old drug lord looked at him, frowned and finally answered: "Ich bin Johann Radowicz."

"Herr Radowicz. Wo kommen Sie her?" (where are you from?)

"Ich bin in Wredenhagen geboren, in Prussia." (I was born in Wredenhagen, in Prussia) It was interesting to Fred that he pronounced Prussia the English way. Probably been away too long.

For a while they exchanged pleasantries, but for the sake of his staff, Johann, Lucky, changed to English and continued questioning Fred.

"Would you like a glass of wine or some whiskey?" he asked.

"No, but I'd love a beer, thanks."

"Why are you dressed like that?" Lucky wanted to know.

"Dressed like this? " Fred looked down at his ridiculously colorful outfit and answered. "Well, it was clean until those guys dropped me in a pickup truck."

It earned him some laughs from Lucky and his entourage, about a dozen men and women sitting around them.

"I mean, before you got dirty. Why do you dress like that?"

"Me? Well, I was on the isle of Saint Lucie with my family, making like tourists and then I got a call to get on a plane and fly to Colombia to speak German to someone and I guess that someone is you unless it's my friend Enrico in the little waterfront bar. I don't know. Anyway, that's how I was dressed, so that's the way I came. Don't you like it?"

"You were asked to come here? By whom?" Vargas' face became stern, very stern. Fred acted as if he didn't notice.

"By Bruce Bongers. He's a Dutchman too and he knows I speak German and his father was an interpreter during the war and I said okay."

"Who's Booze Bonger, or whatever his name is?"

"I'm not sure but I think he's in the Narcotics business in the United States and I ran into him while I was doing research for my latest book."

"Your book? What book?" The facial muscles in Lucky's face relaxed a little.

"I'm an author. I write books. The one I am working on now is about drugs and how they affect teenagers in America." He accepted a cold beer from a young dark haired lady and nearly gulped down half of it.

"Why?"

"Why what?"

"Why you write about drugs for teenagers?"

Fred was surprised by the question, looked at his hands for a few seconds before he answered: "Because my beautiful teenage daughter and her beautiful teenaged friends nearly wrecked their lives, certainly wrecked my life and my marriage and some of them killed themselves by overdosing. That's why." His voice got louder and his eyes started blazing. "I hope to help educate young America to the danger of drugs and that's what I told Bongers. I said: 'Call me if you need me.' So he called. I don't know what I can do, but I do know I have a screaming pain in my neck and I have to go to the bathroom too."

Vargas looked down at his feet and said something about *'bagno'* to his aides and Fred was escorted down the hall. He nearly collapsed. His legs were so wobbly, he could hardly stand. Twice he stopped to shake his head because he got so dizzy standing up.

When he returned, he was directed to a more comfortable chair and in front of him was a tray of fresh fruit. Apparently, Vargas had changed gears.

While he watched Fred chew on a papaya, he asked: "You were in Bogota, last week, yes?"

"Yes," Fred answered while wiping some juice off his mouth.

"You were in the Hotel Domani? Yes?"

"Yes. Nice place, we had a goo.."

Lucky interrupted: "I burn it down."

"You what?"

"I burn it down."

"Why? Burn it down, why?"

"People spy on my business and you may be one of them because you were there and you spy on my pilots and you spy on my operation in Cartagena in the harbor and you ask too many questions from my friend Enrico and I think, you're not an innocent writer, I think you work for the CIA and I think I'm gonna kill you for that."

"Can I call my wife before you shoot me?"

Fred's answer baffled Vargas. "You wanna call? We have your phone and one of the numbers is for Meester Bonger, so you wanna call heem too? Whacha gonna tell him?"

"I'll tell him I think he's mistaken. Mr. Vargas is really a nice man, although he shouldn't go around burning down nice hotels."

Vargas looked flabbergasted. "Are you being funny with me?"

"No, I think you're a nice man, like I said, but I don't have to agree with your business or the way you conduct your business. Besides that, I really don't know what business you're in. Heinrich said you trade in mahogany from Brazil and that sounds like a good business to me. Whadda you think?"

Vargas didn't answer, but snapped a few orders at his audience and got up.

He motioned with his right hand and two of his male servants made sure that Fred followed without falling on his face.

The pain in his shoulder was nearly gone and his neck was less sore than it was when he was first brought in. He made a sincere effort to walk on his own, but the strong hands under his arms came in handy from time to time.

The dining room was most elegant and reminded Fred of some of the old castles he had visited in Spain. Lots of wrought iron and dark mahogany furniture. Most beautiful. They sat, six of them, around an oval table in hand carved armchairs, covered with dark red Moroccan leather. Lucky hadn't bothered to introduce the others in the luncheon party and Fred didn't ask.

A cold soup was offered first and it was delicious. Then little lamb chops and asparagus. This was first class, all the way, Fred said to himself.

While waiting for desert, Lucky asked: "Where are you from in Holland.?"

"I grew up right along the German border, just a few kilometers from Borken and Bocholt. Were you ever in Holland?"

"Just briefly. I had to inspect some camps in Amersfoort and Vucht. I was an adjutant to an SS Colonel and I do remember staying in a pretty medieval castle in Vucht. Most delightful. But that's about all I saw of Holland. How come you speak German so well? Is that usual over there?"

"No, not quite usual. Most people learn several languages in school, but we had a small Hotel-Café-Restaurant and we had German soldiers in the house at all times and we listened to the German *'Sondermeldungs'* (newscasts) day after day, so I simply grew up with two languages. When did you come over here Johann?" Fred felt more and more at ease and addressed him on a first name basis.

"I came over in forty-five. I got caught in Italy when the Americans bypassed Rome, but got across the Adriatic into Greece and from there on a ship to Argentina. I worked my way north and got into Colombia in early forty-nine. I've been here ever since."

A fruit salad dessert was brought in and as they started to eat, Lucky asked: "What happened to my sons?"

"Your sons? I never met your sons."

"Fred, you're not in a position to lie, so you better level with me. My sons disappeared over the last few days and I want to know what happened to them."

"I have no idea. I was in Saint Lucie for the last few days and I am not aware of anything that happened elsewhere. Where were your sons and how many are you talking about?"

"Are you playing with me?" His lips became one straight line. A cruel straight line.

"No, I never met any of your children and I haven't heard anything about them either. Where were they? Here or Stateside?"

The steel grey eyes tried to intimidate Fred, but he didn't blink. "I'll tell you what. Your life is in my hands, right?" Fred nodded. What else could he do?

"We are under siege. Your CIA and our own police forces are all set to storm this place. I surprised them by closing up my business two days ago and now you are my hostage, my bargaining chip. Do you understand?"

"Well, I understand that I'm your captive, but I don't understand all the rest. What do you mean: 'siege'? Are we under attack?"

"Not yet, but they're getting ready. My problem is, I can't get out of here. With all the modern facilities nowadays, they'll track me in no time. Helicopters and satellite cameras would immediately inform them if I left my compound. If I decide to fight, they'll blast me with rockets and kill all my people. I used to think that an escape tunnel would get me out of here, like in the old movies, but infra-red cameras would catch me very quickly, so I'm trapped. I don't want to die yet and I don't want to go to prison, so what do I do, Fred?"

Fred shrugged his sore shoulders: "I don't know. What can you do?"

"I'm going to negotiate, but first I have to know the truth about my two boys."

"Two? Where are they?"

"That's what I want to know. They were in Biloxi and New Orleans, but I can't reach'em anymore. They're either dead or in captivity. I have to know. So, Meester Fred, this is what we're gonna do. I have here your phone." He reached into his vest pocket and produced a cell phone. "You call the big chief in America and ask about my sons. What you learn will determine whether you live or die."

"The big chief? I don't know the big chief, all I know…"

"Who's in charge here? Who brought you to Colombia?"

"That's Mister Bongers, he's the New Jersey Chief."

"New Jersey? What's he doing here?"

"I don't know the connections, but he's the only one I know, he's the son of the Dutchman that I told you about. He's the man who called me to translate when we would meet…. You, I guess or some other German speaking person. He wants me to interpret."

"Okay, you told me that story because you want to write a book, right?" He chewed on a slice of tangerine and continued: "Here's what we'll do. You call Bonger or whatever his name is and tell him you're here and you will probably die before the day is over, unless he gives me the details about my sons, you understand?"

"Perfectly."

"Here's the phone. Show me Bongers' number. I'll copy it in case your batteries go dead."

Fred flipped opened the phone, pushed a few buttons and handed it back to Vargas, who wrote down the numbers. He pushed the little button with the green phone on it and waited.

"Bongers."

"Mister Bongers, Lucky Vargas here, someone wants to talk to you." He handed the phone to Fred.

"Bruce, Fred here.... Okay, but sore... no, no, .. I was knocked out in his office on the docks and had a rough ride over here.... No, no, I think this is his house, I don't know... I was out..."

Vargas interrupted with a snarl: "My sons, where are my sons?"

"Could you hear that? He wants to know about his sons, I don't... why don't you talk to him yourself?" He handed the phone back to the Columbian/German.

"My sons? Where are my boys?" He paled visibly as he listened. His breathing became more rapid. "Drowned?.... In his plane...?" He moved the phone momentarily and wiped his eyes with his shirt sleeve. "And Geraldo? Jerry?..... How bad?.... In prison?... *Caramba! Verdammtnochmal!*" He slammed the phone shut.

Questions sprung up all around the table, all in rapid fire Spanish, so Fred couldn't understand what was going on but he did grab the gist of it. Everyone wanted to know what had happened, including Fred, but he didn't dare to ask. Finally, the master of the house looked at Fred again and with that same cruel look in his eyes and his lips drawn tight, he hissed: "You didn't know? You didn't know one died and the other is in prison and wounded? You didn't know?"

"No one told me. I'm sorry. What happened?"

Vargas stood up on the other side of the table and shouted while leaning across: "YOU DIDN'T KNOW?"

"No. No one discussed your sons with me." Lucky sat back down, deflated.

"Enrico crashed in his own plane in Louisiana. Geraldo was shot in the casino in Biloxi. He's in prison." He broke down. "*Mi ijo está en una carcel en America. Quizas por vida.*" (My son is in prison in America, maybe for life.) His head dropped on the table and his body shook as he wept silently.

"He crashed?" His head shot up again. "He was a good pilot. The gringos probably shot him down. *Que maricónes!*" (The faggots) The look on his face changed. He sat erect and a determined look came over him.

"Herr Fred. Listen. This is what we'll do. I make a plan. You tell Mr. Bonger and if the plan fails, I will die, but you'll die first. Okay?"

"Okay? Are you kidding? I have no intention of dying. I have to write a book about you first."

"Good, then we'll both live, *verdad?*" (true?)

Chapter Forty-Five

Cuartel Militar de Cartagena

"Well, that changes everything."

Bruce was sitting in the luxurious office of General Umberto Di Vasco. They had been exploring various ways of smoking Vargas out of his compound, while at the same time wondering what became of Fred. Their latest reports were that Fred was having a beer or two at the docks and had strolled over to some of the warehouses and that was the last of it. No cars had left the piers without being searched and Fred wasn't in any of them. No vehicles had been spotted going into the 'fort' except an old empty pick-up truck. So, they had no Lucky and no Fred until all of a sudden one phone call placed them in the same locale: "The Fort."

"As you may have gathered, Fred is in Vargas' custody and Lucky is madder than hell. He hadn't heard from his boys for two days and now all of a sudden he knows all the gory details, that his operation is no more and that both sons are out of commission. One dead, one in the can." Bongers shook his head. "Heaven knows what he's gonna do now. Is he going to make a break for it? Is he going to hold Fred as a hostage? Is this going to be another mass suicide affair? Is he dumb enough to fight to the last man? I don't know. What do you think, gentlemen?" He looked around the room. Besides the General, there was another high ranking officer, addressed as 'Commodoro',

Colonel Armando, Bruno, Special agent Grossmann from Central America, a CIA official stationed in Columbia, George Paperious and another half dozen police and Army officers. There was enough brass there to start a war.

Mr. Paperious spoke up first: "I don't think a group suicide is up his alley. He's too much of a murderer. He'd rather go down shooting and killing ten others before he goes. A hostage for a guaranteed way out? That looks to me like the strongest possibility."

"*Momentito!*" One of the local police officers spoke up. "Was he calling from his house?" Bongers nodded. "Then we better be ready. He has a secret tunnel through the hill that comes out in a little farm, north of the fort. It's not secret any more, because we have known about it for a long time. He may be stalling with negotiations while he escapes through the barn. We also suspect that he has a lot of cash and gold in the tunnel. We better be ready.."

"Good point. Colonel, can you get men out there in a hurry and catch him if he tries?" Bongers took the initiative again. "Good. Meanwhile I'll call him and see what he's up to. Quiet, please." Four uniformed men hustled out of the door, while Bruce tried to reach Vargas again. After five rings: "Alo?"

"Mr. Vargas. I'm sure you understand the seriousness of the situation and why don't we settle all of this peacefully, so we won't have anymore bloodshed. Let's start by allowing your people to leave your compound…"

"You peeg! You keell my business, you keell my sons and now you tell ME what to do? Well, I tell YOU what to do. You come close to thees place and I'll keell as many of you as I can, including you and Fred and then you can all go to hell together." Click.

Bongers looked a little sheepish: "That didn't go too well." He chuckled, "Obviously."

Back in the dining room at the fort, Lucky grinned across the table at Fred. "It's like poker. You bid, you raise, you bluff and the one with the biggest balls and the best cards wins. That's why I'm gonna win. We're going to let them stew a little and then we call'em back. How about a brandy, Fred? Did you ever have '*Asbach Uralt*'? NO? You must have been young when you left Holland." He snapped his fingers and one of the men produced brandy snifters and a bottle. "*Asbach Uralt* is a bit sharper than French Cognac, but it is excellent." He poured half an inch in the bottom of the glasses and handed one to Fred. "Prost!" He extended the glass and Fred clinked with him: "Prost."

They sipped silently for a minute and the writer said to himself: "This is the weirdest situation in the world. Toasting your potential killer. I hope I put that in writing some day. Of course, first I have to keep on living. Priority number one."

Lucky lifted his glass, swirled the amber liquid and admired the color, sparkling in the lights of the chandelier overhead. "Do you know how I got into this nasty business?" Fred shook his head. "Not a clue."

"You put it in your book? For sure?" Fred nodded. After another lingering sip, he continued: "My first wife was a pretty girl from the mountains where I first worked in the goldmines. We had three children and I saved a leettle, so I could start a business one day. In the mountains, lots of coke was grown and the dealers sold the dope right there amongst the miners. I didn't touch the stuff. Everything was fine until the drug cartel decided they wanted to get into the gold business. First they tried to mine themselves, then they tried to buy the mine where I worked and when that didn't work, they took it over by shooting the owners and most of the foremen. What could I do? I kept working, but they paid less than what I was used to and I decided to leave. I went into the office and resigned and asked for my pay. Well, they grabbed me, slapped me around and told me they would teach me a lesson as an example for others. They tied me up in front of the building while three of them went to my house, raped my wife in front of the children and turned me loose. I was helpless. I didn't even have a gun. We escaped one night, caught a train in the village below and I made up my mind, I would come back by myself and keell all of them. We went all the way down to the sea and settled in Cartagena. My wife found out after four months that she was pregnant because of the rape and she had an abortion without telling me...." His voice started to waiver... "and she died." He stopped and whipped out a white handkerchief to dab his eyes. "That's when I made up my mind, I would put them out of business by becoming the biggest drug dealer in the country and have all those bastards killed." He took a swig from his glass and swirled it around his tongue. He clucked with satisfaction.

"I nearly succeeded. I'm not the only one in Colombia, but I'm the beegest one and I have knocked off dozens of those animals. I have a lot of satisfaction. They call me ; *El cochino de oro*, the golden peeg! I made a lot of money, married again twice and have thirteen children.... Wait a minute... now I have eleven."

"Eleven? Your son in prison will live, won't he?"

"I hope so but I lost one daughter. *Que puta!*" (The whore)

"Huh?"

"I no talk about that!"

Another half inch was added to the bottom of the nice crystal bells and Vargas looked up at Fred: "What do you think? Time to negotiate?"

"Negotiate what?"

"Whether you live or die?"

"I vote to live!"

"Hahahaha! You're not afraid? That's good."

"I told you I lived with German soldiers for years, didn't I?"

"Okay, okay, muy bien. Here we go. We call. They provide a plane, fly us to Costa Rica. I have a house and friends there and you fly back in the plane if everything goes right. Bueno? If things go wrong, you die and the plane can take your body back to your wife. That would not be good. You wouldn't have finished your book. Let's call."

He opened the cell again, scrolled down to 'Bongers" and pushed green.

"Bongers here."

"Ah, Meester Bongers? Meester Vargas here. Are you ready to leesten?"

"Of couse. Go ahead."

"I will leave here with my wife and Meester Van Dyke in one hour. We will drive to the airport... remember, my car is bullet proof, no point trying to shoot the driver, you understand? You'll have your plane ready to fly. Enough fuel to make Costa Rica. Meester Fred will be tied up and have an explosive device on him and I carry the remote control. One thing goes wrong? Fred goes poof! You can pick up the pieces. Okay, so far? Meester Bongers? Okay?"

"Mr. Vargas, you hurt one hair on Fred's head and I'll have Jerry executed in the U.S."

"Good. Death is better than life in prison. He'll appreciate that. Any other questions Meester Bonger?"

"I have a question for you? Would you like your wife to continue to live?"

"My wife? *Carajo*! My wife? What's you want with my wife?"

"Fred dies, we'll shoot your wife. It'll be painless. Smack between the eyes."

"*Maricón!*" (Faggot) He slammed the phone shut. "Would Americans shoot an innocent woman?"

"That American would. He lost relatives, male and female, in Japanese and German prison camps during the war and he's itching to get even."

"*Carajo.*" He opened the phone again. When it connected, he spoke up. "I know Colombian police and army and I know they would like nothing better than come in here with tanks and rockets and shoot up everything and keell all my relatives and personnel, so I'll let them go. Please let them go to their homes. Don't shoot anybody. After they're gone in peace, we talk again." Click.

He called a tall elderly man over to the table and gave some rapid instructions. After the servant left, Vargas turned back to Fred: "I told heem, take all you want. Money, food, silver, cars, furniture and leave. No tears. Tell everyone. Take everything you can carry. I won't need it any more. I have my stuff packed. I sent my valuables away yesterday and we should be ready to travel soon. First I wanna make sure, the police don't come and rob my people. Let's go and look." He got up and walked toward the back of the room.

"Don't think of escape Fred. My guards will shoot the moment you come in the open. They're good."

After turning into a hall with a beautifully arched ceiling, they reached an elevator that was also dressed out in wrought iron and Moroccan leather. Lucky pushed four and surprised Fred, because he had not expected the building to be so tall. Then again, he realized he hadn't seen the outside of the building, just the tile floor and the interior. On the aerial photographs it had looked more or less like a two story adobe hacienda with a number of adjacent buildings. Certainly not four stories high.

When the arrow in the elevator hit '4', the door opened noiselessly and they both stepped forward on a narrow balcony. It wasn't but five foot wide and three feet deep. The front was draped with hanging plants and they formed a fairly solid curtain. Vargas stepped forward, moved the vines a little bit and asked: "See what I mean?" He waved his right hand from left to right as if he was showing off the whole country. Actually, by peering through the opening in the greenery, they did have quite a view. It encompassed the whole compound and many miles in three directions. Fred realized, he was standing in a narrow cave in a huge wall of reddish sandstone. No wonder the pictures didn't show that. The angle from outer space and the overgrowth kept the cave well hidden. If they had rockets up here, they could pick off tanks three miles away. He wondered how many of these caves they had and if they were defended with modern weapons. Looking down, he could now visualize that half of Lucky's house was built into the hill, the way the Pueblo Indians built their homes. Very clever! And the police probably didn't have the foggiest about this layout. In case of an attack, there might be many unexpected casualties. Fred said to himself: "Let's hope it won't come to that."

"See the helicopter? He's standing guard over us. Very efficient."

Lucky pointed up and to the right. "He theenks we don't know."

On the left side of the balcony was a door and a pair of binoculars was dangling from the doorjamb. Vargas picked them up and locked onto the scene where the road from the house intersected the highway.

"*Caramba!*" he shouted, "just as I thought. The police is arresting my people and taking their belongings! *Que puercos*! Those peegs! Bongers, you be sorry." He swung his lenses to the left and handed them to Fred. "One half mile out, you see a farm? Yes? "

"Got it!"

"You see the barn with red roof?"

"Got it!"

"You see all the police cars? That's the entrance to my tunnel. They expect to get in there and sneak up on me. Hahahahaha! They theenk I'm stupid. And now you see what I mean. Bongers, he lie to me. The police? They lie to me. The army? they lie to me. I know what they want. They theenk I have much gold and money een thees house and in the tunnel. Surprise! I send it all away. They will find nothing. Time to talk to Meester Bonger again." He flipped open the phone.

"Meester Bonger? Why do you lie? I ask, let my people go in peace and now the police is already picking them up. Why? I tell you why. I allowed my people to take all valuables with them from the house and now the police are stealing them. Meester Bonger, the Colombian police and army are corrupt. Very corrupt. They have one interest: MONEY! And they don't care who they steal it from. They will not work with you, they will only work for their own interest. Let that be a lesson to you. Now, are we ready to negotiate?"

"Mister Vargas, I was not aware that your people were being targeted and...."

"I know, I know... ! Same bullsheet. Is the plane ready?"

"It's ready to fly."

"Which tarmac?"

"It's at 'Camino Aereo."

"Good, I know where that ees."

Chapter Forty-Six

A Taste Of Hell

The elevator slid down noiselessly and Fred wondered what was on the third and second floors as they passed them by. Vargas volunteered no information. He didn't speak a word until they were back at ground level where the tall thin man quietly waited for them.

"On the floor! Face down!" Vargas spit orders and pointed a small caliber pistol at Fred's forehead.

"Why?" The command startled him right out of his white shoes.

"Down!"

The pain in the shoulders returned with a bang as his hands were being pulled back and shackled.

"Up!"

With the help of the lanky man, Fred got to his knees and then onto his feet.

"Damn, this hurts, can't you loosen those…"

"Don't worry, it'll worsen." A set of suspenders was thrown over his head and fastened to the top of his colorful shorts. In front of him, a little canvas bag was fastened to his suspenders and Vargas showed him a gadget that resembled a small TV remote.

"One push on thees button and you'll be with Abraham or the devil. One of the two. One thing's for sure, you won't be on earth any more. Now you talk with Bonger."

Fred's cell phone was produced again and within seconds...: "Meester Bonger?"

Fred wants to talk to you." He held the instrument next to the Dutchman's face.

"Fred? Are you okay?"

"Okay's not the word. My hands are cuffed behind my back and a bomb is hanging around my neck while Mr. Vargas is waiving a detonator in front of my eyes. Is that okay?" Vargas moved the phone to his own mouth.

"You say the plane is ready, yes?"

""Yes.'

"We're leaving now." Vargas clicked the phone shut and grabbed one of the aching arms and marched through the foyer like room into a garage. To Fred's surprise, the lanky man got into the black Mercedes and started up while Fred was steered in the opposite direction and put in the back of a dual-cab Nissan pick-up truck. A rope was attached to the handgrip on one side and Lucky expertly wove it between Fred's arms and fastened it on the other side. The great author was suspended between the two doors. It hadn't taken but ten seconds.

Vargas climbed behind the wheel and started up, but instead of following the Mercedes, another garage door opened and the car disappeared into a wood framed tunnel. Fred could hear the door closing behind and asked: "Where's your wife? Weren't you going to bring your wife?"

"My wife? She's in Guatemala waiting for me."

"You mean Costa Rica? Right?"

"You gringos really theenk I'm stupid, no? Now shut up. It's going to be a rough ride."

He wasn't kidding. The tunnel wasn't too bad, but once they went through another garage door and out of a barn, the road got pretty rough. Fred wished he had asked for a painkiller. They might have given him one.

For a moment, Fred was disoriented. The sun was to his left.

The Golden Pig

They were heading east. They must have come through another tunnel and exited on the country side of the hill. The road was a dirt track through a small forest, because they were in the open in five minutes. Another bouncy mile through a pasture and they were onto a paved country road, no lines or any kind of markers, but it was smooth at least. Fred said a silent prayer of thanks. Vargas drove with confidence and in spite of his misery, Fred admired the old guy. He had to be at least eighty years old, but he seemed as spry as a teenager. The road turned and turned, but the general direction changed to the south, because they had the sun in their faces and the road edged further and further away from the blue Caribbean. After a forty minute trip, (Fred was guessing) Lucky turned onto a gravel drive and after passing through another small strip of trees, they faced a pretty valley with a shiny silver river that flowed out of a lake to the north. A nice size two-story home stood at the water's edge where a seaplane and a speedboat were moored at a dock behind the house.

Vargas pulled up to the house and got out. A younger man, maybe forty, came out of the front door and embraced the older man as they met halfway up the walk. They turned around and approached the back seat.

"You're going flying. Have you ever flown a floatplane before?" Vargas asked as they undid the cord from both ends.

"I have a seaplane rating."

"You do, Señor Fred? Too bad I can't let you sit in the front seat to help us fly it. Too bad."

The two half-lifted their victim out of the backseat of the truck and walked him around the house, onto the dock. The plane was what Fred had always dreamed of owning. It was 'LAKE' with a push propeller behind the cockpit.

"What a charm!" He thought as they helped him into the backseat and this time they didn't tie him down. The younger man did his preflight check while Vargas remained on the dock, ready to untie them when asked. With a groan, the propeller turned over and the engine kicked into action with a smooth-sounding roar. Fred was loving it in spite of his pain and discomfort. He had never flown that type before, but he had dreamed about it. Unfortunately, he didn't have the kind of money it took to live on the water with a floatplane on a ramp.

The engine warmed up nicely at a thousand RPM and when the pilot was satisfied, he signaled Vargas, who undid the tie down ropes and climbed in. Without giving it much throttle, the craft glided away from the shore and when it drifted toward the middle of the stream, the pilot added power and turned north toward the lake. The windsock at the dock just hung down, so the wind wasn't a factor. The two men up front locked the canopy and while the engine powered up to full throttle, Vargas turned around and shouted at the Flying Dutchman: "WE'RE GOING TO SEE THE FIREWORKS."

*

In the pompous quarters of the General, Bongers was arguing with Colonel Armando: "This is not what we had agreed on. We were going to let his people go in peace and that's not…"

"Meester Bruce, we don't bargain with creemeenals."

"But I gave my word…"

"But I didn't and.." They were interrupted by a messenger who stuck his head around a door: "The Mercedes left."

"Let's go!" Bongers addressed Bruno and along with Armando and a police officer, they rushed from the room.

In the van to the airport, the Jersey FBI man reiterated: "One man and one woman are on the plane, dressed as pilots. Two plain cars are standing by and I hope we can somehow get the detonator away from Vargas or the bomb from Fred."

"The only way is to shoot the creemeenal in the head. Your sniper is on the roof of the hangar and he will have the best shot."

The radio on the dash crackled and uttered a few garbled words.

"He's on the highway. We have five minutes, he has ten. The copter is overhead. Everything ees going well." The colonel seemed very pleased with himself. Five minutes later, the van pulled in back of a hanger and Bongers walked along it's south side to the ramp, while Bruno took the north side. Bruce was the only one in sight as he slowly approached the entrance to the plane. He stood with one foot on the step as relaxed as could be. The idea was that he would walk up to the car and expose the back of Vargas' head to the hanger where the sniper would have a clear shot. He didn't have long to wait. The black sedan slid to a stop, some fifty feet from the jet and Bongers walked toward it. The driver door opened and a tall thin man stepped out and held out his hand. He was taller than Bongers expected and he looked more Spanish than Germanic. "Mister Vargas? " He asked.

"No, I'm his assistant, Orlando Ortega. Mucho gusto!" He shook Bruce's hand. The Fed opened the passenger door, but nobody else seemed to be inside the vehicle.

"WE'VE BEEN HAD!" Bongers shouted and ran back to the van in back of the hangar. "WE'VE BEEN HAD!"

"Surround the house!" The colonel shouted into the radio. "Prepare to attack!" He turned to Bruce and shouted: "He lied! That creemeenal! He lied. I knew it, I knew it He doesn't know how to speak the truth."

Bongers said to himself: "Whaddaya know? Who's calling the kettle black?"

Armando kept yelling into the microphone and looked back at his American colleagues, "I ordered them into the tunnel. Vargas won't expect that and he'll send all his fire power to the front, so we'll catch them from both ends."

A blue flashing light had been put on the roof of the speeding vehicle as it raced from the airport in the direction of the fort. The radio again spit out some gunfire Spanish and the colonel spit right back at it.

"My men said there's a beeg iron gate. They can't get in. I said, blow it up. They have anti tank weapons. No problem." He was enjoying himself. He was acting like a field general. Every time a message came in, he translated and apparently, some of his men were on the premises. They also had to blow the door that led to the tunnel in the barn and he hoped that Vargas would not have heard that inside the house. The van had reached the overpass and stopped. "You," he pointed to the Americanos, "stay here. You can see with the binoculars what is happening." Each accepted a pair of powerful binoculars and climbed out. They walked to the railing and started to study the scene, while the van continued the turn onto the country road. Within minutes they saw the van disappear behind the compound walls. Several other army and police vehicles had already passed through the gate and a few more followed. They couldn't hear any gunfire so either there was none or they couldn't hear it from that distance. Everything seemed so peaceful, till suddenly a huge explosion collapsed the barn and another one, more muffled, came from the innards of the main house. The gate blew up in a big ball of fire and the buildings inside the walls exploded, one after another. The main building was next and the two story structure and half of the hill behind it exploded outward, resembling a volcano eruption.

"Good God!" Bongers and Garcia were mesmerized by the spectacle. "Good God! Nobody is gonna survive that." They remained frozen in their stance on the overpass, as they saw fire spread through the whole compound. "I hope Fred's not in there! Great Scott!"

Fred was at five thousand feet, about three miles to the south, staring in disbelief.

"How do you like German/Colombian fireworks, Fred?" All he could do was shake his head.

Ten minutes later the 'LAKE' landed on the river and steered to the east bank, Fred was untied and helped onto the dock. He looked around and saw they were at a little ramshackle building in the middle of tall reeds and small trees. The engine was kept running and Vargas took Fred's hand and said: "Walk due east for about five miles. You will then be on a country road, where you can hitch a ride. In the pouch on your belly is some good Colombian chocolate and some money and when you get home, I hope you write favorably about me, Herr Van Dyke. I'll get a hold of the book somehow when you have finished it and I'm anxious to see what you have to say about the Golden Pig." He grinned a friendly smile. "I'm sorry I can't let you have your phone," he tossed it in the river "and I don't need this anymore either." He tossed the remote after it. He shook Fred's hand one last time: "I wont say: "*Auf Wiedersehen*", because we'll never meet again, but "*Grüss Gott.*" (God bless)

With that, he climbed aboard and they took off.

THE END

Epilogue

Fred decided to visit the smugglers in prison in order to wind up his story.

The one he didn't know at all was of course, Geraldo, Jerry, Radowicz/Robinson.

He was sitting across from him in the prison visitation room, trying to look pleasant.

At first Jerry wanted nothing to do with him, thinking it was just another way for the government to pump him for information. When Fred told him about his visit with his father, Jerry became all ears. At times he had a look on his face like: "You kiddin' me?" and sometimes he grinned.

He finally asked: "How many people do you suppose he killed?"

"In the house?"

"Yeah, in the explosion."

"Forty, fifty? I don't know."

"I guess that's what Hitler taught him, taking pleasure in killing other people. Disgusting! I suspected that he had my sister Julia killed, and I had just made up my mind that I was gonna quit the business and disappear when the ceiling fell in on me. One more day and I would have flown the coop. One more day.

The Golden Pig

Now I rot. They assigned me a lawyer, a Public Defender. They claim I have no money to pay for a lawyer, because all my money and assets have been confiscated. I know they can't do that. You know I'm an attorney myself, so I know they can't do this, but they're milking all the legal strings to keep me from getting any bail. I've had a five minute court hearing and the judge simply ruled: "Bond denied" without waiting for my defender to say anything in my favor. That bunch of crumbs are all in cahoots together, you know?"

He sighed a deep sigh. "My brother is the only one who could have gotten me out and who had all sorts of money, but he's dead. They claim he drowned. I don't believe it. I betcha they killed him. Now I have nobody in the States who can help me and from Cartagena I can't expect much help either. Lack of jurisdiction, they call it."

He suddenly looked up: "Hey, will you have contact with my father again?"

"Doubt it." Fred was sincere about that. There was no way he could get through to Vargas, wherever he was. He was sure he could locate the house with the seaplane again, although he did not reveal to the authorities where that was, and maybe he could meet up with Enrico again in the little pub on the docks. Instinctively he felt his neck again, right below his skull. It had hurt for a long time and he wasn't too anxious to take that chance again.

"I doubt it." He said again. "I doubt it very much."

"I'm sure the old man has plenty of money stashed and I'm sure he would spend it to get me out of here, but how do I get hold of him?" He grabbed Fred's hand across the table. "You said you were going to write a book about all this, right?"

"Right."

"Right now, I couldn't tell you a damn thing, because if it became public, it would haunt me in court, you understand? But…. But, when I get out and I'm safely in another country, I could tell you things about the ins and outs of the drug business that would give you enough material for two more books." He hesitated. "Mr. Van Dyke,"

"Fred."

"Okay, Fred, I'll tell you what. If you can get word to my father and in turn he gets some money to a good local defense lawyer, you have my word that I'll give you an exclusive on all the inside knowledge I possess."

"How about your wife?"

"My wife? Ingrid? Up in Chicago? She despises me and everything I ever stood for. No, no! She would like to see me rot. No, not a chance. She's a good lawyer, did you know that?" He looked into Fred's eyes as if he could read an answer there. "Damn good lawyer, but she hates me. Deservedly. I really hurt her." He stood up suddenly. "Fred, you know I can't tell you anything more, you understand? They have recorders going everywhere and you may be on the level, but the authorities are not. They wanna see me burn. Nice meeting you." He started to walk away, but turned around and said: "Remember what I promised?" and he was out the door.

Fred had not made one note.

In a similar room in the Century Correctional Institution in North Florida, he was sitting across from Leroy Anders. The man looked terrible. He must have lost forty pounds and his eyes were set deep in their sockets. He ignored Fred's hand and just sat slumped on the metal chair with his elbows on the table and his head in his hands. He didn't say a word. He wouldn't answer any questions like: "How are you Leroy? Is there anything you need?" No reaction whatsoever. Fred had to decide on a different tack.

"The place burned down the following night, you know. You and I got out just in time." Anders stiffened somewhat. Something must have registered. Fred continued: "They shot the hotel manager and his wife as they were trying to escape the flames."

The man across the table shot erect: "What are you talking about?"

"The Domani. The hotel we were staying in. The place where

we met, remember?"

"Who did what?"

"We may never know for sure, but the police think it was rival drug cartels and we nearly got caught at…"

Leroy was all ears and interrupted: "What are you saying? Are you telling me that we got caught in a drug war?"

"Yeah, my brother and I flew to Medellin and nearly got kidnapped by a couple of sharpies, so we hauled out of there and then we were arrested when we landed back in Bogota. This time by the airport security. They suspected us to be cartel members and advised us to get out. You were already gone, I think, so we got on the first plane out, although we had a three day reservation paid for. We didn't feel so good about the place anymore and that night, it burned to the ground."

"Jeez." He put his head back in his hands. After a full minute he looked up again. "It would have been better if I had died in the fire too."

"Holy Moses, how can you say a thing like that? What are you thinking…?"

"If I had died, my wife would not be in prison, my kids would still have a home, my boys would still be in college and…" He collapsed on the table and burst into tears…

Fred didn't know what to do, so he did nothing but watch the skinny body across the table from him, shaking and sobbing. Another two minutes passed before he looked up and wiped his face with a red handkerchief. "My wife had nothing to do with this. If I had taken a taxi home, she would not be in prison today. Conspiracy and accessory to murder? Come on! We didn't have anything to do with the killing of a mechanic in Tampa. All she did was she came to pick me up after I came back from a trip. Right now there are hundreds of wives that go to the airports to pick up their husbands. Do they go to jail? Do they rot in prisons? This isn't right. This isn't right. My kids are with four different families. What have they done? They don't have a mother any more." He collapsed again and cried. "This isn't right." He looked up again. "Couldn't they put all the blame on me and give me a longer sentence and let her out, so she can look after the kids? This isn't right. It just ain't right!"

Fred got up and left. He felt destroyed.

The federal prison in Georgia looked more like a country club than the prisons in Mississippi and Florida. Men were strolling around in a sort of a sports complex and a lively basketball game was going in one area and a soccer match was in full action in the distance. Fred would have liked to tour the facility, but that wasn't allowed. He watched though as he saw Harry Weaver come out of a building accompanied by a guard. Much to his surprise, the guard didn't carry side arms and wore a simple brown uniform and no hat.

Harry was looking good. He wore blue shorts, a white T-shirt, white sox and blue boat shoes. He looked as if he just stepped off his yacht. Fred moved away from the barred window and sat down with his back to the entrance. He heard the two come in and saw them coming around the table out of the corner of his eye. Harry stopped dead in his tracks.

"YOU?" He shouted and for a moment it seemed he was going to jump at Fred. The correction officer grabbed his arm and said: "Easy or I'll cuff you."

"I don't wanna see that bastard." Weaver hollered, "Get me outta here." He started back toward the door and the officer let him.

"What was that all about?" He asked as he saw the prisoner walking back through the window.

"I can only guess at this point. He probably thinks I'm responsible for his arrest. He may not realize that I was kinda in the same boat, except, I got out in time."

The guard looked puzzled. "What is he in for and are you an attorney?"

Fred chuckled. "No, not by a long shot. No we were in the same hotel in Colombia and I was arrested by the cops and nearly kidnapped by some gangsters, but we all got out in time and that was a good thing, because that night they burned the place down and shot the managers."

"Then what is he so mad at you for?"

"He probably was arrested and never heard about the people in Bogota, but my brother and our wives, we fled to one of the islands, so we're okay. At one point we jumped from island to island, because we were afraid they would come after us."

"God Almighty!" He looked baffled. "Then what do you wanna talk to Weaver for?"

"Oh, I'm writing a book about the whole mess and I have permission from the FBI and the CIA to interview anybody connected with this."

"He doesn't know that, does he?"

"No, I guess not. I didn't give him any advance notice. Didn't have to."

"I'm gonna tell him about that and maybe he'll come back and talk to you."

"I'd be much obliged." The guard took off.

Fred stood by the window and waited patiently. Ten, maybe fifteen minutes went by and he rehearsed in his mind what he would ask and what he really wanted to know. There was no way to know how Weaver would react the next time. Finally the two of them reappeared and came strolling toward the interview room. The dapper author sat down on the same bench as before and didn't turn around when the door opened. He kept staring at his note book and drew circles. Harry walked to the opposite side of the table and remained standing. When Fred didn't look up, Weaver hissed: "What's all this shit?"

"Huh?" Fred looked, stood up for a sec and sat back down. "Yes, Harry?"

"I wanna know what kind of cock and bull story you told Mr. Myers here."

"Oh, I was telling him how we, you and my family, got out of there just in time before they torched the building and shot the managers. We had two more days to go on our reservations, but the Security Captain told us to get the hell out and we did. We took the first flight out and ended up in Saint Martin, which is not where we wanted to go, but... "

"Who torched what and why?"

"I can only tell you what we were told, because I don't know any of those people personally, but I do know that my brother and I were nearly kidnapped at the airport in Medellin and then got arrested at Bogota International. They thought we were part of a drug cartel and apparently they're feuding and killing one another. The captain who arrested us and later came by the hotel when you were there, was ambushed and shot up. He'll live though. When did you get out? That same day when we did?"

"I took off at seven-fifty." He sat down.

"Well, then we were at the airport at about the same time, because we boarded at eight-thirty and we were in the terminal for at least an hour, I think." Fred saw how Harry was dropping his protective armor. The guard stood by long enough to see that there would not be any hostilities and disappeared through another door into the building.

"Why are you here?" Harry was still not relaxed.

"Here? With you?"

"Yes. Why?"

"The same reason why I was in Bogota. I'm an author. I write books and I'm working on a book about the drug trade in America and my research led me to Columbia. When it got too hot there, I contacted an FBI agent for an interview to learn what was happening and when he found out I speak German, he asked me to come along as an interpreter, because they expected to capture some hotshot who used to be in Hitler's Waffen SS and who might talk to me in his native tongue more freely than he might in English. Well, they never did get the guy, but I had an interesting outing, I guarantee you."

"Then how did you find out about me?"

"Oh, I was privy to a lot of their files and when I came upon your name, I said: 'I know that guy' and I asked permission to interview you. Permission granted and here I am. Now Harry,

I've already learned that a lot of these places are bugged and if you told me something that might be held against you later, you shouldn't tell me. I have immunity. They cannot force me to reveal anything you said to me, but the bugs all around the room," he swung his hand in a big circle, " can record every whisper, so if it's okay by you, I'd rather sit on one of the benches under that tree."

"I don't know if I wanna tell you anything. I forgot your name?"

"Fred."

"That's right. The clown is Ted. You're Fred."

"Even if you don't want to talk to me, I can deliver a message for you or if there's anything else..."

"Yeah, I'd like you to deliver a message!" He grew hostile again and got up. "Let's go outside."

Together they walked about twenty steps to a concrete bench in the shade of an old linden tree. As soon as they sat, Harry turned to Fred and with their faces only a foot apart, he said: "Yeah. I'd like you to deliver a message to Hilton Head."

"What's in Hilton Head?"

"My bitch. My ex-wife, my partner, my cutthroat."

"All four of them?"

"NO, NO!" Weaver screamed. "It's all one and the same."

"Sorry, I..."

"You said you read files about me? About us? Carol and me?"

"I glanced through them. Didn't read them word for word yet. Why?"

"When you read them through, you'll see she sold me out. For her testimony against me, she went free after about a month. She got to keep her big house on Hilton Head Island and an income providing portfolio. Everything else was confiscated and I was told in no uncertain terms, that if they found out that I or her or both had some other hidden assets, my time in prison would be doubled. As it now stands I got five years, I may be out in three and a half and I won't be worth a plumb nickel when I leave." He stopped and looked around. Even looked up into the tree. "This is between you and me, okay?" He lowered his voice. "What I didn't tell the Feds is that I own, or owned, a nice piece of property near Macon that I planned to develop into a residential golf course some day. I bought it for two hundred grand, but by now it is worth at least two-fifty. Once it's developed, it would probably be worth a mil, before we start building. Nice deal. The Feds have no idea of its existence." Harry looked around again. "Here comes my darling wife last Sunday, all decked out and looking good. She chats a little and then she says: "Honey, that piece near Macon? I says: What piece? And she says: That piece that you bought two years ago, for two big ones cash, remember? Was that your money or my money you bought that with? I says to her: How do you know anything about that? Man I was getting mad, but it was visiting day and there were at least four other couples in the room, so I had to keep it down. I says: So what? She says; Honey, here's the deal. If the Feds find out that you lied about it, they take it away from you and double your time, right? I say: Whose gonna tell'em? She says: Not me, if you sign it over to me. I jumps up and say: Are you crazy? It's mine and that's it! She says, with that sweet seductive voice of hers: Now honey, be reasonable. If you don't sign, you'll spend ten years. You don't wanna do that. I got it all drawn up, nice and legal and all you do is sign and you'll be out in three and a half. I got up and walked around the room and talked myself out of choking her in front of all these other people. I sat back down and said: You bitch. She keeps right on smiling and says: Here it is. She opens an envelope, shows me enough of the paper inside to see that the legal description is correct and she points at the line on the bottom and says: Honey, this'll save you five years. I signed. Sonofabitch. I signed."

Weaver stood up panting as if he had jogged five miles. "Fred, you tell my bitch, that she can croak and if she doesn't, I'll help her do it when I get out. Tell her!"

He got up and walked back to his quarters.

Fred got up and walked in the opposite direction and was about to reach for the doorknob as the guard came out and asked: "Are you actually grinning?"

"I would never have believed that I would one day walk out of a prison, laughing."

Fred.

The following are some excerpts from Frits Forrer's other books

Excerpt from:

Five Years Under The Swastika

Pappa has preceded him down and is warming milk on the electric stove. Mama and Jopie file into the kitchen too and Mama begins again: "You should…"

"HUSH!" Pappa interrupts softly, but sternly. Mamma gets cups down from the cupboard and puts cocoa mix in them, waiting for the milk to get warm.

"Why Pappa? Why? What have they done? And that little girl, what's her name? The granddaughter? They hurt her Pappa! Why Pappy, why? What did SHE do?"

Pappa stirs the chocolate milk. "Come sit at the table."

Frits turns, Joop and Mama are deadly quiet.

"Drink your cocoa! Watch it, it's hot. Hold it…. let me add some cold… here you go. Stir it! Okay, okay."

"Why Pappa, why? I know what you're gonna say: They're JEWISH right? But what did they do? They're not rich Jews that ruin the world and all that garbage. They're poor working people. He's been working for the County-Water-Department for as long as we've known him. He goes to work on his bike at four in the morning, every morning, I know Pappa, he's not rich, I know! Why then Pappa, why? They'll never come back, I know it. They're gonna kill'em!"

Tears are running down his cheeks, Mama is not doing much better and Jopie is staring in his chocolate milk as if there's something fascinating in it.

Mama hands Frits a handkerchief: "Here, dry your tears. Drink your cocoa."

"There's nothing I can say, Frits… nothing! Goddamnit!"

Pappa's last word shoots out with such vengeance that all three of them look up at him, startled.

"Sit down, Herman, drink your cocoa too!"

She's worried that his ulcer will flare up. "Why don't we all drink up-up-up and go to bed. It's too cold in here. Take your cocoa if it's too hot and let's go. Come boys."

Frits is still crying uncontrollably.

"Come in bed with us."

For the first time in years, he's in bed between his father and his mother, his skinny body shaking with the sobs that won't stop.

Finally, with his head against his father's chest, he falls asleep, blissfully.

The WOHLSTEINS were the first.

Excerpt from:

Smack Between The Eyes

"Now comes the hard part!" Frank walked away from Joey, who looked like a businessman on his way home. Nice suit, white shirt and a very conservative tie. His brown briefcase and a laptop bag swung over his shoulder completed his disguise.

Several detectives, including a cleaning lady, were posted near the arrival spot and two were at the end of the ramp, in case anyone wanted to escape from the rear door.

The large bus slowly rolled to a stop. The door opened and Frank stepped up to give the folks a hand, exiting the bus. Some refused his hand, some gratefully grabbed it.

Frank looked at each face as they unloaded and tried to match it with the pictures he had received on the fax and the e-mail.

The only one who bore the least bit of resemblance was an elegant gentleman in a light suit, blue shirt and white tie. His white fedora and his goatee gave him the look of a Caribbean planter.

After the last passenger descended, Frank boarded the bus, scanned it quickly and jumped off.

"Joey! That's the one! The guy with the black hat!" He mouthed it, rather than holler it, but Joey got the message. He ran after the disappearing figure in the crowd. Frank followed. Luck was with them. The elegant planter stopped to look around.

"Probably looking for Nita." Frank thought.

The man reached into his coat pocket and Frank as well as Joey pulled out there guns. The man's hand came out with a cell phone that he flipped open in order to dial, so he never saw the two officers rushing toward him until he heard: "Hands up! You're under arrest!"

His reaction was swift. With his left hand, he threw the cell phone at Frank and with his right hand he reached in his pocket and fired a shot at Joey, hitting him in the hip.

Frank ducked and the phone hit him in his bus driver's hat. In that very second, Hotta Hotta fired off one more shot, turned and disappeared in the crowd.

PANDEMONIUM!

People falling to the floor, officers shouting orders, women screaming and Frank jumping over bodies, trying to get to the fleeing man. An off-duty policeman tackled Frank, thinking he was the culprit and the gunman escaped.

All the police ended up with was a white hat and a cell phone.

Frank was sooooooo mad, he could have spit bullets.

ISBN 0-9714490-6-6

Excerpt from:

The Fun Of Flying

Pieter drove around, looking for a quiet spot and settled for a corner lot, surrounded by trees. From the debris on the lot, they built a campfire and concentrated on the task of opening up their beer bottles without the benefit of a bottle opener. That was an interesting challenge!

Two guys would take a bottle each, hook the 'crown-caps' together and pulled till one of them came off, while the they other guy got sprayed with beer. Harm was soaked in no time flat and took off his beautiful jacket and threw it someplace. Soon, his shirt was soaked as well and inasmuch as he couldn't handle the buttons in his inebriate state, he tore the shirt to threads.

Meanwhile, some 'serious' singing was being done by the campfire and everybody was in 'excellent' voice that night.

Somewhere during the evening, it was decided that throwing beer bottles all over the place was not very civilized, so they improved the situation by organizing a 'trapshoot'! One guy would throw his bottle in the air, while others threw theirs after it, trying to hit it in mid-air.

Their 'hit' averages stunk, but it felt like a refined kinda way to discard the empties.

Just as the averages were improving by the light of a bigger and improved campfire, sirens started screaming in their direction and soon two police cars ran unto the sidewalk, spitting out four bulky policemen.

"Hands up over your heads!" They meant business!

The boys didn't.

"So nice of you to come! Find a seat and we'll see if we can find you a beer."

"Shut up and raise those hands!"

"In our country, we are more polite than that!"

"We don't give a shit about your country! UP! Up! Now! Put your hands on top of the cars! Now!"

"That won't be necessary, Mr. Policeman. We believe that they're your cars."

"Shut up, I said. Put those hands on the cars!" They were getting mad and rough and started pushing.

"After you, sir!"

"Like hell! Up! Up!"

"Officer, all we were doing was singing a few songs. Is that so bad?"

"You're all under arrest for 'Disturbance of the peace'"

"Officers, if you ever came to visit in our country, we would treat you a lot nicer, I'm sure."

Meanwhile the cops felt them down, but other than 'hiccups' they had nothing on them.

"Get in the cars!"

"After you, sir. After you!"

"Negative. Get the hell in!"

On the way to the station they asked the cops if they had any special requests and they would gladly perform them for'em.

The total ride only took only five minutes and they were put in a big cage with just one more occupant; a dead down drunk who stared at them with wide eyes and a dumb look on his face. He had probably never seen a spectacle like that before in his entire life.

Seven guys, profusely thanking the cops for the ride and offering to pay the cab fare.

Once left alone, the songs started up again and at the stroke of midnight, they stood at attention and sang the American and Dutch National Anthems.

The policeman on duty thought it was very funny and kept supplying them with ice water. Nice touch.

ISBN 0-9714490-3-1

Excerpt from:

Tampa Justice
No Money, No Justice.

Your Honor, I was not informed of all the things that are involved in probation and I want to change my plea to Not Guilty, so I can have a trial and that will clear me for sure."

Well 'Fisheyes' objected vehemently. He had his 'conviction' and he was not about to take a chance on losing it.

"Mr. Fernon?"

"Your Honor, I do not want to represent Mr. Forrer in a trial, because I told Mr. Forrer that I don't do criminal work."

"Then why the hell did you take my case?"

"Mr. Forrer, you will maintain order!"

"Yeah, but Judge, I hired him to…."

"Mr. Fernon, raise your right hand. Is the testimony you're about to give, the truth, the whole truth and nothing but the truth, so help you God?"

"I do."

"Go ahead Mr. Fernon, state your case."

"Your Honor, I told Mr. Forrer, I don't do criminal work and I can not represent him in a trial."

THAT LYING BASTARD! I presented him with two CRIMINAL summonses and he took my thousand dollars to represent me.

"Very well, the motion to change plea is denied and we'll schedule a restitution hearing. Case dismissed."

The bastards! Just like that, in a matter of seconds I'm stuck with a verdict and there's not a damn thing I can do about it. I'm on a five year probation and I'm stuck with it.

To make matters worse, I received a notice from the Department of Professional Regulation that because of my "Nolo Contendere" plea, my Contractors License was revoked.

Apparently, when someone pleads "No Contest" in a construction case, it is assumed by the Department that the person is Guilty and it calls for an automatic revocation.

In other words: I was put out of business.

ISBN 0-9714490-5-8

Excerpt from

To Judge Or Not To Judge

Pandemonium

J.F.K.
1:30 PM

Three people down! Two shot and one knocked unconscious. Two on the outside of the x-Ray check-in, one on the inside. For a minute or two there was so much confusion, that undercover security police nearly tangled with undercover FBI agents. The problem was everyone was incognito. Nobody was in uniform, not even a jacket with FBI on it or an I.D. card around their necks or pinned to their chests. Bongers' loud voice finally restored order and had the law enforcement officers holster their pistols again without any more friendly casualties.

Peter was the only one so far and Bruce wanted to make sure it stayed that way. It took a little while to convince the locals that Peter was NOT with the FBI and NOT a suspect, but he DID work with them and shouldn't have been shot in the first place. Ambulances roared up to the entrance, EMS personnel raced in with stretchers, I.V. bottles and medicine bags. City police officers tried to take control, than backed off and offered help and cooperation and ten minutes later, all there was left to do was clean the blood off the floors and get the passenger lines moving again.

The Feds had cuffed the captives and moved them into the Rembrandt room temporarily, much to the frustration of the KLM personnel, who had to transfer their cherished first class customers to other, less luxurious quarters. Bruce had everything under control again except; *what to do with the two terrorists?* If the CIA snatched them from his possession, which was certainly within their rights, he might be limited in his access to them. If the New York City police took over, defense lawyers would immediately be informed according to the law and of course, they would tell their clients to zip their mouths.

He called his New York counterpart and got some good advice. The City police would just hold them in *protective* custody in their maximum security prison at Rikers Island and that way, the FBI and CIA could interrogate them while awaiting transportation to Guantanamo Bay where al the Taliban and al-Qaida prisoners were being held. Federal laws provided them with that loophole and Bongers would have at least a few days to put their noses to the grindstone and find out what that whole plot was all about.

A police paddy wagon was provided and while the city cops transported the culprits, Bruce had a chance to track his shooting victims, Peter and Sahira, to the Queens Hospital where emergency surgery was scheduled to take place any minute.

In Washington, Travis washed his hands of the transactions, 'cause he would have to inform the CIA immediately and Bongers had begged him for patience.

"I gotta have some time with them, Lester. If the CIA big shots get involved, the Arabs may clam up altogether and I need to find out what this is all about. I'll get it out of them. I know these clowns, I've worked in the Middle East long enough to know how to deal with them. I'll play one against the other. Just buy me some time

Lester. Stall them by saying ; *'There is an operation in progress, details will be released as soon as they become available.'"*

"Okay, Bruce. I have to trust you on that, but keep me posted immediately, okay?"

"Will do. Thanks."

The New Jersey Bureau Chief knew he was walking a thin line, but he had seen it too often, that when too many different agencies or individuals get involved, the suspects tend to draw into a shell and that wouldn't really help anybody.

"Bruno," he asked his sidekick, "get me a ride to Queens Hospital and hold it for a trip to Rikers Island. Preferably a local cop who knows the territory. Thanks."

He reached for the coffee pot that was ready to serve some first class customers and filled a tall mug. "Good God, I'm hungry. Forgot to eat. Well, it'll have to wait a little longer." He finished the hot tasty liquid. "Good stuff. Must be Dutch."

Rikers Island was originally purchased by the Rykers family in 1683. It's located in the East River between the Bronx and Queens and had many different uses over the years. Most memorable was the training of African-American soldiers during the civil war and the conversion to a prison in the 1930's. The facility houses over 15,000 inmates and is now connected to Queens by a bridge. With the cooperation of the Warden, Bongers should be able to keep his culprits secluded and hidden from the press and over ambitious lawyers.

"So far, so good!" He said to himself as he climbed into a patrol car for the trip to Queens Hospitals and his innocent victims. "Let's hope they're alright."

ISBN 0-9714490-7-4

About the Author

Born in Belgium of Dutch parentage, Frits grew up along the German Border in Eastern Holland, enduring five years of German occupation and relentless bombing by the Allies.

This led to his first book, ***Five Years Under The Swastika.***

At age twenty, the Royal Netherlands Air Force shipped him to the U.S. for training with the U.S.A.F., earning his wings in October of '53. After completing 'gunnery' in Arizona, the young pilots returned to their home country flying the F-84 Thunderjet. Result; ***The Fun Of Flying.***

Upon completion of his military duty, Frits came back to America, this time as an Immigrant. After twenty years in the New York Metropolitan Area, Frits and his young family, (one girl, one boy,) moved to Tampa, Florida, where he became a General Contractor, which was the basis for; ***Tampa Justice, No Money, No Justice.***

He stayed active in the flying business, maintaining a Commercial and Instructors' rating, flying with many Flying Clubs and the Civil Air Patrol.

On a trip to Arizona, he met his present wife Katy whom he married in 2000.

During Hurricane Ivan, they lost their home and most of their possessions and decided to spend the rest of their lives on a boat. They now live on a 51 foot Cruiser, where Frits hammers out his novels and they sing their hearts out with several choirs and entertainment groups. He visits his old Squadron and his many relatives in Holland on a yearly basis and lives a happy and active life, speaking, singing, boating and writing.